PRAISE FOR SUSY SMITH

"Susy Smith 's latest beautifully written novel book picks right back up where readers were left wanting more in *Asylum*. This page-turner keeps you engaged until the end and cheering for Lacy and Jace to find their way back to each other....This story has action, romance, and suspense that all readers will love."

— SHELLEY LEVISAY, AUTHOR OF *LOVE ISN'T ALWAYS THE ANSWER*

"In Susy Smith's second dystopian thriller, a pair of courageous lovers fight to save each other from an evil U.S. Senator on a power trip. Fast-paced, entertaining, and tense."

— MARCIA PRESTON, AUTHOR OF *THE SPIDERLING*

WOW! *Asylum* by Susy Smith knocked it out of the ball park. I am impressed and will be marking her as a must-read author....I am eager to see what she comes up with next."

— SHERRY FUNDIN, VERIFIED PURCHASE AMAZON REVIEW

ASCENDANT

ASCENDANT

THE ASYLUM SERIES
BOOK TWO

SUSY SMITH

BABYLON BOOKS

For my kids …
Samantha, Tanner, Sarah, & Cady
*Zhi*ⁿ*gá zhí*ⁿ *wíta óshka*ⁿ *da*ⁿ*hé ablí*ⁿ *akhá.*

PART I

THE GAME

"Hell is realizing you've been captured in a game where leverage is King."

1

Monroe Farm — Shidler OK

Control over one snot-nosed, almost adult, shouldn't have been this hard. Control. Simple, really, in its complexity. But as Senator Thomas Monroe walked through his niece, Lacy's, deserted bedroom, its emptiness mocked him, reminded him control could be elusive without a defining show of strength. He would show her the cost of disobedience.

He had that right, after all, even if the girl knew nothing about how close their familial bond ran. Shifting to the broken window, he lifted the tarp's corner flap where she'd made her escape. The unforgiving February wind had whipped its edges into tiny white strips. Deep in

thought, he didn't feel the frosty air blowing against his face.

When he'd hatched his plan to foil the president's military state, the idea of using his niece to complete certain delicate tasks, hadn't occurred to him. He trusted no one. He couldn't.

But the leverage he used against her and Jace Cooper

provided the assurance to facilitate his plan. He couldn't afford to fail.

The boy would go to any lengths, even if it meant his death, to keep her out of danger. Case in point, he'd killed his own brother for her. Reports on the murder of his long-time friends, Jake and Hannah Cooper, had shocked and saddened him. Not long after, a report filtered in that their oldest son, Zach, had been killed. By Jace. The report went on to speculate the reasons why, none of which he believed. When Jace showed up in Texas looking for him, it wasn't difficult to surmise the boy had something to do with it. After interviewing him in the jail cell, in which he'd been detained, he knew Jace had killed his brother. It wasn't until he'd reached the farm that he learned the reason why. He didn't blame the boy. If Jace hadn't done it, he'd have seen to Zach's punishment.

And Lacy? It was apparent she'd risk everything for him. She'd defied his direct order to stay at the farm. Instead, she escaped out a broken window, out of his grasp. The thought irked him.

The bond between the two couldn't be broken. He didn't want to break it, he wanted to exploit it.

He shut the bedroom door against the icy wind blowing through the broken window and walked into the kitchen. His euphoria diminished somewhat as he contemplated his current situation. He'd had no idea Manuel Nieto, a highly respected Mexican politician, ran a human trafficking ring. Pulling Nieto into their country's problems was risky. Dicey. The man controlled most of the Mexican drug cartels and had unfathomable connections.

He wrinkled his nose, disgusted. Distasteful, and so very cliché. Of course, he should've expected Nieto was involved in something illegal. But he'd weighed the alternatives, and none had the outcome he desired most. Total control over the United States.

He grabbed a clean coffee cup out of the dish drainer and plunked it down on the counter with extra force. The full carafe released the coffee's pungent aroma. It beckoned him. A cup of coffee and a cigarette would go a long way to calm his rattled nerves.

He pulled out a chair and sat at the kitchen table, mulling over his problem. He reached for the pack of cigarettes in his shirt pocket, grabbed the box of matches on the table, then struck the red tip. Fire flared, much like his temper. He lit the cigarette, inhaled deep, then flicked ashes on the floor.

Lacy and Jace were together. How had they slipped through his fingers so easily?

He sipped on the hot coffee, savoring the fresh beans he'd brought. The rag-tag bunch Lacy had given asylum to were an annoyance he'd deal with later.

The question now was, would Lacy and Jace complete the mission and deliver the payment he'd promised Nieto? Or escape with his gold and disappear? He couldn't afford to wait and find out. He needed that payment secured and on its way to Nieto. The man wouldn't tolerate delays.

The brief calm the cigarette afforded vanished. He dropped the spent cigarette on the floor, crushed it out with his heel.

"William!" he bellowed.

His loyal assistant rushed into the room. His long, surfer-blond hair had been secured on the top of his head into a man bun. His untucked shirt and oversized khakis added to the sloppy look so many in his generation sported these days.

He'd been reluctant to hire a twenty-something, green behind the ears assistant, but he was the Texas governor's son. One hand washes the other had given him the short end of the stick this time. But having the governor in his back pocket was worth putting up with the son.

Thomas narrowed his eyes. His aggravation over his current conundrum shifted to his assistant.

"Yes, sir?"

"Find Bryan and bring him to me. He just returned with the chopper."

"Yes, sir."

"And did they secure the governor in the main house?"

"Yes, sir."

The wide-eyed assistant stood at attention, hands clasped behind his back, waiting for further instruction.

"Well? What are you waiting for? Go get Bryan Rash!" he thundered. "And get a haircut," he demanded at the young man's retreating back.

He shook his head. The younger generation's mindset baffled him, and he thanked the stars above he'd never been saddled raising a child. His wife, Geneviève, begged him for a baby.

Currently, he'd tucked his beloved wife away from the country's turmoil and danger in one of their smaller homes in Texas. He loved her, and only her. Wanted her undivided attention in all things. A child would've stolen her love and devotion from him. So, he'd refused to accept her reasons and incessant pleadings that a child would enrich their lives.

The snap of the back door's slam reminded him of the task at hand. He rose to meet his pilot, strategizing his next move. He would make certain Lacy and Jace would not clear the border into Mexico.

Bryan strode into the cramped kitchen, overflowing with boxes containing canned goods, dried milk and potatoes, flour and sugar, tea and the most coveted thing among men, coffee.

He motioned for the younger man to take a seat at the Formica-chipped table.

Bryan lifted two stacked boxes off a green vinyl chair and let them fall to the floor with a loud thunk. He scrubbed his hands across his face, took a seat, and looked with impatient expectancy at the senator.

"I need you to fly me to the border."

Bryan crossed his arms. "Why?"

"Change in plans. We need to catch Jace and Lacy before they cross into Mexico."

"Look, I just got back. I'm tired. I need rest. Food. Coffee."

"You can have the food and coffee. If you hurry. I want to leave in the next thirty minutes."

"The chopper needs to be refueled."

"That will be taken care of."

Bryan let out a long sigh. "Fine, but after —"

"After, you will pick up my wife and fly her to another secure location. I fear she's been compromised where she is now."

The fear might've been irrational, but it didn't matter. He'd move her anyway.

Bryan rose, made his way to the coffee pot, poured the steaming liquid into a silver thermos, then turned back to the senator.

"I gotta be honest, Senator. I'm not comfortable with all this."

Thomas walked over and stood in front of him. "I don't care what you're comfortable with, you'll obey my orders. I've paid you a handsome sum for your services. I expect a comparable payout."

"Fine," he huffed. "Meet you at the chopper."

Thomas watched the young man stomp out the door, trying to screw the lid onto the thermos as he went. He shook his head, searched his pocket for the pack of cigarettes. There was a fine example of why he needed someone with whom he could control. No amount of money could buy what leverage could.

He needed Lacy and Jace separated. Jace proved to be a promising militia man with a sniper's eye. He needed him for his next step.

And Lacy would soon learn why no one crossed him.

Ever.

2

The El Paso-Cordova border crossing appeared over the freeway's horizon, its four-lane check points deserted. No lights shone from the building, no driver's instructions flashed over the lanes. The abandoned freeway looked like a stricken Walking Dead set, wiped clean, waiting for the next scene. Nothing could shock Lacy now, not even a horde of zombies.

They'd driven in silence, both exhausted and lost in thought. The landscape had changed little as they drove through the northern part of Texas. Winter had painted the plains a dull, boring brown.

Jace pulled the car to the road's wide right shoulder. The Cadillac idled, a quiet hum against the silence as they stared at the checkpoint. Beyond lay a straight shot down to Mexico City.

Hot air blew from the vents across her already warm face. She reached forward, pushed both vents away, then shifted to face him. Her arm's mangled flesh, wrapped too tight with gauze, burned, and throbbed.

"This is weird, right? Where are the guards? The MP?"

His tone darkened. "Probably inside."

The short, clipped answer sent tiny needle pricks up her spine.

He cut the engine then turned, his darkened blue eyes locked on hers, searching. "Lace."

The desperate edge in his voice sliced straight through her. She reached over and ran a hand down his spine then back up, her touch feather light. Her hand wandered to the back of his neck. She stroked his hair, curling the ends around her fingers. He took her face between his hands, thumbs brushing her temples. She closed her eyes, turned her face into his calloused palm.

"Are you really sure about me?"

Her eyelids snapped open. "What?"

After everything they'd been through, he still questioned her decision to be with him, her love for him.

"I'd understand if you're having second thoughts or changed your mind."

His tormented face tempered the heat racing through her veins. "About what?"

"Me. Running. Everything."

"Stop. Just stop."

He dropped his hands. "This won't be easy and you," he swallowed hard, "you deserve better."

"Jace," she said on a sigh, "there's no one better than you."

She leaned forward, brushed her lips against his, then slipped over the console into the back seat. Although the pained look never completely left his eyes, his face broke into a grin.

"What are you doing?"

With a smirk, she lifted her T-shirt over her head, let the material slide down her bandaged arm. Cool air hit her bare skin and instant heat flared in his eyes.

"Appealing to the wolf in you," she said, voice soft and low.

"We're meant to be together. I know it. The wolf in you knows it. Can't you stop fighting it?"

His shoulders sagged. "I'll never stop thinking you deserve better."

She leaned forward, grabbed his hand, and tugged him over the console. They fell together onto the back seat.

Laughter bubbled up her chest and she gave him an alluring grin.

Gently, he tucked a wayward strand of hair behind her ear.

She wrapped her legs around his waist, leaned up, and gave him another quick taste of her lips.

"I love you, girl," he whispered.

A wicked smile lit her face. "I know."

He shook his head, a bemused look on his face. "You're a witch, sometimes. You know that?"

She widened her eyes in mock innocence. "Who better than a witch to enchant a dragon?"

Her hands slid under the back of his shirt, fingers tracing the wolf-dragon tattooed there. He'd explained the tattoo's meaning to her one autumn afternoon they'd spent at Lymon's pond. The dragon in him needed her just as much as the wolf did.

"God help me," he chuckled.

She pulled his head down and their lips met again.

A FINGER TRACING lazy circles around the small of her back woke her. She cracked an eyelid open, and found herself face to face with Jace, watching her sleep. Lying side by side with Jace's arm wrapped around her, she'd dozed off. Had he done the same? His handsome face marred with worry and fatigue, suggested he hadn't.

"Stalker," she teased, a smile playing around her lips.

She stretched a cramped arm above her head, wincing at the sharp pain running down her injured forearm as the tight skin expanded.

He raised up on an elbow, leaned over, and whispered, "Not a stalker when the girl just —"

Heat flooded her cheeks as he tugged her closer and leaned his forehead against hers.

"You're thinking too hard again," she murmured, running a hand through his hair.

"No, I'm not," he denied.

"This is where I want to be, Jace. Need to be. So, get over it."

"That's not it," he insisted.

"What then?" she asked, leaning back until her head hit the seat's back.

"I'm just so damn grateful you're here with me."

"You better be," she quipped, giving him a peck on the lips.

"Hey, Lace?"

She shifted, trying to free her trapped arm. "Yeah?"

Jace moved back to give her more room, then fell onto his back into the floorboard with a grunt. She pushed herself up, tangled hair falling over her shoulder and laughed at his compromising position. She scooted to one side while he fumbled his way back up to sit on the other side of the bench seat.

He ran a hand through his hair and grinned. "Ha, ha," he mocked.

"It was pretty funny," she goaded.

He rolled his eyes. "Anyway, where do you want to go?

After we drop this payment?"

She considered a moment then thought of the movie *The Shawshank Redemption*. Andy Dufresne said the Pacific Ocean had no memory. That's what she wanted. A place where her bad memories could be tossed into its fathomless depths and never thought of again.

"Anywhere warm, along the Pacific coast."

He moved closer, grasped her hand in his, then laced his fingers through hers.

"I'd take you anywhere, as long as we're together," he murmured.

She drew in a deep breath and gave him a wan smile. "We'd better go."

He released her hand, drew his shirt from a crack in the seat, and shrugged it on. She retrieved her shirt from the floorboard, then searched for her jeans. They'd been tossed over the back of the passenger seat. He grabbed them and handed them over with a knowing smile.

Desire spread like warm whiskey through her veins as she remembered his gentle touch. The musky scent, unique to only him, drove her heart into a gallop. She craved his strong arms around her, his body, flush with hers, his hands exploring every inch of her. The longing to reach for him was difficult to resist, but they had to go.

He found his jeans, tugged them up to his waist, then pulled on his boots.

"Can we just drive through the checkpoint?" she asked as she struggled to get her shirt on with one arm.

"Probably not." He looked out the windshield. "There are guards on top of the building. They'd shoot us if we drove through without stopping."

He opened the back door. A cool southern breeze blew inside. Further south, winters were mild compared to Oklahoma's. She watched unabashedly as he adjusted himself, then buttoned his jeans.

She turned when he shut the door, pulled on her jeans, then crawled back into the front passenger seat for a better look at the guards.

He slid into the front seat. "You ready?"

"As I'll ever be."

He gave a short nod as he started the car, then pulled into the first lane. When he reached the building, a guard so tall it looked as if he could've fallen down a beanstalk, stepped out. A maroon beret hid his cropped, sandy blond, hair. He stooped to look inside and gestured for him to roll down the window.

"The border's closed," the man snapped in an intimidating baritone voice.

"Wait. I'm going to get a letter from the glovebox."

In slow, deliberate movements, he leaned over Lacy and pulled a white envelope from the glove compartment, then handed it out the window.

The guard snatched it out of his hand, turned without instruction, and marched back inside.

"Chatty," Lacy groused. "What now?"

"We wait, I guess."

The guard returned with two more men at his back. "Step out of the car," he boomed.

Jace glanced at her. "Let's go," he said, voice low.

As they exited the car, the distant whir of chopper blades sliced through the air. She lifted her head, eyes trained on the familiar orange and white helicopter. A tidal wave of dizziness crashed over her, and she gripped the open car door to steady her shaky legs.

Jace sidled up beside her and slipped a comforting hand into hers. "No matter what happens," he started.

"No," she ground out. "Don't finish that sentence."

"Lacy, we're outnumbered with nowhere to run. We have to play this smart."

Tears stung the back of her eyelids. "But he'll separate us."

"Only for a time. We'll find a way out of this. You have to believe that. I'll find you and we'll look for your parents like I promised." He stopped, took her face between his hands. "I love you."

She nodded, unable to get words past the lump in her throat.

Jace laced his fingers through hers then they turned together and faced Thomas Monroe.

Monroe jumped out of the chopper. Downwash whipped his hair to one side. In a quick gait that belied his age, he strode toward them, a revolver aimed at Jace's head.

"I have no problem pulling the trigger," he warned.

Cold, auburn eyes locked on hers. The dispassionate look set a chill in her bones, colder than last autumn's blue norther.

Jace held his hands in the air then turned his head toward her. Love radiated from his eyes as he said, "Remember I love you."

"Get in the car, Jace," the senator demanded waving the gun toward the Cadillac.

The lump in her throat grew. Jace had just made love to her in that car. She couldn't let him go.

She grabbed his arm, pulled it down in a bruising hold against her chest. "No, no, no. Please," she begged. "Please don't leave me again."

"You're breaking my heart," he choked out, then disengaged his arm.

"Please," she whispered.

His eyes sought hers. "Stay safe. Stay alive."

"Let's go," Monroe barked, then turned to Bryan. "Did you get the payment loaded onto the chopper?"

Bryan gave a nod in affirmation. "The black trunk is loaded in the back."

Monroe withdrew a letter from his breast pocket and handed it to Bryan. "Give this to Nieto."

"You have no right to do this!" Lacy screamed at her uncle's back. "You're such a bastard!"

Thomas turned on his heel and in two swift strides had his

finger in her face. "I have every right. And you," he snarled, gritting his front teeth, "are going to learn respect."

"Not from you," she spat. "You're no family of mine."

He took a step back, regained his cool composure, and gave her a thoughtful look. "You're too much like the man who raised you. That's the problem with kids. They inherit all their parent's flaws. And I assure you, I am more family to you than you realize."

"Is that why you never had kids? Or is it because your wife figured out what a psycho you really are?"

She never saw his hand strike, but the blow buckled her knees. She fell hard onto the black asphalt.

He bent over her, face mottled red. "Don't you ever speak about my wife again."

She heard him retreat, slam the car door shut, and drive away. She couldn't bear to look, so she kept her eyes trained on a fissure in the asphalt.

Bryan walked over, steps cautious. "Lacy." He said her name, low, soothing. "I'm sorry."

3

Bryan lifted Lacy off the gritty asphalt. He carried her to the chopper, strapped her in, then placed a set of bulky headphones over her ears. As the helicopter rose into the air, she closed her eyes, leaned her head against the seat's headrest. Too numb, too tired to fight. Defeated. She'd lost Jace. Again.

The first time, he'd left the farm after Christmas without a word. He'd deserted her. She thought he didn't want her anymore, that he'd given up on their relationship. A small part of her didn't blame him, but it stung thinking he'd taken a coward's way out, sneaking off in the dead of night. He couldn't let go of the fact she'd been raped. It ate at him. She hadn't told him it was his brother who'd raped her. He 'd found that out on his own.

Being without him hurt more than she ever imagined it could. He'd burrowed his way into her heart, and she'd foolishly thought he'd stay with her through anything. Learning he'd exacted revenge on her rapist had been little consolation.

"Are you okay?" Bryan asked.

They'd flown over nothing but vast canvas of land, painted a dull brown.

His voice echoed through the earpieces. Was she okay? Tears rushed to her eyes.

"No, not really."

"We're at the halfway mark."

She nodded.

"I'll get us in and out as fast as I can. I'll refuel the chopper at the Mexico City Airport. I'll have you home before you know it."

His comforting words were pointless. A dread she couldn't shake draped itself on her shoulders and bore down. Why had her uncle stopped them at the border? He'd blackmailed Jace into kidnapping the Oklahoma governor. They'd been on their way to deliver the payment to Raul's father just as he'd commanded. What more did he want? It puzzled her why he wanted to use them in his political game.

They were mere pawns in a chess game she didn't understand. She knew her uncle wanted control of the United States. He didn't believe in the current president's totalitarianism, so he'd gathered the Texas militia and anyone else he could find to try and stop the president.

On paper, her uncle's plan looked noble, like he was trying to save the country for the people. The president had sequestered U.S. citizens into work camps, state by state.

In reality, he was a ruthless, power-hungry politician with an 'ends justifies the means' dogma.

A bone numbing silence passed before Bryan spoke again.

"There it is," he said, pointing down.

As she looked down, a swarm of angry bees launched from her stomach to her throat. Panic bloomed in her chest. She glanced at Bryan. He caught her gaze and gave a reassuring nod. But his eyes tightened in apprehension. He banked the chopper, and they landed in a lush courtyard behind a light brown three story stucco. Its beautiful red clay tiled roof was breathtaking. Porticoes ran the length of the house along every floor, giving the mansion an open, airy look. Three-tiered stone steps led up to the back yard gate.

Bryan yanked his headphones off and unstrapped himself from the seat. He reached over to help her unbuckle. She removed her headset then pointed out the window at five men striding toward them in line formation.

"I see them," Bryan half-shouted as he throttled down and set the collective controls.

The helicopter's dying rotors roared in her ears. Bryan climbed out, ran over, and opened her door. Air whooshed down on her shoulders as she jumped out. Dry desert dirt swirled in the air. She covered her head with her arms, shielding herself against the downwash.

"This is bad," she warned, pinching the bridge of her nose.

They walked up the terrain's incline, shoulder to shoulder.

The men, armed with AK-47's, met them.

"Who are you?" the man in the center demanded in broken English.

The man to his left and right had drawn their weapons.

"We have a payment for Nieto from Thomas Monroe," Bryan answered.

His unflappable demeanor impressed her. His military training must've schooled him in the art of self-confidence. She tried to hide her growing fear by mimicking his staunch posture. She spread out her stance and lifted her chin.

The lead man motioned for them to follow him by flicking his wrist toward the estate. He turned and walked back up the slight slope to the lit porch. She glanced over her shoulder at the four remaining men walking behind them. Their weapons weren't trained at her back, but she still didn't like the feeling of being hemmed in.

A man who looked like an exact replica of Raul, except for the silver streaking his hair, sat in a black and white lounge chair. A slim cigar hung in a blasé manner between his fingers.

Whisps of white smoke curled in the air, its herbaceous scent mixing with the earthy notes of the dry desert air.

A gold rimmed lowball glass filled with amber liquid sat on the table beside him. In his white linen suit, he was the essence of opulence, posing for a photographer from the *Lifestyles of the Rich and Famous.*

He spoke to the lead man in spirited Spanish then turned to them.

"My name is Manuel Nieto," he said, eyes trained on Bryan. "I assume Senator Monroe sent you. Where is my payment?"

"In a black trunk in the helicopter," Bryan replied, returning Nieto's hard stare.

Nieto spoke to the lead man again who then turned and led the other four back toward the chopper.

Bryan stepped closer to Nieto and pulled a white envelope from his back pocket.

"I have a letter from the senator," Bryan said.

She admired his steady voice and hand. It exuded an unshakable confidence that defied the precarious situation in which they found themselves.

Nieto's brow rose. He placed his cigar on an elegant glass ashtray, then picked up the lowball glass, and downed the whiskey. He set the glass next to a round crystal cut decanter that reminded her of a Genie bottle.

The five men returned, two carrying the black trunk between them. They stepped over and placed it beside Nieto. The lead man with a mustache thick enough to house a large bird disappeared inside the house, then returned carrying bolt cutters. He bent beside the trunk and snapped the lock. Discarding the broken metal, he lifted the lid.

"*Gracias*, Miguel," Nieto murmured.

He peered down, surveying the contents. Satisfied, he gave a short nod and two of the five men stepped over and carried it inside.

Nieto turned his attention back to Bryan.

"The letter," he demanded, snapping his fingers.

Bryan placed the letter in Nieto's outstretched hand. Nieto tore open the flap and pulled out a single tri-folded sheet of paper. Judging the fury that rode across the older man's face as he read it, she guessed her uncle broke their agreement by detaining Raul.

He swung his gaze to Miguel and spoke in fast, rapid-fire Spanish.

Miguel rushed over and before she could react, he jerked her hands behind her back and held them in an iron grip.

He gave her back a rough shove toward the house. "Go!"

She wrestled against his hold, tried to wrench her hands free, but her efforts were useless pitted against the man's strength.

The two other men drew their weapons on Bryan.

Twisting her head around, she tried to see where he'd been taken.

"Bryan!" she screamed, writhing against the man's hold.

Breaking free, she swung around and saw the two men herding Bryan back down the lawn toward the chopper.

"Hey!" she shouted. "He's not leaving without me!"

She lurched forward, ready to sprint, but Miguel wrapped his thick arms around her waist. His hot breath on her neck reeked of tequila and cigars. She kicked him in the shin and got a satisfying grunt out of him. He released her waist, then grabbed a wrist and held it in his meaty hand.

Raul's father rose, walked over, and made a slow turn around her, in assessment. She spat obscenities at him, but instead of incensing him, he just laughed.

He grabbed her chin. "What a fighter," he said in a delighted voice.

"Let me go!" she shouted, jerking her chin out of his grip.

His face turned to stone. "No. Your uncle kept my son. So, I'm keeping his niece."

"I'm not his niece. You have the wrong girl," she lied.

He laughed as if she was a small child telling an amusing joke. "Oh, but you are. And much, much more. I've done my homework, *cariño mío.*"

Nieto turned to the man holding her and nodded his head.

"You're making a mistake," she said in a pleading voice. "The senator doesn't care about me!"

"Then that is your misfortune," he said coldly.

Manuel Nieto turned and strode into the house. The man who held her wrist like a manacle pushed her forward.

She thrust her elbow into his ribcage. "Stop pushing me!"

He hustled her into a black SUV with dark tinted windows. It blocked her view of the landscape whizzing by.

He stopped the car, opened her door, and jerked her from the seat. They'd pulled into an abandoned warehouse. Miguel strong-armed her down a set of stairs. Before she reached the bottom step, she was hit by the strong stench of mold and sewer water. He manhandled her into a tiny room, then locked the door behind him.

She sized up the tiny room. Dust hung in the air, thick with rotten smells she couldn't decipher. A pathetic cot with a stained pillow lined the far wall. Her feet felt like lead as she trudged to the sorry cot. With a sigh of defeat, she laid down, and let a single tear fall down her fevered cheek.

FROM THE CADILLAC'S passenger seat, Jace got a familiar sense of déjà vu. Hard to believe only a few days had passed since he'd been in this exact position. The difference between now and then was, before, the miles drew him closer to the farm, closer to Lacy. Now, every mile widened the gap between them. Leaving her was like being cut open and watching the blood pour out all over the ground. The pain worsened with every mile marker they passed.

He gave the senator a sidelong glance. "Bad Moon Rising" drifted from the speakers. *Appropriate,* he inwardly scoffed.

"Why are you so hellbent on keeping Lacy away from me?" he asked.

Monroe reached down and grabbed a silver Yeti coffee mug from the cup holder and took a cautious sip of the steaming liquid.

"There's a thermos in the back with coffee in it if you want some," he offered, as if he hadn't heard the question.

"Where the hell did you get coffee?" He sniped, running a hand through his tangled hair. "You know what? It doesn't matter. I don't want your damn coffee. I want answers!"

"I don't like your demanding tone," he reprimanded.

He fisted his hands, trying to subdue the rage threatening to erupt. He wouldn't get answers if he lost his temper.

"I'm sorry," he muttered. "But could you please answer the question?"

"You both have parts to play," the senator replied.

The older man's vagueness nettled him. "We didn't ask to play in your political game."

"You were drafted."

"How do we buy out of your game?"

Thomas replaced his mug and ran a hand over his mustache. "Interesting question. There is something else I had in mind for you to do."

He figured. The man's treachery had no bounds. He could try and argue his way out of whatever the senator wanted him to do, but why waste his breath? Monroe had all the power because he controlled Lacy's security. Because of his love for Lacy, he was an unwilling participant in whatever the man chose for him. He'd been captured in a game where leverage was king.

He despised the man. He had ruthless ambitions, and total

disregard for others, unless he had something to gain from them.

"I need you to take out the New Mexican governor,"

Thomas continued, ignoring his damning silence.

He placed a hand on his forehead. "Jesus Christ."

Thomas narrowed his eyes. "Hold your tongue. You'll not take the Lord's name in vain."

"Whatever," he muttered. "I don't want to do it. I *can't* do it."

"You don't really have a choice, do you? If you want to be with my niece, that is."

"Why? Why do you need New Mexico?"

"I'm taking control over the whole southwest region. As we speak, I have a team taking over Arizona."

"You want to barter the land with Mexico for their help. You're taking control of the whole country?"

Thomas raised a brow. "Yes, that is my current plan. I have back up plans in place if this falls through."

"What do I have to do? You said, "take out" the governor. You know I won't kill him."

"Well, I can't put every governor on ICE. I'm having a hard enough time restraining Harding."

He gritted his teeth. "I can't."

"Then have someone on your team take the shot. But the shot must be taken. Everything rides on your actions."

He was so screwed. Thomas Monroe had him by the hamstring. If he wanted Lacy, he'd have to play Monroe's game. And the likelihood of the senator continuing to use him over and over didn't escape him.

He laid his head against the window and watched scrub brush swish by in a brown blur. He closed his eyes and conjured Lacy's image, vowing to get back to her.

4

rip, drip, drip … Drip, drip …

DLacy counted the monotonous plinking sound as water drops fell from the leaky faucet into the dirty, stainless-steel basin. Her head ached from the strain. She'd counted the droplets until she lost track, then started over. Three long drips, one break. Two short drips, one break. And on and on.

Hard water residue clung around the basin's drain. The stainless-steel had lost its luster to a collection of dirt, piled on year-by-year, until it no longer resembled shiny metal.

The bare light bulb, hanging on a wire from the ceiling, did little to beat back the darkness. As her eyes adjusted to the low light, she saw mold on the walls, creeping and spreading its thin, feathery black veins across the concrete like a spiderweb.

The room looked eerily alive. The walls seemed to expand and contract, each breath blowing out musty air in metronome time with each drip in the sink.

In the far corner, a piece of rotted plywood, black with mold and crumbling around its edges, lay on the floor. She approached it with caution, then squatted down beside it. Did she want to know what was underneath? What if a snake lived under there? Plugging her nose against the stench, she lifted the damp wood with caution and found a hole underneath, no bigger than a dinner plate. Rancid air whooshed up, blasting her in the face with enough force to blow hair off her shoulders.

It smelled worse than rotten eggs. She stumbled backward, turned her head, and gagged. It was used as a toilet. Revolting. What type of creepy, crawly thing would jump out and bite her? She shivered and shoved the plywood back over the scary hole.

She curled into a tight ball on the old cot in the corner, ignoring the urine, sweat, and dirt stains. Wrapping her arms around her head to shield her ears from the dripping water, she let pent-up tears fall. They puddled on the cot's musty canvas, adding to its tapestry of stains. She missed Jace, hungered for the way he touched her, looked at her like she was the only thing that mattered. It would devour her if she gave in to the hopelessness of her situation, cloud her thinking. If she had any hope of escape, her thoughts must be sharp, clear.

This situation was her uncle's fault. He knew Nieto. No politician decided to get into bed with another without doing their homework. Venomous hate spread through her system. A familiar feeling. She'd had the same hatred toward Zach after her assault, but that wasn't something she wanted to think about. Remembering recreated the horror of that night and she didn't want to relive it. Not now.

She choked on a sob as she remembered watching Jace walk away, shoulders slumped in defeat. It was intrinsically woven into her to fight. She would've fought until the last drop of her blood stained the asphalt. He knew they'd both die if they'd tried to fight their way free. His was the smarter move.

She shifted onto her back, throwing an arm over her face.

What had her uncle done to him? Where was he now? Worry settled over her like a fog rolling in off the sea.

She lifted her head at the sound of heavy feet shuffling against the floor outside. She shot up, heart thudding in painful thumps against her ribcage. The feet stalled, then the lock clicked and the door opened.

Miguel walked in carrying a metal lunch tray. He set it on the floor beside the cot then spoke something in Spanish, pointing at the tray.

She eyed the strange concoction oozing from a weird looking shell, then shook her head. "I'm not eating that."

His brown cowboy boots scuffed the concrete as he shuffled closer.

She scooted to the end of the cot until her back touched the moldy concrete. A shiver from the cold rolled down her back.

His eyes roamed up and down her body, making her feel dirty. The sexual hunger, evident in his deep brown eyes, frightened her.

She snatched the coarse, smelly blanket and clutched it to her chest like a shield.

"Don't try it," she warned.

He cocked his head, smoothed his mustache, and gave her a calculated stare. Finally, he stepped back and motioned to the food.

"Eat," he said, then turned and left, locking the door behind him.

She eyed the bluish, black taco shell and her stomach pitched. Its contents oozed out, looking like something that would crawl out of the toxic toilet hole. At least they gave her bottled water.

She stood, fished the pack of antibiotics from her pocket, grateful Jace had thought to look in the care package Cat had sent. She grabbed one of the two water bottles. The stubborn orange cap refused to twist off.

"Damn it!" she shouted and almost threw the useless bottle against the concrete wall.

Instead, she bent and switched bottles. This time, the orange cap twisted off with ease. She popped the pill in her mouth and downed it with a few gulps of the water.

Something in that moment reminded her of Cat and the welcoming numb of alcohol. Her body craved a shot of whiskey, the burn as it traveled down her throat, then the sweet release as her worrisome thoughts drifted away. What was the older woman doing now? Throwing a fit because of her absence, she hoped. Jace would know by now she'd been kidnapped by Raul's father. As much as she tried, she had a difficult time reconciling Raul and his father. Raul acted nothing like the unscrupulous Nieto. But did she even know Raul? Doubt crept in and she began to wonder if she knew Raul at all. He could be exactly like his father.

Anger's familiar acidic sting exploded in her gut. The need to escape burned her thoughts like wildfire consuming dry Juniper trees on the prairie. She'd been buried alive in the middle of Mexico. Even if she managed to slip from the tiny room, then what? She had nothing, no form of protection, no transportation. She couldn't even protect herself from the man who brought her the tray of disgusting food. And the look he gave her made her skin crawl.

She eyed the tray, then picked it up, tested the metal's sturdiness. It might come in handy if she could hide it somewhere. The vision of whacking the bushy moustache man upside his greasy head sent a satisfying tingle through her.

She turned with trepidation toward the hole, then approached with caution. She slid the lid over, exposing the small drain.

Pinching her nose, she breathed through her mouth as she disposed of her uneaten food. Her full bladder demanded release, so she dropped her jeans and squatted. Never had she been exposed to such a foul odor wafting up the drain hole.

She slid her jeans up, shoved the rotten board in place, then stumbled to her cot.

She slid the empty tray underneath the stained flat pillow, sat down, and waited. And waited. But Miguel never returned.

Her back numbed against the freezing wall and her eyelids drooped. A song played in her head, and it brought memories of her parents, dancing in the living room to the haunting melody. Her body relaxed into its strange and mysterious lyrics. As the song shifted to the chorus, she imagined AJ in the room with her, watching over her.

He bent over her slumped, languid frame and whispered, "I'm coming to get you, sis."

Then, he vanished. The vision took a turn.

She pictured her brother creeping through a long hallway. Low light radiated from the wall's faux sconces and gave the narrow hall a tunnel effect. As he drew closer, a door opened in front of him, then a gunshot cracked. He stopped and clutched his chest.

Heart pounding, she jerked upright. Sweat beaded her forehead.

"AJ, no," she choked out.

The dream felt real, but she knew it wasn't. AJ didn't know she'd been kidnapped. He was in California with her parents. She chalked it up as desperation fueling the dream or vision.

Pounding on the wall against her back yanked her from the haunting dream. She heard a hoarse, disembodied "hey," come from the other side of the wall.

She pressed her ear against the cold concrete and listened.

Had she hallucinated the voice? She fisted her hand and pounded against its crude, rudimentary roughness. One, two, three, four.

A few seconds passed. Nothing.

Then a dull one, two, three, thud answered.

"Who are you?" she asked, trying to keep her voice low.

"Willow," the voice answered in a soft, southern drawl.

"Who are you?"

"Lacy. Do you know why we're here?"

The girl didn't answer.

"Hey," she tried again. "Where are you from?"

The girl wasn't Mexican. She ascertained that from her intrinsic southern lilt. How did she end up in Mexico City mixed up with a dangerous man like Nieto?

"Texas," Willow replied. "I was kidnapped near the Laredo border."

"Do you know why they're keeping us here?" she tried again, "or what they want?"

"They hold us here and either sell us or keep us for their high-end clients. They just sold the girl on the other side of me."

An electric shock buzzed from the top of her head down to her toes. Her breaths came short and fast. It sounded like Nieto ran a sex trafficking ring. She dropped her head into her lap, squeezed her eyelids shut, and swallowed the scream building in her chest.

She took a deep breath, counted to five, then let it out as she counted. One. Two. Three. Four. Five. She repeated the exercise until her chest relaxed.

She'd find a way out. Somehow. She wouldn't let herself become a victim again.

"How long have you been here?" she asked.

"I don't know. What month is it?"

"February."

"Four months." Willow's small voice cracked.

Lacy digested the information. Nieto wouldn't sell her, would he? She felt a raging panic attack clawing her chest, demanding release. She shoved down the reaction. She had to know more.

"Have you met any of the high-end clientele?" she asked, afraid of the answer.

As the silence stretched, she thought the girl hadn't heard the question. Or just didn't want to answer.

"Many times," Willow answered in a shaky voice.

"I'm sorry," she commiserated. "I know you don't know me, but I get it."

"Thanks."

A thought occurred to her. A long shot, but she had to ask.

"Do you know if there's a way to escape?" she asked, trying to rein in the hope building in her chest.

"No," Willow said at length. "They come and take us to a hotel where their clients are. The men guarding us watch us shower and dress. There's no privacy."

If they came for her, they'd have a hell of a fight on their hands. There must be a way out of this mess. One thing she knew for certain. She couldn't wait around to be rescued. Her uncle had orchestrated this and had Jace in his clutches. There was no one else who knew where she was. The odds of escape were stacked against her.

JACE LED HIS HORSE, Josie, from the crude makeshift stall in the shop building, into the biting February wind. The drive from Texas back to the Monroe farm had been pure torture. Leaving without Lacy shredded his heart. It was a pain that superseded his soul. It bled into the physical. He counted on Bryan to bring her home safely after they dropped off the senator's payment to Nieto.

Unable to stand being in the senator's presence another second, he'd bolted for the shop as soon as the car rolled to a halt. He'd choose bone numbing cold over the man's company any day.

Jace turned and watched Raul struggle to lead Lacy's horse, Acer, out of the shop building. The incensed horse threw his head and reared, jerked the lead rope from Raul's hands, then bolted for the pond in the far pasture.

"Crazy horse," Raul shouted, chest heaving.

He wiped his dusty hands across his jeans.

Jace watched the stubborn horse race across the brown, deadened prairie grass, his russet mane flying free. "Just let him go."

"I am glad to see you. How was your trip?" Raul asked.

He shook his head. "I'm so screwed, man."

Drawing a curry comb from his back pocket, he began combing hitchhiker burrs from Josie's coat. Bryan should've been back with Lacy by now. Why weren't they back? Unease niggled its way into his heart. He'd give Bryan one hour. After that, he'd confront the senator.

Cold air crept underneath his Carhartt jacket, sending a chill up his back. His head shot up at the staccato wop-wop, wop-wop of chopper blades as the orange and white helicopter came into view. It descended into the pasture, and he ran to meet it, mindless of the gusty downwash whipping his chin length hair into a wild tornado.

The chopper's skids met the ground. Bryan tore off his headphones, opened the door, and jumped down.

Jace craned his neck forward, searching for Lacy. Where was she? Why hadn't she exited yet?

The urgency in Bryan's stride made his knees weak. Adrenaline thrust its way through his system.

"What took you so long? Where's Lacy?" he shouted over the chopper's dying rotor.

Bryan shook his head slowly, his brown eyes darkened with sadness. "Raul's father kept her."

The words shot through him swifter than a bullet. "What?"

Memories flashed, and all he saw was her. Everything he wanted, everything he needed was wrapped up in her.

"He wants his son," Bryan explained. "Monroe keeping Raul was a deal breaker."

He wanted to punch something. The senator knew this would happen, probably counted on it. How could he do that to his own flesh and blood?

Jace took a menacing step forward. "Why didn't you do anything?" he yelled.

"I couldn't!" Bryan shot back. "Five men escorted me *at gunpoint* to the chopper. Starting a fight would've gotten us both killed."

He ran his hands through his hair, feeling helpless, and hating it. "She can't handle this."

"She'll handle what she has to, Jace. She's strong," Bryan said.

"But that's just it. Every time something happens, she loses a piece of herself. How much is she gonna have to lose before this ends?"

Raul walked over and stood beside Jace. "What's going on? Where's Lacy?"

Jace turned, eyes shooting daggers, and pointed a finger at him. "Your father kept her," he seethed.

Raul's face blanched. "*Qué?*"

"He kept her! Why?"

"*Esto no está bien.*"

"English!" he shouted.

Raul rubbed the back of his neck. "This isn't good. My father can't be trusted. If he kept Lacy, she's in danger."

Jace turned to Bryan. "Get back in the chopper. Let's go get her."

"Shut up, man!" Bryan barked.

The command brought him up short. "The hell you say?"

Bryan's eyes shifted to the side. "Look around you."

Jace turned. Militia men headed down the pasture, guns drawn.

In slow, careful steps, Raul backed away, then turned on quiet feet, and made his way back to the shop building.

Bryan rubbed his chin and said in a low voice, "We have to be smart. We'll get her back. But it's not gonna be today."

Jace recognized the senator's assistant, William, leading a team of four men, their semi-automatic weapons pointed at Bryan. The young assistant reminded him of a skittish cat. How he scored a position as a U.S. senator's assistant, he had no effing clue.

"Bryan." William called before coming to a full halt in front of them. "The senator needs you."

"Yeah, yeah. I know," Bryan groused.

"Well, let's go. He doesn't like to be kept waiting."

Bryan cursed. "I'm exhausted. I've been up way over twenty-four hours. I need food and sleep."

"You can discuss that with him," William said in a no-nonsense manner.

Bryan looked at Jace, rolling his eyes. "He wants me to fly his wife to a more *secure* location," he said, using air quotes.

Jace watched the men retreat up the pasture thinking about Bryan's statement. Why did the senator feel the need to sequester his wife?

Josie whinnied and stomped her feet by the shop door, ready to get out of the biting cold. He started the trek back up the pasture. He needed to talk to Travis and Cat before the senator ordered him to New Mexico. They'd been staying in the large farmhouse, along with Edwards, Dylan, Matty, Ethan, and Hailey. A tight fit, but they all agreed it best to stay out of the senator's way.

He led his horse into the shop. After the barn burned a few months before, they'd made the two horses makeshift stalls in the shop building. Not ideal, but it worked.

The fire had reduced the barn to nothing but ash and took with it all their fishing, hunting, and trapping equipment. The president's military police had wanted to starve them out. And it almost worked.

The shop building had been a bitch to clean out. Piles of newspapers, magazines, empty milk containers, and all manner of trash littered the building. It had no insulation and any heat traveled straight to the high ceiling. They'd built makeshift stalls out of wooden pallets. Raul had constructed the front enclosures from old wooden doors he'd found in the trash pit.

He walked out of the shop, headed for the larger house. He had no idea how much time he had before Thomas Monroe shipped him out. His strides lengthened. He needed ideas on how they could rescue Lacy. Anguish's iron fist squeezed his heart. It was a pain he felt past his soul and into his spirit. He had to get her back.

5

Jace sat in the farmhouse kitchen with Cat, Edwards, and Travis in a semi-circle around the large iron stove. The afternoon's gusty wind blew in a storm and night fell in inky darkness as heavy, snow-laden clouds shrouded the moon.

Travis raised out of a flimsy folding chair, opened the stove's iron door with an ancient poker, and threw in two logs. He shut it with a clang and dropped back into the chair with a heavy sigh.

Cat raised a vodka bottle to her lips, took a pull, then let out a martyred groan.

Jace smirked. "What's the matter, Cat? Not a vodka fan?"

She turned to him with a scowl. "I haven't been able to sneak into the cellar for my whiskey lately. The senator's goons follow me everywhere I go. They even watch me gather the eggs, the Cretans. Then after supper, I'm shuffled down here like a prisoner."

With her last declaration she flipped her hair back with an indignant humph. Her silver-streaked chestnut hair fell in loose waves around her shoulders. Jace had never seen it down and thought she looked ten years younger.

Edwards grabbed the bottle from her and downed a healthy dose. "Whoo-wee! That'll hit ya' for sure and certain."

He passed it back to Cat. "Come on, Kit Cat. It's not that bad."

"Not that bad, he says," she muttered, then took another swig. She turned, and with a twinkle in her eye said, "you think you'll turn me into a vodka drinker like you, don't ya, you old coot."

He chuckled, reached over, and patted her hand. "I just might."

"Yeah," she agreed with derision. "Because it's all you brought."

"And you should thank God for that," he said with a mellow smile.

"I just might," she parroted, tongue in cheek.

Jace scooted his kitchen chair forward. "How do we get Lacy? What's our best move?"

"We're basically on lockdown here. Everywhere we go, we're followed, watched, questioned," Travis said, then turned to him. "It sounds like you're being shipped out. I have no idea what Dylan's been up to, and the senator uses Bryan as his personal pilot."

"Thanks for the rundown," Jace groused.

Travis shot him a scornful look and asked, "Where's Raul?"

"Haven't seen him all day," Edwards said.

"I haven't seen him since early this morning when Bryan got back," Jace admitted. He looked around the circle. Something in Cat's expression caught his attention. "What's up, Cat?"

She folded her hands in her lap. "Well, I kind of did a thing for him."

Jace raised a brow. "What kind of thing?"

"I warned ya' bout gettin' too involved," Edwards admonished.

Cat looked askance. "He asked me if I had access to anything that could knock someone out for a while. I said, yeah, sure. A healthy dose of any opioid would do the trick. And I have access to the pharmacy raid medicine."

"Why? Who did you dose?" Travis asked, scooting to the edge of his chair. "This may be our ticket out of here."

"I only dosed his personal guards. No one else. And it's already done. I mixed it into their oatmeal at breakfast. If it worked, Raul's probably long gone."

"Damn it," Travis growled and flopped back into his chair.

Jace studied the small group with dwindling hope. Edwards couldn't make a trip all the way to Mexico City, his age and health wouldn't allow it. Monroe used Cat to run the household, so she was out.

That left Travis.

Friggin' hell.

He bent down, cradled his head in his hands as tension rolled up his neck into his head He had no clue how to get along with Travis. How was he going to plan and execute a rescue mission with him?

They both loved the same girl.

They'd kill each other.

But the fact remained, he needed the younger man's help. He saw no way around it.

And it sucked.

He turned to Travis. "I guess that leaves us."

The younger man jumped to his feet. His chair folded, then fell to the floor with a pitiful clunk. He paced to the opposite side of the kitchen, placed his hands on the sink, and looked out the window. Then he turned, stomped back, and pointed a finger at Jace.

"This is all your fault," he exploded.

Jace bent his head and stared at his hands. Callouses had formed over softer flesh from hard farm work. Strange how proud he felt over those stupid callouses. The hard labor they represented helped him earn Lacy's trust. Travis spoke the truth. He could stand up, face the younger man, punch his lights out. He itched for it.

But he felt the same.

It was his fault.

"If you hadn't come around and screwed everything up, she wouldn't be in this mess," Travis seethed.

"Now hold on," Edwards interrupted.

"That's not true and you know it," Cat cut in. "That makes as much sense as two turtles in a relay race. She was in trouble the second she stepped foot on this farm."

"Don't misplace your anger, son," Edwards said. "Aim it toward the senator. I ain't never seen a man more power hungry. He's ate up with it."

Jace looked at Travis. "You may be right. Fact is, I feel the same. But will you set aside your hatred for me so we can save her?"

Travis looked around the circle and swore under his breath. He picked up his chair, unfolded it with excessive force, and sat back down. Travis's face mirrored a child who'd just swallowed a dose of castor oil.

Jace stifled the laugh crawling up his throat. If Travis only knew how mutual their feelings ran.

Travis folded his arms over his head. "Yeah, okay, I'll help," he finally yielded. "I still don't know what the hell she sees in you, man."

To the younger man's credit, it looked like he muzzled the rest of his comment. Smart, because he still might knock him ass over tit if he said the wrong thing.

"Sometimes, neither do I," Jace admitted, instead of firing the scrappy comeback clawing up his throat. He needed to nix his combative attitude. They'd never reach the border if he didn't.

The back door opened, and an icy wind gust blew Dylan

inside. Edwards rose and helped him close the swollen wooden door still hanging since the 1920's. Its single glass pane rattled against the force. Cracked lime and lead putty littered the floor.

Sleet pelted the tin roof and slid in icy trails down the kitchen windows. They all stared at Dylan dressed in Texas militia clothing, a side piece hanging from a black officer belt.

Jace shook his head, then lifted his eyes to the ceiling. Dylan joined the Texas Militia?

"You gotta be kidding," Travis muttered, scrubbing his hands over his eyes.

"What?" Dylan asked, flinging his hands in the air.

"What the hell, man? You a part of the militia now?" Travis demanded.

"It's not what you think."

"I think you're dressed like those following the senator.

You gonna go out and join the fun sleeping in one of those tents in this storm?"

Dylan walked over and stood by the stove. "I made a deal," he admitted.

"What have you gotten yourself into?" Jace asked.

"Honey, that man doesn't make deals." Cat said, voice somber. "He'll use you until he no longer needs you. Or until you're dead."

Her words rang in Jace's ears, and a lead ball settled in his stomach.

Dylan turned to Cat. "He's sending men tomorrow to get Gracie out of Fort Sill."

"We could've worked on something," Travis said, voice low.

"She's pregnant! Who knows what's happening to her? It's making me crazy." Dylan raked a hand through his wet hair.

"I know, man." Travis conceded.

Dylan bent down in front of Cat and laid a gentle hand on her knee. "He agreed his men could bring your husband back if they found him. They'll bring back Ben Wirtz if he's there."

Jace watched the interaction play out like a dramatic movie scene. He knew how much that statement meant to the older woman. He'd witnessed her heartache. She'd pined for her husband, grieved for him. She threw herself into farm work, taking care of Lacy. Busy work kept her mind off not knowing if Ben was alive or dead.

Cat's grey eyes filled with tears. She rose from her rocking chair and pulled him into a tight hug.

"Thank you is not enough, but it's all I have." She walked around the kitchen table to the living room entrance, then turned. "I'm kinda tired. I think I'll go lie down."

"Of course," Edwards said gently. "You go on."

Jace looked at Travis. "That still leaves only you and me."

"Just me if Monroe decides to send you to New Mexico before we have a chance to get away."

He cursed then turned to Edwards. "You think Cat could find my truck keys?"

The old man adjusted his black and white checkered hat. "Maybe. I think I might could help with that. Create a distraction of sorts, ya know. Yeah, we'll work on that tomorrow."

"The sooner the better," Jace agreed.

"Hey," Travis said, "what about my truck? I still have my keys."

"That old white Chevy under the carport?" Jace scoffed.

"It wouldn't make it out of the state let alone Mexico City."

Travis cracked a small grin. "Yeah, maybe not. But my sound system blows yours away."

Jace nodded in agreement, surprised by his civility. "Hey, you know how to hotwire?"

"I do," Edwards piped up.

"Then let's get the hell out of here. Before Monroe has a chance to send me to New Mexico."

Dylan blocked the door. "Sorry guys. Can't let you leave."

Without thinking, Jace turned and rushed at him, pinning his neck tight against the door with his right forearm. The glass pane rattled and shifted. "What the hell!" he shouted. "We trusted you, Lacy trusted you!"

Travis pulled on his left shoulder. He swung his arm around and pushed him away.

"Just wait until I get Gracie back," Dylan choked out.
"Please."

Jace applied more pressure to his neck, then released him.

"I ought to knock you on your ass. We'll leave whenever we damn well please and you better stay out of my way. Are we clear?"

"Yeah," Dylan rasped, then took a seat in Cat's rocker, rubbing his neck.

He turned to Edwards. "Later tonight."

Edwards nodded his head.

He and Travis would head for Mexico City tonight. He didn't know how they'd cross the border, but he couldn't wait any longer. He feared for Lacy, couldn't think of anything else.

What had Raul's father done with her?

6

Lacy was beginning to hate time, forever moving in one direction, each second pulsating with her heartbeat. The quiet darkness amplified the sensation. When the dim light shut off, she assumed night had fallen. She scooted down the cot from her vigilant sitting position and laid down to rest her aching back. She stared up into nothing, the darkness so black she couldn't see her hand in front of her face. She knew because she'd tried.

Miguel hadn't returned since he'd brought her food. The two bottles of water were long gone. If the empty minutes didn't drive her madder than a hatter, her aching thirst would. She refused to drink the water dripping from the faucet.

Seconds ploughed into minutes, into hours, with nothing but her myriad of jumbled, often morbid, thoughts. Ludicrous what the idle brain conjured in the night's stillness. It painted tucked away memories on a blank canvas. Memories long forgotten.

Junior basketball homecoming had been a huge deal in her sixteen-year-old world. When her peers voted her queen, she'd been euphoric. She'd driven her mother crazy with the details; decorations, gifts for the homecoming court, the luncheon. But buying the perfect dress had been paramount.

And she'd found it, the palest teal blue with a laced back, her favorite feature. Afterward, Jace had been with her family during the long picture-taking process afterward. He'd insisted on one, just the two of them. Too preoccupied with Travis, she'd never considered why he'd wanted it. The memory pushed its way forward.

The old Bias Gymnasium overflowed with alumni and students. The giant overhead heaters blasted blistering air against Lacy's back. She'd taken pictures with the homecoming court, then with her parents and AJ. By the time her dad snapped the last photo, her lips felt paralyzed into a smile. She raised up on her toes, searching the crowd for Travis. He said he'd take pictures with her and her parents, but so far, he'd been a no-show. Their friendship had shifted into something more the summer before. She liked him. Kissing him was a new experience she enjoyed, but something was missing. And when he flaked on her, she wondered if they'd be better off as friends.

Then warm hands snaked around her waist and pulled her back against a hard muscled chest. She inhaled her favorite Versace cologne. Jace. Heat flooded her cheeks, and she felt her heart kick up a notch.

He leaned down and said in a low voice, "Hey beautiful, can I get a picture with you?"

She'd never guessed his feelings for her. AJ always made sure she understood her place where his friends were concerned.

Where was the photo now?

Where was Jace now? What if her uncle had thrown him in a military prison? Or worse, sent him on another one of his missions? She would never underestimate him again.

In the darkness, minutes ticked by with every drip in the

sink. Somewhere in the dreary hours she dozed into a fitful, half-sleep, her mind awake, her exhausted body at rest.

The lightbulb buzzed on, and she rocketed up, scraping her elbow against the concrete wall.

"Shit," she muttered.

Blood bloomed in a checkerboard pattern across her skin. She reached behind her, slipped her hand under the flat pillow for the metal tray, then shoved it underneath her. How long before someone came and checked on her, she wondered?

Would they leave her here to starve to death? Or just go mad?

The locks clicked, then the door swung open. Miguel walked in carrying another tray with the same disgusting fare as the day before. She eyed the black corn tortilla with revulsion.

He sat it on the floor beside her. "Eat," he commanded.

She swung her legs over the side of the cot, careful to keep the tray hidden underneath her, then grabbed the two bottles of water. She uncapped one and drank a small portion. Ration it, she reminded herself.

"Eat," he insisted.

"No."

He stepped closer.

She slipped her hands underneath her, fingers wrapping around the warmed metal of the tray. One step closer and she'd clock him.

"You must eat. *Señor* Nieto wants to see you."

Another step. The tips of his boots almost touched her toes.

Too close.

"Don't come any closer," she warned.

Her muscles bunched, ready to strike.

"If you refuse to eat, you will come now," he insisted.

His hands reached down to grab her shoulders. She shot up, and with unabated fury, shoved him in the chest hard enough he stumbled backward. Before he gained his footing, she swung the tray like a melee weapon and bashed the side of his face. He dropped like a bag of bricks thrown from a skyrise. Blood trickled from his temple.

"*Puta*," he spat, struggling to rise.

She swung again connecting with the top of his head. "I'm not going anywhere with you," she shouted. "Get the hell out or let me go!"

Miguel inched backward on his knees. When the heel of his boots knocked against the door, he catapulted up, rushed out, then clicked the locks in place.

The fear that twisted into rage died, and in its place, a dark sinkhole threatened to suck her will to fight like water spiraling down a bathtub drain. The tray slid from her sweaty palms and landed on the concrete. The clatter hurt her ears. Her pulse decelerated and she tripped back onto the cot, completely spent.

"You okay?" Willow asked from behind the wall.

"Just peachy," she sniped, then rolled over, and propped herself up against the cold concrete.

Her arm throbbed, her head hurt, her mind screamed. She felt like a hot mess. What the hell was she doing?

"I heard a noise," Willow continued. "Did he hit you or something? Nieto's men aren't supposed to touch us."

She ran a hand through her greasy hair, dug into her pocket, searching for a rubber band. She'd never been one to frequent beauty salons, letting her hair grow until her mother complained. A sob rose at the thought of her mom. What was she doing right now? She longed for her like a missing limb.

Her fingers found a small band in the corner of her back pocket. She drew it out, gathered her mass of hair and wound it atop her head into a messy bun.

"Nope," she answered when she'd finished with her hair. "I beat the crap out of him with a metal tray."

"No shit? Damn. Why didn't I think of that?"

"Yeah well, it didn't get me out of here. I'll no doubt pay in spades for it. What do you do to pass the time? 'Cause I'm gonna lose it, especially in the dark."

"The food," was all she said.

She waited for her to continue. She didn't.

"What about the food?" she finally asked.

"They drug it. I don't know what they use. I didn't like it at first," she admitted. "But now it helps numb the pain."

"Yeah," she muttered to herself. "What I wouldn't give for some of Cat's whiskey right now."

"You got a guy back home?" Willow asked, voice wistful.

A lump formed in her throat. Thinking about Jace hurt too much and made her impossible situation seem insurmountable.

Instead of answering she asked, "Do you?"

"I did. I doubt he'll want me now. Nieto sold me to a man that lives in the states, so he keeps me for him." She choked on a sob, then fell silent.

"Sure, he will," she said, trying to sound convincing.

Truth was, she understood how the girl felt, and often wondered how Jace could be with her after what his brother, Zach, had done. Zach had raped her, gotten her pregnant. A wave of shame washed over her at the thought of her miscarried baby. She still thought the miscarriage a blessing. She couldn't help it. Zach had said he'd done it because he knew Jace loved her. In Zach's twisted mind, he thought he was taking what belonged to him, what was owed him. His haunting words played through her mind. *"Never could stand that little shit getting anything before me. He wanted you. Badly. I made sure I had you first."*

"No, he won't," Willow continued, jerking her from the memory. "How could he? I feel … I feel so dirty. I was a virgin. Before this."

The pain in the girl's voice was palpable. It swept through the wall like wildfire smoke, saturating her tiny space. Its wispy, elongated fingers wound around her throat, threatening to cut air from her lungs.

She thought of Jace. "If he loves you, he won't throw you away. He'll help you heal. You're not trash, Willow," she said in a soothing tone. "Your life still has worth. Don't define yourself by what these sick bastards do to you."

"Thanks, Lacy," she whispered.

She believed her own words, but a darkness circled the rim of her mind looking for a weakness, a way to pour itself into her. She stubbornly denied access to the thought scratching, digging, worming its way into her consciousness. Eventually, she'd have to deal with it. The stark realization that odds of her escaping this prison unscathed were dismal.

She eyed the food on the tray. Globs of cold onions and something green spread out of the black corn cocoon. It looked like *Jabba the Hutt*. Knowing the food could knock her out didn't make it any more appetizing. But hunger and a desire to be oblivious gnawed at her until she caved. She sat the tray on her lap and broke off a piece of tortilla. She stuffed it into her mouth before she could change her mind. It tasted bland. She couldn't even detect salt. She ate half, then laid back and waited for oblivion.

7

Jace slipped out the back door into the sleet-driven wind. Its force pummeled tiny ice pellets into the side of his face like a sandblaster, the air so sharp it hurt to breathe. He pulled his beanie over his ears, rounded the side of the house, and tried to search the gravel drive for a viable vehicle to swipe. Dylan said the senator anticipated his getaway, so he'd locked his truck in the shop building. Nothing would keep him from Lacy. His every thought concentrated on getting her back.

A lone floodlight situated atop the dilapidated carport shone against the pitch-black night. An eerie wind whistled between the house and carport, shoving him forward. He stumbled down the gravel drive lined with Humvees, Rangers, and Ground Mobility vehicles, but the senator's Cadillac, usually parked beside the smaller farmhouse, was absent.

He hunched his shoulders, intent on turning around to go back, but before he could, someone jerked him backward.

"What the hell!" he shouted.

The words carried on the wind and a hand slammed down hard over his mouth. He rammed an elbow into a ribcage, heard the return of a gratifying grunt.

"Shut up," a familiar voice hissed.

Bryan grabbed his arm, propelled him to the side of the wash house, then released him with a shove. He whipped around ready to knock out the large, linebacker outlined against the darkness.

"What the hell do you think you're doing?" Jace demanded.

"Saving your dumb ass, that's what. The senator will throw you in the closest brig if you try to leave. He's pissed about Raul and knows someone helped him escape. He's gonna question Cat tomorrow. I was on my way down to tell her when I saw you."

"I don't care!" he yelled. "I've got to get her back."

"Hold your voice down," Bryan barked. "You wanna get caught? I told you we'd get her, but it wouldn't be today. You're gonna have to play by Monroe's rules. Or act like it anyway."

Jace shoved his hands deep into his coat pockets. The cold crept into his bones causing them to ache. "Come on." Hestepped around Bryan. "Let's get inside."

Bryan grabbed Jace's coat sleeve and set a brisk pace down the drive. He jerked his arm out of Bryan's hold, took the two-step cinder block back porch in one leap, then opened the door. Bryan tumbled in at his back. Edwards, Travis, and Dylan sat at the kitchen table, each nursing a cup of coffee, waiting for his report. He glanced at the old, wind-up pendulum clock hanging on the kitchen wall. The varnish had faded from the dark-stained wood showing the passage of time in a different, more visceral way. The shorthand rested on the two, the long hand crept toward the six.

Every passing minute without Lacy cracked his heart like a chisel on glass. When he'd left the farm to hunt Lacy's rapist, he left secure in the knowledge she was safe, surrounded by those who loved her and would protect her. It made the pain of separation bearable. It was different now. Now, he feared for her safety. He stripped off his coat, threw it on the rocker, then pulled a chair from the table and sat.

Bryan gravitated to the coffee pot, pulled a mug from the cabinet, and filled it to the top. Steam rose from the hot liquid, its scent overriding the cold mustiness of the old shotgun shanty farmhouse. The coffee sloshed over the rim onto his fingers as he sat. He wiped his hand on his jeans and looked around the table.

"What's going on?" Travis asked. "Are we leaving or what?"

"The senator knows what you're planning. He's prepared to throw all of you in jail," Bryan answered.

Jace scratched the little hairs on the side of his jaw. "We've got to come up with another plan. One he won't expect."

"We need more than that," Bryan said in a conspiratorial tone. "We need an exit strategy. At least I do. I know you and Lacy do too. Don't know about the rest of you, but I'm done with the senator."

"Lacy comes first," Jace said with resolution. "Whatever it takes."

"I'm curious," Edwards mused, turning his sharp eyes on Bryan. "How much did the senator pay you? American dollars aren't worth piss in a pot."

"He didn't pay American," Bryan explained. "I had him pay me in Euro Dollars and deposit it in an offshore account. All upfront. Didn't trust him then, don't trust him now. He paid me a lot, so he thinks he can drag out our arrangement."

"Smart," Travis muttered. "But we still have to figure out how to get Lacy out of Mexico."

Dylan shifted uneasily. "Jace will have to go to New Mexico. There's no way around that. The senator has hemmed the state in with the Arizona takeover. He expects the governor to put up a fight. He wants us on that pretty quick."

Jace rubbed the back of his neck. "Shit."

"I'm sorry, Jace," Dylan said.

Before he could respond, Edwards cut in. "Dylan, why don't you go to bed now."

Dylan gave a curt nod, rose, and walked into the living room.

Jace appreciated Edwards tactful dismissal of the young man because Jace could barely restrain himself from knocking him senseless. Wouldn't take much effort either. The guy had no sense to begin with.

"So that leaves me," Travis said, running a nervous hand through his hair.

Bryan scooted up his chair. "And me."

All eyes turned on Bryan like he'd just transmitted a homing beacon.

"How you figure?" Travis asked. "The senator's not gonna let you just up and fly out of here."

"Not unless he thinks I'm going somewhere for him," Bryan said, raising a brow.

"Hold up," Jace interjected. "What about me? I'm going to get her."

"No," Bryan said slowly. "Not this time. Not if you want this done fast."

"What are you proposing?" Edwards asked.

"Edwards," Jace said, voice on edge.

Edwards shifted his chair sideways to face Jace, stretched his knees out. "You gotta hear him out, son. I get that ya wanna run outta here like the devil was chasin' ya to save your girl, but your way may not be the best way."

Irritated at the older man's rationality, he rubbed his hands up and down the legs of his jeans, the friction warming his hands. Never one for coffee, his mom had always made him hot chocolate instead. He missed warming his hands around a hot mug.

He missed her.

Part of him still couldn't believe his parents were gone. His brother, Zach, had orchestrated their murder. A part of him felt justified, yet another small part would always regret killing him. No matter how he tried to reconcile killing Zach, he came to the same conclusion.

Zach assaulted Lacy because of the sick, twisted jealousy he had for him. Zach wouldn't stop until he'd destroyed Lacy, which would've destroyed him. All forms of law enforcement had been dismantled and replaced by the military police which Zach held in his back pocket. He'd had no other choice. It still saddened and sickened him to think about.

He narrowed his eyes at Bryan. "Fine. What did you have in mind?"

Bryan cleared his throat. "The senator wants me to fly to Arizona, pick up Corporal James and take him to New Mexico. He'll meet you and the others he sends to take out the governor and assist if necessary."

"You have to make that trip," Jace said.

"I know," he agreed. "But once I make my drop, so to speak, I'm supposed to fly back here. Instead, I'll fly to Mexico City. Travis and I will have to do some recon to find out where Lacy's being held, but we'll get her."

"Why can't I load up with you in New Mexico?" Jace asked.

"There's no way." Bryan shook his head. "I overheard the senator. The whole reason for me dropping James in New Mexico is to watch you. The senator's eyes are trained on you. Let that be his mistake."

"Won't Corporal James notice I'm with you?" Travis asked.

"Yeah," Bryan said. "That's a wrinkle. You'll have to hide in the back of the chopper. It won't be comfortable."

A look of uncertainty crossed Travis's face.

Resentment rose inside him like a nuclear cloud, over the younger man's previous relationship with Lacy, and the fact he was being stymied. He'd give anything to trade places with Travis. He made Lacy a promise he'd find her.

"Can't handle it?" Jace scoffed before he could check it.

Rising, he paced a small circle around the table. "I'd give anything to trade places with you and you're hesitating! Wondering if you should take the risk. She's worth the risk. I'd die for her. Would you?"

"You don't know what the hell I'm thinking!" Travis shouted, standing to face him. "She was my girl first. I got a stake in this too. She hasn't married you yet."

Edwards's admonishing, "Boys," went unheeded.

"That you know of," Jace taunted. "This has been a long time coming. Let's get this hashed out, right now."

Travis balled his hands into tight fists. "Fine by me."

Bryan looked at him, a warning in his eyes. "You really think this is a good idea?"

Jace cooled like dry ice, took a seat, and kicked his legs up on the table. "I always wondered what happened between the two of you," Jace started. "You had a leg up being her friend first. Took AJ by surprise when your friendship shifted into something more. Not a lot he could do at that point. So, I know it wasn't his interference. What was it, then?"

Travis's face grew bright red. He raised a fist and took a step forward.

Jace hid anger's burning forge behind a cool, unflappable mask and continued his interrogation. "I watched her around you. She was into you. So, what happened?"

How he admitted Lacy had a thing for Travis without showing how much it gutted him was a miracle.

"That's none of your business," he shot back.

"Come on, Travis. She didn't break your heart." He lowered his feet. The chair's metal legs banged against the floor. "It was the other way around, wasn't it?"

"Why? What did she say?"

"That's just it. She never said anything. Not a word to her brother. Nothing. Which tells me something."

"Yeah?" Travis challenged. "What?"

"It was you. You broke it off. You dumb sack of shit."

"You have no idea what you're talking about," Travis seethed, taking another step toward Jace.

Jace smirked. "I think I do."

"You don't know what it's like living with my family. I'm a rez dog. Our ways are different."

He stood and ran a hand over his stubbled chin. "What do you mean?"

Travis's eyes darted to the floor. "My dad. He didn't like …"

He let out a derisive snort. "You mean she was too white? You're an idiot and don't deserve her."

He saw the right hook in time to dodge it, then jumped up, and rammed his fist into Travis's stomach doubling him over.

Jace shoved him to the ground, towering over him. "You have no claim over her, got it? Let it die right here."

The door opened, slamming against the wall as a strong gust of winter wind blew inside. He turned and stared into a pair of eyes he never thought he'd see again.

"AJ?"

8

The Day Before...

The one-hundred-acre dairy farm in Tulare, California was a perfect place to start over. AJ picked up his steaming coffee mug off the breakfast bar and opened the French doors to the dark-stained deck overlooking a small valley. Their new home. Three dairy cows meandered in slow placid motion across the lush, green grass.

His mom and dad really lucked out.

Anticipating the big crash, his dad, Emmett Monroe, withdrew all the money they'd saved in stocks, bit coin, and IRA's. At the time, AJ had scoffed at the blue duffle bag stuffed with American bills and gold coins, and thought Emmett Monroe was out of his mind. Now, he thought him nothing less than a genius.

California's struggling economy still relied on American dollars so when they'd reached Tulare, the young couple who'd wanted to consolidate and move in with their parents, happily accepted the ten thousand dollars his dad offered them. They'd bought the grey brick ranch house and farm for a penny an acre. Unbelievable. The notarized deed lay in a safe in his dad's

new office.

His dad sat on a white wicker chair, balmy air ruffling his salt-and-pepper hair, enjoying his coffee. Probably his third. AJ shook his head. His mom, Lila, would detonate if she knew how many cups of coffee he had each morning. Caffeine raised Emmett's blood pressure and he'd run out of medicine long ago. It worried his mother and for good reason. A history of sudden heart attacks ran in the Monroe family.

"Hey," he greeted his father as he wandered to the deck rail.

"Mornin'."

AJ blew on his coffee then took a cautious sip, contemplating the dream he'd had the night before.

His sister was in trouble.

A million army ants marched across every inch of his skin as he remembered the lucid dream. She'd called to him, and he'd answered, told her he was coming to get her. He tried to recall her surroundings, but they were fuzzy, like looking through a shroud or an unfocused lens. She should be on the Monroe farm in Oklahoma where they'd left her. She wasn't. Call it intuition, but he knew she was in danger. If she wasn't on the farm, then where the hell was she?

Heat flared up his neck. If his uncle harmed her in any way, there'd be hell to pay. His dad didn't trust his brother for reasons he refused to name. He'd only met Thomas Monroe once when he was five, but he never forgot the cold steel in the man's gaze. His uncle had an unscrupulous reputation as a senator, often using questionable tactics to get what he wanted.

He knew that much because Jace's dad, Jake Cooper, and his uncle, were friends from high school. Besides that, CNN ran reports on Thomas Monroe daily, it seemed. He had no reason to believe his uncle would harm Lacy. But that didn't mean he hadn't.

"Don't think too hard," his dad commented.

He focused on his dad who'd always been a man of few words, but when he spoke, they packed a punch. He didn't want to talk about the dream, or his sister. It would accomplish nothing except trouble his dad.

Emmett rose in slow motion, his arms stretching above his head. "Guess I'll run to town. Need anything?"

"Nah, I'm good, Dad. Thanks," he said, distracted, as he followed him back inside.

"I'm meeting a man in town about a horse and trailer," Emmett said, grabbing his keys from the key hook next to the door. "Tell your mom."

He donned a blue and gold Shidler Tigers baseball cap, opened the door to leave, then stopped. "Sure you're okay, son?"

"Yeah Dad. Fine."

Emmett nodded once then left.

AJ's thoughts returned to the disturbing dream. He'd experienced this type of surreal connection with his sister on two other occasions.

The first occurred on one of their camping trips in the Arbuckle Mountains. She'd fallen into the rushing water of the Washita River after refusing to listen to him. He'd warned her not to hunt arrowheads. Debilitating fear had stopped him dead in his tracks and he knew without a doubt his sister needed him. He turned on his heel, rushed down the trail to see Jace walking up the bank, Lacy clinging to his neck, dripping head to toe, and scared to death. He'd wanted to throttle her but knew the near-death experience was punishment enough.

He'd never asked Jace how he'd gotten to her before him. Love for his sister, written all over his best friend's face, had shocked him at first. But after a while, the idea of Jace and his sister together pleased him. He'd waited years for Jace to say something, but he never did, and he'd never gotten a chance to ask why. The American way of life disappeared overnight, and they'd moved to California.

The other occurrence happened the night they crossed into California. Sleeping in a truck with his parents was a fresh hell he never wanted to experience again. They'd bedded down in the truck bed while he tossed and turned in the cab on the back bench seat. Still in love with each other, their muffled private conversations and love making scarred him in ways he'd rather not think about.

He'd just fallen into a fitful sleep when Lacy floated into his dream. She seemed to be in a free fall. The height and depth of her fall, he couldn't see. Her hand reached for his. He'd tried to grab it, but she vanished in a thin wispy line of smoke. The mental image bothered him so much, he almost suggested turning around, but the trip from Oklahoma to California was

arduous. They'd had to think smart, and travel small, dirt, county roads to cross three state lines. Interstates and high-ways were too dangerous. If they saw military police or national guards, they backtracked and found another route. It took them a week to travel fifteen hundred miles. As his dad drove, AJ took notes, drew rough state maps, wrote down operable, deserted gas stations, and chronicled their route.

He knew how to get back home. But did he have that kind of time?

Urgency heated his blood, quickened his heartbeat. He flipped his black bangs out of his eyes, glad they were finally recovering from the butchering his mom had called a haircut. He grimaced. God, never again. He tapped his fingertips on the black speckled granite breakfast bar and considered how to tell his parents he was leaving without distressing them. His mother would worry regardless. Leaving a note might be best. No discussions. A pen and yellowed notepad rested by the old black wall phone. Landlines were ancient technology and he'd never used one. He couldn't imagine being tethered to the wall to make a call.

He dumped his cooled coffee in the sink, rinsed out the cup, and put it in the drainer next to his father's. His mother was a stickler about dirty dishes and had trained him well.

Grabbing the paper and pen, he moved to a bar stool and sat. What to say? Lacy is in trouble and I'm going to rescue her? No. His parents regretted leaving her behind, they'd suffered over it. He scratched the pen's tip over the paper, testing the blue ink, then began to write.

Mom and Dad,

I'm going to bring Lacy home. It's time. Please don't worry.

AJ

There. Simple and to the point.

He left the pad where it sat and went to his bedroom. Throwing a few changes of clothes in a backpack took less than a minute. The chest of drawers creaked as he jerked them open. He stuffed underwear, socks, T-shirts, and jeans into the ratty Nike bag he'd had since high school. He changed his tennis shoes for boots, grabbed the keys to the truck his dad bought him when they arrived, and shot out the door before his dad returned and he changed his mind.

He took their five-day journey in under thirty hours, racing through the day into the night. His recklessness almost upended his truck in New Mexico on a rutted gravel road. He slowed his pace after that, but the urgency racing through his blood never abated.

Shock barreled through him as he pulled into the main gate at the Monroe farm.

What the bloody hell?

Military vehicles lined the drive and tents spread across the forty acres like a brown speckled disease over the pasture.

He turned off his headlights, pulled into the yard, and bumped his way to the side of the larger house. His windshield wiper's swift whap, whap, whap, motion kept the onslaught of sleet at bay. He cut the engine, grabbed his jacket from the back seat, and shrugged it on. Steeling himself against the cold, he opened his door, and ran around the side of the house. The force of the wind all but tossed him inside as he opened the door.

Jace craned his neck over his shoulder and looked him square in the eye. He towered over Travis.

"AJ?"

What the hell was Travis doing here? Had the whole world gone bat shit crazy? It looked like Jace was giving the younger guy a beat down. He couldn't help the smirk that pulled at his lips. Not for a million bucks. He'd wanted to give the guy a swift kick in the ass the year he'd dumped his sister.

Shock registered on Jace's face first, then AJ swore he saw guilt flash through his eyes.

"What's going on here, brother?" AJ asked as he banged the door shut against the driving wind.

Jace turned and grabbed him in a bone crushing bear hug.

Travis picked himself up off the floor. "Yeah, Jace," he taunted. "What is going on?"

Edwards rose from his position at the table, walked over hand outstretched. "Name's Edwards." Without waiting for a response, he continued. "Who are you?"

"AJ," Jace answered. "Lacy's brother."

"Well," Edwards said with genuine delight. "I sure am glad to meet you. Travis and I was just about to hit the hay. Glad to meet ya, sure am. Hope we get a good visit in tomorrow."

Edwards limped to Travis and placed his hand around the scruff of his neck.

Travis tried to shrug off Edward's hand. "I'm gonna stay. I want to hear this."

AJ watched the old man give Travis's neck a light squeeze. "Come on, boy," he said, voice lowered and gruff. "Let's go."

"Whatever," Travis muttered with a heated face and stormed off. Edwards trailed behind.

AJ's brows rose. "What the hell was that all about?"

Jace ran a nervous hand through his hair.

Damn, the guy looked rough.

"Probably ought to sit," Jace suggested and pulled a chair from the table.

AJ looked around. "Got any coffee? I'm freezing. Temperature took a dive right when I crossed into Oklahoma."

Jace motioned to the half-full carafe on the counter. "I think it's still hot."

AJ walked over to the counter, pulled a cup from the cabinet, and poured a cup. He rounded the countertop and sat opposite Jace. No one had mentioned Lacy or offered to wake her up. Something was wrong and he needed answers. He wrapped his hands around the cup's warmth and looked his best friend in the eye.

"Where's my sister?"

Jace turned his head. "I'm not sure," he said, voice raspy and hoarse. "Somewhere in Mexico City."

AJ jerked up, toppling his chair to the floor. "What the hell?" he shouted. Confusion muddled his thoughts. "How? Why?"

Jace scrubbed his face with both hands, then motioned for him to sit. "A lot has happened since you left. It's a long story. And a hard one to tell."

9

The phrase, 'you can't make this shit up,' kept circling Jace's thoughts as he watched his best friend right the chair and sit. AJ pinned him with eyes that ran hot or cold, depending on his mood. Much lighter than his sister's, they were peridot green with a sunflower ring around the pupil. Right now, they ran furnace hot. Jace turned his head away from his penetrating gaze.

"When you called and said you were leaving and Lacy was staying at the farm, I wanted to move out here that day. I couldn't stand the thought of her being alone."

"Did you?"

"No, I —" A lump formed in his throat, and he swallowed hard. "My parents were murdered, so I stayed at the ranch a little longer than I should've, trying to figure out who killed them. And why."

"Shit." AJ blew out a breath. "I'm sorry, Jace."

He nodded, fighting for breath. "Yeah. Me too."

"Did you ever figure out who did it?" AJ asked, quietly.

"Not then, no. Zach was being an ass, as usual, so I left and moved here."

He didn't know how to tell AJ his sister had been raped. It

still scraped him raw, tortured him like a splinter that couldn't be dug out. Agitated, he shoved his chair back and walked around the table to the kitchen window. The storm had covered everything in a glistening sheet of ice, but the volcanic storm inside him still raged.

"Go on," AJ urged, his tone impatient.

He turned and braced himself against the sink. "When I got here, everything had changed. Lacy wasn't the same. I thought she hated me. I couldn't figure out why. I kept trying to talk to her, trying to find out what happened. She'd given shelter to a few people, Travis included."

"I don't like where this is going," AJ muttered, gripping the coffee mug until his knuckles turned white.

Jace took a deep breath and ripped off the Band-Aid. "Lacy was raped."

AJ bolted back up. "No." He shook his head over and over. "Hell no. You're lying."

The back of his eyes ached with tears. "I wish I was. AJ—" He stopped, caught his friend's gaze. "It gets worse."

"How the hell could it get any worse!" he exploded, pacing the floor. "What else is there?"

"She got pregnant." His quiet words echoed in his ears and he swallowed convulsively.

It still razed him to think of Zach and what he'd done.

AJ's eyes widened in disbelief. "Lacy's pregnant?"

"Not now. She miscarried," he choked out, remembering all the blood, the pain she'd suffered. He knew she still carried guilt over the loss of the baby. Guilt because she'd been relieved when she'd miscarried. He didn't know what he would've done if she'd carried Zach's

baby to term. He didn't want to look that far inside himself to find out either.

Zach had said he'd taken every one of his firsts. Zach had killed his first dog, his first horse. And he'd taken Lacy. The only woman he'd ever loved. He'd been her first, taken her virginity, then gotten her pregnant. Another first ripped from him.

AJ fisted his hands. "I'm gonna kill whoever did this," he growled. "Who was it?"

"She wouldn't say."

"God damn it!"

Tension radiated from Jace's shoulders to the base of his head. The story went downhill from here, and he didn't want to finish it. Hated reliving it. But his friend deserved to know.

"The bastard came back for her when we were away, hunting. He caught her alone, but she was ready for him. He left with buckshot in his foot."

"Damn straight," AJ huffed. "That's my sister."

"I pressed her for a name, but she never did tell me. Then, the MP came and stole our food. We couldn't easily replace it and it weighed on her. The responsibility of the farm and everyone here was breaking her. So, I decided to go find your uncle. But first, I did track down who raped her."

AJ paced to the ancient iron stove, then back to the table. "How?"

"Blown-up foot was a dead giveaway."

"Who. Was. It," AJ demanded.

Jace rubbed the heel of his hand against his chest. He felt like it had been ripped wide open. He pushed off the sink and walked to the giant iron stove's warmth.

AJ sidled next to him. "Jace. Who was it?"

"My brother," he whispered, remembering Zach's confession. *I never could stand you having anything I didn't have first.*

Lacy was raped because of him. Tears he'd fought formed and blurred the stove's black iron in front of him.

"Where is he?" AJ asked, voice low.

The tears vanished and his face hardened. "I killed him."

AJ's head snapped back like he'd been sucker punched. "You killed Zach?"

He'd never tell AJ the entire truth. That belonged to Lacy

and him alone. Some things were meant to stay in the dark. Some things were just too ugly to bring into the light.

"Truth is," he paused, ran a hand through his hair. "I'm in love with your sister. I have been for a while. There's nothing I wouldn't do for her, and that includes making my brother pay
for what he did."

He turned his head to hide the sheen of tears that returned to his eyes. Talking about Lacy made his heart ache. What was happening to her? Raul said his father wasn't a good man. But
what did that mean? Mexico was known for its drug cartels and often used humans as mules to transport their illegal narcotics across the border. He cleared his voice and turned back to AJ who gave him a strange look but didn't say anything.

AJ lowered himself into Cat's rocker, body tense, pulled tight like a tripwire. "What else is there?"

Jace sat in the chair beside him. He leaned forward, rested his hands between his knees.

"Jace?" he pressed.

"Your uncle found out I'd killed Zach and threatened to throw me in jail if I didn't help him with certain … missions. He's using Lacy as leverage."

AJ pinched the bridge of his nose. "This is insane. How is he using her, and why?"

Jace told him of Monroe's plan to start a civil war using the Texas militia and Mexico. He relayed how his uncle black-mailed him into abducting the Oklahoma governor and that
he'd go to jail and never see Lacy again if he didn't do as he'd been told. He left nothing out, not even the part where Lacy held Governor Harding at gunpoint.

"Then we tried to run."

AJ rubbed the back of his neck. "What went wrong?"

"We were supposed to deliver a payment to one of Monroe's contacts in Mexico City. After, we were going to try to find you and your parents in California, but your uncle

intercepted us at the border. He sent Lacy to Mexico City with the payment and brought me back here."

"How'd she get there?"

"I flew her there," Bryan said, walking into the room.

"Walls are pretty thin. I could hear your conversation and figured Jace could use a little help."

"This is messed up," AJ muttered. He ran both hands through his hair causing it to stick up in clumpy black spikes.

"It is," Bryan agreed as he gravitated to the coffee pot.

"How do we get my sister back?" AJ demanded.

"Monroe's sending a group of us to New Mexico. He wants control over the whole southwest region," Jace said.

Bryan looked at AJ. "I'm flying to Arizona, then New Mexico to drop off one of Monroe's men. After that, I'll fly to Mexico City. I'll get your sister back. I only have room in the chopper for one other person. Travis said he'd go with me, but I figure you'd want to go?"

"Hell yes, I'm going," AJ bellowed.

Bryan nodded. "I'll tell Travis."

Jace inwardly rejoiced Travis wouldn't be on that chopper to Mexico City. He wished he could go with Bryan and AJ but wishes weren't horses. He was trammeled, and he

hated it.

"You better hide your truck, AJ," Bryan said. "It'd be better if the senator didn't know you're here."

AJ rose from the rocker. "Any suggestions on where?"

"Hide it down the road in Diehl's barn," Bryan suggested.

AJ rose and headed to the door. "Be right back."

Bryan crossed the room and sat in AJ's spot. "You ready for this?"

Jace sucked in a deep breath. "Every minute that goes by I wonder what's happening to her and it kills me. I want her back. I don't care what it takes. If it costs me my own life, I'll lay it down. For her. So yeah, I'm ready."

"Whatever it takes, then," Bryan declared raising his coffee cup.

"Whatever it takes," Jace echoed thinking further ahead. He needed a strategy to buy out of the senator's game. Monroe had to have a weakness, something he could use to his advantage. There had to be a way out.

THE PENDULUM CLOCK chimed four times, its somber echo bouncing off the kitchen walls into the living room. Jace adjusted the flattened pillow underneath his head for the zillionth time and tried to adjust his six-foot frame on the small cot. The rusted springs creaked like a field of crickets on a sultry summer night every time he moved. His stockinged feet dangled over the edge. Huffing out a frustrated breath, he bent his knees and curled up his feet.

"Stop rolling around," AJ complained from his spot on the floor.

Seven makeshift beds consisting of cots and pallets lined the small living room like mummies in a tomb. It created a claustrophobic air. Cat slept along the far wall. AJ's pallet, made up of two blankets and a musty couch cushion, completed the human sandwich.

Bryan let out a loud snore, then snorted, and tossed his arm over his head, muttering in his sleep. The air hung thick with carbon dioxide and produced a smell that would rival any horse barn.

Jace thought about his earlier conversation with AJ. His friend hadn't said a word about his admission he was in love with Lacy. It was almost like …

"You knew," he said quietly.

AJ rolled over to face him and propped up his elbow. The

pallid moon peeked through the rolling clouds, casting enough light Jace could see the smirk covering his best friend's face.

"Of course, I knew, dumbass. And I respected the hell out of you for not making a move on my sister when she was in high school. Why do you think I worked so hard keeping all those other assholes away from her?"

"I just thought you were being the overprotective brother you always were."

"Well, yeah, that too," he admitted. "After she graduated, I thought you'd ask her out, but you didn't. A whole year passed. I was getting kinda pissed and was gonna talk to you, but then all this shit happened."

"Yeah." He let out a heavy sigh. "How did you know?"

"Are you shittin' me?" AJ scoffed. "Looking back, I know the second it happened. When we walked into the auditorium for the first time as seniors. You stopped in the middle aisle and just stood there, starin' at my sweet little sister. Mouth hanging open like the dumbass you are in front of God and everyone. As if that wasn't enough, as soon as the principal finished his welcome speech, you lit outta there and found ..." he paused.

Jace could hear his nails scraping his scalp.

"What was that cheerleader's name? The super-hot one. Sharon. No. Shelly?"

"Shannon."

"Right. You threw away a whole year full of fun, meaning-less sex to pine over my fifteen-year-old sister."

Jace barked out a short laugh. "True."

"Creepy," AJ mocked. "Really. I put it all together though during that camping trip where you saved *her* dumb ass from drowning. You walked around all moon-eyed ..."

"Oh, feck off," Jace muttered good-naturedly.

Cat sat straight up and Jace didn't have to see her face to know she wanted to box their ears.

"You all have the manners of two pigs at a tea party.

There are five others in this room and as much as it warms my heart to hear you catch up, we all need as much rest as we can get so

stop yapping and go to sleep. Oh, and I'll meet you properly in the morning, AJ."

"Yes ma'am," AJ muttered.

Jace smothered his laugh and apologized. "Sorry, Cat."

"Don't be sorry," she groused, "just go to sleep."

He forced his body to remain still. If only he could freeze his chaotic thoughts, then maybe he could forget Lacy long enough for his mind and body to rest.

10

———

orning light cascaded through the dingy east window warming Jace's face. The wind blowing through the trees caused sunlight to dance in shadows behind his eyelids. He threw his arm over his face, shielding his eyes, hoping to catch a few more minutes of sleep before the tidal wave of reality crashed over him. But even in sleep, he couldn't escape. Lacy haunted him, her eyes begging him to catch her.

He sighed and rolled over. AJ lay flat on his stomach, with the faded floral couch cushion flopped over his head. Coffee's bitter aroma hit his senses, and lowered voices floated from the kitchen. Coffee never sounded good, but a mug of hot tea did. Better get up and face the day, because he sure as hell wouldn't get a pass.

Edward's voice halted his inner monologue. "Are we gonna talk about it?"

A dish rattled in the sink. He couldn't hear Cat's response, but Edward's disgruntled words filtered back to him.

"Woman. You know what. We've danced around it for 'bout an hour now."

Jace imagined the older man tugging the hat off his head.

He strained to hear more and tried to swing his feet to the floor, but his threadbare blanket wrapped around his ankles, binding them together. Flummoxed, he laid both feet flat against the mattress, then bent his knees. He inched forward, slowly unwrapping the material. He leaned forward to free himself. Big mistake. The bottom half of the cot collapsed while the top half flew upward, folding him in half. Cursing softly, he wrestled his way out.

AJ rolled over and flung his cushion into the side of his head. "You are without a doubt the worst roommate ever."

"Shh," Jace said, tossing the dusty cushion back at AJ's head.

AJ rolled onto his stomach. "Whatever."

Jace picked himself up, righted the cot, then tuned his ear back to the conversation. He edged to the kitchen doorway on silent feet.

"I can't talk about it," Cat said, frustrated. "I feel guilty. I love Ben, but I ..."

"We'll deal with it, Cat."

"There will be nothing to deal with. I can't abandon him. If you're thinking I have a choice, I don't."

Jace heard Edward's boots scuff against the floor.

"Shh, now. You've got nothin' to feel guilty about."

He couldn't hear Cat's muffled response, then the kitchen went silent.

Who would've thought Cat and Edwards would fall for each other? In her mid-fifties, Cat still held a youthful look. Laugh lines around her eyes and the grey streaking her hair were the only things indicating her age.

Edwards was older by about ten years, he guessed. His hair had greyed, but women seemed to love grey-haired men. His mom gushed over how hot Brad Pitt was with grey hair. He couldn't imagine his mom thinking men were hot.

Lacy would love this. She adored Cat and hated watching her mourn over her husband. The MP had electrocuted the older man several times, then threw him into a boxcar headed for Fort Sill, when Lacy and Travis had found Cat. She was certain his weak heart couldn't handle the strain and assumed he'd died. Today she'd find out if he survived.

A delicate situation Jace didn't envy, and his heart went out to Edwards who'd be on the losing end if Ben Wirtz was alive.

Bryan rose from his pallet and joined Jace by the wall.

"What are you doing?"

Bryan's raspy morning voice brought Jace out of his thoughts. He raked his fingers through his messy hair and looked around the room. Travis still slept on his cot, blanket pulled over his head, but Dylan's spot was empty.

Jace pointed to the rumpled cot. "Where's Dylan?"

"Left about an hour after you guys wrapped up your little convo. Guess he went with the militia selected to go to Fort Sill. They should be back today sometime. I heard Monroe made the governor write a letter demanding the release of Dylan's girl and Cat's husband."

Jace cocked a brow. "Well Dylan did sign his life away by joining Monroe's militia. He better get something out of it."

Bryan huffed a laugh and nodded in agreement. "Better get what you can from the governor now. I don't know how much longer Monroe will let him live." He turned and glanced at AJ's covered head. "AJ better get up and hide before Monroe's men come and do a head count. His best bet's Matty's room. They never check on him."

Jace walked over and nudged AJ's shoulder with his foot. "Did you hear that, r-tard? Get up. Matty's in your dad's old room."

AJ shoved Jace's foot away and sat up. "I heard," he grumbled.

"Can I get some coffee first?"

"I'll bring you some," Bryan offered.

AJ stumbled along the north end of the wall dragging his blanket and couch cushion.

Jace grabbed his boots, then turned and walked into the kitchen, Bryan trailing behind. Cat and Edwards sat at the kitchen table with their heads bent toward each other. She pulled away as soon as they entered, wiped her eyes on the side of her sleeve, and gave Jace a stern look.

Dropping his boots, he raised his hands. "Before you say anything, I wanted to say I'm sorry for keeping everyone awake last night."

Her wrinkled brow smoothed. "All right then. I'm glad we got that settled. No more late nights, Chatty Kathy."

"Sounded like two chicks having a sleepover," Bryan sniggered, pouring coffee into a thermos.

Jace flipped his middle finger toward Bryan, then bent and pulled on his boots.

Frigid morning air blew inside as two militia men and the senator's assistant, William, walked through the back door. The assistant's attention focused on Cat.

Bryan swore under his breath. He'd never had a chance to warn Cat that Monroe wanted to question her about Raul.

"Cat, the senator would like a word," William said.

She crossed her arms and lifted a brow. "About what?"

"Just come with me, ma'am."

The young assistant took a step forward, smoothing his hair back with an air of importance.

"Now hold on. You're not taking her anywhere," Edwards interjected, rising from his seat.

William turned a condescending eye on Edwards. "She'll come, willingly or in handcuffs." He shrugged his shoulders. "It makes no difference to me."

Jace stepped forward. "I'll go with her. I need to talk to the senator anyway."

Cat rose, stepped over, and gave Edwards a quick hug. "I'll be okay."

"I'm comin' up there if you're not back in twenty," he grumbled.

"I'll bring her back," Jace assured him.

Taking the lead, William opened the door and led them out. The two militia men brought up the rear. Ice crunched underfoot as they walked up the drive. Their breaths came out in misty puffs.

"You know what they want?" Jace asked.

Cat huffed and rubbed her hands up and down her arms. They'd been ushered out the door without coats.

"I have a good idea," she said through clenched teeth.

"Got a defense?"

"Just denial."

They walked up the porch steps into the kitchen where Monroe sat at the table sipping coffee. A lit cigarette dangled between his fingers.

He raised a brow at Jace. "I didn't send for you."

"I need to talk to you," Jace shot back.

Monroe pursed his lips, then took a long drag off his cigarette. "Make it quick," he said blowing smoke through his nose as he spoke.

"When are you sending us to New Mexico?" he demanded.

"I thought you said it would be today. I need this done and over with so I can go get Lacy."

Monroe took his time stubbing out his cigarette on his empty breakfast plate. Jace shifted his feet and let out a loud breath.

"Dylan went to Fort Sill early this morning. We may be able to move on New Mexico tomorrow."

"What does Dylan going to Fort Sill have to with the price of rice in China?" he blustered. "You have enough manpower. We could leave today. I'm surprised you're helping Dylan at all," he added, bewildered at the man's seeming sensitivity to Dylan's plight.

Monroe steepled his fingers together. "I believe my niece promised Dylan help. I try to honor family debts."

Jace shook his head. "Your family views are so screwed. You'll honor her promise to help Dylan yet trade her off to a Mexican thug. Why?"

The senator's blatant lack of concern for his niece threatened his barely controlled rage. He fisted his hands together until his knuckles cracked.

"She disobeyed me and needs to learn I'm never crossed." He pinned Jace with cold, flat eyes. "You better remember that as well. Raul was my bargaining chip to get her back, but it seems someone helped him escape." He turned his attention to Cat. "Which brings me to you."

"How do you figure?" Cat asked.

Monroe's lips folded down. "His guards were drugged."

She shrugged, but never looked away from the senator. "So?"

"Did you drug them?"

"How would I have done that?" she deadpanned.

"You tell me."

"Look, Senator, I'm sorry Raul's gone, but I had nothing to do with it," she insisted.

Monroe eyed her, brows drawn together like the Grinch.

Clearly, he didn't believe her, but didn't have enough evidence to place the blame on her.

"Fine," he conceded, waving a dismissive hand. "Go."

Jace wrapped an arm around Cat and led her out the back door.

"Watch your step, Cat," Jace counseled as they headed back down the drive. "He doesn't believe you."

"I know. I'm sorry I helped Raul. I had no idea he wanted to use him to get Lacy back."

"It doesn't matter. Everything that comes out of that man's mouth is either a lie or a half-truth."

"What are you going to do now?"

Jace sighed, hating the helpless feeling washing over him. "He has me by the throat, Cat. All I can do is play his game and hope Bryan and AJ can get her out of Mexico City."

The senator was artful and a master at his own game, and Jace felt like a blind man walking through a mine field.

11

Warm hands roved over Lacy's face, then down her neck. She'd been screaming for Jace. Was he here? Or was it a trick of the drug that dragged her down the dark hole she was now struggling to crawl out of? The euphoric numb had been sweet when it first hit her system. It was a saccharine, blissful high. But then it took a nasty downward turn and threatened to consume her with a completeness she was unwilling to surrender. She wrestled against it, but the drug proved too powerful. It chained her to her darkest demon. Zach.

He tormented her, hunted her. She hid behind her grandmother's old leather couch, praying he wouldn't find her. But he did.

"You want this." He leered at her as he unzipped his pants.

"You know it. I know it. You're nothing. Worthless."

She relived the vile act he forced on her as if it played on repeat, shaming her over and over.

"Stop!" she screamed. "Jace!"

Then, she found herself sitting in her grandmother's claw foot tub. Cold water running from the faucet mixed with the blood pooled around her bare legs. Zach circled the tub, ogling her naked body.

"You want this miscarriage," Zach sneered.

"I —"

She let out a blood-curdling scream as her abdomen contracted. Sweat dripped down her brow. She couldn't deny it, couldn't make herself say she wanted to have his child.

"You don't deserve my brother," he sneered. "You don't deserve anyone."

"Stop," she begged weakly. "Please. Just go away."

She covered her eyes, bent over, and sobbed. When she rose, Zach was gone, and she was in the cab of Travis's white Chevy truck. His onyx eyes bore into hers with an intensity that made her tremble.

"You betrayed me," he accused.

"No," she whimpered.

"I took care of you when you needed someone the most. How could you choose Jace over me?"

Hands moved down and cupped her breasts. Fingers pinched her nipple, a painful twist that forced Travis's image away and pushed her mind to the surface. She slapped at the hands on her breasts, struggling to open her eyes.

"Stop," she rasped through cracked lips.

The hands dropped from her chest. "Get up," the man commanded.

When she didn't move, he grabbed both ankles and jerked her body sideways. She rolled onto her side. Stars burst behind her eyelids as pain from her injured arm rolled through her in a harsh wave.

"Shit," she gasped, as she pushed herself into a sitting position.

She weaved back and forth, struggling to gain her equilibrium. Her eyes wouldn't focus. Her head sloshed in painful swells against her skull. Whatever drug they used held a hell of a backlash.

The burn hit her cheek before she realized the man had slapped her. Her eyes popped open.

"Wake up," the man ordered.

Her bleary eyes focused on Miguel. "Screw you," she rasped out.

This time, the back of his hand split her cheek open. Her neck snapped sideways at the force of the blow.

"Do not speak again," Miguel threatened. "*Despiértate.* Wake up."

She wiped blood from her cheek onto her T-shirt. Dirt clung to it like dust on a windowsill and reeked of mold and sewage. She raised her eyes to his.

Remembering a few Spanish words from school, she gritted out, "*Porqué?* Why?"

"As I told you, *Señor* Nieto wants to see you."

How long had she been asleep? Time would kill her in here. No way could she survive being held prisoner. She had to think of something.

"Fine," she spat, waving her hands at him. "Bring him in. What are you waiting for?"

"You come with me," he said, eyeing her warily.

Her eyes focused on his swollen cheek and sizable cut on his forehead. She couldn't help the smirk forming on her lips.

"Wash your arm," he instructed. "I'll be back."

She looked down at the blood tracking down her arm. "Shit," she muttered.

It seeped its way through the dirty brown gauze. Cringing, she peeled it inch by inch, away from the wound, wincing each time it stuck to a newly formed scab. She dropped the gauze on the filthy floor, approached the grimy sink, recoiling at the layers of dirt. The four-pronged knob on the right stuck like welded steel. She gripped the left knob and twisted hard. Brown water gushed from the spout. She waited until it ran clear, then dipped her shoulder under the stream. The cold water felt good against her fevered flesh.

She looked around for the square cloth they'd sent with the food. Their version of a napkin, she guessed. The grey material peeked out from under the cot. She shuffled over, picked it up, and shook it. Dust from the fabric flew up her nose, causing her to sneeze. Wiping her nose against the side of her sleeve, she moved back to the basin and lowered the cloth into the stream. After soaking and wringing it several times, she lowered her shoulder back under the spout and scrubbed until tears streaked down and stung her split cheek.

She wrapped it around her arm and tucked the end inside the material, hoping it would hold. Although still angry, the offended flesh looked to be healing. Cat's antibiotics were keeping infection at bay at least.

Outside, a door banged shut and Miguel's strident voice filtered inside commanding someone to *apúrate*! Hurry! Something soft thumped against her door, then she heard feet scuffle away. The locks clicked and Miguel entered.

"Go," he said, pointing to the open door.

She stepped out, drew in a lungful of cleaner air. As her eyes adjusted to the bright hallway lights, she noticed a petite blonde. Willow. The girl in the cell next to hers. Clumps of limp, dirty hair covered her face. Her body slumped against the concrete wall and her head hung sideways.

Pity flooded her. The girl reminded her of a rag doll abused at the hands of a callous child. She stepped over and wrapped an arm around her waist. The girl leaned into her and raised her head. Mystifying blue-grey eyes under long black lashes looked up and she offered a small smile. Beautiful, even in her broken condition. No wonder they kept her. She looked like a China doll.

"Hey," Willow said through parched, cracked lips.

"Nice to finally see you face to face," Lacy said. "You okay?"

"Dunno," she slurred.

Miguel nudged her in the back. "Go."

She tightened her grip on Willow and stumbled forward. They moved through the small hallway to the steep wooden staircase. Miguel poked her in the back. She swung around and smacked his hand.

"Don't touch me!" she shouted.

His brown face flushed bright red, but he didn't retaliate. Instead, he shoved past them and up the stairs. They trailed behind, fumbling their way up. The large expansive warehouse was deserted except for a dark, nondescript SUV. The service door was up, and the vehicle idled, its gritty exhaust clouding the enclosed space.

She looked outside. A group of rough teens loitered on the corner across the street. Miguel moved past her and opened the SUV's back door. He pulled a weapon from the back of his waistband and motioned them to get inside.

She adjusted her steps to Willow's smaller ones, helped her inside, then reached over, grabbed the seatbelt, and buckled her in. She settled in the seat beside her. No longer able to hold herself upright, Willow slumped against her and let out a small sigh.

Miguel backed the SUV out of the warehouse, then made a sharp right turn. Straining her eyes against the darkened window, she saw rows of tiny houses lining the streets as they sped by. Graffiti in bright bold colors blurred in a muted kaleidoscope. The atmosphere was oppressive. It seeped into her soul. The thought of being trapped here brought tears that burned the back of her eyelids. Jace. Her heart called out to his through the long miles, and she hoped he heard.

The SUV turned into an underground parking garage. Miguel rolled down his window, swiped a card, and the white and yellow striped bar rose. He pulled forward then parked by a service elevator and cut the engine.

He exited, then opened their door. "Out," he commanded in an impatient tone.

She unbuckled, then stumbled out on rubbery legs. "Shit," she muttered, gripping the open door.

Willow slid over.

"Here," Lacy said offering her hand.

Willow's small hand latched on to hers and she stepped down. Miguel punched the elevator button. The doors clanged open and he motioned for them to step inside.

"Get in," he said, pulling a pack of cigarettes from his front shirt pocket. He fished for his lighter, then lit the tip.

Willow wrapped herself around Lacy like a boa constrictor as they stepped onto the elevator. Miguel got in, swiped another card, then punched the top floor button. The doors clanged shut. It registered that no one could get to the top floor without a special card. Her heart plummeted as she realized Jace would never find her, and she couldn't hold him to his promise. These circumstances were beyond their control.

"No, no, no," Willow mumbled.

"Shh. It's okay," she murmured in soft, soothing tones.

The elevator stopped but her stomach kept its upward trajectory. As it came back down, the sudden urge to throw up overwhelmed her.

Frantically, she disengaged herself from Willow's grip, stepped out the doors, and doubled over. Vomit spewed onto her shoes, the plush red carpet, the white walls, and Miguel's scuffed leather boots.

"*Mierda*. Shit," Miguel muttered stepping over the green curdles of half-digested food. "This way."

He sped down a long hallway. As she looked around, something familiar tugged at her. The hallway resembled the one AJ had snuck down in her dream. And was shot. She shuddered as dread settled over her shoulders.

Miguel knocked three times on the door at the end of the hall. It opened and a man stepped out. A wicked smile played about his lips.

Manuel Nieto.

"Welcome, welcome," he said in a buoyant voice that made her want to scream obscenities at him. She scowled but bit back her scathing remark. She helped Willow past the threshold into a large living area. A wide, open window with white ironwork let in sunlight. She gravitated toward it, pulling Willow with her. She looked out on a courtyard filled with vibrant trees and flowers of every color and species. A slight breeze blew in its robust scent and filled the room with false cheerfulness.

"No," the girl whimpered. "Please."

She squeezed her hand. "I'm here," she assured her, then turned to Nieto.

"Why are we here?" she demanded.

She tried to sound stern as if this situation didn't scare the hell out of her. Fake it until you make it.

"I wished to speak with you, and we have need of the girl."

"The girl has a name," she snapped. "Willow. Her name is Willow."

"I don't care what her name is," he replied, and took a seat on the white sofa against the wall. "Miguel, take the girl."

"No," she protested, pulling Willow closer. "She stays with me."

"You're in no position to bargain with me."

Miguel stubbed his cigarette into a glass cut ashtray sitting on a round breakfast table. He strode to the window and snatched Willow from her grip. The girl stumbled and fell to her knees. He jerked her up, ignoring her cry of pain, and shoved her through a door opposite the sofa.

Nieto's dark brown eyes, a mirror image of his son's, never left hers. "Have a seat," he said, motioning to the white chair next to the sofa.

"I'd rather stand, thanks."

"As you wish."

His smirk grated on her frayed nerves.

She returned his hard stare. "What do you want?"

"I want my son. Why did your uncle keep him?"

"How am I supposed to know?" she sniped, folding her arms across her chest. "I'm not his personal secretary."

"You know something," he returned with confidence.

"I assure you," she said, sarcasm rising to the surface. "I don't."

Nieto sniffed. "You will stay here until my son is returned."

"You can't hold me prisoner in that hellhole basement!" she shouted.

"I assure you," he tossed her words back at her. "I can. But," he continued before she could respond, "Will this do?" he asked, gesturing to the room.

"Whatever," she muttered.

Miguel returned and at Nieto's nod, grabbed her arm and propelled her toward the same room he'd taken Willow. She dug her dirty, vomit-stained Converse into the white carpet and jerked her arm back.

Looking over her shoulder at Nieto, she said, "You have no right to keep me here. I won't be used for sex."

He lifted a brow. "I hadn't considered that, but maybe it's a good idea."

"Liar," she accused. "You thought of it. But I'm telling you, if anyone comes into that room for me, they'll go out in a body bag."

Nieto threw his head back and laughed. "So feisty."

Miguel jerked her arm and half-dragged her into the adjoining room, then slammed the door. The knob was reversed so it locked from the living area's side. She heard the tumbler click in place.

Willow rested on the far side of the bed in the fetal position, hiding from their absolute dire situation. Fear sledgehammered through her. Anger born from helplessness rose from the pit of her stomach and she doubled over and screamed until her throat was raw.

She raised up, completely spent, the drugs from the food still wreaking havoc in her system. She sank into the luxurious bed, felt the white down fluffiness of the comforter underneath her fingers, and cried. She fell asleep. Dreams rose to the surface, but this time, they weren't the drug induced nightmares that lingered and tormented her waking hours.

This time, they were comforting because Jace was with her, back at old Lyman's Pond. Sitting on the pier, Jace reached over and twined his fingers with hers. Her heart skyrocketed at his touch. No one had ever made her feel the things he did. She knew he had lingering doubts about Travis.

But Travis had never touched her soul.

Only Jace.

He was reading The Adventures of Huckleberry Finn by Mark Twain. *'Jim was most ruined, for a servant, because he got so stuck up on account of having seen the devil and been rode by witches.'*

The soothing sound of his voice washed over her. She closed her eyes, squeezed his hand, and soaked in his reassuring presence. The faint sound of crying lifted her from the dream like a hot air balloon.

She rolled her head to the side to see Miguel shaking Willow by the shoulders. Tears dripped through her closed eyelids and ran down the girl's sunken cheeks.

She pushed herself up. "Leave her alone," she croaked.

Her throat felt like she'd swallowed a handful of hot coals. Ignoring her, he grabbed the front of Willow's shirt and dragged her into a sitting position. Moving her head to the right, she noticed a lamp with a heavy iron base on the nightstand.

She inched her way off the bed, crawled along the baseboard to the outlet, and unplugged the lamp. Made of wrought iron, the heavy lamp would make a viable weapon. She raised up and peeked over the bed's edge. Unaware she'd left, Miguel scooped the slight girl up and carried her to the bathroom.

When he shut the door, she jumped up, grabbed the lamp, and ripped off the shade. The bathroom door swung inward, so she flattened her back against the wall, held the lamp upside down like a baseball bat. And waited.

The rush of water muffled Willow's sobs. She tracked Miguel through his heavy lumbering movements in the small interior. Something soft and wet smacked the door. Had he undressed the poor girl? Lacy shuddered at the memory of his hands tracking down her neck, violating her breasts.

Miguel opened the door. Steam rolled out in a misty wave. Lacy swung fast and hard as his face emerged through the steam. The impact reverberated up her arm as the lamp's base smashed into the side of his face. He dropped to his knees, screaming in Spanish.

Hefting the lamp above her head, she brought the wrought iron base down over his back. He dropped to the floor, and in a swift move, she wheeled it across the other side of his face. Blood splattered over the side of the door, the wall, the carpet, her clothes.

Horrified, she dropped the lamp and ran into the bathroom. Willow lay naked in the bathtub, eyes open, staring at the ceiling. Bruises in various stages of healing marked her torso.

"Willow, get up," she urged.

They needed to move. Now.

She crossed to the sandstone tiled garden tub, grabbed her shoulder, and gave it a shake. "We have to go."

"Can't go," she mumbled. "No way out."

"Yes, there is. Get up!"

Her eyelids fluttered, then bloodshot eyes focused on hers. "Huh?"

"I knocked Miguel out with a lamp. We need to leave. I don't know how long he'll be unconscious."

She yanked a towel off a shelf and handed it to the stunned girl, then stepped out to check on Miguel. Blood poured from his skull, staining the white carpet a dark crimson. He lay still. Too still.

No.

She stepped back in, sucking in breaths, fast and short. She rubbed the heel of her hand over her tightened chest. Willow stepped out of the tub, wrapping the towel around her slender frame.

Lacy doubled over, muttering, "Shit, shit, shit," over and over.

What had she just done?

Willow stumbled to her side. "What's wrong?"

She looked up. "I think I killed him."

PART II

THE STAKES

"Better hedge your bets because high stakes are heart driven and winning the game depends on how far you're willing to go."

12

How many murderers were born exactly like this? Lacy rose from her knees, slow and steady. She couldn't think about the dead body lying in the next room. Not if she wanted to escape.

Willow stepped over her pile of wet clothes into the bedroom. Lacy followed, averting her eyes from the copious amount of blood pooling around Miguel's head. Willow walked to the closet and started ripping clothes off hangers as if she was well acquainted with its contents.

"Here," she said and threw a pair of jeans at her with the tags still attached.

"I don't need to change, and we don't have time to look through all this," she said, tossing the jeans on the bed. "We have to go."

"Your clothes have blood all over them, and I'm not walking through the hotel naked."

At least Willow sounded more coherent. She stepped into the closet beside Willow and started rifling through the long row of seductive dresses and lingerie.

"This is repulsive," she muttered, raising a blood red teddy from the rack.

"Most clientele have certain appetites that aren't socially acceptable."

Lacy shuddered and picked a heather grey long-sleeved T-shirt, then grabbed the jeans, and hurried into the bathroom. Her reflection in the mirror stopped her short. Disheveled and dirty, she looked like a crumpled piece of trash. Blood spattered her white T-shirt, now muddled grey from the basement's grime. Horrified, she wrenched it over her head and threw it in the bathtub. She plunked the toilet lid down, sat, and changed into the soft, designer jeans, then pulled the new shirt over her head.

A brush lay near the sink. She grabbed it and ripped it through her long, black locks. Tears welled as knotted hair ripped from her skull. Gathering it at the back, she parted it into thirds and quickly braided it down her back.

How many minutes had passed?

The urgency pulsing through her made her body quake. She rushed through the bedroom, careful to avert her eyes from the blood soaking into the white carpet. She couldn't think about what she'd done. She'd leave it for another time. Or maybe never. She could justify killing Miguel. He'd been her captor. Or one of them. They needed to escape, no matter what it took, and she'd done it.

Willow sat on the couch in the living room, dressed in a pair of jeans and a non-descript black hoodie. Her blonde hair, prone to curls, bunched on top of her head in a messy bun. She tugged on a pair of black, vintage Justin Roper boots. Although it would be impossible not to notice the blond beauty, she'd done a good job dressing down.

"Let's get out of here," Lacy said, walking to the door.

Willow nodded and pulled the hood over her head. Lacy cracked the outer door and peered outside. The hallway was ghost-town silent. She stepped out on cautious feet. The coast seemed clear, so she bolted for the elevator, praying she didn't need one of those cards Miguel had used.

Willow stuck close to her heels. She should've looked for his but the thought of touching his dead body revolted her. She punched the down button, bounced on the balls of her feet, and eyed Willow. The fog in her eyes had lifted but her body was frail from malnutrition and misuse.

"Could you take the stairs down?"

Willow's eyes sought hers. "Could you? How many floors?"

"Honestly, I don't know the answer to either question."

The elevator's vibration rumbled under her feet. It stopped with a whoosh. Heart thudding in her chest, she pulled Willow against the wall. If someone was in the elevator's car, escape would be impossible.

The elevator down button turned green and the doors opened with a ding. No one exited the elevator's car, so she took a tentative step forward. Seeing no one, they both bolted inside the elevator. Lacy punched the lobby button and waited. The doors closed, and the elevator began its descent.

She turned to Willow. What would happen when they reached the bottom? She took a deep, calming breath, and closed her eyes. She needed to focus. She couldn't dwell on the fact she'd just murdered someone. They needed a plan. She opened her eyes and forced out the breath she'd been holding.

"When we hit the bottom, we walk out of here like nothing's wrong. Don't attract attention and we can't call the police."

"How are we getting out of the country then?" Willow panicked.

"I don't know," she muttered.

Willow turned her back to Lacy, lifted the oversized black hoodie to reveal a gun tucked in the back of her waistband, and said, "This might help."

"The hell you get that?" she asked, nonplussed.

"Lifted it off the stiff while you were in the bathroom. Got his knife, hotel card, and money tucked in my boot."

An unbelieving laugh escaped her lips. "You got moxie."

The elevator slowed and she grabbed Willow's hand, heart thundering in her ears. They were so close to freedom.

The car stopped. The doors opened with a ding.

Together, they stepped out.

A bell hop stood to her right. His large frame, stuffed into the white hotel uniform, was hard to miss.

He tipped his red and black cap at her. "G'day, miss," he said in an Aussie accent.

She gave him a curt nod as they stepped into the lobby. Workers at the front desk, busy assisting travelers, didn't notice them or even look their way. She turned her attention toward the magnificent wrought iron front doors, then stumbled to a stop.

"What's wrong?" Willow whispered.

"Look." She motioned with her head toward the door.

Manuel Nieto waltzed in like he owned the place. A white man with bleached blond hair strutted at his side.

Shit.

Where could they run?

She scanned the hotel's open layout. There was no place to hide. Had he seen them yet? Willow's face blanched. Her feet started to backtrack, but Lacy held her in place. They could run to the front desk, beg for help, or pull the fire alarm next to the elevator.

She looked back to Nieto. The cold smile on his face didn't reach his eyes.

Her stomach plummeted.

"How nice of you ladies to greet us," he gushed, walking toward them at a pace that belied his casual appearance.

The false sincerity fooled his companion who gave them a suggestive grin. But she read anger in Nieto's eyes. And questions.

Her body trembled as a shot of adrenaline singed through

her blood. Could she play this game and win? Probably not. But she had to try.

She cleared her throat. "Willow and I were just going to sit by the pool." Lacy nudged her. "Right, Willow?"

Willow's lowered head bobbed up and down in silent agreement.

"Of course," he said easily. "But first, won't you join us upstairs?"

Nieto's guest adjusted his tie, his hungry eyes roving over Willow like he wanted to devour her.

"Nice to see you again, Willow." The man's words slid off his tongue like an oil spill, slick and deceptively shiny on the surface.

Nieto ushered them back into the elevator. As her foot crossed into the car, the burly bell hop stepped forward and placed a beefy hand on the door, holding it in place.

"Is everything all right, miss?"

His concerned gaze caught hers, and she darted her eyes to the floor. Nieto would harm the bell hop if she involved him and she wouldn't be responsible for that.

Nieto wrapped a possessive arm around her shoulder.

"Everything is fine."

The bellhop nodded once, released his hold on the door, and stepped back. The elevator doors closed. The sound, a death knell in her ears.

"Where is Miguel?" Nieto asked, close to her ear as they ascended back to the top floor of the hotel.

She shrugged his arm off and stepped away. Tapping her chin, she said, "I think he's taking a nap."

She hadn't thought of the consequences of killing Miguel. Escaping was her objective. Her spirits sank. She'd never get out of here. He'd kill her before he'd let her go. Hope fluttered away like a butterfly through a window and took with it any regard she had for her own life. Jace's entreaty that she stay safe and alive dissipated like an apparition in the sun. A disconcerting calm slipped over her. Her body stopped quaking and her mind cleared.

As the elevator slowed, Willow began to whimper. She stepped over, placed her arm around Willow's slim waist and squeezed hard. The pressure drove the hidden gun's metal into the girl's back. A reminder.

"You're stronger than you think," she assured her. "Don't be afraid."

Nieto and the man Lacy surmised was a client, stepped off the elevator. They had no choice but to follow them out and down the long hallway. He pulled his key card from his suit coat's breast pocket, tapped it over the door's lock, then ushered them inside.

He went to the bar, poured the blond client a drink from a crystal cut decanter. "Make yourself at home," he said, gesturing to the couch, then turned and walked into the bedroom.

Lacy stood by the door with bated breath. Pins pricked her scalp as she waited for Nieto's return.

The blond man patted the cushion beside him. "Willow, come and sit by me. It's been too long."

"Not long enough," Willow muttered.

"Now, now," he crooned. "You know the rules."

Willow shuffled to the couch and sat on the edge, her entire body rigid. The man reached over and pulled her into his lap. His hand skirted up her leg in a way that made Lacy physically ill. Willow turned her face, eyelids squeezed shut.

Nieto strode out of the bedroom, talking on his cellphone in low tones. He pushed the end button, shoved the phone in his pocket, then turned to his guest.

"John, let's use this room," he said motioning to an adjoining door.

The man nuzzled Willows neck, then bit down so hard she cried out. He shoved her off his lap and she landed on the glass coffee table with a thud. She started to rise, but he slammed a hand down on the side of her face, shoving her head into the table so hard the glass cracked. He flipped his hair back, face flushed, eyes bright with excitement.

"Who's your master, Willow?"

Lacy lurched forward but Nieto grabbed her by the waist.

"Let them be."

Silent tears washed over the splintered glass. Willow remained mute.

Incensed, the man grabbed her hair, and yanked her head backward. Willow's reddened, tear-streaked face screwed up in pain.

Lacy heard the pop of Willow's neck and struggled against Nieto's muscled arms.

John leaned down, spittle dripping from his mouth onto Willow's cheek. "Say it, Willow! Tell me I'm your master. Tell me I'm the only one who gets to play with that ..."

"Stop!" Lacy screamed.

John turned his fiery gaze on her. "You shut the hell up!"

She rammed an elbow into Nieto's side. "Get your hands off of me," she shouted.

Nieto swung her around and forced her into a chair by the breakfast table. He pulled a gun from his waistband and pointed it at her head.

"Shut your mouth and don't move," he commanded, then turned to John who still held Willow's head at an awkward angle. "I think it's time you move into the other room, John, don't you?"

"Sure," he agreed, jerking Willow up as he stood. He shoved her toward the adjoining door. "Let's go. I'm looking forward to this."

Willow glanced at Lacy before disappearing into the other room. Her eyes flat-lined and her jaw set in a determined line. She wondered what the girl was planning. Pull the gun and shoot the man, or stick the knife in his gut? Either one suited her. The monster didn't deserve to take another breath.

Nieto moved to the bar, pulled a roll of duct tape from under the sink, then turned to her.

She lifted her chin. "You don't scare me," she bluffed.

His cold brown eyes searched hers. She held his gaze, unwilling to look away. He walked over, jerked her hands behind the chair's wooden back.

"God dammit," she protested as he wound duct tape around her wrists.

The tape cut her skin and stayed the blood circulation. Her hands tingled from fingertip to wrist. Pain radiated down her arms.

"You wound the tape too tight, asshole," she bit out.

He chucked the tape onto the sofa. "You killed Miguel," he accused, circling the chair.

She stared out the window. The words were more statement than question, so she offered no reply. A soft breeze blew the tops of the trees and the waning light danced in shadows across the table.

He stood in front of her. "Why did your uncle keep my son?"

Her eyes lifted to his face. "Jesus, this again?" she challenged.

"I told you already. I don't know."

He brought his open hand down hard against her cheek. The sting swept upward bringing tears to her eyes.

"Why?" he shouted.

She stared him down. "I. Don't. Know."

This time, his fist hit the side of her cheekbone. Stars exploded behind her eyelids. The flesh beneath her eye swelled, and the laceration on her cheek left from Miguel's strike split open further. Warm blood mixed with sweat slid down her neck, soaking into her shirt collar.

His raised hand stopped midair at the muffled pop of gunfire. The adjoining door flung open, and Willow walked through. Her ashen face was highlighted by bright red blood smeared all over her forehead. Red dots speckled her blond hair. The front of her black hoodie, saturated with red liquid, dripped onto the carpet.

In a slow, steady move, Willow raised the gun, the barrel aimed at Nieto's chest.

"Let us go or I'll kill you too."

13

W hen Willow walked through the door, time stretched like taffy in a puller. She saw Wiley Coyote step off the ledge, and in a heart-stopping moment, realize he was going to fall. She felt like that. The fall was inevitable.

Where was Jace? He'd never failed to catch her. Despite the bleak circumstances, she held on to that ember of hope. The room was pin-drop silent. The blood dripping from the hem of Willow's hoodie formed a Rorschach pattern on the white carpet.

Lacy twisted her bound wrists. "Do something," she pleaded.

Willow stepped toward Nieto. "I mean it. Untie her. Now."

The main door's lock clicked. Willow jolted, swung around, and aimed the gun at the door.

Nieto's shocked demeanor shifted. "That will be my cleanup crew," he said with smug confidence.

The door swung open, and Lacy's heart stuttered. Raul stepped into the room. His eyes darkened as his gaze swung from his father to Lacy. Rushing to her, he spat something in Spanish.

His father replied in a nonchalant, dismissive voice. Raul reached into his back pocket and drew out a knife. Snapping it open, he cut her free.

"Who are you?' Willow shrieked, eyes wide, hands shaking.

Raul hadn't noticed Willow standing by the adjoining door, gun trained on his head. Lacy unwound the tape, balled it up, and dropped it on the floor. Massaging her abused wrists, she glared at Raul who'd backed away with his hands raised.

His brown eyes locked on hers. Concern etched a V on his forehead. "Are you okay," he asked, sparing a glance at Willow.

"Am I okay?" she choked out. "Are you serious right now? Your father's holding me hostage! He threatened me, beat me. *No!*" she shouted. "I'm not okay!"

His pained face turned to Willow. "I am sorry, *senorita*," he said, tone gentle. "No further harm will come to you."

"Not good enough," Willow growled. With swift steps, she moved to Raul and placed the 9mm to his forehead. "Someone's gonna pay."

"Let's be reasonable," Nieto entreated, hands outstretched.

Willow's eyes darted to him. "Don't say another word."

Lacy rose from the chair. "Willow," she began, tone low, soothing. "I think Raul will help us. Killing him won't fix anything."

With a defeated sigh, Willow lowered the gun and turned to Nieto. "You're a monster."

Unfazed by the accusation, he tipped up his shoulders. "Me? You're the one who just killed your benefactor."

Willow's eyebrows shot to her hairline and her lips pulled

back in a snarl. "*Benefactor*? You call that sadistic piece of shit a benefactor? He tried to kill me!"

She pulled the hoodie's material away from her neck. Purple marks in the image of four fingers bloomed around the left side of her delicate, porcelain skin. A faint thumb print splotched the right.

Lacy covered her mouth, trying to suppress the rage bubbling within her. She stepped to the trembling girl, reached down, and with a gentle hand, retrieved the 9mm pistol from her lax fingers.

"I will take that, *mi cariño*," Nieto said, voice an insufferable calm.

"No." Molten lava raced through her veins as she turned on him. "On your knees," she demanded. "Now."

His face blanched and he dropped to the floor, his suit's white linen fabric wrinkling at the knees.

"Lacy," Raul interjected.

"Shut up!" she screamed. "Not. Another. Word."

Her sanity was slipping. She planted her feet in front of the kneeling man, and placed the barrel's cold tip to his temple. Hate swelled in her heart like an over-inflated balloon.

She inhaled.

Exhaled.

Then raised the gun and swung like a top major league hitter. Steel met skull with a satiating thud. Blood flowed from the gash the steel ripped into his temple. Nieto crumpled forward, face down.

Raul rushed over and checked his father's pulse. Lacy read relief as his eyes lifted to hers.

Adrenaline darkened the edges of her vision and she swayed. He rose, took a step toward her, then stopped at her warning glance.

"Don't touch me."

Steadying herself, she tucked the gun in her waistband, then inched with caution to Willow. She placed an arm around the girl's shoulder in a slow, methodical way, then urged her

toward the first bedroom. Raul moved to the side and let them pass. She stopped at the bedroom's threshold and turned. Her gaze fastened on Raul's, lips pressed back, teeth bared.

"I'm going to clean her up. When we come out, I want your father gone."

Raul nodded once, face grim. "We will talk then."

"Fine."

"Close your eyes," she instructed Willow as they stepped inside.

She led her around Miguel's dead frame into the bathroom. The room filled with a muted glow as she flicked on the mirror's light over the sink.

Stepping around wet clothes, she guided her to the edge of the sandstone garden tub and plugged the drain. The knob at the tub's foot turned with ease and hot, steamy water flowed out.

Willow sat on the tub's edge, her body slumped against the wall. Pity swelled in Lacy's heart as she took in the abused girl. She reached over and pulled the blood-soaked hoodie from

Willow's body. The strong scent of salt and rust wafted over her as she tossed it to the floor.

Her thoughts turned. She'd taken a life, and whether Miguel deserved it or not, she would never forget. His blood stained her. It tainted her soul like tattoo ink. She couldn't wash it off. Now she knew how Jace felt about killing his brother. It was twisted, but she felt closer to him.

She shut the water off. "Stand up and I'll help you out of your jeans."

Without a word, Willow stood. Lacy stripped her then guided her into the hot water. Willow lowered into the steam with a sigh.

Lacy took the scrunchie out of her hair, dipped a washcloth into the water, and wrung it out over her head. Blond hair hung limp across her forehead, and she smoothed it back. A helpless feeling tumbled over her as she took in the bruises in various healing stages marring Willow's slight frame. Hips sunken, skin on bones, the girl looked anorexic. What type of human treated another this way? She knew Willow wasn't the first to be stolen by Nieto and wouldn't be the last.

Lacy heard muffled footfall outside and hoped they were removing Miguel's body and cleaning up the blood. Nieto could throw her in a Mexican prison for killing Miguel, for

assaulting him with a deadly weapon. He could conjure a list against her long enough she'd rot there for the rest of her life. Guilt weighed her down, a permanent anchor from which she could never be free.

How had Raul escaped her uncle? How much sway did he have over his father? Enough to get them home? A nagging thought surfaced. If Raul wasn't the man she thought, if he took orders from his father, then there was no hope of escape.

Water lapped Willow's bruised body. Tears dripped from her closed eyes. She lifted a hand, and a sob escaped her lips as she touched the bite mark on her neck. It had swelled into the

shape of a dark purple grape.

"I'm so sorry, Willow," Lacy whispered, returning her attention to the girl.

Eyelids fluttered open and sad, red-rimmed, eyes fastened on hers.

"When I was little, it was my older sisters' job to give me a bath." The pained lines around her mouth softened. "They hated it."

"How many sisters do you have?"

"Two. Both older. Olive and Laurel." She bit back a laugh that turned into a sob. "My mom's sort of a tree hugger, hippie type."

"They sound amazing," Lacy said in a soothing tone.

Willow wiped her nose against her bare shoulder and nodded. "Yeah, they are."

Lacy raised up and grabbed the small bottle of shampoo from the tub's side. The fragrant tang of citrus and sage lifted from the open lid. She poured a large amount into the palm of her hand then bent over the tub's edge and soaped Willow's hair. She massaged her scalp in gentle methodical circles.

Willow's shoulders shook with silent sobs, and she sucked in a shivery breath. "I miss them."

"I know," Lacy said softly, dipping her hands into the warm water to rinse them. "Finish up. Take as much time as you need. I'm going to talk to Raul."

She needed to find out if he'd help them, or if she'd end up fighting him too.

When she exited the bathroom, Miguel's dead body had been removed. The room on the other side of the door was quiet.

She turned the door's knob and stepped into the living area. Her eyes widened. Disbelief washed over her.

What. The. Actual. Hell?

Raul was gone.

14

Jace sat on the back porch steps and watched the sun creep across the sky, agonizing over every lost minute. Even the painful cold seeping through his jacket couldn't distract him. Three days. That's how long he'd been separated from Lacy. She needed him. He could feel her desperation crawling under his skin.

He pulled the watch from his pocket she'd given him for Christmas, rubbed his thumb over the engraved Monroe crest. It was an heirloom, a gift to her from her grandfather. He still couldn't believe she'd given it to him. He opened the case, every secondhand tick dropping into the past. Time. It was a blessing and a curse.

Staring at the picture inside made his heart race. He remembered the day she'd taken it. AJ had complained nonstop about her fussing over her appearance.

"Why does my sister need five thousand friends over just to get ready for a stupid senior picture?" he'd grumbled over the phone.

Jace had been on the road pitching for the University of Central Oklahoma. He had a fast arm and even faster swing. He loved playing baseball and still missed it.

"I don't know." He enjoyed the mental picture AJ painted. "I wasn't blessed with a sister."

He loved her then.

He loved her even more now.

Another memory flooded him. He missed her seventeenth birthday party because of baseball practice, but stopped by to see her as soon as he returned the following weekend.

She opened the door, fastened those expressive emerald eyes on his, causing his heart to jackhammer in his chest. She grabbed his hand and pulled him inside. He remembered the explosion of nerves that hurtled through him. He handed over his gift wrapped in pale pink and waited while she opened the complete Harry Potter DVD set.

"You got me HARRY POTTER!" she squealed, launching herself at him.

Laughing, he caught her, savoring the feel of her arms around his neck. She grabbed his hand again and pulled him inside, insisting they watch the first movie together. During the second movie, she fell asleep tucked into his side.

Every minute spent with her was precious to him.

Matty bounded out the back door with Castiel trailing close behind. He skidded to a stop when he saw Jace and plopped himself on the porch step beside him. The dog bounded down the steps, then turned and gave the boy an expectant look.

"Go on," Matty told the dog. "I'll catch up."

The long-haired Rottweiler turned and raced through the brown grass toward the shop building. Matty was Ethan's little brother. Their parents had been taken to one of the work camps, so Ethan and his wife, Hailey, took on the job of raising him. Jace thought the boy had adjusted well for a thirteen-year-old who'd lost his parents, his friends, his whole way of life. Lacy and Travis had rescued them the day the National Guard had shown up.

He grinned at the boy and couldn't help reaching out and

ruffing up Matty's wild blond hair.

Matty mashed it back down, a scowl on his face. "Y'all need to stop doin' that."

Jace let out a soft chuckle. "Where you going?"

"Gonna go take care of the horses." He drew in a deep breath. "Geez, have you noticed how hard it is to breathe in there with all those people?"

Concern flashed through him. "How do you feel, kiddo?"

The boy was still recovering from a long illness. What would've been a manageable case of pneumonia with a doctor and proper medication had almost killed him. Cat, a retired nurse, had done her best to bring the boy back to health. But if it weren't for Lacy raiding the town pharmacy and getting the necessary nebulizer and medication, he would've succumbed to the illness.

Pride and consternation over Lacy's reckless actions warred within him. He could've

strangled Travis. He could've gone alone, taken that risk himself.

Matty rolled his eyes. "I'm fine."

Before Jace could suggest he go back inside and rest, the boy leapt up and raced across the yard toward the shop building. He heard Castiel's excited yip, greeting the boy he'd adopted as his own.

He heard the group of men walking down the drive before he saw them.

Rising slowly, he went back into the house, closing the door on a soft click.

AJ sat at the table playing poker with Travis and Bryan. Cat sat in her rocker watching the game, laughing at the taunts Bryan threw AJ's way.

"AJ get in Matty's bedroom. Now," Jace said, urging him forward when he stood. "Hide under the bed."

"What the … but I'm winning," AJ groused, dropping his hand on the table.

Edwards walked from the iron stove to stand beside Cat, resting a protective hand on the back of her chair.

"What's going on?"

"We've got company," Jace said.

As soon as the words slipped from his mouth, the door opened.

AJ froze in the archway that separated the kitchen from the small living room. In a slow deliberate move, he turned, hands clenched at his side. His face flushed a bright red when he saw his uncle stride in with his assistant. Two militia men flanked their sides.

Jace leaned against the kitchen counter and rubbed the back of his neck. He didn't know what his best friend thought would happen, but a confrontation with the senator never ended well.

Cat reinforced his thoughts with a muttered, *"Scheisse."*

Thomas Monroe's eyes darkened at the sight of his nephew. A frown dipped the corners of his lips. "When did you get here?"

AJ stepped forward, but Edwards held up a subtle hand and gave him a meaningful look. "I'm here for my sister," he said, voice granite hard. "Where is she?"

Monroe drew in a breath through his nose. "Hmm," he said as he let his breath out in a slow exaggerated way. "Currently, I believe she's being held by Manuel Nieto, a high-powered

Mexican human trafficker and drug dealer."

Jace's temper snapped at the man's smug attitude. He bounded forward, crossing the distance between them in two swift strides. He rammed a right hook at the senator's head, then turned and glared at the assistant who raised his hands and took a step back.

AJ came and stood beside Jace as the militia men jumped forward. AJ lunged at the one on the right with a swift upper cut to the jaw.

Jace stepped back as the man crashed against the counter hitting his head against the chrome side as he fell. He placed the heel of his boot against the man's throat.

AJ turned on the second man and punched him in the gut then kicked him to the floor.

The lightning-fast altercations shocked the room silent. Travis's mouth gaped as blood from the senator's nose dripped all over his gingham button down shirt.

"Enough," Thomas barked, pinching the bridge of his nose to staunch the blood flow.

AJ rounded on him, fury causing the yellow in his eyes to blaze. "I don't take orders from you. Why is my sister in Mexico? What have you done?"

"I've done nothing," he responded in a cool manner that contradicted the steely glint on his face. "I told Lacy to stay here. She didn't listen. Now she's suffering the consequences."

"Why didn't you bring her home when you flew to the border?" he shouted with enough volume to bring the roof down. "You knew what she was walking into."

"She needed to learn a lesson."

Jace had heard enough. If Monroe valued his life, he'd shut the hell up because the rage boiling in his chest was about to erupt. The man at his feet started to rise. He thrust his boot heel against his esophagus.

"Stay down," he ordered then snapped his attention back to the senator. "You better stop talking," he warned in a low growl. "Don't place the blame on Lacy. We both know you let her walk into a trap because you're keeping her from me."

Monroe considered him. Before he could respond, AJ stepped over and pointed a finger in his face.

"I'm going to find my sister," AJ seethed through clenched teeth. "After that, I'm coming for you."

Monroe's face burned red. "Don't threaten me, boy. You'll regret it."

"That," AJ bit out, "was not a threat. It was a promise."

The low rumble of a diesel engine and heavy tires crunching on icy gravel caught the room's attention. The team sent to retrieve Dylan's girlfriend and Cat's husband was back.

Jace focused on Cat. He worried what her reaction would be to the news of her husband, Ben. Good or bad.

Face pale, she looked at Edwards and stood on shaky feet. His hand rested on her lower back in support.

Monroe turned and opened the door wide.

Vehicle doors slammed shut. Suspense hung thick in the icy air. Dylan walked in first with an emaciated pregnant girl leaning against his side. Gracie.

Jace sucked in a breath as his gaze shifted over her form. Dull brown hair hung against a pale, sunken face. Her brown eyes carried pain, both physical and mental. A loose shift dress, faded and dirty, hung limp against her bony frame.

He couldn't imagine the kind of hell she'd endured. She lifted her head, licked her cracked lips and tried to smile as Dylan helped her into a kitchen chair.

Cat hurried to the girl's side, lifted her wrist, and checked her pulse.

"Thank you, Cat," Dylan said.

Dylan ran a hand over his upper lip, then reached in his back pocket and pulled out a crumpled white envelope. Catching her hand in his, he gave it to her. His eyes met hers and he gave a slight shake of his head before releasing her.

With trembling hands, she drew out the single sheet of paper. Even from the short distance, Jace could tell it was a death certificate. Ben was dead.

Cat blanched. The ecru colored paper fluttered to the floor.

Edwards rushed over and caught her before she collapsed.

"Come on, Kit Cat," he said in a soothing lilt. He lifted his eyes. "We need somewhere quiet."

Jace cleared a path to the living room then opened the first bedroom door. "You can use this room. Hailey and Ethan are feeding the chickens. I know they won't mind."

Cat rested her head on Edward's shoulder as he led her out of the room.

Watching Cat and Edwards tore at Jace's heart. He needed Lacy. She was his other half. He strode into the kitchen and punched an angry fist in the air, then turned to the senator.

"You have no control over what happens to Lacy now. I'm not going to New Mexico. I'm leaving with AJ."

Blood had dried around the rim of the senator's nose. His right hook shifted it a little to the left. If he hadn't broken it, he'd come close. Monroe said nothing, just studied him like a
bug under glass.

Then Monroe's gaze connected with Dylan. "I've delivered on my end of our agreement."

Dylan nodded in acknowledgment.

"Bryan, help Dylan detain Jace in the wine cellar until we are ready to move on the New Mexico mission."

Dylan walked over to Jace, blocking his way to the door.

"Get out of my way, Dylan."

Sorrow masked Dylan's face. "I'm sorry, Jace. If there were any other way —"

Jace struck out, putting all his weight into the force of the strike. Dylan dropped to the floor with a heavy thud.

He looked down as Dylan struggled to rise. "Stop being sorry and start playing for the right team."

He stepped around Dylan. The two injured militia men stood in front of the door.

"Let me out," he ground out.

"You'll stay right here," the senator said at his back, "and fulfill your mission."

He turned. "What difference does it make now? You have no control over the situation in Mexico or what happens to Lacy. I'm going."

"I'm *letting* AJ go."

AJ snorted at the comment.

"The odds of his success are slim, but he can try. Only I have sway over Manuel Nieto. It will take some bargaining, but I think I can retrieve her." The senator looked at Jace and Bryan. "After I have control over the southwest region. Then I'll have something Nieto wants."

"Sick sonofabitch," AJ muttered as the senator spoke to the two men at the door. "Trading my sister like chattel for land."

Monroe sighed and faced his nephew. "You have no idea what's going on. Don't be so quick to judge me."

"All I know," AJ said, voice low, deadly. "Is that you didn't protect my sister. You're using her like a piece of property. I don't give a shit about your politics. When my dad finds out

what you've done, he'll slit your throat without blinking an eye."

"Empty threats have no effect on me, boy."

"You have no idea," AJ warned, "what my father will do."

Ignoring the last comment, the senator turned to William. "Let's go."

The men at the door moved so they could leave. The finality of the door closing was like listening to the seal of his own tomb.

Jace turned on his heel, shoved his way past Travis, then hoofed it to the bathroom. He sat on the toilet's lid, head cradled in his hands.

AJ walked in without knocking.

"Glad I wasn't hittin' the head," Jace snarked.

He needed space. Time to wrap his head around what needed to happen next. If there were any way to save the governor of New Mexico, he couldn't think of it.

AJ smirked. "Stop moping."

He lifted his head. "Feck off."

AJ let out a sharp laugh and punched his shoulder. "Snap out of it. I need to talk to you before I leave."

Jace groaned into his hands. "What?"

"There's a map I want to give you."

"Of what? Buried treasure?" he asked, voice heavy with sarcasm. "How to save the governor of New Mexico? Because that one would be helpful."

"No dumb ass. It's directions on how to get to our new home in Tulare."

He raised his head and looked at his friend.

"I want you to know where to find us. I'm taking Lacy home."

Tears burned the back of his eyelids and a hot lump formed in his throat. His damn emotions were all over the place.

He cleared his throat and swallowed hard. "Thanks," he said, voice hoarse.

His friend studied him in silent regard.

"I miss her," Jace admitted quietly. "I'm losing my mind worrying about what's happening to her. All the 'what if's' are messing with me and I'm so angry I want to kill something." He huffed a short laugh. "The senator mainly."

"I had a vision of her," AJ said. "That's why I came. It was so real."

"You need to hurry. I can feel it." He raised up and grabbed his friend in a tight hug. "Get her back for me. It's killing me that I'm not going."

He released him and stepped back.

AJ gave him a short nod and turned to leave.

"Hey AJ," Jace said, stopping him. "Tell her I love her."

He nodded again and left.

AJ and Bryan rescuing Lacy should've given his heart something to hold on to. But it didn't. His heart was shredded, and the weight of sorrow and grief threatened to consume him.

15

The shot of whiskey burned, leaving Lacy's throat scorched and lit a fire in her empty stomach. She set the cut crystal glass on the coffee table beside the bottle, then leaned back into the couch's fluffy cushions with a long sigh.

The expensive Buffalo Trace she'd gleefully plucked from the bar seemed like a good idea a few seconds ago.

Not now.

She groaned and doubled over, her stomach rebelling against the shot of alcohol. Drinking on an empty stomach. Not her best idea. She needed food. Her system had gone too long without it.

The whiskey's distinct smell of vanilla and oak still permeated her nostrils, and she tried not to gag. Cat would've appreciated the flavorful notes. She didn't care if it tasted like unicorn rainbow juice, she craved the high.

Fatigue slammed into her like a crash dummy hitting a wall. Her body slumped over, and she curled into a tight ball on the couch. Questions swirled in her semi-coherent brain. Where had Raul disappeared to and why? The niggling fear he wasn't the stand-up guy he'd played at the farm wormed its way forward.

How the hell was she going to get home without his help?

The question brought her up short. She had no home. Her parents fled to California, and she had no way to contact them. Searching for them would be like looking for Waldo. She'd rather chew her arm off than go back to the farm and live under her uncle's thumb. So, where did that leave her? The silence mocked her. Why had Nieto and his men left them alone?

Her eyelids drooped. She was so tired. Conjuring the image of Jace, the curve of his soft lips and the way they tasted, and his wolf-dragon tattoo, comforted her. She craved his touch like an addict craved heroin. He was her home, remembering her revelation at the lake.

She'd been so angry with him when he'd followed her there. He'd been holding her at arm's length, and she couldn't figure out why. He wouldn't talk. Ironic, given the fact his *modus operandi* was needling her into talking any chance he got. She'd thought he couldn't handle the fact she'd been raped. It still stung to think about. He'd bulldozed his way into her life the moment he'd shown up at the farm asking for a place to stay.

A smile curved her lips remembering his bulldog tenacity. Despite her brokenness, her heart had fallen hard. It hurt when he started avoiding her. Confused, she'd decided she needed distance from him. She'd taken off on her horse toward home and ended up at the lake.

He'd followed. They'd fought. She'd thrown wet sand in his face. Then he'd told her he loved her and gathered her into his arms.

Whatever it took, she'd get back to him.

Willow walked into the room. "Where'd that guy go?"

Lacy lifted droopy eyelids and tried to focus. "Hmm?"

"Where did that guy go? The one you know."

"Dunno. Don't care. No one's coming back today."

The sun had set and the automatic lighting around the garden below cast an ethereal glow through the window. Raul had left with his father, and she had no way of knowing what that meant.

Willow sat beside her. "Are you okay?" she asked, concern lacing her voice.

"Sure, sure," she mumbled.

Willow's response got lost somewhere between the whiskey's ether and fatigue. Awareness of her surroundings didn't filter through exhaustion's haze until someone nudged her wounded arm.

"Wake up," Raul commanded, aggravated.

What the hell did he have to be irritated over?

She kept her eyes closed, smothering the overwhelming desire to strangle him. How long had she slept? Her whole body ached.

Willow's soft footfall drew near.

"Leave her alone," the girl said sternly.

"Respect," she muttered, surprised at Willow's mettle.

She opened her eyes, one at a time. The room came into focus in a dizzy, merry-go-round sort of way. The faux candles in the elegant chandelier above swirled in streaks of white light.

She clutched her head and swore on a soft moan. "The gods hate me."

"We need to talk," Raul said in a flat tone.

She rose in slow increments into a sitting position, cradling her head in her hands.

"Ugh, my head," she whined.

Its relentless pounding made her want to hurl. In fact, there was a ninety-eight-point three percent probability she would throw up soon. She kept her mouth closed and breathed in through her nose, willing her stomach to stop its angry sea enactment.

"What did you do?" asked Raul, picking up the Buffalo Trace bottle. "You didn't drink enough to make you like this."

She raised her head and shot him a death glare. "That's what happens when alcohol hits an empty stomach. I haven't eaten in …"

How long had it been? She'd lost track of time. It couldn't have been more than a couple of days.

"How many days have I been here?"

"Three days." His brows furrowed. "You haven't eaten in three days?"

He moved to the wall safe, punched in the code, and withdrew a hotel telephone. Crossing to the end table beside the couch, he pulled out a phone cord, then snapped the end into place. He dialed room service and ordered breakfast for her and Willow.

"It better be food I recognize," she mumbled.

Willow sat beside her with a glass of water. "Sip slowly."

She took the glass, drew in a small mouthful, swishing it around to clear the funk from her teeth, then spit it in the trashcan Willow had retrieved from under the bar's sink. She took a cautious sip and swallowed.

Raul replaced the phone, closed the safe, and sat in the chair by the sofa. "Breakfast will be here shortly. All American."

She pinned him with a hard stare. "Let us go, Raul."

He looked away, muttering in Spanish, then turned to her with regret written in his eyes.

"My mother died when I was very young. My *abuela* raised me. My father, Manuel, was always away on business, and I believe my grandmother shielded me from him. I am not like my father."

Her face flushed and she pushed the lingering fatigue away. "Look, Raul, I don't care if you were born under a bridge and raised by trolls. Let. Us. Go!"

"I can't. But —"

Her fisted hands pushed down against the plush cushions. Rage continued to build, pushing her wall of control. Like rushing water pounding against a levee, she was about to break.

"But what?" she spit out.

"My father's business dealings are dishonorable. I have nothing to do with them. But I can't cross him. He's too powerful. I can't just let you go."

"How can you say you have nothing to do with them? You may not kidnap the girls your father sells and abuses, but having that knowledge and doing nothing? That's just as despicable. You are dishonorable, Raul."

Maybe calling him out wasn't the best idea, but when shit's being slung, she'd rather get out a shovel than risk being buried in it.

He leaned forward, placed his hands between his knees. "My father has spoken to me about you."

"*What?*" Lacy ran both hands through her dirty, tangled hair. "Why?"

"He likes you," he said quietly.

"I cracked his skull open and killed one of his men. How could he like me?" she asked incredulously.

Raul's lips tipped in a sad smile. "That's *why* he likes you. You're a fighter. It …" He paused and his cheeks stained red in embarrassment.

"It?" she prompted.

"It excites him," he said in a slow measured way.

Willow sucked in a sharp breath.

Realization slammed into Lacy, knocking the wind out of her. Her hands clenched into tight fists. Long nails bit into her palms. Her thoughts reeled.

"Lacy." Raul moved and knelt in front of her.

Her fist rammed into his cheek. The impact cracked her knuckles. She shoved his shoulders and he fell backward. "Get away from me!" she shouted, chest heaving. "Let me out of here!"

Tears streamed down her face. She would die before she let anyone touch her against her will again. Panic clawed under her skin. How was she going to survive this?

He stood and rubbed his reddened cheek. "If you don't agree to his arrangement, he will sell you to the highest bidder. I cannot protect you."

"I'm not his property. I'm not his to sell and I will *never* be his plaything."

His mouth pressed in a fine line. "He said you have twenty-four hours to decide."

She turned and her eyes locked on Willow. "What happens to her?"

A light tap on the door interrupted them. Raul walked over, opened it, and took the tray of food from the bell hop.

Lacy jumped up before he could close the door. "Please!" she screamed. "We need help!"

Raul slammed the door, set the food on the bar, then turned on her. "That won't work. My father owns this hotel."

She sat back down. Her mind wanted to shut down. How the hell could they escape? She needed time to think.

"You never answered about Willow."

Raul stood by the door. "I don't know."

"You tell your father I want forty-eight hours to think about his proposal." She spat the last word out. "And Willow stays with me. No one touches her."

He nodded, then held out his hand. "I will need the gun."

"What if I don't give it to you?" she challenged.

"My father will send his men to take it by force. There wouldn't be enough bullets to kill them all."

Her shoulders slumped. She reached behind her back and retrieved the weapon, then stepped around the coffee table. Her heart felt like it was being run through a shredder as she handed over the one thing that could've protected her from Nieto.

"You better watch your back, Raul," she said, as he snatched the gun from her hand.

"I know," he acknowledged, and slid out the door.

Bile and water slid up her throat. She half-ran into the bathroom, knelt at the toilet, and vomited until dry heaves ripped her stomach muscles in half. She felt Willow's hands lift her hair away from her face.

She looked up at the girl. "I have no idea what to do now."

16

Rage blistered Jace's skin as he watched the two militia men through the door's single pane. The wind whipped at their worn grunt style hats. The sentinels stood as a reminder of the senator's warning. No one would leave unless given permission.

Reality rolled in painful waves, and his shoulders fell under the strain. The senator had him fettered.

"Why did you confront Monroe that way," Travis complained to AJ. "It could've ended badly for all of us."

He turned and walked to the giant iron stove.

AJ stalked from the coffee pot to the kitchen table and leaned over the back of Travis's chair.

"What's your problem Travis?" AJ asked, menace lacing his tone.

Travis huffed and shifted away from AJ's imposing frame. "I don't see the point in angering the man who's letting us stay here. He could force us to go on suicide missions like Jace. I just don't feel like getting killed."

AJ straightened, walked over, and stood beside Jace. "Speaking of missions, Travis. I'm going with Bryan to get my sister. There's room for one passenger. That's it. So, you're out."

Jace folded his arms across his chest. "He didn't want to go anyway."

Travis stood, fists flexing at his side. "Go to hell, Jace. First chance I get, I'm outta here."

He stalked out the back door. One of the guards grabbed Travis by the arm.

"I'm going to check the horses," he snapped, jerking away from the guard.

The guard nodded and stepped out of the way.

"Hey," Dylan interjected. "Gracie needs to lay down. Can we use Matty's room?"

"Go ahead," Jace said. "I'll let Hailey know when she comes in."

Hailey, Ethan's wife, had hated the farm when she'd first arrived, but after Matty's illness, she seemed more accepting of her new way of life.

"Thanks," he said, then shuffled out of the kitchen with Gracie in his arms.

"Anyone want a cup of coffee?" Bryan asked, moving to the empty pot. Not waiting for an answer, he began filling the carafe with water. "Travis has a point," he said over the gushing water.

"Meaning?" Jace prompted, although he doubted Travis had any good points. The guy was a pain in the ass.

Bryan poured water into the reservoir then shoved the pot under the basket. He turned, leaned his elbows on the counter.

"We need to think beyond the crisis happening right now. No one can see the forest for the tree up their butt. Bigger picture says everyone here needs an exit strategy and we need to evacuate soon."

"I can't think of anything except getting Lacy back," Jace admitted.

Bryan lifted an insulated cup from the dish drainer and set it by the coffee maker. "Yeah, but then what? You'd be a complete idiot to come back here."

"You're right," he conceded. "I'd go to California with Lacy and AJ."

Bryan tapped his cup on the counter. "Okay. But that's not going to stop the senator. If he's not finished with you, he'll find a way to reel you back in. He's a master at the game he's playing. We may not be able to stop him from taking over the United States, but we sure as hell better figure out how to stop him from messing with us. Permanently."

Jace scratched his head. "I don't think Monroe cares about Cat, Edwards, and the rest. They should be able to leave without causing much of a dust-up."

"Agreed," Bryan said, hovering over the percolating coffee. "But where would they go?"

Edwards walked into the kitchen. "I smell coffee."

"Hey Edwards," Jace started. "We're talking about evac plans. Can you spare a minute?"

Edwards's brows knitted together. "Sure. Let me go get Cat," he said, stepping back through the doorway.

"She okay?" Jace asked.

He sympathized with the older woman. The loss of his mom and dad a few months ago still slit his heart like a razorblade.

Edwards gave him a crooked, half-smile as he walked through the doorway to the living room. "She's tough. She'll make it."

He returned with Cat, hand in hand. Tears left tracks down her pale cheeks and a bright sheen covered her swollen eyes. Edwards dragged two chairs from the kitchen table to the semi-circle of disparate furniture facing the giant iron stove and motioned for everyone to sit.

Bryan brought over two mugs of coffee, one for Edwards and the other for AJ, then returned for his own. He sat beside

Jace, took a huge scalding gulp, then sucked air through his teeth to cool the burn.

Jace rolled his eyes. "That stuff runs in your veins like motor oil through a car engine."

Bryan grunted, slouched down in his seat extending his long legs, and took another swig, then went through the whole air sucking process again.

Ethan and Hailey walked through the door, the basket of eggs swinging from the crook of her arm. Ethan bent, whispered something in her ear, and a pretty pink flushed her cheeks as she smiled up at him.

God, he missed Lacy. The scene drove home the fact his soul's other half was missing. He almost hated them for their easy display of affection. He shook off the morose feelings and concentrated.

Everyone needed to start thinking about relocating. He wondered if Edwards would open his home to the rest of them. Soon, Gracie would need Cat's help delivering her baby and Matty still suffered with his breathing. It would be a good place to start the conversation.

"What about your place, Edwards?" he asked, jumping in.

Edwards scratched his stubble-covered chin. "Well, I've thought about that. I'm thinkin' it might work. That is, if Cat will come."

Edwards' hand reached out, covered her folded hands with his, and gave a gentle squeeze. She looked up, and Jace read a myriad of emotions. Acceptance settled on her face and her shoulders relaxed.

"Of course, I'll come, you old goat."

"Old goat," Edwards mimicked, chuckling.

Cat gave him an exasperated look. "Well good God! Someone's got to keep everyone organized. Lord knows you'd all starve if I didn't come, and I don't want that on my conscience."

Jace looked around the circle, then at Ethan and Hailey,

listening from the kitchen. "So, if that's cool with everyone?" he trailed off, waiting for confirmation.

Ethan stepped around the counter. "We'd be grateful," he told Edwards. "Matty still needs Cat's watchful eye. He's not out of the woods yet."

Jace looked at Cat. "You'd need to take Dylan's girlfriend. She'll need you. Dylan won't be much help if he's off on one of the senator's missions."

Cat nodded. "If she's agreeable."

"She will be," Dylan said, walking into the room. "And thank you for thinking of her."

Dylan's gaze locked with Edwards, his guilt, palpable. He'd stolen the older man's truck and left him stranded by the roadside in a snowstorm. It was the night he'd attacked Lacy. It still amazed Jace that she'd forgiven Dylan.

"It's more than I deserve," he said, lowering his eyes.

"Put the past where it belongs, son."

Dylan nodded, eyes still averted, but his shoulders sagged in obvious relief.

Matty burst through the back door, cheeks ruddy from the wind, eyes bright with excitement.

"Guys!" he shouted. His breath came short and shallow.

"Matt, slow down," his brother cautioned. Concern etched grooves between his eyes.

"But —"

"I mean it," Ethan commanded sharply. "Take a slow deep breath."

Matty rolled his eyes but did as his brother said, locking his hands over his head.

Satisfied, Ethan made a rolling motion with his finger, a clear indicator for Matty to continue.

"Travis took off with Acer and hasn't come back. He was headed toward Kaw City."

"He probably won't be back," Jace muttered.

"He knows how to live off-grid," Dylan said, shaking his

head. "His home life was pretty rough. His dad used to drive for miles out into the Osage, kick him out of the truck and make him find his way back. He missed his fair share of school trekking back from as far as Okmulgee. No money, no phone, no hitching allowed."

AJ ran a hand through his hair. "Lacy mentioned that once. I thought he was feeding her a line, playing some kind of sympathy card."

"Nope," Dylan confirmed. "His dad beat the shit out of him once for hitching to make it back in time to play in his basketball game. He was in bed for a week."

"Guys," Matty interrupted bouncing on the balls of his feet.

"Damn," Jace said under his breath.

"Guys," Matty tried again.

"Don't interrupt, Matt," Ethan admonished.

Jace had to admit, Ethan had the dad voice down to an artists' perfection.

"BUT ETHAN!" Matty shouted and wrenched open the back door. "Those military guys are doin' something to the governor!"

Jace sprung up like a mountain lion jumping over a boulder and bolted out the door, the others on his heels.

In the southwest corner of the property, a semi-circle of militia men had the governor cornered. On his knees, hands up in surrender, the governor begged for his life. Jace watched in stunned horror as a bullet ripped through the governor's skull, exploding out the back. Blood, brain, and skull fragments rained down on the ground.

Jace grabbed the sides of his head. He fisted large clumps of hair in each hand, then pulled hard. He fell to his knees, heedless of the wet soil seeping into his jeans, and let out a

painful shout. It ripped from his gut, ruptured blood vessels in his eyes, and shredded his vocal cords. Anger clawed inside his chest, craving release. He sprang up, then turned toward the smaller farmhouse where the senator likely lounged on the dirty, leather couch, smoking a cigarette.

"Don't do it," Bryan cautioned, reading his thoughts. "You can't confront the senator. That's what he wants."

"He killed the governor!" Jace shouted. "For no reason. It's senseless. The man needs to be stopped."

"We can't stop him," Bryan shot back. "We can't change the backdrop. The die for this country has already been cast. The best we can hope for is to fall off Monroe's radar. Think smart. Think strategically. He killed the man to send you a message. Think about what that is."

Jace's face fell. "He's forcing me to kill the New Mexico governor."

"Maybe," Bryan said. "If that's the case, think about how to outmaneuver him."

"God damn it," Jace shouted at the top of his lungs. "*How?*"

The senator was playing dirty to get what he wanted. Well, he could play dirty too. He just had to come to terms with what that meant. He was going to have to find a way to flip the script.

17

The bathroom floor's cold tile felt good against Lacy's battered cheek. With reluctance, she forced herself up and crossed to the sink to rinse her mouth out. Careful not to let any unfiltered water slip down her throat, she swished and spit, then reached for the hotel's tiny bottle of courtesy mouthwash. She unscrewed the cap and gargled the whole bottle, letting the minty sting numb her tongue, wishing it could numb her heart as well.

Willow's watchful gaze never left her back. Lacy could see the petite blond studying her in the mirror.

She lifted her head and raised a brow. "What?"

Willow gave a slight shake of her head. "Nothing. I just wondered if you wanted to take a bath or a shower. Wash off the blood and grime. Plus ..." she trailed off, looking embarrassed.

"Plus?" Lacy prompted.

"You stink," she blurted.

Laughter with a tinge of hysteria bubbled up her throat. After spending two days in the underworld's seventh circle, the foul odors had seeped into her clothes, hair, and skin, along with blood, not only from her own injuries, but also from the man she'd bludgeoned to death. If she smelled horrid enough Willow felt compelled to mention it, she should shower.

Walking through the bathroom door, she opened her mouth to agree, then snapped it shut.

"I think I'll pass," she said over her shoulder.

Smelling like a dead carcass could work to her advantage. The stench might repulse Nieto or at least annoy him. An involuntary shudder skittered down her spine as she passed the darkened spot on the plush white carpet. She could still see Miguel lying there. A bloody stain forever burned into her brain.

The breakfast Raul ordered sat on the bar, cold and unappetizing. Still, her stomach cramped with hunger. She grabbed a piece of dry toast and took a small bite. It tasted like sawdust. Grimacing, she searched the small refrigerator tucked under the bar and pulled out a bottle of water. She took a swig then pressed it to the cut on her cheek, let the cold soothe the constant throb.

Sunlight poured through the terrace windows, warming the room. She took her toast and water and sat at the small high table by the window. Willow brought the breakfast tray and joined her.

"How did you end up here?" Lacy asked without preamble, munching on another bite of dry bread.

Willow picked at a piece of bacon on her plate. "I'm not sure. I've gone over that night a million times in my head. My boyfriend, Scott, and I were on a date. It was our three-month anniversary, so he'd taken me into Laredo to celebrate. My dad's a large animal vet and owns a ranch near Cotulla, about an hour north of Laredo."

Willow's brows puckered and her mouth tipped down into a frown. She speared scrambled eggs onto her fork and took a bite. A grimace replaced the frown as she chewed. She reached over, picked up a saltshaker and shook a generous amount onto the pile of eggs.

"What happened?"

She cocked her head. "I didn't want to go to Laredo, but Scott had heard about a great Mexican place he was dying to try. Supposed to be authentic, not the tex-mex stuff we're used to. So, I agreed."

The toast had settled in Lacy's stomach without upset and she felt a little better. It was enough to clear the fog from her mind. She took another piece of toast from the plate.

"Was the restaurant in a bad part of town? How'd you get nabbed?" she continued, crunching on another bite.

"It was a nice place in a good part of town. The maître d' settled us into a cozy booth and Scott ordered some wine. The waiter asked to see my ID. I'm only eighteen, but I had a fake one. I left my purse in Scott's truck, so I walked out to get it. That's when three men grabbed me, shoved me into an SUV, and took off."

"You were in the wrong place at the wrong time." She gave Willow a wry smile. "Makes you wonder what we did to piss off the Fates, huh?"

"Yeah maybe," Willow said, doubt tainting her tone.

"You don't think it was just bad luck?"

She let out a gusty sigh. "It could've been, but it felt like they were waiting for me." She crumbled a piece of bacon, then pushed the plate back. "It felt … deliberate. I swear I heard one of them say, 'that's her.' But that doesn't make any sense, does it?"

"No," Lacy said slowly, "it doesn't. But that doesn't mean it's not possible."

"What about you?" Willow asked. "How did you end up in Nieto's crosshairs?"

Her face puckered. "Long story short? My uncle. I made the mistake of trying to help family."

Lacy slid off her chair and wandered to the television. Her mind needed a diversion, a break from thinking so hard. A DVD player hooked up to the set with a small stack of movies beside it caught her attention. She picked out a comedy, *Liar, Liar,* inserted the disc, turned on the set, and beckoned Willow over.

"Let's watch TV and I'll tell you the whole shitty tale."

As they sat and watched the movie, Lacy unfolded her story. She found welcome release venting pent-up anger at the twisted nightmare that summed up the last half-year of her life.

Willow folded her legs in, tucked her feet under her, and leaned back on the couch's plush back.

"Tell me more about your brother," she encouraged.

She suspected Willow's curiosity had more to do with needing a distraction rather than actual interest in her brother. Talking about her uncle made the acid in her stomach boil and her hands twitch. She closed her eyes and visualized AJ. To her, he was the perfect brother.

"What do you want to know?"

"Does he look like you? I look nothing like my two older sisters. They're both cut from the same tall brunette cloth. They have the most beautiful sloe eyes like my mom. My dad says I look like his mother. She died before I was born."

"She must've been beautiful," Lacy mused.

Willow lifted a shoulder and shrugged off the compliment. "So they say."

"AJ and I both have the same black hair, but his eyes are different. They're a much lighter shade of green. Like a peridot. It gives him a very jungle cat vibe." She gave Willow a wistful smile. "It pisses him off when I say that."

The girl's eyes saddened. "I wish I could meet him."

Her eyes traveled the room. It was easy to believe they'd never see their loved ones again from this vantage point. Maybe they wouldn't. She reached over and patted the girl's knee.

"It's better for you if you didn't. AJ is overbearing and overprotective to a fault. He'd steamroll right over you."

"He sounds great."

"He is," she agreed, her tone melancholy.

The door swung open, interrupting their exchange. She looked over expecting to see Raul, sharp tongue ready, teeth bared. Her heart plummeted to her stomach then bounced back up blocking every cutting remark.

Nieto strolled in, two henchmen at his sides. The yellow linen suit he wore gave off a Colombian drug lord impression. He looked like a walking lemon. Lacy rolled her eyes. Could he get any more cliché?

He jerked his head toward Willow. "Take the girl into the bedroom and leave us."

Willow backed away, melting into the back of the couch.

Lacy narrowed her eyes at the men. "Don't touch her."

She said it with as much power as she could muster but knew it wouldn't do any good. They were outnumbered. Willow leaned into Lacy and whispered in her ear as one of the men wrenched her arm forward.

She stumbled off the couch. "You're going to dislocate my shoulder, you idiot," Willow snapped.

The man ignored her, propelling her into the bedroom. The other followed and slammed the door shut.

Nieto sauntered to the couch and took a seat beside her. "Have you considered my proposal?" he asked in a careful voice.

She folded her arms. "I asked for forty-eight hours. It hasn't even been six."

"There's no point putting off the inevitable," he said, breezily waving a hand in the air.

He inched his way closer, leaning his body into hers. Vomit pushed its way up her throat and tiny pinpricks of fear traveled over her body. Zach had violated her, overpowered her in a way she never wanted to experience again, yet here she sat in the middle of friggin' Mexico with a sex-trafficking drug lord leering at her with the same intent. In the past, anger had fueled her, pushed her into action but all her rage seemed to dissolve into blinding, muscle frozen, terror.

"You know you don't have a choice, *mi amor*," he murmured in a low seductive voice. "I always get what I want."

Her throat contracted, restricting her breath. Blood rushed from her head, dimming her vision. His arms snaked around her, forcing her into him.

He leaned his head back. "*Apestas*, you stink."

The action woke her. As she slid sideways, her hand reached beneath the couch cushion, pushing backward until she found what she sought.

In a quick move, she retracted her hand. With all her strength, she thrust the knife Willow had hidden under the cushion into Nieto's chest. It sunk between two rib bones.

Shock covered Nieto's face. "*Puta*," he rasped.

She pushed him away and jumped off the couch. Black eyes glittered dangerously at her. In a slow, deliberate movement, he pulled out the knife and stood. Blood bloomed, soaked into his yellow suit jacket.

In sharp Spanish, he called for his men. They opened the door, then rushed to their bleeding employer. One grabbed a bar towel and pressed it to his wound, talking rapidly in Spanish.

Lacy didn't think she'd struck hard enough to do serious damage, like puncturing a lung, but she'd gotten his attention.

"I will be back tomorrow to get you," he warned.

Although his face blanched in pain, his words still carried a weighty threat.

"I will fight you every step of the way," Lacy shot back.

"Hmm," he purred. "I'm looking forward to it. And bathe," he commanded. "*Apestas*."

His men put an arm around each shoulder and helped him out the door.

Falling to her knees, she screamed. Her head fell forward,

tears dripping off her nose. The situation was hopeless. Suicide seemed the only way out of this screwed up mess.

Willow laid a comforting hand on her back. "We'll find our way out. I can feel it."

She raised her head and trained her eyes on Willow's. "I don't know. Maybe I've cashed in all my chips. I don't see a way out."

"Then we'll make our own way."

But how? The question tormented her. She laid her head on her knees, closed her eyes. The question still bounced around her brain like an annoying ping-pong ball. How? It taunted her, challenged her. Could she find a way out? Did she have enough fight left in her? She didn't know.

18

Dry New Mexico air infused with the earthy scent of creosote blew under Jace's jacket conjuring the image of bony phantom fingers sliding up his back.

Dylan and three militia men Jace didn't recognize, made up their small team of five. They'd unpacked their gear out of the black Expedition and trekked through sand and sagebrush to the gates of the governor's mansion. Speed demon Dylan had driven the eleven-hour trip in nine and they'd arrived around midnight.

A long driveway meandered up a hill, hiding the square dwelling that sprawled across the desert like a red clay snake. He stood staring at the iron gates, his mind numb. Thinking on his feet was exhausting. His mind, severed between Lacy and trying to figure a way out of killing again, had taken a vacation.

Catching a solid thought was like chasing fireflies. The men around him began talking to Dylan, but his mind refused to focus on their words.

A coyote howled in the distance and in the heavy darkness, the senator's parting words echoed through his brain. '*You have no choice,*' the senator said in his careless, offhand manner.

'*There's always a choice,*' Jace muttered. '*Just like you* chose *to kill Governor Harding. You didn't have to do that.*'

'*I tried to persuade Harding to join me, but he refused. He no longer served a purpose, and I don't have the manpower to set up a POW camp.*' His cutting gaze lasered in on him. '*And you needed to see that any attempt on your part to sabotage the New Mexico mission is futile. You will* do what you're told.'

'*I'm not going to kill New Mexico's governor for you!*' he shouted. '*I won't help you destroy our country.*'

'*Destroy? You have no idea what this country will become if the president has his way. You're a part of this whether you like it or not.*'

He clenched his fists until his nails bit into his palms.

'*I'll do what it takes to restore our country,*' the senator continued. '*It takes sacrifice, sometimes even the sacrifice of your own moral code, to get the job done.*'

He'd been shanghaied.

He had no choice if he ever wanted to see Lacy again. He raked his hands through his gritty hair trying to get a handle on the staggering mix of anger and helplessness impaling his gut.

Dylan broke from the conversation and motioned Jace to follow him into the desert's darkness.

"We're waiting on Corporal James," he said, voice low. "Bryan left before we did, so he should be here soon."

Buzz Cut. Damn. He'd hoped they'd go ahead and get this over with. Now, they were stuck in the desert, in the middle of the night, waiting for a man he knew would force his hand. He still hadn't figured a way to flip the script.

"Where's he going to land? The governor will hear the chopper."

"Where we left the Expedition. He'll drive up." Dylan placed a hand on Jace's shoulder. "Look, Jace," he hesitated, cursing under his breath.

"What?" he barked.

"I just wish —"

"What? That you could help? You could help me, but you won't."

Dylan rubbed the back of his neck. "I have a lot at stake."

"And you think I don't? Lacy has been taken by *a human trafficker*! Do you understand what that means? If she's sold, I doubt I'll ever find her."

He ignored the tears burning the back of his eyes and pinned the younger man with a hard stare. At least Dylan had the decency to look ashamed.

"Whatever you're planning, I'll try to cover for you. That's the best I can offer."

Jace nodded. He'd take all the help he could get. His mind whirled like a pinwheel, trying to figure out a way to warn the unsuspecting governor.

The metallic grind of an engine filtered through his thoughts. Corporal James had arrived, and his time was up. Bryan and AJ should be on their way to Mexico to rescue Lacy now. He ground his molars. He should be on that chopper. Depending on someone else to recover his girl made his blood boil. He blew out a long breath to ease his tight chest. Bryan and AJ wouldn't fail, he reassured himself, despite the senator's disheartening words. They couldn't.

Dylan squeezed his shoulder then walked back to the group of militia men. They stood at attention waiting for Corporal James to exit the SUV. The senator had trained the men to work, not think. They would follow orders without question, relying on someone above them to make all the important political decisions.

The door opened and a large black boot hit the ground quickly followed by the other. James unfolded himself out of the car and strode toward the militia team standing stiff, hands at their sides. As one, they saluted him.

James looked over the group. "Where's Cooper?"

Jace moved out of the shadows but didn't fall into formation. "Right here."

"Fall in," James commanded.

"No."

Fury crossed James's face, coloring it ruby red. The older man marched to him and pointed a finger in his face.

"Do as you're told."

He took a step back and bunched his hand into a fist, ready to take a swing. The scar on James's face running from eye to chin stood in stark relief against the moon's light. For a fleeting moment, he wondered what James had done to acquire such disfigurement.

The man studied him for a moment, sized him up, then shook his head. "The senator wants you to go in alone," James informed him.

Shock ricocheted through him. Why would the senator send him in alone? As punishment?

Before he could respond, James continued. "We're here for back up only. If you fail, we'll finish the job."

"Okay," he said dragging out the word.

His mind began to calculate. He could work with this scenario. All he had to do was help the New Mexico governor escape. Undetected. What were the odds of success? Dismal, at best. Still, he had to try.

"And Jace, if you fail, you better be dead."

Buzz Cut's smirk said it all. If he didn't complete the senator's task, there'd be hell to pay. And the older man would be more than happy to deliver it.

"Fine," he said, eyes flat, face schooled in indifference.

He walked over to his backpack, unzipped the front pocket, and pulled out the tranquilizer gun he'd used on the Oklahoma governor. That was the first job he'd completed for the senator, and he'd thought it would be the only one. But Thomas Monroe played a dirty game, and somehow, he'd landed right in the middle of his crosshairs. He loaded it and stuffed it in his back waistband.

Buzz Cut leaned over his shoulder. "What are you gonna do with that thing? You need your MP7."

Jace pulled out the MP7, screwed on the barrel, and slung it over his shoulder. "Satisfied?" he asked, brows raised.

Buzz Cut just humphed and crossed his arms. "Go," he commanded.

He surveyed the gate and the adjoining stone wall, looking for possible ways inside. The iron gate's bars were set too close together for anyone to squeeze through. Stones jutted out of the wall that surrounded the property. Scaling it might work. Two camera's set atop the iron gates blinked as he jogged by, acknowledging his presence.

If someone was monitoring those cameras …

He let the thought drop, unwilling to focus on the possibility of getting shot. Two yards from the gate, he found a spot suitable to scale. He hefted himself up, threw his pack over, then jumped down the eight-foot wall. His feet thumped and sank into the desert sand. The sand provided a landing buffer and took much of the shock from his feet. It still stung like a bitch.

Grabbing his pack, he sprinted down the long drive. As he topped the hill, the sprawling mansion took shape. He had no intel except the governor was alone. He didn't know how the senator's goons got their information, or if it was reliable. He could be walking into an ambush the senator set up for all he knew.

He cut away from the drive and ran along the mansion's southern side. A darkened window, possibly a bedroom, seemed like a good place to enter. Not bothering with the cutting tools, he pulled out a spare T-shirt from his pack and wrapped his left elbow. He jabbed at the glass, breaking through. Broken shards littered the sand beneath his feet and the carpeted floor inside. Clearing the frame, he stuck his hand through and unlocked it. The noise so far had been minimal, but the need to hurry pushed against his back.

In the dim moonlight, he observed a small library with floor to ceiling books lining the walls. Dust crawled up his nose, and he stifled a sneeze. His feet moved with quick silent steps to the door. He cracked it open, peered out into the hallway, lit by a small nightlight.

A Doberman Pinscher crouched in front of the door, a low snarl ripping from its chest. The dog's hair stood straight up along its neck. His keen ears had picked up the sound of glass breaking.

Shit.

The dog hadn't made the intel list. What other information had the senator failed to reveal?

He reached around slowly and pulled the tranquilizer gun from his back waistband. The dog lowered a fraction, showing his teeth. His hands shook as he pulled the trigger, aiming for the dog's muscled shoulder. The dart hit its mark. The large dog fell with a whimper and Jace let out a long gusty breath. He'd seen the layout of the mansion once on the drive to Santa Fe. If he remembered correctly, the governor resided in the east wing. The hallway gave way to a small sitting room.

He crossed it and moved down an eastern hallway. He could see large wooden double doors at the end. The governor's suite.

A wave of familiarity washed over him as he crept toward the doors. He'd snuck through another governor's mansion not long ago, searching for his target. He'd try to avoid getting into a brawl this time.

The Oklahoma governor knew how to throw a right hook. His nose still ached from the blow. Lacy had been with him then and had saved him from further damage. A small smile tugged his lips as he remembered her aiming a Sig at the governor. They'd made it out and delivered Harding to her uncle. Something he'd never forgive himself for.

The dark wooden doors loomed ahead, and he shook off the memory. He needed his mind focused on the task at hand.

He cracked open the door just enough to look inside. A woman and girl, no more than twelve, huddled together on the massive four poster bed.

Confusion fused his feet to the floor. New Mexico's governor was a *woman?*

"What do you want?" the woman croaked, voice heavy-laden with sleep.

The girl hid her face against the woman's arm. Long, rich brown hair cascaded over her shoulder hiding her profile.

"Take whatever you want, just leave us alone."

She thought he was a thief. Where the hell was his target?

He gave himself a mental shake. "Where's the governor?"

"I am the governor," the woman said.

"Bloody hell," he muttered, dropping his hands.

He cursed the senator under his breath. Thomas Monroe knew he'd fail, had set him up to fail. The man wanted him incarcerated. A deafening roar filled his head. Why would the senator do this? He already controlled their immediate future. What could he gain by throwing him in jail?

Rage boiled over. If the senator wanted to play dirty, the man had better hedge his bets, because he was about to double down.

19

AJ would never think of coffee the same way again. He let out a sharp breath through his nose to clear out the mixture of smells crowding his nostrils. He'd hidden from Corporal James, the formidable man they'd picked up in Arizona, by cramming himself into a small corner. Huddled under a thick tarp behind supplies meant for the senator's wife, he'd tried to stifle his claustrophobia.

Closing his eyes, he imagined he was floating down Missouri's Elk River with his friends instead of flying in a tin can death trap. The tarp trapped the earthy scent of potatoes, carrots, and onions as well as the musty aroma of coffee. The combination was enough to put him off the brew for the next decade.

The helicopter rose into the air leaving Corporal James by an SUV in the middle of the New Mexico desert. AJ slipped out from under the tarp, took a deep, cleansing breath, and situated himself in the passenger seat. The helicopter hovered above the ground for several seconds and he white-knuckled the seat. His body felt weightless, leaving him suspended. Then the chopper burst forward, shoving him back into the seat.

His family had never taken lavish, fancy vacations like some of his friends. He'd never been on an airplane, and if it felt anything like this, then his butt would happily stay planted on the earth. His eyes focused out the window. Nothing but inky darkness ahead.

Bloody hell.

He gave Bryan a sidelong glance. "How long does it take to get to Mexico City?"

Bryan smirked. "Four hours, give or take. Don't like the bird?"

Shit. He wished he had a Xanax. Those things would chill out a cheerleader. But he vowed never to take them again. Prone to addiction, he had to watch his ass.

He flipped him the bird.

Bryan's laughter echoed through the headset. "Fair enough."

His mind's sole focus was his sister, getting her back. The fury he felt toward his uncle would be fractional compared to his father. Emmett would burn the little kingdom Thomas had built for himself until nothing, but ashes remained.

He shifted from the question of why his uncle had chosen to exploit Lacy to the more pressing matter of how the hell they'd rescue her with their lives intact. He knew the man that held her wielded massive power and would have her guarded around the clock.

He shifted in his seat. The chopper's dashboard lights glowed soft blue, creating enough light to see Bryan's face.

"What's our first move?"

Bryan scratched the top of his head, adjusting the headset's band. "Well, we'll get there around sunrise. We'll have to hide the chopper somewhere. We can't just land it on Nieto's lawn. If we use the airport, they'll inform him of our presence. He's got ties all over the city."

He cursed under his breath. "So, we'll have to land in the desert and pray no one notices?"

Bryan's head bobbed up and down. "Then hike in several miles unless we steal a car. Which we'll have to at some point. But that could also bite us in the ass."

"We're making this up as we go?" he groused. "Great."

"Hey, if you have any better ideas, let's hear 'em."

"Will she be at Nieto's house?" he wondered aloud. "Or will we have to do recon all over the city?"

"We should start at Nieto's and work from there. We have packs in the back with binoculars." Bryan gave him a wolfish grin and continued. "Let's hope you're better at recon than playing football."

"Feck off," AJ shot back trying not to return the smile.

"You're still just as big a dick as you were in high school."

"Thanks," Bryan said, adjusting his crotch in an obvious, vulgar way.

Laughter burst from his chest. "Yeah, I walked right into that one."

He rested his head against the side window and closed his eyes. Worry for his sister consumed his thoughts. Spunky and high-spirited, it troubled him to think what she might do to escape. Never bending to anyone's will but her own, she wouldn't survive in captivity. Like a raccoon in a trap, she'd chew her arm off to gain freedom.

The next time his eyes opened, the sky before him looked like a watercolor painting. Enough light from the emerging sun back-lit the clouds and atmosphere in orange, purple, and dusty blue. He gave a loud yawn and stretched his arms over his head.

"I've been looking for a place to land," Bryan informed him.

"How far from Nieto's place?"

Bryan banked the chopper east and headed toward a hilly, wooded area. "We'll land out here and hike in. Probably three miles, maybe more."

"Awesome," he muttered.

The last time he'd hiked had been on a camping trip with his family. Looking out over the rugged terrain, he knew this hike would be more intense than the Kay Starr Trail in Oklahoma's Arbuckle Mountains.

Lacy almost drowned on that trip. He shook his head at the memory. Jace had braved the swift undertow to rescue her. His brows tipped down. He hadn't been paying attention. In over his head, the addiction to alcohol had controlled his entire life. It started in high school and didn't end until the forced move to California.

He'd experimented with pills, but it was the alcohol that called his name. It still did. Jace recognized his problem and tried to help, but at the time, he hadn't wanted anyone's help.

Bryan landed with relative ease. He lowered the chopper straight down into a gap between a copse of trees.

The drop made AJ queasy.

"Grab those backpacks in the back, will ya?" Bryan asked, studying his face. Humor danced in his eyes. "There's some nausea pills in the first aid kit," he added and pointed to a white steel box that hung on the back wall.

He unbuckled himself and muttered, "I'll be fine."

Bryan left the cockpit to search a small supply bin for a change of clothes. He threw a pair of tan camo pants and T-shirt at AJ's head.

"Change."

He caught them before they smacked him in the face. "Why?"

"Number one, because I don't think you've changed or bathed in a week. Two, look around you. We're surrounded by desert terrain. You'll stick out like a sore thumb."

He raised the crimson Oklahoma University hoodie over his head, sniffing as he threw it down. He huffed a laugh and finished changing. Maybe Bryan had a point. He did stink.

They exited the chopper. Bryan studied the sky, drew a

pair of sunglasses from his pack's front pocket, and took off straight into the rising sun.

An hour later, breathing heavily in the dry air, they dropped their packs and flattened themselves in the desert sand. AJ peered over the small rise and judged Nieto's house lay about half a football field away.

"How are we supposed to see this far out?"

Bryan unzipped his military pack and pulled out a pair of binoculars. "There's a pair in your pack," Bryan instructed, adjusting the eye cups.

They settled in and surveyed the house. No one stirred.

"Where is everyone?" AJ whispered.

"Still a little early. We'll need a car. If Nieto leaves the house, we need to be able to follow him," Bryan said, rising to his feet. "I'll hike into town, boost a car before everyone wakes up."

"What if he leaves while you're gone?"

"Stay put," Bryan instructed. "I can't find you if you move."

Sweat trickled down his face. He wiped it away with the back of his hand and nodded. He watched Bryan jog down the slope to the road they'd walked up.

Hot and miserable, AJ rose to a crouch, dusted the sand sticking to his clothes, arms, and face and searched his pack for something to drink. He found a hydration pack, drew the straw out, and drained the bladder.

Surveillance work sucked. It was boring, and even in February, Mexico was too warm. He thought of his sister and calmed his antsy nerves. She needed him and he'd do whatever it took to get her back.

A light-yellow scorpion scuttled under his feet. He stifled the girlish squeal rising in his throat but couldn't resist the urge to jump up and dance like his feet were on fire. He shook out his shirt and brushed off his pants. Uncomfortable and now wary of creepy, crawly things that could sting the bejesus out of him, he laid his pack down and sat.

Bryan panted up the hill. "Got us a ride," he said dropping his pack.

"What do we do now?"

Bryan pulled out the binoculars, laid down on his belly, and said, "Now we wait."

AJ raked a hand through his hair. "I hate waiting."

20

By the time Willow placed the third movie into the DVD player, it was well past midnight. Lacy reached for the bottle of Coke delivered with their supper and topped off her glass. She hadn't realized how much she'd missed the acidic drink until the first sip's harsh bubbles hit her tongue.

She sat back on the plush couch and watched the fizz dissipate into the air. Where was Jace? Was he coming to rescue her or on one of the senator's missions? Her heart ached. Her whole body ached. Craved his touch, his mouth on hers. A whimper escaped her lips as a tear ran down her cut cheek. She couldn't stand one more minute without him.

Willow reached over and grabbed her hand. "Maybe *The Notebook* isn't what we should watch right now."

She rose to change the movie, but Lacy stopped her. "Leave it," she sniffed.

"You sure?"

She cleared the lump from her throat. "Yeah. This has always been one of my favorites."

Ryan Gosling's determined character reminded her how

Jace had pursued her. He'd been persistent, yet so aware and careful of her brokenness.

Willow sat again, plumped a pillow, then laid her head down. The scrunchie holding a messy bun atop her head hung loosely to the side. Blonde hair escaped, framing her face.

Lacy still thought she looked like a pretty porcelain doll. She smiled as Willow's eyes closed when her head hit the pillow. Just like a doll's eyelids that blinked open and shut.

"Think Nieto will come back?" Willow mumbled in a drowsy voice.

Lacy ran fingertips over her battered face, checked the swelling and winced. "Yeah. That stab wound won't slow him down much."

"What are you gonna do?"

She laid her head back and stared at the ceiling. Ryan Gosling's voice melded with the roar in her head until she could no longer make sense of his words.

"I have no idea." Her words leaked out low and weary.

Jace had told her to stay safe, stay alive. How could she agree to Nieto's proposal and stay safe? The man threatened her in every way conceivable. But to decline would put her life in danger. No matter what she chose, she'd lose. A pawn couldn't check a king, not without help. And no other pieces lined the chess board.

She was alone.

The seed of revenge took root in her gut and grew with every hour she spent in captivity. A niggling worry kept cropping up she couldn't dispel. The scene at the border with her uncle replayed in her mind over and over. With a meticulousness that bordered on neurotic, she examined his every word.

When she screamed, he had no right to control their lives, he'd erupted like the Chernobyl Nuclear Power Plant. Why did he feel he had any say over her, any right to tell her what to do? She'd seen the man a handful of times in her short twenty-year life and met her aunt once when she was little.

She leaned her head back and closed her eyes in concentration. He'd turned savage when she'd mentioned her aunt. Why?

Then he'd called her father 'the man who raised you.' What the actual hell? Was he so angry with her dad he couldn't speak his name?

The man must be on a Napoleon Bonaparte trip, thinking he was lord and emperor over everything. Nothing made sense when it came to her uncle.

The television's white noise lulled her into a fitful sleep as she forced her turbulent thoughts into a box and slammed the lid shut.

WILLOW NUDGED Lacy awake with her foot from the couch's opposite end.

Lacy cracked open an eyelid to morning light streaming from the wide window. The sun seemed too bright in Mexico. She wanted more sleep. In slumber, she found blessed relief from her heartache. She wasn't sure how much stress her mind could take before it cracked open like an egg on a hot sidewalk.

"What?" she muttered.

"I think someone's outside the door," Willow rasped.

She tuned her ear toward the door and listened. A man's voice filtered in. He spoke Spanish. Two female voices answered in a questioning tone.

How had this awakened Willow? She had to concentrate to hear the meaningless conversation. The man spoke in low tones making it impossible for her to identify the speaker.

She propped herself up on her elbows, staring at Willow who'd sat and drawn her legs up to her chest.

"Do you have Vulcan hearing? How did that wake you up?"

"I've been awake for a while," she answered giving her a small smile.

She rubbed her eyes and rose to a sitting position. "What time is it?"

Willow shrugged. "I'm not sure. I'm used to getting up early and helping my dad with farm chores before school. It's around seven or eight."

"Fantastic," she grumbled. "Next time don't wake me up. I don't care if the building is on fire."

Willow's smile grew. "Not a morning person?"

"No," she said in a clipped tone, knowing sleep would not return for her.

She rose and made her way to the bathroom. After using the facilities and checking her slow-healing arm, she returned to the living room. Willow had shrunk as far as she could into the back of the couch.

Nieto stood beside the bar with two women. Two bags sat at their feet and a rack full of evening gowns had been rolled in. She didn't miss the shock on their faces as they took in her appearance. Bile burned her throat as Nieto turned his gaze on her. The look he gave was feral, predatory.

She was just another man's prey.

Why did this keep happening? She was beginning to think the gods really did hate her.

"What are you doing here?"

"I need the two of you this evening. I'm hosting a party and you will help me entertain my guests."

"No," she said, tone flat. She crossed her arms, determined not to give in to his request.

He gave a dark laugh. "You will *mi amor* or I'll auction both of you off to the highest bidder."

She sucked in a sharp breath. "That's what tonight's party is? A human auction?"

Where did he keep his girls? Only Willow and herself occupied the underground cells in the warehouse.

Unless …

He'd kidnapped more. She'd been naive to think they were the only girls he kept. He had scores of men working for him. She wondered if Raul helped capture the women to be auctioned tonight. Her first instinct was to save them. She knew the impossibility of it. She couldn't even save herself. First rule in any dire situation; save yourself first, then help those around you.

She dropped her arms. Her shoulders slumped forward as resignation poured over her. "Fine."

"Excellent," Nieto said in delight, clapping his hands together.

She kept a sharp eye on him, looking for any weakness the stab wound might've caused. He turned and spoke to the women. His breathing seemed labored, and he favored the injured side.

"The girls will do your hair, makeup, and help you dress." He pinned her with a hungry look. "I'm looking forward to seeing you, *mi amor*."

She swallowed the gag forming in her throat. His insinuation shone through his dark eyes. He intended to have her, no matter the cost. How was she going to get out of this?

"Stop calling me that," she snapped. "I'm not your love or anything else. I'm warning you. You touch me, you die."

His sultry chuckle filled the room. "I do love a challenge."

He stepped into her space and ran a finger down her jawline to her neck. She cringed and stepped out of his reach.

His eyes narrowed and she read the warning in them. He would get his way, one way or another.

"I'll be back to escort you," he said then walked out the door.

She blew out a breath as the door closed behind him.

One woman ushered her into the bathroom and began filling the large tub with steaming water. She poured a fragrant bubble bath into the stream. The woman spoke to her and pointed at the bath. Her lipstick shone bright red in the bathroom's light as it tipped into a friendly smile.

"No." Lacy crossed her arms.

The woman's smile faded, and worry crept into her wideset eyes. "You must, *chica*."

She wondered what Nieto would do if she refused to go to his party. Bathe her himself? She shuddered. It might be smarter to comply. Would there be a way to escape? Maybe. It was worth finding out.

She undressed then stepped into the hot bath. Her body sank into the rose and citrus water. It soothed the tight muscles in her neck and shoulders, and she could feel the grime from the past few days lift off her skin.

The woman pointed to herself. "Maria," she said.

She nodded and said, "Lacy."

Maria scrubbed her body and hair, all sense of modesty lost. She didn't care. It felt amazing, her body soaking up the attention. The woman spent the day giving her a massage, manicure, pedicure, and haircut. Willow received the same treatment.

They sat in the living room wrapped in luxurious cotton robes from the hotel. The women braided their hair into intricate up-do's and applied generous amounts of makeup. Lacy never wore makeup and when Maria lifted a mirror for her to inspect her work, she didn't recognize the reflection staring back at her.

She turned and appraised Willow, brows raised. "You look like the goddess Aphrodite."

"Thanks," Willow said with a smile. "Maria did a spectacular job covering up the bruises on your face."

Maria wheeled over the cart and lifted a beautiful silk dress with crystal embellishments along the dipping neckline and shoulder straps. The straps wrapped around the neck and became one strip that centered down the back. The gown flowed from a high waistline and pooled at the floor.

She fingered the material fascinated by its deep purple color. It almost looked black. Maria held it up, said something she didn't comprehend, and motioned for her to try it on.

She took the gown into the bedroom. Placing it with care on the bed, she shed her robe. She stepped into a fresh pair of underwear then the gown. The zipper snagged on a piece of fabric. Twisting, she released it then finished zipping it up. She stood in front of the full-length mirror attached to the back of the bedroom door. The gown's silk fabric dyed a deep purple brought out her eye's green color. They popped bright emerald and it fit with flawless perfection.

She hated it.

Her mind teamed with memories of proms and coronations. Happy times she wished she could relive. Anything to escape.

The setting sun's light dappled through the window, dancing on the bedspread. What would happen tonight? A buzz ran through her body. Could they find a way to escape?

Male voices filtered in from the living area, then someone knocked on the door. She remained silent, standing in front of the mirror. Her chest tightened, breaths short and painful. If she didn't start counting, she'd pass out. Taking a deep breath, she held it, counted to five, then released it.

The door opened and Nieto stepped into the room. His hungry eyes traveled over her body.

"You look *perfecto*," he exclaimed walking into her personal space.

She tried to step back, but his arm snaked around her waist, holding her in place.

He tsked. "No running tonight."

"Let me go," she hissed, trying to twist out of his hold.

His hand squeezed her hip bone, and she gasped in pain.

"You will play nice tonight, Lacy, or suffer the consequences. I'd hate to put you back in lockup."

He lowered his head and placed soft kisses against her

neck. Tears sprang into her eyes as his mouth traveled to her collarbone.

"Stop."

The command came out weak and breathy.

He rose in slow increments, then released her. "Ah, Lacy. By the time I'm finished with you, you'll beg me for it."

He tipped her chin and forced her to look at him. His eyes smoldered with lust, mixed with malignity.

Anger pushed fear aside. "You're a pig," she spat. "I'm not your property to do with as you please. By the time I'm finished with *you*, you'll be dead."

For a split second, his face betrayed his feelings. He believed her but quickly recovered and smoothed his face into an indifferent mask.

"We shall see."

He took her elbow and guided her out the door. Surprise slammed into her when she saw Raul standing by a resplendent Willow. The girl glowed like a star in a shimmery silver dress that hugged her slim frame. The glow didn't reach her eyes.

She glared at Raul. "Figures."

He looked at her with sorrow in his eyes. She wasn't interested in his regret or giving him absolution. Tonight, she'd look for a way out. She had to find one because she'd rather die than be at Nieto's mercy.

PART III

DOUBLE DOWN

"*For where no hope is left, is left no fear.*" *John Milton*

21

"I'm not a thief," Jace informed the cowering woman and girl in a low, non-threatening voice.

The girl raised her head and looked around. She turned back to her mom and whispered, "Where's Jupiter?"

The woman crossed her arms over her chest, raised her chin a fraction, and gave him an appraising look.

Vocal cords frozen, he just stood there, his mind splintered. What in the hell was he supposed to do now? He couldn't hide them. Corporal James would search the property until they were found, and the men outside didn't discriminate. They'd shoot her and the girl. No questions. Harming a woman and child defied everything decent.

The girl rose to get out of bed, but the woman placed a firm hand on her arm, stopping her.

"Mom," she protested. "I gotta go find Jupiter."

The woman narrowed her eyes at him. "What've you done with our dog? How'd you get past him without being attacked?"

He cleared his throat, tried and failed, to erase the guilt he felt. "He's not hurt, ma'am."

"Ma'am," she snorted, running a hand through her hair.

"So, you're a polite thief? And that doesn't answer my question."

"I'm not a thief," he denied again, disgruntled.

The woman gave him a disbelieving look. "So, you just break into people's houses to frighten them for fun?"

"No, I —"

"Or is it for the rush? Are you an adrenaline junkie? Or just a junkie in general looking to score some pills?"

Her gaze settled into a hawkish glare.

Affronted, he shifted from foot to foot. "Does it look like I'm tweaked out on drugs? Just let me explain."

She rubbed the heel of her hand against her forehead and let out a deep sigh. "Let me guess. You're one of Thomas Monroe's henchmen."

His eyes widened. "You know why I'm here?"

"I've heard the rumors. Despite the communication break-down, there's still a grapevine running from state to state. Louisiana's governor was the first to fall, followed by Okla-homa's. He's gunning for the southwestern states. So, this isn't altogether unexpected, although you caught me unguarded and unprepared. If you'd been one day later, I wouldn't have been here." Her shoulders fell. "One lousy day."

The gun strap shifted. He hadn't even drawn his weapon. The question what to do bounced in his brain like a clown on a Pogo stick. Just standing here would get him nowhere. He needed to act.

An idea formed then crystallized. "Where would you have been?"

She folded her arms across her chest. "I'm not telling you that."

"Look, we don't have time for this. You're just gonna have to trust me. Please," he entreated with outstretched hands.

"My husband is in Colorado," she relented. "He secured a cabin in the mountains for us. Kylie and I were leaving in the morning to meet him there."

He gestured toward the girl. "She can go check on her dog. I shot him with a tranquilizer in the hall by the library."

Kylie let out a sharp gasp and gave him a look that portrayed all her little girl fury.

"He'll be fine," he assured her with grave solemnity.

Not waiting for her mother's approval, she jumped up and ran out of the room, calling the dog's name. He watched her hair flying behind her as she raced away. The long, pastel pink nightgown she wore almost tangled between her legs, but she managed to stay upright. A slight smile tugged his lips. She reminded him of Lacy. Everything he cast his eyes upon reminded him of her in some way.

He turned to the woman. "I didn't want to say this in front of your kid, but I was sent in to kill you. There are men outside, waiting to hear a gunshot. If I don't do it, they will."

"What then?" she demurred.

Not one emotion skittered across her face, and he wondered how she could stay so calm. She must've dealt with some dicey situations as New Mexico's governor to remain as unflappable as she appeared.

"Is there a back road out of here?"

"Yes, it goes straight from our driveway to the side road."

"Where's your car?"

She rose and donned a robe. "In the garage, already loaded with our stuff. Why?" she asked, suspicion lacing her tone.

"Are you going to let us go?"

He had no idea if his plan would work and knew the risk of trying. If they were caught, they'd all pay with their lives.

"I'll let you go on one condition. Take me with you."

"Why?" she demanded.

His mind leapt to Lacy. The thought of never seeing her again ripped his insides to shreds. He'd told her to stay safe, stay alive, and he needed to do the same, or they'd never see each other again. The thought spurred him on.

"Because they'll kill me for letting you escape. And I don't want to die."

She studied him for a beat too long.

"Ma'am, we've got to move. Cover your ears."

He raised his weapon and shot three times at the ceiling. Sheetrock and plaster fell in large clumps onto the bed and floor. Dust plumed and filtered down in a whitish cloud covering everything in sight. Coughing, he waved a hand in front of him trying to clear the air.

The woman had moved to her closet, grabbed a set of clothes, and disappeared into what he assumed was an adjoining bathroom. He had to admit, her nerves were steady. She hadn't blinked an eye when he told her he'd been sent to kill her, nor had she flinched at the gunshot.

The woman returned wearing a black jogging set and tennis shoes. She thrust her hand toward him. "I'm Mira Deschene."

"Jace Cooper," he said, shaking the offered hand.

"Well, what now, Jace Cooper?"

Her head swiveled to the door as Kylie burst into the room, tears streaking her face. "He won't wake up!" she shrieked.

"I'll get him," Jace offered.

He jogged out of the room and found the dog where he'd shot him. He let out a grunt as he hefted Jupiter off the floor, then carried him back into the room. The tranquilizer must've been more potent than he thought. The dog's large gangly limbs folded together like a roped calf and his head lolled against Jace's chest. He laid the dog on the bed and swiped at his shirtfront checking for dog drool.

He bounced on the balls of his feet. "We've got to go now. They'll be coming in to check on me to make sure I've done my job."

His last words disgusted him and tasted bitter on his tongue. Only a few minutes had passed from the time he'd fired the shots into the ceiling until now. Precious minutes they couldn't afford to waste.

Mira grabbed her purse off a wide, ornate dresser that matched the massive four poster bed.

She turned to her daughter, brows furrowed. "Kylie, we need to move quietly. No more shrieking, okay? There're men outside and they want to kill us."

The girl nodded, eyes wide with fear.

"Follow me," she ordered.

The tone brooked no argument. He picked up the dog and hurried after them. They moved with quick, quiet steps through the kitchen then out a door that dumped them into a large three car garage.

A black Lincoln Navigator's lights blinked, and he heard the doors unlock. Why did all powerful people drive black SUV's?

He opened the back door, dumped the dog into the floorboard, then hopped into the cramped back seat. The butt of his gun dug into his back, and he shifted it to the side. Carving a place to sit amidst boxes, blankets, pillows, and a stuffed pink monkey holding a banana proved to be a challenge. No matter how much he rearranged it, the banana still ended up falling in his face. His feet hovered over the large sleeping animal in the floorboard. His abs started to burn from the strain. He twisted sideways placing his feet in the middle and leaned against the door.

Lacy would've doubled over laughing at his absurd circumstances. The dog would gnaw his face off once the medicine wore off.

He huffed and strangled the chuckle building in his throat. No matter in what situation he found himself, he could always find a reason to laugh. But it felt sacrilegious to find any humor now. Not while Nieto held Lacy. There was a very real chance he'd sell her. And then? Lacy was his whole world, and without her in it, all color faded into shades of grey. His world would topple. His mind stayed in crisis mode, because every time he thought of her, his heart shattered. It was like jumping off a high-rise, over and over, then lying on the concrete, broken and bleeding. Then as if someone kept pushing the start over button in a video game, the process would begin again.

Mira and Kylie buckled their seat belts. She twisted the rear view mirror. Her gaze zeroed in on him. Her head nodded once, then she pushed the start button and revved the engine.

The garage door lifted on silent hinges.

"Turn off the headlights," he advised.

He rolled down his window, pulled the gun slung over his back, and stuck the barrel out the window. The thought of shooting Dylan, or the men he'd become acquainted with during the long drive to New Mexico, twisted his stomach into a pretzel. Dylan's girlfriend needed him, and the others had family and friends who cared about them. Although, he wouldn't lose any sleep if a bullet hit Corporal James.

The car crept out of its slot onto the slightly sloping driveway. He looked over his shoulder and his heart thundered as Dylan burst through the back door.

"Go!" he shouted.

Mira punched the gas and everything in the car shifted backward. Something thumped against the rear door. He muttered a curse as Dylan jumped on the back bumper.

"We got company."

"I know," she grunted and swerved to the left then right in sharp succession.

Dylan shouted as his feet slipped off the bumper. He rolled several times on the concrete.

Jace shifted his gaze out the side window and saw the militia's SUV bouncing over the lawn gunning straight for them.

"Damn it," he muttered under his breath.

The Navigator's tires screeched as she turned out of the

drive onto the narrow side street. Mira punched the gas and maneuvered down the road. His doubts about her driving skills vanished as she took the next turn, not bothering to use the brakes. They drifted for a few seconds before the SUV's tires gained traction. That bought them a few seconds as their tail fell behind when they tried to match her maneuvers.

"I'll make a few more turns before we hit the freeway. I'll lose them," she said with confidence.

The car raced up the I-25 north on-ramp. He looked behind them and saw nothing. She'd done it. A professional couldn't have done better. A tsunami wave of grief mixed with anger rose when it dawned on him, they were headed to Colorado. He lowered his head lacing his hands around his neck. Something in him buzzed, igniting every cell in his body. Energy he couldn't contain built, threatening to erupt. He had to get Lacy back. Trusting AJ and Bryan proved harder than he could ever imagine.

Mira pushed the SUV to its limit, flying down the highway and he was grateful. He needed to find a way back to Lacy.

But would AJ and Bryan take her back to Oklahoma? Or make the journey through the closed states to California? He remembered the map AJ had wanted to give him but never had the chance. He cursed. How would he find her now?

22

Waiting had never been in AJ's wheelhouse. As a child, his mother had told him on more than one occasion if he didn't develop some patience, she'd lose her ever-loving mind. They'd been watching Nieto's three-story home for hours and although the household had awakened, no one had moved in or out. The antsy feeling started in his feet, and little by little crept up his legs until it had consumed his entire body. He shifted his elbows, resting on his backpack into a different position, then wiggled his legs.

"Stop fidgeting," Bryan ordered in a harsh whisper.

"The house is dead, man. Can't we at least go get some food? Take a break? Move around?"

He tried to keep the slight, degrading whine from his voice, but Bryan's arched brow told him he'd failed.

"Not until we've exhausted the possibility that Nieto's here. We need to give it at least a couple more hours," Bryan returned with a hint of amusement. "You're acting like a two-year-old."

He rolled his eyes. "Feck off."

Bryan's shoulders shook in silent laughter.

The rumble of a car engine caught their attention and they both ducked their heads, molding their bodies into the sand. The car sounded like it turned into Nieto's long driveway.

He raised his head little by little until he could see. A black SUV with dark tinted windows pulled up to the front door. The driver jumped out and hurried around the hood, assisting an older man from the vehicle.

Clipped conversation between the two men carried on the breeze, but he couldn't understand a word of it. They walked up the sandstone steps and disappeared inside.

Bryan scuttled backward then popped onto his feet. "Okay."

"Okay what?" he asked, mimicking Bryan's actions.

He pushed off his arms and stood beside Bryan, brushing sand from his hands, shirt, and pants.

"The older man, who got out of the backseat, was Nieto. Did he look injured to you?"

He shrugged. "I don't know, maybe. He held a hand against his side."

"Yeah." Bryan turned his head with a slight grin lifting his lips. "I think your sister stabbed him."

His head throbbed with sudden shock. "How do you know that?"

"Nieto said the word puta and I caught a word I think means stab. They were too far away for me to hear but I bet he was talking about your sister," he said, smirking. "They also said something about leaving at five. So, we have a couple of hours to waste."

"Wait," he said holding up a hand. "Lacy stabbed Nieto?" He shook his head. "No way. And did you just call my sister a bitch?" He gave Bryan's shoulder a solid punch.

"Hey," Bryan protested, rubbing his arm. "I didn't say it. Nieto did. Your sister's a certified badass. No offense," he added.

"You're on crack. There's no way my sister would stab someone," he said in disbelief. "No way."

Bryan's smile dropped. "A lot has happened to change her. She's not the little kid sister you left last July. I could be wrong and misinterpreting what they said. But I wouldn't put it past her."

Bryan had been a part of Oklahoma's National Guard stationed near the Monroe farm. He and Lacy had been enemies at first. Then she learned he worked for her uncle as a mole and their relationship had morphed into frenemies. Bryan had told him that much during the flight to pick up Corporal James.

He hefted his backpack off the ground and followed Bryan down the slope toward the boosted car. Could Lacy stab someone? The sister he knew never would. He couldn't wrap his mind around the possibility.

Something tickled his right ankle. He lifted his pant leg and before he could shriek, swat it off, or blink, a light-yellow scorpion raised its tail and struck. The venomous strike took effect immediately. His eyes burned, and he muffled a shout, as pain shot from the entry point on his lower shin to his knee. He shook his leg in a frenzied panic. The arachnid lost its grip and fell to the ground. Sweat beaded his forehead and along his upper lip. Bending at the waist he sucked in long, slow breaths. Bryan stopped, then turned around when he realized AJ wasn't following.

"What the hell happened?"

He lifted his head. "Scorpion," he said on an exhale.

Bryan's brows furrowed. "Damn. You allergic?"

"How could I possibly know that?" he snapped.

He lifted himself to a standing position. His body swayed back and forth, and bright lights dotted his vision.

"I need a sec," he said.

Bryan shuffled through the sand and grabbed him by the elbow, supporting his weight. "I'll help you to the car."

"Thanks," he said, grateful for the assistance.

The sting radiated white hot streaks of pain up his leg. He'd been stung by red wasps, hornets, and bees, but this one felt like a million red fire ants attacked him. He limped with Bryan's help to the car, his ankle swelling with every step.

His eyes focused on the black vehicle, his mind flipping through makes and models. This one looked old, like a classic. He stopped, causing Bryan to jerk back a step.

Dumbfounded, his jaw dropped. He stared at Bryan like he'd grown two heads.

"What?" Bryan asked, eyes wide in mock innocence.

"How are we supposed to stay under everyone's radar driving that?"

"Relax. No one will—"

"Relax? How the hell am I supposed to do that? We're responsible for rescuing my sister!" His voice rose. "Which means flying under the radar. We can't do that driving around town in a restored Corvette!"

"I found it parked in a vacation home's garage. I made sure no one was there before taking it. I also switched license plates from a random car, parked next door. We're good for the day at least."

He wanted to knock the smug smile off Bryan's face. And he didn't even ask why he'd been at a vacation home. That's not where people on the lam looked for cars to steal.

"This is a bad idea," he grumbled, making his way to the passenger seat.

Bryan laid the top down and hopped behind the wheel. His face turned somber.

"Look," Bryan started, turning toward him. "We don't have a snowball's chance here. This is a suicide mission. This car won't get us caught. It was easy to steal. No one will even notice it's gone. Not for a while. We'll get some food, then go back. It's the one chance we've got to follow Nieto. He'll lead us to Lacy."

"Then what?"

Bryan reached under the steering wheel and grabbed two wires. They sparked and the car rumbled to life.

Bryan's gaze locked with his. "I don't know."

THE FIVE PORK tamales AJ had consumed sloshed up his stomach, then back down, as Bryan raced the Corvette down the old highway, headed back to Nieto's house. He glanced over at the odometer and blanched.

Bryan pushed the restored eight-cylinder engine well past one-twenty. Stomach acid mixed with tamales gushed up his throat and he let out a loud belch. The orange needle crept toward the one-eighty mark.

He was gonna barf.

The thought of a Mexican prison cell did little to settle his stomach either. Bryan insisted they blow off steam before heading back. He could think of a hundred different ways to accomplish that goal, none of which included racing down the highway at breakneck speed. He'd much rather spend his extra time in the arms of a well-endowed senorita.

Bryan turned his head with a shit eating grin plastered on his face.

"Keep your eyes on the road," he shouted over the wind.

Lyrics to Falling in Reverse's song "Popular Monster" played in his memory about crashing a car, and he belted out "*I am terrified*!" at the top of his lungs.

Bryan gave him a sidelong glance, still grinning. He slowed the car and turned onto a compacted dirt side-road near the place he'd parked earlier.

"We'll have to sprint back when they leave."

AJ nodded then jumped out of the Corvette. He'd never admit it to Bryan, but the ride did help his nervous energy.

They traipsed back up the incline, dropped their packs, and sat.

"How's the sting?" Bryan asked.

He pulled up his pant leg. "My ankle's swollen. I'd forgotten about it 'til now," he admitted. "Your driving would make a math teacher forget how to add two plus two," he tacked on with dry humor.

He settled in, binoculars in hand, and looked down the hill. Several catering vans were parked in the circular drive, and maids in black and white uniforms bustled in and out of the porticoes on level one and two.

"Looks like Nieto's throwing a party," Bryan observed, ignoring the dig about his driving skills.

AJ, still shaken from the Fast and Furious drive from hell, rolled his eyes. "Ya think?"

They laid flat on the sand and watched the organized chaos below until the sun dipped toward the west. Restlessness built inside him again. If Nieto didn't move soon, he'd explode.

"You know, this party's a good thing," Bryan said, breaking the silence. "If Nieto brings Lacy here, we might be able to pass as one of the caterers or servers."

His brows rose. "In tan camos? C'mon."

Bryan snorted. "No."

When Bryan didn't continue, he hefted himself up. "What then? Knock out a couple of servers and steal their clothes?"

Bryan's jaw hardened. "Yes."

He coughed out a disbelieving laugh. "Okay then."

Although he loved a good fight, he'd never used violence against someone who wasn't deserving. In his opinion. Before he could think on the situation further, Nieto exited the house with his two bodyguards. An SUV pulled up and the men stepped inside.

Bryan popped up and grabbed his arm. "Let's go."

They sprinted down the hill. Sand flew behind him, some

lodging in the heel of his shoe. He made a sharp turn. His feet slid and he took a nosedive into the dirt. Ignoring the sharp pain that blasted up his leg, he pushed ahead and caught up to Bryan who already had the car started.

He jumped in and Bryan threw the car into reverse. The car's back end dipped into a culvert. Bryan punched the gas pedal. Dirt and rocks flew behind the car as its wheels grabbed for purchase. They fishtailed, and for a second, he thought the car would spin out of control. Bryan righted the car, then pulled around the corner in time to catch Nieto's SUV turn toward the downtown area.

Bryan expertly trailed behind, not so close to draw attention, but not so far, they lost sight of them. The SUV turned into the swanky Four Seasons hotel's parking garage and stopped next to a non-descript steel service elevator. Bryan found an empty parking space and cut the engine.

They watched as Nieto's driver helped him out of the backseat, then step up to the elevator. Nieto swiped a card and the doors opened. The elevator swallowed them inside and started its ascent.

"Let's go," Bryan said as the doors shut.

They got out and surveyed the garage.

"This must be a private entrance for employees," AJ commented.

Bryan strode to the elevator and looked up. Red neon numbers ticked off the floors as it rose, then stopped on the twelfth floor.

"Or hot shots like Nieto. Did you see him swipe that card? He went to the top floor," Bryan said.

"Are we gonna wait here or follow him inside?" he asked.

Unease crept up his spine.

"We'd have to go through the hotel's entrance and then it would be iffy getting to the top floor. You gotta have a card for top floor access, I bet."

"So," he drew out the word. "We stay?"

"I don't know," Bryan returned, his tone brusque. "I'm talking out our options here."

"If we left and they came back, we wouldn't know if he has Lacy for sure."

"True."

"One of us could go and one could stay," he suggested.

"No." Bryan shut down the idea. "If they came out and one of us was gone, we couldn't follow them."

"Our safest bet would be to wait here then," he surmised.

"Yup," Bryan confirmed. "We wait."

The unease he'd felt moments before, ratcheted up. This game was dangerous, and he'd be a fool to forget or lose sight of it. The sting sent out a painful jab, but it became background noise as they settled back into the Corvette. His mind centered on his sister. Would she be with Nieto when he returned? The tamales turned over in his stomach. He hoped she would, and yet part of him hoped she wouldn't. Would she be injured, or in pain? Had Nieto hurt her? He had a feeling he'd find out soon.

23

Lacy glided past Raul as gracefully as she could in the ridiculous stiletto's Maria placed on her feet. She'd pleaded for flats, but the woman wouldn't budge. After walking two steps, she knew without a doubt a man had crafted the horrible shoes. Why would anyone subject themselves to a punishment like this?

Her mother would've been impressed that she walked from the bedroom to the door without falling ass over tit. She rubbed the heel of her hand against her chest. She missed her mom. The weight smothered her when she let herself dwell on it. With a deep breath, she sucked it up and blocked the debilitating desire to fall apart. She'd face her shame and regret later. She couldn't bear to dwell on the grave disappointment she knew her mother would have in her.

Nieto's hand on her back felt like a branding iron, hot and unyielding. Her hand snaked around, grabbed his fingers in a painful twist, and pushed them away. He leaned over her shoulder and placed his lips to her ear.

"Remember what I said," he purred in a low voice.

"Keep your hands off me," she hissed.

His arm wrapped around her waist, fingers digging deep

into her hip bone. He gave a warning squeeze. She resisted the urge to spit in his face. It would get her nowhere. She needed to remember he fed on violent reactions.

Nieto turned to Raul. "*Listo?*"

His son nodded. "*Sí.* Let's go."

Nieto ushered them out the door, then pulled a card from his front pants pocket and swiped the elevator fob. The left heel of her shoe stuck in the crack between the elevator and floor as she shuffled through.

"Dammit," she muttered, bending down.

She raised the silk fabric, freed the mangled heel, then stepped inside with extra care. She threw Raul a nasty look as the elevator fell to the ground floor. He lowered his eyes unable to hold her gaze. She felt no satisfaction from the flash of mortification in his eyes when he turned away.

"Tonight is important. I will need you and the girl to stay with me or Raul. No wandering off. No conversations with anyone." Nieto's expression flattened as he locked his gaze on her. "Do I make myself clear?"

She crossed her arms and pressed her lips into a fine line. He chuckled and tightened his grip around her waist. Her hands curled into fists at her sides. Arrogant prick.

The elevator dinged and the doors opened at the garage level. Nieto's two bodyguards waited beside a long, sleek limo parked at the curb. Raul opened the back passenger door on the driver's side for Willow.

Willow's eyes surveyed the garage, then sought out hers. Their gazes connected like magnets. The girl was scared. But underneath Lacy read steely determination. Willow nodded at her, then ducked inside the limo. Raul followed, leaving her alone with his father.

Nieto guided her around to the other side then stopped. She gasped in surprise as he trapped her against the side of the limo, grinding his pelvis against her. His fingers wrapped around her wrists like manacles and held them in place at her sides. She started to struggle, then stopped. He wanted her to react, to fight him. It fueled his sick desires.

She recoiled. Forcing her muscles to relax, she turned her head and worked her facial features into a mask of boredom. Beads of sweat pricked her forehead.

One hand reached up and gripped her chin. She didn't resist as he jerked her head back to him. She combated the overwhelming urge to knee him in the balls and run, but now wasn't the time. If her and Willow were going to escape, the timing needed to be perfect.

His hot breath fanned her cheek. The scent of scotch and peppermint made her nauseous. She closed her eyes, trying to remain calm. His touch, like dull razorblades, scraped over the never-ending wound deep inside her from Zach's assault.

"You will be mine tonight," he whispered. "I will treat you like a queen. *My* beautiful queen."

This couldn't happen again.

Zach's assault was more than enough. He'd taken control of her. Violated her. She swore she'd never let anyone take advantage of her again. She forced those memories away. They would only add fuel and make this situation worse.

She squeezed her eyelids until they ached. Fingernails sliced into her palms, breaking the skin. Still, she said nothing. Did nothing. The messy cyclone of emotions begged for an outlet. She felt like a car, spinning out of control. She needed to get a grip, lock everything down before she lost it.

He lowered his head, then his lips crashed into hers. The kiss was brutal, dominating. His tongue thrashed against hers, demanding a response. She tasted the minty sting of peppermint on his tongue. Tears leaked from her closed eyelids. Her body remained rigid as his hand slid along the slit in her dress. What would Jace think? She was letting this man grope her. But what could she do?

Nieto pulled back. Her eyelids snapped open as his hand

struck her cheek. The sting caused her eyes to water. He'd smacked her in the same place several times now.

She wanted to kill him.

"You *will* respond when I touch you," he snarled.

He squeezed her wrists until her hands tingled. Her heart hammered against her ribcage as adrenaline dumped into her system. Controlling her fight or flight instinct took all her concentration. She had to smother her hostility to appear docile.

"Let go of me," she breathed. "You're hurting me."

His eyebrows rose. "Do you think I care if I hurt you?" He leaned in. "I know what you're doing."

Panic slammed into her chest. She couldn't breathe.

"You're controlling your reaction to me. Quite well. I know you'd like to stab me again. But," he sighed, tracing a finger across her forehead, wiping away the beads of sweat. "I'll have fun breaking you. And I will break you."

The window rolled down at her back. "Is there a problem?"

Raul asked, leaning over Willow. "*Padre*, we can't be late."

His eyes narrowed on his son. "I am aware of the time."

He released his hold on her bruised wrists. She turned, opened the car door, and escaped inside the dark interior, sliding across the black leather seat. Nieto followed then slammed the door.

"Go," Nieto ordered the driver.

Nieto's tense silence infused the cab. Raul studied one of his gold cuff-links, rubbing imaginary smudges from its surface. Willow folded her shoulders inward and bent her head.

Breathing became difficult. The heavy air soaked up the strained atmosphere until it morphed into something unfit to consume. She breathed in, held it five counts, then counted five as she exhaled.

Willow turned her bent head toward her. "Does it work?" she asked in a soft voice.

The corner of her lips turned down. "Does what work?"

"The breathing and counting," she returned.

"At times," she said, drawing in another breath. "Other times, circumstances are too heavy for it to calm my anxiety."

"Is it working now?"

Willow's curiosity annoyed her. Why did it matter? Why ask about something so inane?

"Not with you asking questions," she huffed.

Willow laughed quietly but didn't ask anything else.

The limo pulled into Nieto's drive and parked at the front entrance. The two men in front stepped out, then opened their doors. Nieto stood then extended his hand to assist her. She slid to the door. Ignoring his offer, she planted her stilted shoes on the concrete, and hefted herself out of the car, clinging to the door for support. She straightened her dress and thanked the stars she remained upright. Her right foot wobbled a little.

Nieto reached to steady her, but she sidestepped his touch. Her throat thickened and she swallowed hard. She couldn't think about his kiss or the way his body had pressed into hers. If she did, she knew without a doubt, she'd lose the last shred of her sanity and either kill him or kill herself. At this point, she had no idea which way she'd swing. She'd never considered suicide. Until now. But one way or another, tonight she would free herself.

She felt his hard stare at her back but refused to acknowledge him. Instead, she sidled up beside Willow, and walked through the front door. Raul positioned himself next to Willow while Nieto paused to speak to a guard holding a clipboard.

Beautiful marble tiles the color of sandstone covered the entryway. A dazzling chandelier hung from the cathedral ceiling, casting bright prisms of light across the floor. Twin staircases graced the foyer leading to the second floor. The open floor plan would make sneaking away difficult.

A man stood guard at the foot of each staircase, preventing access. She looked up to the second story mezzanine. Men milled around, cigars hanging from their fingertips, glasses of scotch or whiskey in their other hand. Only certain people were allowed upstairs. The auction must be up there in one of the back rooms.

Servers milled through the downstairs crowd, trays held high, filled with hors d'oeuvres or glasses of champagne. She rolled her eyes. How chic.

She turned to Nieto. "Why am I here?" she demanded.

He turned and studied her, his eyes cold chips of brown. "Many reasons," he evaded.

She grabbed Willow's hand. They'd stay together tonight. And find a window, a door, an opportunity to escape. They mingled through the crowd with Raul and Nieto. His hand never left the small of her back.

Willow jerked to a stop. Her eyes tracked someone in the crowd.

She leaned into the girl's shoulder. "What is it?"

Willow turned to her. "Um, nothing. I just—"

"What?" she asked tensely with nerves strung high-wire tight.

Willow shook her head in disbelief. "I think I'm seeing things. There was this guy in the parking garage when we left." She paused, her eyes scanning the crowd. "I think he's here."

Nieto turned, grabbed her wrist, and yanked her forward.

She stumbled a step.

"Let me go," she snapped. "You've bruised my wrists, if you haven't noticed."

He spared them a glance, shrugged his shoulders, but released her. "Stay with me if you don't want bruises on your body, too," he warned.

"Fine," she bit out.

After a few turns around the large, open room, Nieto stopped to talk to a large man, stuffed into a tux that looked two sizes too small. The black fabric stretched over the man's muscles, seams straining to keep the jacket and pants in one piece. The man seemed uncomfortable. If he moved the wrong way, she swore he'd split his pants in two. He looked familiar.

"What did the guy you saw look like?" she asked Willow, returning to their interrupted conversation.

"He had short black hair, tall and built. I don't know. He was too far away from me to get any other details. His eyes, though," she gave a self-conscious laugh, "they were piercing, like he was seeing right through me."

"That could be half the men in here," she muttered.

"It looked like he was looking for someone," she added.

She scanned the crowd. Then, a pair of light green eyes snagged her attention. Their gazes locked.

Her breath froze in her throat.

AJ.

Her brother was here. Fear from the nightmare she'd had a few nights before barreled into her. He'd been shot. What was he doing here? Her heart plummeted.

Where was Jace?

24

Dawn burst from the eastern horizon in a dazzling array of dusty purple and pink. From the compacted back seat, Jace watched the colors turn to a muted orange as the sun peeked over the skyline. The Spanish Peaks jutted upward from the ground to his left. A dusky grey shroud clung to them like Dr. Doom's cloak, hiding their mysteries from prying eyes below.

Jupiter stared him down from the floorboard. A growl rumbled from his throat every few minutes. His lips curled back in a menacing display of sharp fangs and drool. He minimized his movements to appease the large animal, but after three hours, his cramped legs and bowed back begged to be stretched.

"Mom, I gotta go to the bathroom," Kylie whined.

"There's a Loves Station ahead. I'll stop there."

"I don't think we should stop," he warned. "Those men are behind us somewhere. They won't stop searching for you."

Mira said nothing as she slowed the car and turned off the interstate. The Loves Station's neon sign stood in immutable darkness. Only the pumps shone against the encroaching dawn. She pulled up to one and cut the engine.

Reaching under the seat, she pulled out a Glock 19, checked the safety, then stuffed it in her back waistband. She turned in her seat to face him. Her bobbed hair, the same rich brown color as her daughter's, swayed from side to side. Brown coffee-colored eyes bore into him. The longer she stared the more exposed he felt, as if she were reading his soul, uncovering his darkest secrets. He wondered if Zach's murder had left a stain there. If she could somehow see his deep-seated sin.

She cleared her voice and broke the silence. "If they do catch up to us, I'll be ready."

He raised his knees to his chest, still sitting sideways in the seat. She had no idea what kind of men hunted her.

His brows turned down and he pinched the bridge of his nose. "You'd be dead before you could draw your weapon," he stated resolutely.

Ignoring him, she turned to her daughter. "Take Jupiter and run to the side of the building. Keep me in sight. And hurry."

The girl nodded then reached into the back and tugged on a pink quilted duffle bag wedged between the door and seat. The stuffed animal along with blankets and pillows tumbled across his lap. The bag loosened then gave way. Kylie lurched backward tumbling into the floorboard, feet flailing upward.

"Kylie, what on earth are you doing?" her mother scolded.

The girl looked up from the floorboard. "I wanna change."

Mira offered her daughter a hand up. The girl scrambled out of the car and ran to the west side of the building.

"Let Jupiter out," she called over her shoulder.

He unfolded himself, turned, and opened the back door. The dog bounded out and ran after Kylie. Hiding his smile with a yawn, he watched Mira pull a card from her billfold then swipe it at the pump.

"Does regular American currency still work in Colorado?"

he asked, surprised when the pump began filling the SUV's empty tank.

The look she gave him still expressed distrust. He didn't blame her. He'd broken into her home with a gun, shot their dog, then forced her to take him with them. Shame rippled through him when he thought about it from her perspective. It wasn't who he was, who he wanted to be. He was better than this.

"All governors received a card like this from the government for travel. I'm not sure if a MasterCard would work or not," she explained in a clipped voice.

He ran a hand through his hair. "I'm sorry about all this. I just couldn't see another way out where we both didn't end up dead. I didn't want to do this."

"Then why did you?"

"I —" He stopped, wondering how to summarize. Telling her every detail would take a while. "The senator blackmailed me into this."

"What's he got on you?"

"That's a longer story. He's leveraged his niece. I love her and he knows I'll do anything to get her back."

The woman seemed lost in thought for a moment. "Where is this girl?"

He hated all the questions, but knew she deserved an answer.

"Right now, she's in Mexico City being held by a human trafficker. He's big into drugs and politics. The senator wants his help."

Mira cursed. "He's leveraging a hell of a lot more than that girl. Damn it, Monroe." She paced in front of him. "It's not that I don't believe in what the Texas senator wants to achieve. I just won't support the way he's going about getting what he wants. His own niece isn't even safe. I can't believe he did that. He's fighting against totalitarianism. I get it. There's just got to be a better way."

The pump clicked off. She removed the nozzle, placed it back into its cradle, then screwed the cap back on until it clicked.

Kylie sprinted to the car with the dog at her heels. A pair of grey track pants and a pink Nike T-shirt sporting the words 'just do it,' replaced the nightgown. She jumped into the back seat with the dog then threw the duffle bag on top of the monkey.

"We'd better go," he said.

His stomach tied into tiny knots and the hair stood on end against his neck. He had a sinking feeling they shouldn't have stopped at all.

Before they could open the car doors, a black SUV shot down the off-ramp racing straight toward them.

He jerked the back door open and reached across Kylie's legs to retrieve his MP7 lying in the floorboard.

"Get in the floorboard with Jupiter," he commanded. The girl looked up at him, her pupils blown wide. "It'll be all right," he said in a softer tone. "Your mom and I got this, okay?"

She nodded then crouched down, cradling the dog's head in her lap.

"How do you want to play this?" he asked Mira as he flipped the safety off.

When the SUV was about twenty yards out, she aimed her pistol at the windshield and fired three shots in succession. The man driving ducked, the windshield shattered, then the car made a sharp swerve to the right.

"Okay," he muttered under his breath. "Guess that works."

The vehicle righted its course, and the driver gunned it straight at them, his intent clear. He was going to run them over.

Jace shot at the left front tire, blowing it out. The car

screeched to a halt then Corporal James swung his car door open and crouched behind it.

Jace scanned Corporal James's vehicle through the broken window, searching for other militia men. It appeared he traveled alone. Where were Dylan and the others?

"Leave now," Mira shouted. "I don't want to kill you."

James's laugh was loud and full of gravel and ire. "I could say the same. Surrender. Now."

"Surrender? Why? To make it easier for you to kill me and my daughter?"

She shot at him again before he could respond. James ducked down and let out a loud curse. The 9mm bullets sank into the door's metal, then stopped. His head bobbed back up.

And Jace was ready. He pulled the trigger, picturing the paper target at the shooting range in place of the man's head. The bullet grazed the upper part of James's forehead. Blood sprayed upward saturating the air with a fine mist. The man fell backward, clutching the top of his head. Vile screams burst from his mouth.

Without thinking, Jace rushed to where the man lay sprawled on the concrete. Thick red blood pooled around James's head. The man's eyes, full of blistering hate connected with his.

"You won't win," the man rasped on a ragged breath. "The more you fight, the more you'll lose." He coughed, and blood spurted from his mouth.

Pity filled Jace despite his dislike for the dying man. Thinking back, he realized he'd wished for this. But now, seeing the man struggle for every breath, remorse filled him.

"You'll never see Lacy again," he gurgled, then choked out a laugh.

The remorse he'd felt seconds before morphed into explosive rage, and he couldn't help the curse that erupted from deep within his chest. He pulled his weapon and shot the man, killing him instantly. The MP7's bullet splintered James's head into a mass of bone and brain, grotesque and unrecognizable.

He wiped blood from his face with the back of his hand. A strong metallic copper scent roiled his stomach and a wave of nausea hit him hard. He looked down on the blow-back covering him. The gun clattered to the ground as he turned his head, bent at the waist, and wretched.

Mira walked up behind him and touched his shoulder. He jerked from the contact. "Thank you," she murmured. "You saved me and my daughter."

He straightened. Using the inside of his T-shirt, he wiped his mouth then almost threw up again.

Tears burned the back of his eyes. "I hate this," he forced out.

He'd told himself he'd never kill again. But Corporal James lay dead in defiance of his wishes. Another stain on his soul he'd bear for the rest of his life. The man might've been a giant asshole, but he was someone's son. Maybe a brother or father. Someone out there loved the man.

"I know. But you saved us. It was self-defense. Nothing more." Her strong gaze locked with his. "Believe that."

He nodded and worked to swallow the large lump in his throat.

She turned and walked to the Navigator and opened the back hatch. She pulled out a pair of faded jeans and a green and black checked flannel shirt, then grabbed a bottle of water.

"These should fit you," she said striding toward him. "They're my husband's."

Relief swept over him. "Thanks."

He wouldn't have to wear the blood-soaked clothing. The strong scent of copper still made his stomach turn.

"Look," she started. "I think now would be a good time to part ways. As much as I appreciate what you've done, I still don't want anyone to know where I'm going to be. You can take that man's car."

He thought about that. She'd been vague on where they were headed. She said Colorado and speculation on the exact location was futile. At this point, he didn't care, either.

"Okay," he agreed.

"Change the tire then pull up to a pump. I'll fill it with my card," she offered giving him a small smile.

He nodded then opened the trunk and retrieved the spare tire along with a jack and tire iron. The spare looked like it belonged on a go kart. It would hinder his travel. So would the broken windshield.

The dead body lay beside the driver's door. He couldn't change the tire until it was move. Steeling himself, he grabbed the body under the shoulders and pulled the wrecked corpse to the side. Pangs of conscience hit him hard. If there'd been another way to deal with the situation, he hadn't seen it.

Shutting down his emotions, he changed the tire and threw the blown one to the side. Scattered bullet holes filled the driver's door. Even the handle had a hole through it. He grasped it and pulled. Thankfully, it worked, and he slid into the seat. The shattered front window was a problem. The glass caved in the center. There was a section in front of him he could see out of, but the rest restricted his vision. He'd need another vehicle soon.

Mira filled the tank, then gave him a curt nod as she walked away. He watched her drive up the northern on-ramp until all he could see was asphalt.

He changed clothes in the front seat of the SUV, threw the soiled ones out the window, then started the engine. Turning the vehicle toward the I-25 north and south on-ramps, a decision warred within him.

Where was he going to go?

If AJ and Bryan were successful in rescuing Lacy, would

they take her back to Oklahoma? He didn't think so. And going back to Oklahoma was risky. But the responsibility of Edwards, Cat, and the others ate at him. Did they make it to Edwards's farm okay? AJ told him he wanted to take Lacy home to California. If he made it to California, he still didn't know where Lacy and AJ's parents lived. All he knew was the town. Tulare.

Torn, he stared out the piece of unshattered square glass. Then he gritted his teeth, turned the steering wheel, and hoped he was making the right decision.

25

The romanticized notion that detective work was sexy withered up and died like the brown, creepy long-legged spiders in AJ's closet back home. In no known universe could waiting below ground in a gritty, smelly parking garage, be considered a lit job. Not to mention lying in the sand for hours and getting stung by a scorpion.

AJ's mind was absolute in this decision. He'd stick with being a cowboy. And now that his dad bought a farm, he could add farmer to his list of jobs that might entice a woman to love him.

Quicker than a blink, he flicked the notion of love out of his head. It wasn't that he didn't believe in it, he just didn't think he'd ever meet a woman he'd want to settle down with. The kind of woman who'd consume his entire being. Heart, soul, mind, body. The certainty she didn't exist made it easier to 'love 'em and leave 'em.' That's how he liked things.

And if he kept up the behavior that fit the dogma, maybe he'd believe it.

He folded his arms over his chest and tried to still his anxious mind and bouncing knee. Every time he relaxed, the pain from the scorpion sting hit him in the gut. His mind wanted to fixate on the pain, so he turned his thoughts to Lacy instead.

What condition would she be in when he found her? She'd suffered enough with Zach's assault and running the farm on her own. He was grateful his best friend had been there for his baby sister.

Now, she was in the hands of a known human trafficker. All because of their uncle. Real worry trickled down his back, like a tiny stream, fighting its way through rocks and dirt. His dad would go nuclear when he found out. Snow colored ash would rain from the sky. There was a stark probability his dad would kill his uncle. He didn't know the whole history behind their feud. It had to be more than just his grandmother leaving the farm to his uncle.

Bryan slid lower in the seat, then nudged his arm, motioning him to do the same. He pointed. "Look."

He peered over the door's frame. A sleek limousine pulled up and parked in front of the elevators. Two broad-shouldered men stepped out and waited beside the curb.

What was he doing tonight? He had a feeling it was something big.

The elevator doors slid open and Nieto, his son, and two women stepped out, all dressed to the nines. He opened his car door and slunk out, needing a better look.

"What are you doing?" Bryan hissed. "Get down."

Ignoring Bryan, he focused on the two women. One had dark hair piled atop her head in an extravagant up-do. She could be his sister. She was the same height, build, and hair color. But he couldn't see her face well enough to determine if it was Lacy.

"Let me see your face," he muttered under his breath.

The other, a petite blonde in a grey shimmery dress turned, and her gaze connected with his like a puzzle piece snapping into place. The air punched out of his lungs and his stomach did a free fall. He inched forward, drawn like a magnet. The dress made her striking blue-grey eyes glow in the darkened garage. She looked ethereal, Elvin, as if she'd stepped out of J.R.R. Tolkien's *Lord of the Rings* novel.

The blonde released him from her intent stare, nodded at the dark-haired woman, then disappeared into the limo's interior.

He sucked in a lungful of air. What the hell was that? He didn't know the girl in the grey dress, but with a single look, she'd captured his attention.

That was … Weird.

Nieto led the other woman around the car. He caught a glimpse of her face as Nieto swung her around and shoved her against the door.

Lacy.

Every single muscle in his body locked. He couldn't even draw a breath. Nieto's head lowered to Lacy's in a savage kiss. She stood stock still, didn't try to fight him.

Why?

He heard Bryan mutter a curse. He'd recognized her as well. Blistering heat raced up his chest to his neck and face, so fierce, he thought he might burst into flames. Nieto's hands had hers pinned to her sides. Bile burned the back of his throat. Without thinking of the consequences, he lurched forward.

Before he made it two steps, Bryan clapped a hand on his shoulder holding him in place. "Not now."

The harsh whisper snagged his attention and jolted him out of the rage induced haze. He turned his head, unable to watch any more. He wanted to kill Nieto with his bare hands. His insides twisted into painful knots for everything his sister had endured. If she hadn't been so stubborn, so dead set on staying at the farm, none of this would've happened. But that placed all the blame on her shoulders, and that wasn't fair.

This was his uncle's fault.

The limo door slammed shut. They ducked between cars

as it sped through the garage toward the exit. Bryan ran around the hood and they both hopped into the Corvette.

Tense silence stretched as they followed the limo back to Nieto's party. His mind flitted from Lacy to the mysterious blonde, then back to killing Nieto.

Bryan gave him a sidelong glance and let out a heavy sigh. "I know what you're thinking."

"I'm ninety-nine percent sure you don't," he shot back.

"Stay focused on your sister," Bryan advised.

He raked a hand through his hair. "I am."

"Not if you're thinking of ways to kill Nieto and his son."

"Can't help it." He turned in his seat to face Bryan. "If I don't, my dad or Jace will."

"Maybe not. Hopefully they'll just be grateful to get your sister back in one piece."

"One piece!" he shouted. "You think she's okay? That she can just brush off what's been done to her like—" He sputtered to a stop and wanted to howl his frustration.

Bryan parked at the end of Nieto's long driveway. "Bad choice of words," he admitted, then jumped out.

Bryan popped the trunk and retrieved two 45 caliber pistols. He handed one to AJ along with a silencer.

"How are we going to hide a pistol and silencer under a waiter's uniform?" AJ asked as he screwed the slim metal tube to the end of the gun.

He tried stuffing it under the waistband at his back, but it felt awkward with the silencer halfway down his butt crack. Shifting it to the side didn't work. In either position, he squirmed like a little kid trying to hold his pee.

Bryan rolled his eyes. "Unscrew the silencer, then stick both pieces in your back waistband. A waiter's jacket should keep it hidden. It's uncomfortable, but it'll work."

He did as Bryan instructed then followed him back up the hill to their surveillance spot.

Twilight blanketed the earth. The sun's dimmer switch lowered and left the sky a dusky grey.

"Nope." He shook his head as Bryan lowered himself on the cooling sand to watch the house below. "Not gonna happen. There's no way I'm going to lay down in that sand again."

"A scorpion never stings you in the same place twice," he mocked in a teasing voice.

He crossed his arms over his chest. "That's such bullshit. You just pulled that out of your ass."

Bryan's lips curled in a smirk as he hefted himself into a sitting position. "Well, I don't think we'll be able to pass ourselves off as servers or waiters."

"Why not?"

"Our skin tone isn't dark enough."

"Huh?"

"They're all Mexican. We'd stick out like a gringo's sore thumb."

The nervous energy in his system rose a few notches and he kicked a short, thorn covered bush.

"What are we gonna do then? Pretend to be one of his pervy, rich clients?"

Bryan's lips thinned and his eyes tightened. "Yup. We'll have to come up with the right clothes, though. We can't waltz in his door in desert camos."

"Doesn't he have some kind of guest list? This looks like a very private party. I doubt we'd get in no matter how we're dressed."

He shifted his weight to his good leg and wanted to cry in relief. The scorpion sting was getting worse.

Bryan's skeptical eyes studied his face. "You okay?"

"Fine," he said, brushing off the concern. He didn't have time to worry about a sting. Not when his sister needed him.

"Then let's go." Bryan rose and started down the hill.

"Wait a minute," he called at Bryan's retreating back. "Where are we going?"

Bryan turned and glanced over his shoulder. "To get suits."

He threw his hands in the air. "With what money? Or are we going to steal those too?"

Bryan continued down the hill. "As a matter of fact, yeah."

He scowled but followed despite the warning bell pealing in his head. "Stupid idea," he mumbled under his breath.

Bryan laughed. "I heard that."

They reached the car and hopped in. He leaned his head against the seat's back, his heart jackhammering in his chest. He hadn't over-exerted himself down the hill, but it felt as if he'd just finished a marathon. He was on the verge of a full-blown panic attack.

"Relax," Bryan said in a breezy tone. "We'll go back to the house where I boosted the car. They'll have what we need, and we can shower, too."

"Perfect. Let's go back to the scene of the crime. You're a genius," he said glibly.

Bryan's face lit with a grin. "I know!"

26

Waiting in the red '69 Corvette in the most uncomfortable suit ever made, AJ worried about their plan. Or the lack of one. Could they slip in with the next guests that arrived? He couldn't imagine the client list being huge. If their assumption was true, the whole party revolved around selling girls.

What if no other clients showed up? What if everyone had already arrived? He cringed. Who in their right mind would buy another human being?

"Dude, you smell like someone beat you with a bouquet of flowers," Bryan teased.

"Yeah? Well at least I'm not wearing frills on my collar," AJ returned, snarky and a little superior.

They'd returned to the house Bryan had robbed, helped themselves to a shower, then rummaged through the clothes closets. The shower made AJ feel a million times better and he'd never been more grateful for a bottle of shampoo. Not even the lavender scent prevented him from using it. The desert's sand and grit tracked down his body until nothing remained but clean skin and hair.

Two sets of men's clothing were in the master bedroom's

closet, one a size smaller than the other. And shorter. The bigger sized shirts had ruffles along the collar and cuffs. Because Bryan was built like an NFL linebacker, he claimed the bigger size.

The petite man's dress pants looked like clam diggers on him, so he dug in all the dresser drawers looking for black socks to help camouflage the problem. He found an assortment of bright colors and bizarre patterns but no black. The tamest pair he could find had little rainbow-colored gnomes all over them and when he sat down the pants rode halfway up his shin. Classy.

The angry red ring around the sting and the swelling around his lower shin and ankle concerned him a little. He shrugged it off because nothing could be done. They had to use Nieto's party to their advantage and rescue his sister. She was his only priority.

Nothing else mattered.

Bryan punched his shoulder. "Hey, you listening to me or what?"

"Gah," he yelped, rubbing the smarting muscle.

He fisted his left hand and landed a jab on Bryan's right arm.

Bryan barked out a laugh. "That didn't hurt. Who taught you how to fight? Yo mama?"

He crossed his arms against his chest. "Shut up, asshole."

"Baby," Bryan taunted.

"Prick."

A pair of headlights snagged their attention. A red Tesla S rolled up to the drive, paused, then continued to the front where a guard waited, clipboard in hand, ready to check off the next guest.

AJ gripped the door handle. "We going?"

"Wait. Let's see who gets out."

Bryan's soft, steady voice annoyed him, and he rolled his

eyes. He wanted to get on with the plan. If they waited any longer, he'd think of another way to access the house.

"Is that …?" Bryan's voice trailed and his eyes widened. "It can't be."

He strained in the day's dying light to focus on the man who'd exited the posh Tesla.

"What are you on about? I can't see shit," he muttered.

"I think that's Oliver Young."

"Who?"

"The MMA fighter from Australia, dumbass. The guy with him must be his trainer. Or a bodyguard."

"Oh, yeah. I totally see it now," he mocked. "Of course. It's the most famous MMA fighter of the decade. Here. Because he can't get a girl any other way. Right. You're the dumbass. A big one."

"Yes, it is," Bryan insisted, jumping out of the car.

He rolled his eyes again but opened his door and stood. "What now?"

"Let's go." Bryan waved his arm forward and started up the drive, his stride widening with every step.

They caught up to the two men and Bryan started to clap the MMA fighter's shoulder in a friendly gesture, but the bodyguard caught his hand mid-air.

The MMA fighter stopped then turned. "Can I help you?" he asked Bryan in a brusque, Aussie accent.

Bryan smiled at the man and AJ coughed down a laugh. He looked like the Joker.

"It's an honor to meet you Mr. Young."

The skin tightened around man's dark-brown eyes. "I think you —"

The guard holding the clipboard took a step off the portico. "Is there a problem?"

"No, no problem," Young assured, then turned back to Bryan. "Look, I'd appreciate it if you'd not tell anyone I'm here."

"Mind if we walk in with you?" Bryan asked.

Tense muscles rippled along Oliver Young's neck. The man towered over them, could snap them like a twig if he wanted.

His brows rose at Bryan's request. "So, you'll keep my identity confidential?"

"Of course," Bryan agreed, still smiling.

Young gave a curt nod, then strode to the man with the clipboard.

"Bring your smile down a couple watts," he whispered. "You look like you just flew over the coo-coo's nest."

"I'm not deranged," Bryan said defensively. "I'm just a little fan struck that's all."

He smirked. "I think the term you're looking for is star struck."

"Whatever."

"Name?" Clipboard Man asked.

A brow rose over his dark, wide-set eyes as he waited for Young's response.

"Oliver Jones," he answered, giving an alias.

"They with you?"

"Yes. They're my bodyguards."

The seconds it took for the man's decision to let them pass felt like an eternity. AJ's skin itched to get inside. Find his sister.

The man waved them through, but AJ knew Clipboard Man wouldn't forget their faces. He'd scrutinized them too long.

Bryan eyed the room they'd just entered, body tense like a coiled spring. Young and his bodyguard disappeared into the crowd.

People milled downstairs in typical party fashion. Guests enjoyed champagne and finger foods served on silver platters by servers in black and white tuxedoes. How much did Nieto pay for their nondisclosure? A pretty penny, he'd bet.

He glanced upstairs. A select few wandered along the rail, whiskey glass in hand, a cigar perched between their lips. They seemed at ease, as if buying a girl was normal, like going to the grocery store.

A man with jowls like a bulldog protected the left entrance to a stately set of twin staircases. The amount of mahogany to make the staircases must've cost a fortune. To his right, another man stood, arms crossed against his thick chest. A tattooed snake wound around his neck.

Men with bank accounts higher than the Empire State building filled the entire house. Two women should stick out in this testosterone-filled crowd, but he still hadn't seen his sister.

What if Nieto planned to sell her? Urgency thrummed through his blood until his whole body vibrated. They had to act fast.

"We need to find a way upstairs," he said quietly.

"Let's check down here first." Bryan stopped a server, grabbed two flutes from the tray, then handed one to him. "We need to act like we belong."

He'd recently sworn off drinking, more a necessity than a conscious decision on his part, to better his life. Alcohol had become hard to find, and pricey when he did. As he stared at the bubbles popping in the air, he realized he didn't need it anymore.

Bryan had wandered toward the back of the open entry space. He handed his full glass to a passing waiter, then followed him through a set of double doors that opened into a ballroom.

An opulent chandelier hung from the ceiling, large tear shaped crystals dripped from its tiers, bouncing refracted light to the floor. A grey marble-stone bar was built into the far-left corner. Men occupied high-backed bar stools drinking from martini glasses. A stage with an orchestra clad in black playing soft music graced the right end. Bouquets of light purple orchids set on tables scattered around the room's perimeter.

His eyes tracked around the area's circumference, then stopped. Tiny pins pricked his scalp. There she stood, her arm linked with the girl with the fascinating eyes.

Lacy.

Bryan sidled up next to him. "See her?"

"Yeah. Right side of the bar," he said, gaze never leaving his sister.

"Ah, okay. I see her. You notice Young behind her?"

"Yup. Wonder what he's doing here? He doesn't seem the type to buy a girl for sex."

Bryan huffed a laugh. "Maybe he wants his own personal merry maid."

"You're twisted."

"Prude."

He shook his head. "Can we just concentrate on getting out of here? This place gives me bad vibes."

"We need to snag Lacy's attention. If she could get upstairs where there's not as many people, maybe we can use the back stairs to disappear."

His eyes lasered on Lacy, willing her to look his way. As if she could feel him, she turned her head and stared right at him.

He placed a hand against his breast then pointed his index finger toward the ceiling. She gave him a slight nod in acknowledgement.

He grabbed Bryan's sleeve and tugged.

"Come on," he said, voice low. "She got the message."

Oliver Young rose, said something to Nieto, then started toward them.

Bryan hesitated. "Is he coming over here?"

He released a breath. "How should I know? Let's move."

"Wait a sec."

"Dammit," he muttered.

Young walked up and stood in front of them. "What are you mates doing here? This isn't a place you want to be."

"Thanks for your concern," AJ returned coolly. "But we have our reasons."

"Why are *you* here?" Bryan countered.

"That's no concern of yours," Young snapped. "Look, you mates need to leave. You're drawing too much attention."

Bryan cursed. "We can't leave. Not yet."

"Well, whatever you're going to do, do it quick," Young advised. "Nieto isn't a man you want to cross."

AJ turned to Bryan. "Let's go."

Young's words stuck like a fishhook in his jaw. They had to move fast. Standing around shooting the shit would get them caught.

"You mates need help?" Young asked.

Young's sudden offer seemed wrong. Why would he help? He just told them to leave. He didn't trust the MMA fighter.

He scrubbed his face, impatience barreling through him. "Thanks, but —"

Bryan butted in. "If you could distract Nieto, that would be enough."

Young nodded. "Right."

Young strolled back with an ease that underplayed his large frame and caught Nieto's attention. He sat beside the man, his suit pants straining against his thighs, and engaged him in conversation.

AJ turned and walked back toward the double door entrance, Bryan at his back. He didn't trust Young but hoped his distraction would be enough for Lacy and her plus one to get away. The prickly sensation on his scalp hadn't left. It moved down his neck causing the hairs to stand on end. How were they going to get past the men guarding the staircases?

Bryan grabbed his sleeve. "Wait."

"What now?" he bit out.

Bryan pivoted. "Let's check out that door. See it?" he asked, motioning with his head to a door adjacent to the bar.

"Yeah. Think it's a back stairwell?"

"Maybe."

They adjusted their course weaving around clusters of talking men. He tried to catch bits of conversation but couldn't decipher anything through the large room's buzzing atmosphere.

When they reached the door, Bryan cracked it open and peered inside.

"All clear," he confirmed.

They slipped through then sprinted up a set of stairs. He scoured his surroundings. A deserted hallway lay in front of him, lined with faux sconces emitting a soft light. To his left, he heard the low hum of conversation. The mezzanine area, he surmised. They needed to find a place to hide while they waited for Lacy and the young girl. She was out of his sight, and it made the acid in his stomach boil. He'd give her three minutes. If she couldn't get away, they'd have to alter their plans.

"Three minutes," he whispered to Bryan.

Bryan nodded in understanding. "Let's find a place to lay low."

On alert, they snuck down the hallway. Bryan checked doors to his right while he checked the ones on his left. All were locked, except one. A janitor's closet. They crept inside, leaving the door open just a crack. The air, thick with chemicals, stifled his breath.

"Come on, Lace," he breathed.

The seconds ticked by.

Where the hell was she?

27

Numbing shock froze Lacy's brain. AJ was here. How had he found her? Her brother rested his hand against his chest, then his index finger pointed upward. He wanted her to go upstairs.

She tilted her head in a subtle move, acknowledging his request. Her eyes focused on the man next to AJ.

Bryan.

He'd come back. How ironic. She never would've guessed the man who'd made her life hell on the farm would be her savior. Gratitude swelled in her breast, and tears gathered in her eyes, wetting her eyelashes. She wasn't alone. For the first time since she'd been placed in Nieto's hell hole, she felt hope.

But …

Where was Jace? Why wasn't he with AJ and Bryan? Her chest constricted, strangling her airflow. It hurt to breathe. A tear escaped and ran down her cheek. Her eyes frantically searched the crowd behind her brother, but her gut told her Jace wasn't there.

What had her uncle done to him?

She needed to gain control over her rising panic before she passed out. Taking a deep breath through her nose, she counted to five, then released it in slow increments through her mouth. She needed to concentrate on getting the hell out.

She leaned her shoulder against Willow. "We need to get away," she whispered.

Willow gave a short nod, then turned to Raul. "I need to use the ladies' room," she announced in a loud, stilted voice.

She grimaced. *Real smooth, Willow.*

Nieto turned from the man with the Aussie accent. "Raul, take care of that, *por favor.*"

She let out a short huff. "I think we can manage without Raul holding our hands."

Nieto raised a brow. "Do you think I trust you?"

She clamped her mouth shut. The acidic remark on the tip of her tongue would garner nothing but trouble and raise his suspicion.

Raul rose and offered a hand to Willow. She accepted it with a grace Lacy didn't possess.

She stood, steadied herself on spiked heels, and trailed them across the dance floor. He led them through a door by the bar, to a set of stairs.

"Quiet," he murmured, as they climbed the steps.

"Why?" Lacy asked. "Who's up here?"

Where were AJ and Bryan? Had they been caught? A foreboding settled over her shoulders like a weighted cloak. Hot, stifling air engulfed them as they neared the top. Beads of sweat formed around her neck.

He stopped on the last step and glanced back. "That's none of your concern."

"Why is it so hot?" Willow asked, fanning her face with her hand.

"You ask too many questions," he snapped. "*Silencioso.*"

He led them down a hall, then stopped at the second door on the right.

She glanced around the hallway, familiarity tugging her

memory. Her heart hammered against her ribcage. The vision of AJ dropping to his knees, as a bullet ripped his chest open, played over in her memory with shocking clarity. Her nightmare.

Could she stop it from happening?

Willow grasped her elbow. "Come on."

Raul opened the door, checked inside, then retreated to the opposite side. He lifted one foot, pressed it against the wall, then folded his arms over his chest.

"There are cameras everywhere," Raul warned. "And guards inside every door along this hallway. Don't try anything stupid." He gave her a pointed stare.

"Wouldn't dream of it," she drawled, in a deceptively sweet voice.

Raul's mouth turned down and he eyed her with suspicion. Shit. What if he suspected something? Bryan and AJ had to be here somewhere.

He waved a hand. "Just get on with it."

Resisting the urge to flip him off, she turned. As her foot stepped over the threshold, AJ and Bryan burst out of a door to their left. Both had weapons with silencers drawn, pointed at Raul. She spun around and looked at her brother. She'd never seen him so fierce.

"Let my sister go," AJ demanded, eyes trained on Raul. He extended his free hand. "Lacy, come to me."

Raul bolted off the wall and grabbed her left arm, twisting it behind her back. Stinging pain radiated from her elbow to her shoulder. She stumbled backward, slamming into Raul's muscled chest. With his other hand, he'd drawn a small pistol from his back waistband. The barrel, warm from his body, dug into her temple.

She'd trusted this man, thought of him as second in command at the farm, and he'd kill her if pushed far enough. Her uncle had sent Raul to the farm. He'd set all this in motion. Fresh rage kindled inside her like wind to a flame. If she survived this, her uncle would pay in spades. She'd make sure of it.

"Who are you?" Raul challenged.

"I'm her brother. Now let her go, asshole."

As AJ and Raul faced off in defiant silence, her gaze snapped to Bryan. He blinked once, then shifted his eyes to the left. His body remained in shooting position, ready to fire. Had he asked her to duck left? Did she trust him enough to let him take the shot? What if he missed Raul and hit her instead?

Deciding to roll with it, she jolted left, then dropped.

"What are you doing?" Raul hissed.

She let out a grunt as her knees cracked on the floor. Raul's grip tightened on her wrist as she fell. Her arm hung at an awkward angle, pain sluicing her shoulder.

Two muted pops broke the silence.

Raul fell backward, dragging her with him. Her head slammed against the carpeted floor, temples erupting like someone had jammed an icy hot poker into her brain. She wrenched out of Raul's weakened grasp and struggled to her feet. Trapped fabric ripped underneath her shoes. As she bent to free her hem, her eyes locked onto her brother.

She couldn't breathe.

He'd fallen to his knees, head slumped forward. Both Bryan's hands lay against the right side of his chest applying pressure to staunch the blood flow. Willow hovered on the other side, brushing damp strands of black hair from his forehead.

No. This couldn't happen. She couldn't lose him. He was her anchor. He kept her grounded when life threw crazy curveballs at her. He always tried to protect her from danger.

A guttural, gut-wrenching cry exploded from her. She lurched forward, then dropped in front of AJ.

"I'm sorry Lacy," Bryan apologized, his face a masked in

grief. "I got one round off. Hit Raul in the chest. He shot at the same time. Dammit! I thought he'd fire at me!"

Raul raised his head. "Go," he rasped. "Guards coming."

Lacy glanced back at Raul, her brows raised in surprise. Why would he help now? She turned back to Bryan, who'd positioned his shoulder underneath AJ's arm, trying to help him stand. AJ cried out, then slumped forward, face ashen.

"He's in too much pain," Willow told Bryan. "You'll have to carry him."

"Hurry," Lacy urged.

She stripped the shoes from her feet, then rose. Running in stilettos? Not an option.

With his back toward AJ, Bryan knelt, grabbed an arm, and pulled it over his shoulder. He raised up slightly, then grasped his leg and hoisted it over his shoulder as well. His breath punched out as he stood with AJ on his back. AJ's head lolled to the side.

Willow adjusted his head to rest against Bryan's back, then placed two fingers against AJ's neck. "He's okay, just out cold."

Lacy took one last look at Raul. His body lay still, arms splayed around his head. Her brain formed another bloody image she'd never forget. Death hovered, watched over him, ready to whisk his soul to the deepest parts of hell.

A chill skittered up her spine.

They'd run out of time.

She lifted her gown, bunching the silk material in her hands. "We gotta go. Now."

Bryan turned his back to her. "Grab my gun," he instructed. "Shoot first, ask later."

She drew the gun from his waistband, measuring the weight of the steel. She knew her way around a weapon. Her dad had made sure of it. She clicked off the safety.

Someone shouted a warning, followed by feet pounding above her head. A door opened ahead of them to the right. A man with a thick frame and wide shoulders stepped out. Lacy took aim at the wide target and shot. He fell against the door frame then dropped like a stone in a pond.

Lacy and Willow charged forward with Bryan behind them. She trained her eyes forward, refusing to look at the man she just killed. Another thing she'd process later. They ran the length of the hall then turned right, away from the balcony filled with Nieto's patrons. Into another long hallway. A scene from *The Shining* leapt into her mind. She could almost see those creepy twins float toward them. Shaking off the image, she charged ahead.

Bryan stumbled, knocking AJ's feet into the wall.

Lacy slowed her pace. "Where's the exit Bryan?" she asked on a labored breath.

"The stairs are here. Just ahead to the left."

She bounded forward, her head twisting side to side, searching. She didn't know how many men were behind them but knew she couldn't wait to find out. She couldn't shoot them all. They were outnumbered. By a lot. They had to get out of this narrow hallway. They'd be fish in a barrel if those men caught them.

Bryan skidded to a stop. "Here," he grunted, adjusting AJ's weight. "Open it."

Willow opened a door on the left, and the pleasing scent of Mexican Honeysuckle drifted inside. Lacy looked back. Five men rounded the corner, the first two had their weapons drawn.

"Shit. Go," Lacy barked shoving Bryan into Willow's back. "We got company."

She let out a short scream as a bullet zinged above her head. They stumbled out the door onto the second story portico.

Bryan darted right, down a set of stairs, then took off in an all-out sprint. He skidded around the corner of the house, then down the long driveway.

She stopped, spun around, and shot three times at the men following. Swinging back around, she caught up to Bryan who'd shoved AJ into the passenger seat of a red Corvette convertible.

"Really?" she panted, as she came to a halt beside Willow. "Where the actual hell are we supposed to sit?"

"Just get in," Bryan bit out, as he raced around the hood. "They can't catch us in this car."

"Willow, sit on my brother's lap," she instructed. "You're smaller than I am."

Willow shook her head. "I don't want to hurt him."

"He's already hurt," she half-shouted. "Just do it."

Willow pushed AJ's slumped form against the back of the seat, then buckled his seatbelt.

"Hurry up," Bryan urged, revving the engine. The Corvette's tires spun on the black asphalt.

Willow hiked her dress up to her waist then bent her legs on either side of AJ. Straddling him, she folded her dress underneath her legs. Lacy hopped over them and sat on the trunk, between the seats. Anticipation's tingling sensation rolled over her, leaving goose bumps in their wake.

"Go!" she shouted.

Black smoke billowed behind them. Burned rubber's sharp, suffocating scent filled the open car. His foot let off the brake and the car rocketed forward. She looked back. Pins flew out of her hair, destroying her intricate up-do. She grabbed her hair and held it in a tight grip.

The men chasing them had jumped into a black sedan and were a few car lengths behind them.

She leaned toward Bryan. "They're following us," she hollered in his ear.

His eyes darted to the rear-view mirror. "I know. I see 'em."

She looked down at Willow and her brother. Willow's hands placed pressure on AJ's chest. Blood leaked between

Willow's fingers. The girl's head rested on AJ's left shoulder. Her lips moved as if she was talking to him. The amount of blood that stained AJ's shirt, jacket, and tie overwhelmed her. Tears smarted her eyes. She couldn't live with herself if her brother died. How much blood could a person lose before it was too late to save them?

28

An elephant hosted a wicked all-night party and used AJ's body as the dance floor. He was sure of it. The pressure on his chest hurt, and his lungs had deflated like a sick balloon.

His head began to clear, and he realized two things. First — he'd been shot, and the shock was wearing off fast. He lifted his heavy eyelids to check out the second thing. A head lay against his shoulder. The wind whipping through the Corvette blew strands of blond hair over his nose and mouth. His heart skipped a beat in his battered chest. The girl with the fascinating eyes sat on his lap. Was this a pain-induced mirage? A dream? If it was, he never wanted to wake up.

"You're gonna be okay," the girl whispered in his ear. "I promise. Just hang in there."

Her sweet southern drawl washed over him like a drug, and his insides melted when she nuzzled her nose against his neck.

"How is he?"

Sweet relief swept over him when he heard his sister's voice. They'd gotten her out. Memories of their rescue came in short bursts, like movie clips. He remembered hiding in the janitor's closet, screwing the silencer on his weapon, then rushing out like he was friggin' Jack Reacher.

The Corvette shot down the highway like fire following gasoline. He tried to raise up, but the girl's head still nestled under his jaw. He flexed his hands, then his arm muscles, testing them. The side with the bullet hole hurt like a mother. He encircled Willow's waist with the arm that worked, then let out a shuddered sigh.

The girl raised her head and fixed her widened eyes on his. The wind caught her hair blowing it like a cyclone around her face. She grabbed it and pulled it around her shoulder. The tender smile she gave him shot straight to his center, lighting a fire. A fire that could blaze into a raging inferno. She was different. He knew it instinctively.

The girl turned to his sister and shouted over the wind, "He's awake!"

Lacy bent down, wrapped her arms around them both, and squeezed.

He let out a sharp yelp.

"Sorry," Lacy apologized, laughing through a sheen of tears threatening to fall.

He gave her the best smile he could muster. It probably looked more like a grimace. Now that his brain had become functional again, the burning sensation in his chest spiked over one hundred on the pain scale.

He turned his gaze back to the girl. "What's your name?" he rasped, resisting the urge to cough.

The wheeze in his lungs worried him.

She laid her head back on his shoulder. "Willow," she whispered in his ear.

Willow. Interesting name.

"I think we lost 'em," Bryan yelled. "I'm gonna head to the chopper."

Oh great. He'd forgotten about the chopper. The long hike back would be difficult at best. Then his body reminded him of the scorpion sting by shooting fiery pain up his calf muscle. He closed his eyes again, concentrating on the nearness of Willow's body. He rubbed his thumb up and down the side of her waist. He'd never see this girl after tonight, so he let himself enjoy the sensations rolling through him. No woman had ever turned him on the way the girl in his arms did, nor had any made him want to run, screaming for the hills.

The car slowed. They'd hit the end of the paved road. Bryan pulled onto a dirt path for hikers and ATV's. They bounced and scraped the bottom of the low set car until AJ thought his ribs would push through his chest.

"This is as far as I can go," Bryan said when the trail gave way to trees and hills.

"How far do we have to hike?" Lacy asked. "AJ won't make it far."

Concern laced her tone and he wished she didn't have to worry about him. It was his job to worry about her. He didn't like the shoe on the other foot.

"I'll be okay." His voice sounded like he'd swallowed a mound of gravel.

"Like hell," Lacy argued. "You've lost so much blood. You need a hospital."

Willow lifted her head. "I've been thinking about that."

His eyes shot open. "About what?"

"My dad's a large animal vet and the closest thing to doctor you'll find quickly." Her eyes searched his. "Bryan can fly us to my parent's house."

"That's the best shot we've got," Bryan agreed.

Bloody hell. A horse doctor. Before he could think on it further, the girls opened the door and climbed out. Bryan popped the trunk open, then hopped over the door, and jogged around the hood.

"Grab the packs in the trunk, will ya?" he asked Lacy.

Willow reached over and unhooked his seat belt. He raised

his hand to the wound on his chest, but she grabbed it before he could touch it.

"Don't," she warned.

"Why not?" he asked warily.

Her eyes locked onto his. "Because you'll panic."

He dropped his hand, not wanting to deal with a panic attack. But the idea of a veterinarian cutting him open, rooting around to dig out the bullet lodged in his chest, was enough to set him off like a rocket. Bryan's strident voice cut through the gory images rolling through his head.

"Where the hell are your shoes?" Bryan barked.

"I took 'em off," Lacy retorted, her voice conveying the fact she thought the reason obvious.

"You can't hike to the chopper barefoot," he said incredulously.

His sister's voice drew near. "I don't know what you want me to do about it."

Bryan came into view and dropped down beside him. "I'm gonna carry you to the chopper."

"I can manage," he tried to insist through a sudden haze of dizziness.

"No, you can't. Plus, Lacy needs your boots. She won't make it without them."

"Fine," he conceded.

He tried to fold his arms across his chest then let out a sharp hiss as pain surged through his chest. Willow pushed Bryan aside, then placed his arms back in his lap. She leaned forward until her nose brushed his.

"Accepting help when you need it isn't a weakness," she whispered on a small smile.

Their gazes locked. How had she read him so easily? He felt like he'd known her for years, not just a few hours. She acted like she felt the connection between them as well. She didn't move until he acknowledged her with a faint smile ghosting his lips.

As she stepped back, he looked down at her feet. They were encased in some sort of strappy heeled silver shoe.

He shook his head. "You can't hike to the chopper in those heels."

"I can make it on my own," Willow said.

"You'll break both ankles," he argued.

Lacy elbowed her way between them, bent down and unlaced his boots. She pulled them off, then plopped down with a grunt. Using the loop on the back of the black utility boots, she tugged them on her feet. She tightened the laces then tied them off.

"Their five hundred sizes too big," Lacy complained. "My feet will be protected but the rest of my body won't when I trip all over myself in these things."

"You'll have to carry Willow," AJ said ignoring her grumbling.

Lacy turned to the girl. "You good with that?"

"I'm sure I can —"

He looked up and caught Willow's gaze. "Accepting help when you need it isn't a sign of weakness," he parroted with a grin.

A fire lit within Willow's narrowed eyes which increased his smile to megawatt status. He liked her stubbornness, was used to it. His sister could be a mule sometimes.

"Fine," Willow huffed.

Bryan paced in the background. "Can we go? Those guys are gonna catch up to us."

Lacy motioned for Willow to jump on her back. Willow hiked her dress up, then holding the material in one hand, she jumped on and wrapped her arms around Lacy's neck.

Bryan maneuvered AJ onto his back, then took off at a fast pace. Every step Bryan took shot pain up AJ's leg and through his chest. Nausea hit him hard. Darkness circled the edges of his vision. He swallowed the bile burning a path up his throat, refusing to barf all over Bryan's back.

He heard Lacy's labored breath behind them. They hiked two miles through sand and rough terrain, until the orange and white helicopter materialized.

With a relieved sigh, Lacy let go of Willow's legs. Willow dropped to the ground and released her dress. It fell, hiding her legs. AJ had been staring at them without an ounce of shame and was disappointed to see them covered. She might be tiny in height, but her body type suggested she'd had curves in all the right places before she was starved half to death.

Lacy rushed to the chopper, opened the door, and hopped in. Willow followed, then Bryan placed him at the entrance.

"There's a first aid kit hanging on the wall back there. You might want to disinfect the wound," Bryan advised Willow.

"There's a couple of headsets in the steel box beside it. Use them because this old bird will make your ears bleed if you don't."

Willow nodded, grabbed the head sets from the box, then moved to retrieve items from the kit. Lacy hopped in the copilot seat and situated her headphones. Bryan jumped out, slammed the door, and rushed into the pilot seat.

The chopper's rotor began winding up as Bryan prepared for lift off.

Willow poured antiseptic into the bullet hole. It bubbled inside the wound like acid eating through rust. He could feel the pain through his bones to the roots of his teeth.

"Gah! God dammit that hurts," he shouted, piercing his own ears as his words traveled through the head set Willow had placed on his head.

Willow patted the wound with gauze pads, poured in more, then repeated the process.

"Jesus, how many times are you going to do that?"

"Until it's clean," Willow replied in a no-nonsense manner.

She lifted off her knees holding the bloody gauze pads, searching for a trash receptacle. As she glanced outside, something drew her up short. The soiled pads fell to the floor, and her face blanched.

"What is it?" he pressed.

"Flashlights. Coming this way," she said in a shaky voice.

"Shit," he muttered.

She swung around, raced to the front and shook Bryan's shoulder. "Get us off the ground!" she screamed.

Bryan glanced over his shoulder. "What?"

"Get us out of here! I see flashlights coming through the trees."

His nostrils flared. "Hang on back there."

Lacy adjusted an earpiece. "What's going on."

"We've got company," Bryan said through gritted teeth.

"Dammit! How'd they get here so fast?"

Bryan shook his head. "Doesn't matter. This takeoff's gonna be rough."

Willow hurried back to AJ, gathered his head in her lap, which he didn't mind in the least. Willow's scent, a hint of lavender and honey, clouded his senses and his eyes drifted shut.

The chopper lifted off the ground, hovered, then lifted higher.

Ping, ping, ping.

The peace surrounding him evaporated. What the hell was that noise? It sounded like hail on a tin roof. Willow screamed as a bullet sank into the chopper's light aluminum side.

His eyelids snapped open, and his muscles locked. Round after round hammered at the rear of the chopper. Nieto's men were aiming at the back. The tail rotor. If they managed to damage it, their escape would end here.

"Shit!" Bryan yelled.

The chopper lifted higher, then shot forward, out of danger. The trajectory forced them backward. They slid along the floor until Willow's back crashed into a bolted bin along the wall.

"Ow!" she cried.

"You okay?" he asked, searching her face.

"Yeah. You?"

He snorted. "Never better."

Her attempt at a laugh washed over him and smoothed out the worry lines bunching his face.

"You'll be fine," she assured him, brushing a lock of hair from his forehead.

And his stupid heart tripped over itself again. This girl. She scared him. He couldn't fall for her.

"Why are you so relaxed around me?" he wondered.

Men had damaged her. That was a given. As beautiful as she looked to him, he wasn't blind. He saw the bruises on her neck and the bite mark. How much abuse had she endured, and for how long? The unfamiliar sting of jealousy pricked his skin. And a rage so strong it rivaled the ocean's swiftest current battered him.

She turned her head and sighed. "Lacy told me what a great brother you are. I said I'd like to meet you someday, but I never thought I'd get to. And you make me feel safe."

Emotion clogged his throat and he swallowed hard. He loved his sister, would move mountains for her if necessary. She talked about him, thought of him as something great, and that meant the world to him.

He cleared his throat, reached up, and touched her cheek. She turned her head and their eyes locked.

"I'm glad you did," he whispered.

29

An hour down the road, Jace pulled to the shoulder, still questioning if Tulare was the right choice. The decision to go to California placed a lot of trust that AJ and Bryan would rescue Lacy and take her home. What if they weren't there? He had no idea where to start looking for them if they weren't. Dammit! Maybe he should've gone back to the farm.

But returning to the farm presented another set of ugly problems. The senator was going to blow a fuse when he learned he'd disobeyed his direct order to kill New Mexico's governor and helped her escape. On top of that, he'd killed Corporal James. How furious would he be over that? Would the senator take out his anger on Edwards, Cat, and the others?

He hoped Edwards and Cat were successful in their escape with Matty, Hailey, Ethan, and Dylan's girlfriend, Gracie. Edwards farm would be a great place for them to start over. Edwards had more than enough room for everyone, plus acreage for a garden and a few cows. He wavered with a powerful desire to check on his friends. Did they need his help?

Lacy needed him more. He had to make decisions based on the assumption AJ and Bryan had rescued her. If they'd failed, he'd deal with it, somehow. The shattered windshield made it difficult to see the road ahead. The dawning sun projected prisms of color through the broken glass. Unbuckling his seat belt, he shifted back and lifted his legs. Gathering his strength, he punched his feet at the windshield. Metal screeched as a corner ripped from the frame. Little shards of glass rained over the hood to the ground, and all over the interior.

"Dammit," he muttered, observing his small progress.

It would take more than a few kicks to remove it. He bent sideways, opened the glove box, and searched for gloves. A black leather pair peeked out from under the owner's manual. He pulled them over his hands, bending his fingers to stretch the material.

He got out of the car, gripped the corner that had given way, and pulled hard. He wrestled the windshield like an MMA fighter executing a cross face crippler on his opponent until he'd won. By the time the last of the glass gave way, his sweaty shirt clung to his back, and he'd spent the last of his energy.

Cold air hit his sweat-slicked skin, causing a shiver to roll through him. Lack of sleep and the absence of adrenaline weighed his eyelids down like an anchor. He shouldn't stop, but he hadn't slept since … He couldn't even remember the last time he'd slept. Had it been the night AJ showed up at the farm?

Five days had passed since he'd seen Lacy. It felt like five years. He missed the stubborn fire that glowed in her eyes. She had a dogged determination to win in any situation and was a force to be reckoned with. But mostly, his thoughts lingered on their shared moments, when she'd given herself to him for the first time. She was equal parts innocence and seductress, a heady combination. He missed her seductive touch.

He moved to the back of the car with sluggish steps and lifted the hatch. Why did it feel like he was wading through wet cement? He unzipped Corporal James's pack. Remorse crept up his back, twisting around his neck like a vine choking off his airway. Could he steal from the man he'd killed less than an hour ago? It was messed up and it jacked with his head. His vision blurred and he swayed back and forth. He needed whatever food Corporal James had packed.

Steeling himself against his warring emotions, he rifled through the pack, grabbed a power bar and a bottle of water, then slammed the hatch shut. He opened the back passenger door and slid into the seat, bone weary.

He ate the power bar in two bites, then chugged the water. It took the edge off his hunger but solidified the fact he needed sleep. Against his better judgment, he let his eyelids droop, let sleep's dreamless depths finally pull him under.

A CAR DOOR's loud slam drew Jace out of darkness into the dregs of the semiconscious. His lethargic brain tried to process the sound and what it meant. For a few fleeting seconds he was cast back to his traveling days, playing baseball for the University of Central Oklahoma. Sleeping in a narrow bus seat didn't bother him. He could sleep anywhere.

Most of those long bus rides he'd spent thinking, dreaming about Lacy and what it would be like when he managed to tell her how he felt. Would she feel the same? The times they spent together included her brother, but he could often feel her eyes on him. She studied him like he was her calculus homework, confused yet at the same time, intrigued.

Someone jiggled the door handle and the dreamworld he'd built with Lacy in it disappeared. His eyelids flew open. With slow movements, he reached into the floorboard for his rifle.

"Cooper! Open up!" someone shouted.

He knew that voice.

Dylan.

How had Dylan found him? How could he have known what route he'd take, or where he'd decide to go? He hadn't seen Dylan following Corporal James. His heart pounded in his ears, pulsating like electromagnetic waves.

He eased into a sitting position and placed the rifle in his lap. Dylan's nose pressed into the passenger door's window.

His lip curled into a snarl. "What the actual hell, Dylan?"

"Open up," he said on a resigned sigh.

Dylan's dejected look sparked a fire in his belly. He didn't get to feel remorse. Lacy had given him a chance to prove himself worthy of their help. But time and again, Dylan chose the easy way, and Jace didn't want to hear whatever excuse the younger man had this time.

"Not gonna happen," he growled.

"What happened to the corporal?"

"How did you find me?" he countered.

"Corporal James gave us short-wave radios. We were in communication with him the whole time. By the time we got to the Loves Station, you'd left. We had to make a judgment call on which road you'd take. I figured you'd try and make it to Tulare."

He balled his fists, heat racing through his veins. "Why did you come after me? You could've just gone back to the farm."

"We had orders to make sure you returned." Dylan lowered his voice. "The other three men are in the car. There's no way they're gonna let this go. You killed the corporal."

"He was gonna kill Mira and Kylie," he shouted.

Dylan's forehead creased. "Who?"

"You stupid shit," he snarled. "The New Mexico governor is a woman. She had her kid with her. I'm not that heartless.

Are you?"

Dylan rubbed a hand over his mouth. "I'm afraid of the senator and what he might do to Gracie if I step out of line. Look what he did to you and Lacy."

He straightened in the seat, his finger on the rifle's safety, tempted to shoot Dylan where he stood. He didn't want to go back to the farm. The senator would punish him or worse kill him. He was sure of that. He killed an important man in his militia. Men were scarce. Every one of them counted.

Fighting his way out of this situation would be the smartest thing to do. His lips turned down on a sigh. He didn't want to kill anyone else, but if he surrendered would he be forfeiting his life?

He flipped his gun, buttstock facing the window, planted his feet on the floorboard, then took a deep breath. Raising the gun, he struck the window where Dylan's nose rested. Glass crunched as the butt's black metal bashed a hole through it.

Dylan stumbled back clutching his nose, cursing the world. Jace swung the door open and punched the man's already offended nose before he could recover. Dylan dropped as if the ground were a magnet, drawing him down.

"I don't want to kill you, so stay down," he ordered.

The commotion drew the attention of the other three militia men. They stepped out, and he braced himself for a bloody fight.

He raised the gun into firing position and flipped off the safety. "Don't come any closer," he warned.

A tall, lanky man with greying hair hanging to his shoulders stepped forward. Dave. He seemed like the leader of their small group.

"You're outnumbered, Jace," Dave said, voice steady and sure. "Don't make this harder than it has to be."

He emptied several rounds at their feet. Sand spit

outward, and dust mushroomed up from the ground, as bullets lodged in the road's sandy shoulder. The men jumped back.

He unleashed several more rounds at their feet, jogging backward to the driver's door. As his fingers gripped the handle, something struck him from behind. Shock mixed with pain disoriented him. What the hell? Warm blood trickled down his neck, soaking into the collar of his flannel shirt.

Dylan's blurry face appeared before him, and he thought he heard an apology pass his lips.

Sonofabitch. Dylan had struck him. That was the last thing he remembered.

SEVERAL HOURS PASSED before Jace regained consciousness. He slowly opened his eyes. The sun, starting its descent into the west, shone cheerless rays through the back window. Gah. He held his head in his hands and ground his back molars. The brightness hurt his head, causing his stomach to pitch. He fought the urge to throw up by taking deep, cleansing breaths.

They'd shoved him in the luggage area. The militia leader, Dave, drove like a man on a suicide mission. The SUV's tires gripped the road, propelling them forward faster than he liked. Each passing mile marker drew him closer to the senator and he wasn't ready to face him.

The motion mixed with the grinding tires didn't help his queasy stomach. He probably had a concussion. He'd suffer a lot worse when the senator got ahold of him.

Dammit.

Every choice he made seemed to catapult him farther and farther away from Lacy. The chances of them seeing each other again kept plummeting. The odds were stacked against them.

His heart clenched as frustration mounted.

He hoped AJ and Bryan were having better luck rescuing her. The obstacles facing them were larger and more dangerous. Better to shut those thoughts down and focus on the present. Good counsel but difficult to execute.

He rose to his knees and looked out the back window. All too familiar landscape rushed by in a blur of naked brown trees and yellow limestone rock. The car's tires drifted as Dave maneuvered a sharp corner. He fell backward as the car shifted the opposite direction around another curve. Highway 11 between Ponca City and Kaw City tested the driving skills of everyone who drove it.

The last leg of the trip passed in swift segments. Kaw City, the bridge over Kaw Lake, then Cooper Road —the road that led home— sailed past his window. His stomach became a swarm of angry bees as they neared the Monroe farm. He knew the senator to be a ruthless man. Would he have him executed in old military fashion? His mind conjured a long line of militia men staring him down through their sights. The car turned into the gravel drive and his heart stuttered.

Dave cut the engine, turned around, and caught his eye. "Glad you're awake."

He said nothing. The back of his head still leaked blood. How much more would he lose?

Dave shook his head. "You're a good guy, Jace. I'm sorry I have to turn you over. And for what it's worth, I admire you for not killing that woman and child."

His admiration wasn't worth the oxygen it took to utter them. He averted his gaze to the side window. Bitter wind blew and rattled the skeletal branches of the mimosa tree in the yard.

He'd drawn deuces in this situation and would have to play them out. The senator walked down the back steps to the SUV.

The men stepped out and gave him their lengthy report.

Dylan opened the hatch. "Let's go."

He turned from the window and faced Dylan. "How could you do this?" he asked through clenched teeth.

Dylan opened then closed his mouth several times, like a fish out of water.

"Bring him to me," the senator boomed.

He shoved his way out of the back before Dylan could lay a hand on him and strode to the senator.

Senator Monroe jabbed a finger at him. "I warned you, boy, not to cross me. You didn't kill Governor Deschene, which you were ordered to do. But you did manage to kill Corporal James, an important man in my militia. Is this correct?"

The senator's cold amber eyes drilled into his.

"It is," he confirmed.

The senator struck fast and hard. His jaw popped as the senator's fist tried to punch a hole through his face. He staggered back. Before his eyes could refocus, two men, one on each side, grabbed his arms.

"Take him to the governor's old tent and guard him until Widow gets there," the senator instructed.

Dave gave him a grave look. "I'm sorry, Jace."

"Don't worry about it," he sneered, as the two men jerked him forward.

They walked the pasture, overrun by tents and militia men, to a larger tent near the ponds. His mind cast back to the blazing bonfire Travis and Raul had built. Sparks flew high into the night sky. Laughter floated on the wind. He embraced the phantom feeling of Lacy in his arms. That night was the first time he'd gotten a chance to hold her.

They opened the tent flaps and shoved him inside.

"Wouldn't want to be you," the larger one said, shaking his head.

"Who's the Widow?" Jace managed to ask after landing on all fours.

"A man who gets off on torture," the other man said in a flat voice.

The flaps closed, leaving him in semi-darkness. His concussed head lured him into sleep, a safe place where he could dream of Lacy, and forget men like the Widow existed.

30

Lacy was no helicopter expert. In fact, she'd never been in one, until now. But she could see the fuel gauge had dipped dangerously low.

They'd been in the air for about an hour. AJ had nodded off with his head nestled on Willow's lap. Sheer exhaustion swept his mind and body away from the relentless pain his body suffered. Willow's eyelids fluttered shut, yet her hand continued stroking his head in a soothing, rhythmic motion.

Bryan eyed the fuel gauge, tapped it with his index finger, then swore. She'd never heard some of the words coming out of his mouth. When he reached his peak, spouting vulgar phrases no woman ever wanted to hear, she tore off the headset.

Lifting a brow, she fixed a pointed stare at him until he turned to face her. He motioned for her to put her headset back on. Rolling her eyes, she slipped them over her head, positioning them over her ears.

"What?" he blustered.

She folded her arms across her chest. "You kiss your momma with that mouth? And what in the hell does TARFU mean?"

His loud laugh chafed. She narrowed her eyes at him until he stopped.

Still smirking, he said, "It means 'Totally and Royally Effed Up.'"

She frowned. "What's wrong with the chopper, Bryan?"

The question sobered him, and he shook his head. She waited as he tapped his fingers on the cyclic lever by his side.

She scrubbed a hand over her face. "Just tell me," she insisted.

"I didn't have time to refuel. But there was enough to get us halfway to Laredo. I knew I'd need to stop, but not this soon." He took a deep breath. "We're about one hundred miles, give or take, from Mexico City. It's still too close to stop," he muttered.

"What are we going to do?" she asked weakly.

The shakes started in her legs traveling upward to her midsection and arms. What if Nieto caught up to them? His resources were mind-blowing. The urge to burst into sobs stuck in the back of her throat and she swallowed convulsively. They wouldn't survive if he caught them.

Bryan laid a gentle, brotherly hand on her shoulder. "Hey, breathe, okay?"

She gave him a shaky nod, sucked in a deep breath, held it, then let it out.

"That's it," he encouraged.

"You didn't answer my question," she said through chattering teeth.

"There's a heliport in San Juan. I've got money to refuel. Maybe Nieto hasn't alerted every airport and police station between here and the border. It's our best bet." He shrugged. "We could get lucky. But —"

"I hate that word," she muttered.

"But," he continued, "When those assholes were shooting at us, I think they nicked the main fuel tank. If we fill up both tanks, we should be good to the border."

The urge to cry came over her in waves. Before she could check them, tears sprang into her eyes. She smashed her lips together, refusing to make a sound. She wouldn't allow herself the luxury of falling apart, but … she couldn't survive Nieto a second time.

If he captured her again, she'd break her parting promise to Jace to stay alive, because she refused to live through another sexual assault. Everyone had their limits, and she was at hers.

"San Juan is up ahead. Go tell Willow we're about to land. There's a blanket in the bin back there. Get it and cover AJ. If they want to inspect the chopper, it would be better if they didn't see that he's wounded."

"Will they want to inspect the chopper?"

"I don't know. Our story is that we're Americans on vacation."

She looked down at her ruined gown. The tattered hem dragged behind her like a wedding gown train when she walked. Blood and dirt covered her arms and neck. Her hair hung in a hot mess down her back. Pins still fought for control over some of it and large, braided strands wrapped around her head resembling a bird's nest.

Fan-friggin-tastic. She looked like a shoddy homeless person.

"What about my clothes?" she asked, throwing her hands in the air. "How am I going to explain why I look like a homeless person who went dumpster diving for a dress to crash a wedding?"

He turned an appraising eye her way. "There're clothes in the bin, but I don't think you'll find the right size. You'll have to make do."

"Make do!" she screeched. "Our lives hang in the balance, and you want me to make do? What are they going to think when they see me in clothes five sizes too big?"

He removed his hand from a lever to throw it in the air.

"How the hell would I know? Can we just focus on one problem at a time?"

Her brows drew together, thinking of everything else that could go wrong. And what could go wrong, usually did. She didn't care if she annoyed Bryan, she'd keep asking questions.

Bryan stared ahead, his fingers fidgeting on the levers at his side. His brows drew down in a sharp V. He was worried.

"They'll see the bullet holes," she stated, voice quiet.

"They will," he responded curtly. "And if they start asking questions, we'll deal with them another way."

"What way?"

He smirked. "For starters, I've got enough of the senator's money to bribe them."

The muscles in her back relaxed as pent-up anxiety drained down her body like water sliding off a duck's back. The thought of shooting or killing anyone else made her sick. A bribe should work. Everyone wanted money, right? The idea was enough to hang her hopes on for now.

She unbuckled herself and moved to the back. Willow's eyelids remained shut, hand resting on her brother's head. They looked peaceful.

"Hey," she whispered, tapping Willow's shoulder.

Willow opened her eyes and flinched. "Sorry. For a second, I didn't know where I was."

"We're about to land in San Juan for fuel. I don't know how this is gonna go, just so you're aware."

Willow eyes widened. "Okay."

She opened the bin, retrieved a grey wool blanket, and covered AJ to the chin, then returned for a set of clothes. After rummaging through pants and T-shirts of various sizes, she found something she might be able to work with.

She slipped out of the dress and tugged the black T-shirt marked medium over her head. It didn't look too bad. She pulled on a small pair of men's khaki pants. They fell to the floor the instant she let go of the belt loops. She drew them up, then continued searching the bin. At the bottom, she found a black adjustable belt. Score.

After adjusting the belt, she put back on AJ's huge boots. The pants pooled at the bottom. She rolled her eyes, glad there wasn't a mirror nearby. All in all? She looked more like a vagrant than a happy vacationer. Great.

The chopper began its descent. A silent prayer formed on her lips as she buckled herself back into the passenger seat.

"Here we go," Bryan said.

"Yeah. It's all or nothing right here," she said, bracing herself for landing.

Bryan grinned as he worked the levers and pedals, lowering them to the ground. "It's the only way I like to play."

She appreciated his optimism, but his tense body told a different story. He started speaking to the heliport's tower informing them they were about to make an emergency landing. Someone responded in broken English, giving him permission and instructions on where to land.

The greyness of pre-dawn bloomed around them like dye soaking into fabric. Another day away from Jace. She closed her eyes and stilled her mind. What happened next would determine their fate. Would Nieto be waiting for them? Her anxiety spiked again, despite her efforts to breathe and meditate. She fidgeted in nervous anticipation, rubbing her hand up and down the oversized pants.

"God," she whispered, desperate for help, "if you're up there, please, please protect us. Help us."

Over and over, she prayed until the chopper's skids hit the ground.

BACK IN THE AIR, profound relief filled Lacy. It pushed away the persistent darkness hovering around her mind. They had enough fuel to make it across the border. Getting

AJ to Willow's father was all that mattered now. He hadn't woken when they landed at the heliport. Willow assured her his pulse was steady, his body just needed rest. It did little to relieve the twisting anguish in the deepest part of her.

The stop at the San Juan heliport went better than expected. They had to sell the honeymooning newlyweds act to an astonished aircraft fueler. Their unexpected presence at the heliport would create a buzz Nieto would hear about. They needed to be out of Mexico before that happened.

Overwhelming odds were still stacked against them. Needing a distraction from obsessing over circumstances out of her control, she turned and gave Bryan a cheeky grin.

"Oh my God, I can't believe we pulled that off," she exclaimed.

He chuckled. "I told you. Bribery almost always works."

She laughed on a relieved breath. "You did. But they were still sketched out enough you had to drag me out of the chopper and introduce me as your wife."

He rubbed the back of his neck. "Yeah, about that. Can we keep that between us? I mean, are you going to tell Jace? Because I'd like to be a healthy distance away before you do," he finished. Sarcasm dripped from his words like a leaky faucet.

She snorted. "Why?"

"Well," he hedged. "The thought of you with anyone else seems to light a fire under his ass."

"Good effing God," she muttered.

"I did put my arm around you," he pointed out.

She rolled her eyes. "I won't tell if you won't. Do you want to pinky swear?"

"What the hell is a pinky swear?"

"Hold out your hand," she instructed.

He complied and she linked her pinky around his.

"I swear not to tell Jace we pretended to be newlyweds,"

she vowed with all the solemnity she could summon without bursting into laughter.

"This is something kids do on the playground," he grumbled trying to pull his hand back.

Lacy tightened her grip. "Come on," she cajoled. "You don't want Jace to know do you?"

"Fine," he relented. "I swear not to tell Jace we pretended to be married."

"Good," she said, pleased he complied. She folded her hands in her lap.

"What *are* you going to tell him?" he asked in a soft voice. "About all the rest, I mean."

She picked at the cuticle on her thumb. The depressing darkness she momentarily escaped wrapped around her like an old friend. What would she tell him? Did she want him to know all the things she'd done to survive? That Nieto kissed her, touched her?

"I don't know," she said on a sigh. Then a thought crossed her mind. "Bryan, why did the senator give you all that money?"

"For fuel and food. I'm supposed to be moving his wife to some cabin he bought in the Teton mountains in Wyoming." He gave her a wink. "Obviously I got sidetracked."

"Obviously," she said in a droll voice.

"Have you thought about how you're going to get out from under your uncle?"

How to escape her uncle's control? It was a question for which she had no immediate answer. It hummed in her mind, just below the surface, like an annoying tune on the radio, or one of those insurance jingles — *"Nationwide is on your side."* Ugh, now that would be stuck in her head.

"It's all I think about," she admitted.

"Got any ideas?"

"No. I wish I knew of something that ..."

Her voice trailed as an idea presented itself. Of course.

"What are you —"

She held up a hand. "Shh."

The solution had been in front of her all along. The one thing that seemed to unhinge the senator was when he thought she disrespected him. She could disrespect him until hell froze over, and all she'd get would be a broken jaw. When she mentioned his wife, however, he went berserk in a certifiable way. What if … what if they could somehow use his wife as leverage?

"Tell me what you're thinking," Bryan urged.

"It's just an idea," she hedged.

"Just spit it out, Monroe," he said, rolling his finger in the air, indicating her to continue.

"You're going to think I'm crazy—"

"I already do," he touted, cutting her off.

She humphed. "Seriously?"

"Okay, I'm listening."

"What is the one thing the senator seems to give a shit about?" she asked.

He scratched the whiskers on his chin. "Well, other than his grandiose plans to take over the world, the one thing that he's concerned with is his wife."

"Right," she agreed, a smile tipping her lips. "And you're supposed to be taking her to Montana."

"Wyoming," he corrected.

"Whatever. What if we sort of keep her?"

He raised a brow. "By 'keep her,' you mean kidnap her?"

"Well, okay, if you have to put a name on it. It's not like my uncle doesn't deserve it," she defended.

"What about your aunt? Does she deserve it?"

Like a match to a pilot light, fire burst upward from within. Blood rushed to her face and the tips of her ears burned. If her aunt became collateral damage in her uncle's game, then that was on him. He'd been using her the same way.

"She's guilty by association," she shot back. "And honestly? I don't give a rat's ass what she deserves!"

He leaned away from her. "Got it."

"Will you help me or not?"

He studied her for a long moment. "Of course I'll help you. This helps me get away, too."

Satisfied, she nodded, then leaned back in her seat and closed her eyes. "Thank you," she murmured.

"Hey, Lace?"

"Yeah?"

"I've been wondering something," he said in a tentative voice.

She turned her head, lifting heavy eyelids. "What is it?"

His face held remorse, and she wondered why.

He ducked his chin. "Have you forgiven me? For what I put you through back at the farm?"

He'd made life harder than it had to be, not just for her, but for everyone living at the farm. He took their food and terrorized them. But the icing on the cake had been when he burned the barn. All their fishing poles, nets, bows, arrows; everything they used to acquire food, to survive, was in the barn when he burned it to the ground.

"Did you have to burn the barn?" she asked. "Raul could've been in the root cellar under there. You're lucky my horse wasn't in there either."

"I know, and I'm so sorry. The governor wanted you out and gave me no choice."

Everyone has a choice, her caustic mind chirped. But the sincerity in his voice touched her. His recent actions proved the words he spoke. He didn't have to risk his life to save hers but he did.

"Bryan, I wanted to thank you for coming back for me. You didn't have to do that. You're a good guy. Yes, I've forgiven you. How could I not?" she said simply.

Relief flooded his face. "Thanks."

She closed her eyes, shut out every thought, and let her mind fade into an exhausted sleep. Jace appeared in her dream and her body relaxed. Further and further, she drifted. In her dream, they rode a roller coaster. Her stomach dropped with every downhill plummet.

She woke on a sharp breath. It wasn't her dream roller coaster causing the free-fall effect.

The helicopter was falling.

31

AJ's first conscious thought was, he couldn't breathe. He opened his eyes, saw silver fabric, and … *wow.*

Willow had folded her body over his head like a mother hen protecting her chicks. Her evening gown's V neck split to the waist. In her current position, the fabric gaped open enough to see the mound of her breast, small but firm, and just enough dusty pink to make his blood heat.

He turned his head and took a deep breath. Her scent etched her name on his soul. He didn't know this girl, but something about her drew him to her, like an inescapable tractor beam. Their souls linked the instant they'd locked gazes in the parking garage. It sounded so cliché, like a trailer advertising a chick flick.

He'd never act on his feelings. As much as he thought about love, longed for it, he knew he didn't deserve it. Besides, with what the girl had gone through at the hands of Nieto, she'd be too fragile for someone like him.

A shiver rocked her body and knocked him out of his lust induced haze. He reached up with his good arm and adjusted her headset.

"Hey, what's wrong?" he asked, fixing his own earpieces.

His voice sounded rough as it echoed back through the speakers.

She rose and wiped her nose with the back of her hand, hiding half of her terrified expression. "Can't you feel it?"

The chopper drifted downward at a steady, pinwheel pace. He turned his head toward the front and saw a frenetic Bryan working levers and pedals.

"What's going on, Bryan?" he asked with caution.

"We're out of fuel," Lacy answered. "Bryan thinks we're over the border but is trying to stay in the air long enough to make sure we've crossed over."

"I thought we had enough to get to Laredo?"

Heat raced up his neck as panic began to dig another hole in his chest.

Lacy turned to face him. "It drained out faster than Bryan thought it would."

The chopper dropped like a plane through turbulence. Bryan muttered a curse and shifted a lever up.

His heart hammered and an ocean roared in his ears. Did they rescue Lacy only to die hours later? No one knew where they were. No help would come if they crashed. His forehead beaded with sweat. He needed to remain calm. But how? They were dropping through the air in a tin can with no parachute, nothing to buffer their free fall.

"How are we still in the air?" he asked breathlessly.

"Auto-rotation," Bryan relayed in a clipped voice.

"How does it work? Are we safe?" Nervous questions tumbled out of his mouth.

"Yes," Bryan bit out. "We're safe. Now shut up so I can concentrate. I've done this maneuver once, and that was in flight school."

They might not crash, but Willow still needed reassurance. So did he. He touched the silken strands of her hair. The length ended just below her shoulder blades. He curled an end around his finger. Concentrating on her took his mind off his physical pain, and everything else. He could lose himself in her. Part of him wanted to.

He looked up to find her watching him. Her ashen face looked translucent in the chopper's LED lights illuminating the cabin. Her lips parted, surprise flickering over her face.

Could she see how he felt?

Planting his hands on the floor, he pushed his body up. Pain exploded through his chest. Every time his lungs expanded it felt like they were being fed through a shredder. He managed to shift his back against the small bin bolted to the floor.

"Come here," he said, motioning with his hands.

She hesitated, eyes trained on his wound. "You want me to lean against your chest? Won't I hurt you?"

"I'll survive," he assured her.

The bandage she'd wrapped around his chest after she'd tortured him with the antiseptic, still held. He looked down to find it soaked with blood. Thankfully, the bleeding had abated. His gaze lifted to Willow. She'd stilled, hands folded on bent knees, eyes trained on the lower part of his bare chest.

A slow grin formed on his face. "Like what you see?" he asked in a light, teasing voice.

The question startled her out of whatever she'd been thinking. "Um, what?"

At least ogling him distracted her. She seemed to forget they were falling from the sky.

Lacy turned, lips pulled down. "Leave her alone, AJ," she reprimanded.

Bryan interrupted. "I'm about to land this bird," he warned. "Hang on. It might get a little bumpy."

The chopper hit the ground, and like a jack hammer against concrete, it bounced back up.

Willow tumbled into his chest.

"Umph," he grunted.

The skids bumped the ground twice more, then slid a few

feet. They came to an abrupt stop in the middle of an open field.

Willow pushed her hands against his shoulders to right herself. Before she could withdraw, he wrapped his good arm around her waist, and drew her close. Her solemn eyes lifted to his. He couldn't explain or identify what passed between them in that moment. His arms tightened, securing her to him. *Mine,* his soul whispered. His possessiveness scared the hell out of him. He wouldn't keep her. But God, he wanted to. He swallowed hard, resisting the urge to kiss her.

Bryan opened the cockpit door, jumped out, then opened the passenger door. Fresh air swept into the cabin, clearing away the stale, coffee-infused air. It also cleared his head as effectively as a sledgehammer cracking a nut. He relinquished his hold on Willow.

She backed away from him with a look of confusion he understood. He didn't understand the instant attraction between them, and by the look of it, neither did she.

Bryan held his hands out. She moved toward him, and he picked her up by the waist and set her on the ground.

He needed to keep his distance. He avoided relationships and didn't form attachments. If there was any other way to get this damn bullet out of his chest, he'd take it. Traveling to her dad's veterinarian clinic with her was going to be the best and worst kind of torment.

Bryan returned to help him. He wrapped an arm around Bryan's wide shoulder and stepped down. The pain buckled his knees. Bryan eased him to the ground. Fire eaters had nothing on the inferno raging inside his chest as broken muscle and bone stretched then retracted. He stayed on his knees until the tears cleared from his eyes.

Willow sat beside him. "You okay?" she asked, placing a gentle hand on his shoulder.

He flinched, then cleared his throat. "Yeah," he managed.

He needed to control his feelings, separate himself, but

couldn't get himself to do it. A lump formed in his throat. He wanted this girl. Distance was the cure. The sooner the better.

———

LACY'S HEART shot upward with the velocity of a rocket as she observed the miles of open, grassy-brown terrain. No blacktop or gravel road anywhere she could see. Where in the devil had they landed?

Her brother sat on the ground with his head bent to his knees. The bleeding had slowed, a good indicator a major artery hadn't been nicked. Willow knelt beside him, her hand rubbing slow circles up and down his back. A gesture of comfort more than anything else. But there *was* something else.

AJ ran hot and cold when it came to women. Normally, she'd warn Willow but reasoned they wouldn't see each other after her father removed the bullet.

Bryan walked out from under the chopper with a scowl.

"Bad news?" she asked.

"Yeah, poor Bertha won't fly again," he grumbled. "I don't have the tools or parts to fix her. No way of getting what I need anyway."

She gave him an incredulous look. "You named the chopper?"

He gaped at her like she'd grown two heads. "Yeah, I named her. We had a good run, Bertha and I."

His genuine affection mitigated her disregard and she swallowed her laughter. "I'm sorry," she repented. "But what are we going to do now? Where the hell are we?"

He raised a hand to his forehead shielding the sun from his eyes. He pivoted on his boot heel and faced northwest.

"A road should be that way," he said, pointing a finger.

"Okay, how does that help us?" Frustration mounted inside her. "AJ can't walk. We need a car."

"Let's see if he can get to the road. I'll carry him. Then you and I can continue walking until we find something." He glanced over at Willow. "She can stay with your brother."

She ran a hand over the top of her head. Ugh. The braids, stubborn enough to withstand the hair-raising car ride, felt like a bird had nested there all night.

"We could walk for days before finding anything," she scoffed, unraveling the remaining plaits.

"I'm aware," he said, derision in his voice.

"Did we overshoot Laredo?"

"I don't think so. Maybe." He patted her arm in reassurance. "Don't worry. There's got to be a ranch or something close."

She shook her head. "I hope you're right."

"Let's get goin' then."

Bryan hefted AJ onto his back, firefighter style, and set off toward the northwestern horizon. The sun, not yet at its highest point, indicated they had hours before sundown but the mild February day would turn colder as the sun set.

The group trudged through endless waves of brown grass in silence. The wind rustled it and her imagination conjured zombies, bloodthirsty vampires, and every other horror movie monster. A chill tickled the back of her neck. She shivered and turned her thoughts to the present. How far had they walked?

She watched Bryan with a keen eye. He flagged under AJ's weight. The guy was no doubt exhausted. When was the last time he'd slept?

Willow picked her way through the grass, dress raised, and … Shit. She forgot Willow wore those ridiculous heels.

She stopped Willow, swiveled her back to the girl, then patted her shoulder. "Jump on."

Willow complied without comment, and they continued at a faster pace. A startled pheasant burst from the grass ahead, its white-tipped russet wings stretched to catch the wind.

After what felt like hours, a structure came into view. Her eyes strained to see what type of building lay ahead.

"Please don't let it be a pole barn," she muttered under her breath.

Energy rejuvenated at the sight, Bryan lengthened his stride. She struggled to keep up with Willow attached to her back like a leach.

The structure materialized into a dull, brown ranch-style house. A white Ford F150 sat next to the porch. Brown, sandy mud caked the side and undercarriage. Other than the truck, there was nothing that indicated anyone occupied the home.

Dry ruts ran through the unkempt yard. A chicken coop lay to the south, several yards out, but no chickens pecked the ground. Spiders had woven their webs on the filthy porch, from corner to corner, in gleeful abandon.

It looked eerily deserted. Her mind returned to *The Walking Dead.* If she'd known the show would plague her like a tick on a hound, she wouldn't have spent so much time binge watching it.

Willow slid from her back and stepped up beside her. "Thank you."

"You're welcome," she said, giving her a small smile.

They shied away from the house, crept to the side of the truck facing nothing but open field. They dropped to their knees. With gentle care, Bryan lowered AJ from his back, then propped him against the truck's back wheel.

"What now?" Lacy whispered. "Do you know how to hotwire?"

"Of course I do," Bryan scoffed. "How do you think I got the Corvette?"

Willow slid to Lacy's side. "We could check the front door. It might be unlocked, or the owner might be home." She gave both Bryan and Lacy a pointed look on the last statement.

"We can't just ask to take someone's truck. No way

anyone's gonna let us borrow it," Lacy argued, whisper rising several degrees.

"Maybe," Willow conceded. "But I'm not convinced there's no one here. That Ford has been driven recently."

"Look around you," Lacy whisper shouted. "There's no one here."

Bryan gave them a trepidacious look, took a deep breath, then scooted sideways to the driver's door. The handle lifted, unlatched.

Turning to them, he whispered, "I'm going to look for a key."

He inched the door open, searched under the mat, the console, then tried the visor. The fob fell and hit his head. Cursing, he picked it up, clenching the electronic device as if he wanted to hurl it against the windshield.

"Got the fob," he muttered. "At least I won't have to hotwire."

"I'm drivin'," Willow announced, eyes sparking.

Bryan threw her the fob with an amused smirk. "What's up with that?" he asked Lacy, throwing a thumb over his shoulder.

She shrugged. "She's from Texas. What'd you expect?"

Willow jumped on the side bar, then hopped in ninja style. She ducked in the seat, waiting for them to load AJ. The truck swallowed the petite girl like a giant Venus fly trap.

Bending down, she assessed her brother. His slumped body remained still. Too still. When had he slipped into unconsciousness? Prickles of heat raced up her neck.

"When did he pass out?" she asked, voice breaking on the last word.

"About the time we came across the house, I felt his body relax. I'll get him loaded," Bryan added.

She nodded, ducking her head. Her throat convulsed as she tried to swallow with no saliva. Dehydration was taking a toll on her ability to think, to keep her emotions under wrap.

He shook AJ's shoulder. "Come on, man. Wake up. Help me out here."

AJ didn't respond, breaths short and shallow.

"I don't like this," Lacy fretted. "Why isn't he waking up?"

"He'll be okay." Bryan's arm wrapped around her in a quick side hug. "Let's get out of here. We need to be quick in case there's someone around."

She nodded, wiping wetness from under her eyes. Makeup clung to her face from the night before and smeared her index finger. She looked down at her T-shirt. Foundation stained the front where she'd used it as a Kleenex. The cuts on her face stung and the bruises throbbed.

Bryan slipped an arm under AJ's legs and lifted him up with a grunt. Muscles in his neck strained with AJ's dead weight.

"Dude, I'm carrying you. Again. I'll never let you live this down."

She opened the back door, then hoisted herself into the back seat. Bryan raised AJ to the seat, then strapped him in.

Grabbing the top of the truck, Bryan climbed up, turned, and quietly shut the door. He clambered over AJ, then squished himself between her and the door.

"Willow, you ready?" Bryan asked.

Nodding, she started the truck. The V8 engine roared to life. She peeled out of the yard onto a long gravel drive. Lacy turned, looked out the back window.

The home's front door opened abruptly. An old woman stepped onto the porch, stature so short Lacy thought she might be a little person. A wiry mass of white hair stuck out in every possible direction.

"Oh my god," she gasped. "Willow go, go, go!"

32

Spiders.

Everywhere.

The kind with the little red dot on their fat bulbous abdomen. Jace crab-crawled backward until he hit the tent's side. Somehow, he knew this was a dream, but his heart galloped in his chest as if it were really happening.

The demon spiders crawled unnaturally fast. He pressed his back against the vinyl. As they edged the bottom of his boot, he stomped on them, smashed them until yellow guts popped, ran out, and stained the floor. No matter how many he killed, it seemed more took their place.

They began crawling up his pant leg. Frantically, he tried to brush them or shake them off, but there were too many. Pain pierced his arms, and he cried out. His heart stuttered to a stop when he looked down. Up and down his arms they crawled, leaving a trail of puncture wounds behind.

Wake up, he commanded himself.

Instantly, the scene switched. Now, he was in the ocean, fighting his way to the surface. The water felt heavy, weighted, like liquid quicksand. He couldn't breathe. He wouldn't make it to the surface before his oxygen deprived body breathed, sucking salt water into his lungs.

Would he ever wake up?

33

Buckshot rained down on the truck like a sandblaster on paint as the little old woman loaded shell after shell into the shotgun with lightning speed.

"Hurry!" Lacy shouted, banging the back of the driver's seat.

"I am!"

The truck's back tires spun, seeking traction, spitting a wake of gravel behind them.

Bryan turned in his seat to watch. "Damn, the woman's ballsy," he said, nodding in appreciation of the old lady's impressive skills.

Small lead balls tore into the tailgate in staccato *ping, ping, pings*, but the truck suffered no other damage. Willow turned off the long gravel drive onto an old county road, leaving the old woman behind.

"Do you know where we are?" Bryan asked Willow.

"Not yet. We'll drive west and try to pick up a major high-way. Then I'll know."

Bryan scratched his head, brows furrowed in skepticism. "Okay," he said, shrugging.

Guilt niggled Lacy's conscience. She lowered her head

into her hands. They'd just stolen a truck from an old lady. It was a despicable thing to do and it felt like she'd dropped from the seventh circle of hell to the ninth. She could justify it any way she wanted, what they'd done still sucked.

She grabbed the front seat and pulled herself toward Willow. "Hey."

"Yeah?" "Is there a way we can return the truck to that old lady? I

feel bad."

Willow snorted a laugh. "I don't know. Maybe."

The answer made her feel a little better. The truck hadn't been well taken care of. Old take-out trash littered the interior's floorboards. The interior smelled like old grease and onions. Even the off-putting aroma in the stuffy cab couldn't refrain the Pavlov response to the McDonald's hamburger wrapper at her feet.

She missed junk food, especially Coke and Snickers. The thought brought Jace to mind, and the familiar wave of grief rolled and tossed inside her. He'd teased her about how many Snickers she'd eaten as a kid.

The truck's tires hit the edge of the road, jerking her attention to Willow. The girl rummaged through a pile of CDs in the console.

"Watch the road," Lacy admonished.

"I got this," Willow replied, inserting a CD into the player, then returned her attention to the road.

Tim McGraw sang in the background, while empty grasslands meant for cattle, flew by in a rush. At least Willow knew how to open the throttle.

Lacy turned to Bryan. "What now?"

"Sleep," he mumbled, eyes closed.

The poor man needed rest, but the unfinished business with her uncle had to be addressed.

"We need to plan our next steps," she said, voice low.

He opened his eyes on a sigh. "I know that."

"Where's my aunt?" she asked, heart pounding like a Led Zeppelin drum solo.

She used her sweaty hands to pull her hair out of her eyes. Could she do this? How hardened would she need to become to kidnap someone? The more violent acts she committed, the more desensitized she feared she'd become. Losing her compassion and empathy frightened her.

In a metaphorical sense, some situations were like rolling down a steep hill. Taking a baseball bat to Dylan's throat after he'd stolen her horse hadn't been the best way to handle that situation. But she'd climbed back up that hill, found a way to reconnect with the good part of herself and move on. She'd forgiven Dylan.

She didn't know if she could absolve herself if she kidnapped her aunt. She'd take a bone-splintering, one-way nose-dive off a cliff.

Bryan shifted sideways in his seat, stretched his long legs, then let out a satisfied groan. He leaned against the door, flopped an arm over his eye.

"Your aunt is in San Antonio." He lifted his arm and leveled her with a questioning look. "You up for this? Like for real?"

"I have to do this, so whether I'm up for it or not, is irrelevant," she said, relinquishing the idea there was a different way to handle things.

Heaviness pressed on her chest. The urgency to cut her uncle out of her life, out of Jace's life, forced her hand. Whether she could live with the trade-off? She didn't have a friggin' clue.

"Your aunt has a personal bodyguard. He's with her 24/7."

"You've been there before?" she asked, crossing her arms.

"Yup. A couple times."

"Is there ever a time he leaves?"

The truck's tires bounced out of a pothole sending them

both upward. Her head hit the ceiling, and the back of Bryan's head smacked the passenger door's glass.

"Ow," Lacy complained, rubbing the top of her head.

Bryan let out a string of curse words.

"Sorry 'bout that," Willow hollered over her shoulder.

She leaned over AJ. His breathing hadn't improved, but it seemed like he held his own. Mollified, she leaned back.

"The bodyguard knows me," Bryan stated. "But we'll either need to take him, which is a calculated risk, or try and give him the slip. He knows the senator moves his wife around, but he always goes with her."

"Does he ever leave?"

"Every morning for coffee, then in the afternoon he goes for a run."

"Can you take him out?"

His brows furrowed. "Maybe. He's special ops though. Our best bet is to wait until he leaves, or just take him with us."

"I don't want to take him," she protested.

"Then we wait and watch. When he leaves, we'll go in," he said directly.

She tapped her index finger against her lips. "What will we tell my aunt? She'll want to take her guard with us."

He raised his arms, lacing his hands behind his head. "We'll say the senator has something else for him to do and he'll catch up to her later. Something like that."

"Will it be that easy?" she murmured, thoughts coalescing.

"If it were easy, you wouldn't need me," he answered with a grin.

She dropped her head into her hands. Guilt tormented her over deceiving her aunt into a hostage situation. Her parents never tolerated dishonesty. The adage, 'It's easier to ask forgiveness than permission,' didn't work with them. They turned that old saying on its head. By painful trial and error, she'd learned there were far more successes asking permission than forgiveness.

Willow slowed the truck, then turned north onto a well-maintained four lane highway. "Hell yeah," she blurted, bouncing up and down. "We're about an hour away from my house."

"Awesome," Lacy exhaled, relieved.

"Rest, Lacy," Bryan advised. "You look like hell."

She kicked a leg at his thigh. He laughed, not even cracking open an eyelid.

She harrumphed. "No wonder women won't come near you."

He inhaled. "I'm waiting for the right one. You can't rush these things."

She snickered at his reasoning, then started to ask him another question, but he raised a hand.

"Lacy, shut up."

She snorted but closed her eyes and mouth. Bryan was right. She needed rest, and the ride would be over just as soon as it started. Taking advantage of the hour would revive her flagging energy. So would food and water. She hoped Willow's family had *something* to eat, because her stomach felt emptier than a gas tank the day before payday. The sharp edges of her thoughts turned fuzzy, and she relinquished her hold on the waking world.

The truck slowing brought her out of her light slumber. Tires crunched on gravel. She opened her eyes and sat up. A beautiful two-story home with light red brick came into view. Two dormer windows graced the front, and two columns held a high-pitched roof covering a wide porch. A huge red barn with pristine white trim, sat in the background.

A corral sat to the side of the barn where a tall brunette brushed down a young horse. Her head shot up at the sound of the truck. She hopped over the fence and booked it to the home's back door.

Another brunette stepped out onto the front porch. Before the truck rolled to a complete stop, she'd raised a shotgun at the windshield.

Lacy glanced at Bryan whose brows had risen to his hairline.

"This ought to be fun," he muttered.

"Texas and shotguns, man," she mocked.

"That's Laurel," Willow said with a grin, rolling down her window. She stuck her head out. "Laurie!" she shouted.

Laurel lowered the gun in stunned disbelief. The woman who'd been grooming the horse took calculated steps out the front door, a small, black pistol in chest ready position.

Willow threw the truck into park, jumped out, and shot toward the two on the porch. Laurel propped the gun against the porch pillar then caught her sister. She wrapped her in a fierce hug and didn't let go. The other woman holstered the pistol then circled them both with her arms.

Lacy's eyes watered. She was happy for Willow. She and Bryan stayed in the truck, allowing them time. Would she be reunited with Jace? Her parents? Would their kidnapping plan work to free them of her uncle, or would it backfire?

AJ's wheezing sped up as if he couldn't get enough air. She bolted out the door.

"Willow!" she shouted. "AJ can't breathe."

Willow broke from her sisters. "One of the men who rescued me was shot," she explained as they half-ran back to the truck.

Laurel took charge without questions, but her countenance relayed an interrogation would come. "Let's get him out and into Dad's clinic."

Bryan jumped out, rounded the hood, then carried AJ around the side of the house to the back. Corded muscled stretched down his neck and his breath punched out in short puffs.

Beyond a kidney bean shaped pool, covered for winter, sat

a structure built from the same brick as the house. A sign with Sinclair Veterinary Hospital in black script hung from two chains on its little porch.

The other sister, Olive, opened the door. Bryan followed them both through a small waiting area to the back of the clinic. Olive opened a door revealing a small surgical room where Bryan laid AJ on a cold, sterile table, normally used for larger animals.

She hated hospitals. They always had a weird smell. Antiseptic saturated the air in this room, leeching oxygen from her lungs. White robot-looking arms hung over the table with lights attached at the end. She shivered. They almost looked alive.

Laurel shoved Bryan out of the way. "Liv, get me the sonogram. Let's see where this bullet is."

She brushed a strand of hair out of her eyes. Laurel cut AJ's shirt off, then began cleaning the wound. She sponged on an orange fluid around the bullet hole.

"I need a CT scan," Laurel muttered as she tossed orange sponges in the trashcan along the wall.

Olive rolled over a cart with the sonogram equipment. "This will have to do. You can find the bullet, Laurie."

Laurel cast a worried glance at Lacy. "Maybe ya'll should go on up to the house and wait. This might take a while."

"No," Lacy objected. "I'm staying."

"Maybe we should," Bryan said as he walked over and stood by her chair.

She looked up, tears falling down her cheeks. "This is my brother, Bryan," she whispered. "I have to stay."

Bryan laid a reassuring hand on her shoulder. "Okay. We'll stay."

The two women worked tirelessly on her brother. They hooked up an IV with antibiotics and fluids to rehydrate and sustain him through the surgery.

Olive prepared the machine, then handed Laurel the

sonogram wand. Laurel muttered to herself as she moved the wand over AJ's chest.

After a few choice curse words, Laurel found the bullet. Lacy turned her head when Laurel started the extraction. She bent her head and prayed. Her mother should be so proud. She never cared about church and God as a child. But now, all she could do was fall back on her upbringing, her faith.

After the surgery, AJ still hadn't woken, but his vitals were stronger. A chest X-ray revealed a small area on his lung that had collapsed.

"His lung should heal with time," Laurel informed her. "He's stable but can't travel. His body needs rest, and that means staying here a few days."

"Thank you," Lacy said, rising from her seat. "You saved his life. I can't thank you enough."

He was going to be okay. Herculean relief and complete exhaustion buckled her knees. Arm extended, she staggered to the nearest wall, and leaned her back against it for support.

Her gaze traveled to Willow who'd held AJ's hand throughout the entire procedure. As if she could feel her stare, Willow's blue-grey eyes lifted to hers, a small smile lifting her pale lips.

"I should thank you. You rescued our sister," Laurel said, raising a brow at the small blond hovering over AJ. "Liv and I want to hear the whole story."

"I just wish Mom and Dad were here," Olive added, a sheen of tears glistening in her deep brown eyes. "They've been out of their minds since Will disappeared."

Then the second part of Laurel's words played through Lacy's mind. AJ couldn't travel. Now that she knew he'd live, her heart turned to Jace.

Bryan stepped around the portable X-ray machine, sidled up next to her.

"We need to go," he said quietly.

"I need something to eat first or I'm going to faint," she snapped, unable to keep the bite from her tone.

Tears she could never seem to shake blurred her vision. She felt an enormous weight of emotions just below the surface.

"Let's go up to the house," Olive offered. "I made soup."

She swiped at traitorous tears escaping her eyes. "Thanks."

Olive led the way out of the clinic. Laurel and Willow stayed behind.

Bryan nudged her shoulder as they trudged through the lawn's dead grass. "You okay?"

"Yeah." She choked on a laugh. "I think this whole shit-show is catching up to me. I don't know whether to laugh or cry."

His arm circled her shoulder. "Aw, don't. It kills me when you cry."

She leaned against him, grateful for his kindness, his friendship.

"How'd your sister know what to do?" Bryan asked Olive as they stepped into a cozy kitchen.

"She trained with our dad," Olive said, crossing to the stove. "Then went to Oklahoma State University for her degree."

"Where are your parents?" Lacy asked curiously.

"Senator Monroe called all medical personnel to the capital. Mom's a nurse, Dad's a vet. Laurie stayed with me even though she should've gone." Olive looked contemplative. She motioned to the brown flecked granite counter that served as a bar. "Have a seat."

She took two bowls from the dish drainer by the sink and ladled soup from a stainless-steel stockpot on the stove. They sat on cushioned high-back bar stools as she served the soup made with beef broth, canned carrots, potatoes, and corn.

"I didn't mean to pry," she repented.

Olive gave her a sad smile. "Mom and Dad were losing their minds here not knowing how or where to look for Willow. At least now they won't feel so helpless."

She nodded in understanding, then started devouring her soup. She didn't notice the mug full of rich, black coffee in front of her bowl until Bryan sucked air through his teeth.

She gave him a sidelong glance. "You're weird. Who drinks coffee that way?"

He shrugged. "My grandpa."

Olive refilled their soup bowls, observing them with a sharp eye. "Y'all need rest."

"I'll rest when I'm dead," Lacy muttered.

Bryan pushed back from the bar with a contented sigh. "I wish we had time to sleep," he lamented.

"Me too. But we don't." She hopped off the bar stool. "I'm going to say goodbye to my brother. Meet you at the truck."

Bryan nodded.

Opening the door, she let the cool, Texas wind sweep her out. She could feel they were nearing the end of a never-ending dark tunnel. New resolve coursed through her, a second or third wind, to finish the game she never wanted to play. Her uncle would suffer for what he'd done. She'd finish the game he started.

She was all in.

34

Bright light wove through AJ's mind like sun-sparkled water, waking him into conscious thought. He tried to hold onto the golden three stranded braids. They reminded him of Willow's hair, but they dissipated, leaving him in the dark.

His sister was talking to him, but he couldn't decipher the words. Yet he could feel the emotion behind the sentences that sounded like nonsense.

Sadness. Worry. Guilt.

The last one stung. Lacy had nothing to feel guilty about. She didn't pull the trigger. Guilt was a tricky emotion and often misplaced. Most who felt guilt misinterpreted the true cause. Guilt wove into DNA, became an intrinsic part of the person, impossible to extract. He should know.

Darkness called again, and he welcomed it. Memories he'd rather forget still lurked in the shadows. The absence of light obscured the overwhelming tide of guilt. It was in the darkness he felt the most relief. It was this absence of light, of feeling, he chased when he drank.

Guilt filtered through his mind's weakened barriers. It had taken on a persona of its own through the years, morphing into a monster he didn't know how to defeat. He'd discovered certain trade tricks to keep the monster chained, but sometimes it failed. Then the monster, free to torment him, crowded his mind with images and damning thoughts.

Time passed, impossible for him to measure, during the ebb and flow of light and dark. Each time the darkness faded, the light remained a little longer. Like the days in early summer, the light lengthened, coaxing his mind into consciousness.

A warm hand grasped his. A lilting voice, soft and reassuring, tugged him into full awareness. Before he could respond, the little bell above the clinic's door tinkled. Heavy footfall traipsed down the hall, then the door opened.

He heard Willow's soft gasp and felt her arm stiffen.

"Will," a male voice sighed.

Instant irritation flared inside him. The man spoke her name like an endearment. Willow's silence made him wonder who the voice belonged to and what he meant to her. Hell, he knew nothing about her. They'd barely met before he passed out. A gorgeous girl like Willow would no doubt have a boyfriend. But he couldn't deny the connection he knew they both felt.

The man drew closer. "I never thought I'd see you again."

Her grip on his hand tightened. He remained still, thinking it best he stay out of their conversation. Okay, that was a half-truth. He didn't move, didn't speak, thinking they'd be more apt to speak freely if they assumed him unconscious. He'd gain insight about the true nature of their relationship. He shouldn't begrudge her happiness with the guy. But the thought charred him inside.

"Hello, Scott," she said softly.

"How are you? Are you okay?" he asked in a disinterested tone.

Of course, she's not okay. He couldn't help but open his eyelid a sliver. He had to see this guy. His peripheral vision caught the guy brushing something off his pant leg. He opened his eye a little more. The dude's blond hair was brushed forward. It looked like he'd wrestled with a giant hairdryer and lost.

"I don't know," she admitted. "I haven't had time to figure it out."

He puffed out a breath as if her answer annoyed him.

Willow's hand remained in a death grip in his.

"Who's this?" Scott asked, tone dropping several degrees.

"AJ. He helped rescue me and got shot," she murmured.

"And that's why you're holding his hand?" Scott demanded.

Anger gathered in his chest. This guy needed to back his shit up.

"Who told you I was back?" she deflected.

"Olive. She came this morning and gave me and the folks the news. Why are you out here?" he continued, the annoyance in his voice clear now. "The guy's obviously okay. You need to go get cleaned up."

"I want to stay until he wakes up," Willow asserted.

He heard the rustling sound of hands being shoved into pockets. Willow's other hand, ice cold, covered his.

Scott sighed. "Fine. I came here to see you, but I guess you're too busy. I'll catch you later."

He shuffled to the door.

Willow tensed. "Wait."

AJ tried to keep his body relaxed, breathing slow and even, as he waited for her to continue. She released his hand and his heart dropped to his acid-filled stomach. She'd fallen for that asshole's obvious guilt trip.

"I'm coming," she said, rising to her feet.

"Good girl," Scott praised with satisfaction. "Let's get you cleaned up. You look like shit."

What the actual hell? Did the douche nozzle just say that

to her? She'd been to hell and back. What did he expect her to look like?

Scott sniffed. "Can't have my girlfriend smelling and looking like a homeless waif."

Protectiveness welled inside him, and his hands closed into fists. He wanted to pummel the guy.

They closed the door, leaving him to stew. He opened his eyes and glanced around. The IV machine at his head dripped steadily. The needle shoved up a vein and taped to his hand stung. He became keenly aware he needed to relieve himself.

He bit his bottom lip as he ripped the invasive needle out of his hand leaving the open vein to bleed. The bloodied needle continued to drip pink saline onto the stone-colored tile. He wrapped the end of the plain white sheet covering him around his hand to staunch the blood flow. Taking a deep breath, he lifted himself to a sitting position. Pain barreled through his chest like a band of wild Mustangs.

"God dammit!" he shouted.

He breathed through the pain, then turned to dangle his legs off the side. He freed his hand and the sheet swooshed to the floor. Electric pain rushed down to the scorpion sting he'd forgotten about, and sliced through his middle, stealing his breath. Every hair follicle on his head vibrated to its beat, lifting out of his scalp, then back down. *Boom, boom, boom.*

Dammit, was there anywhere his body didn't hurt? He took inventory, mentally checking various body parts, and decided the answer. No. Definitely no. His hair even hurt, for Christ's sake.

The small operating room contained state-of-the-art equipment. The Sinclair's must've had a successful practice before the economy took a dive.

He lowered his feet to the floor with care, then shuffled in slow motion to a door he hoped was the bathroom. He opened the door, flicked on the light switch, and let out a grateful sigh. The room, smaller than a closet, held a toilet and sink. His face split into a grin. He could literally use the restroom and wash his hands at the same time.

After relieving himself, he wondered why his sister hadn't been in to see him. Had she left him here? Somewhere in the back of his mind her garbled words returned.

His sister had left with Bryan. Why? He tried to recall what she'd said, but the constant hammering in his head interfered, grinding his brain into mush.

A chair, upholstered in bright brocade, sat in a corner by the door that opened into the hallway. He shuffled over, and using its arms for support, lowered himself down. He closed his eyes. His body throbbed on a cellular level, making him nauseous. He needed pain killers.

Laurel opened the door, sailed past him, her attention focused on the empty stainless-steel table. She jerked to a stop, spun around until her narrowed eyes landed on him.

"What are you doing up?" she accused.

He watched her turn off the beeping IV machine. She picked up the soiled sheet, rolled it into a ball, then tossed it into a hamper by the bathroom door.

"You shouldn't be up," she said gruffly.

He rolled his eyes. Stellar bedside manner. "Where'd my sister go?"

"Her and that other guy left yesterday. They didn't say why, just that it was important." She pulled a stool out from under a medical machine, rolled it in front of him, and sat. "Take off your pants," she ordered.

Stunned, he jerked back. "Huh?"

If he'd been on his game, he would've made a crude joke about her wanting in his pants. Too late. But he couldn't help the smirk covering his face.

Laurel blew a breath through pursed lips. "Knock it off. That guy said you'd been stung by a scorpion. I want to check it."

That made sense. He unbuttoned the tan camos, tugged

them off his waist, then threaded them off his legs and bare feet. He leaned back and closed his eyes as Laurel inspected the wound.

"Ow," he complained when she poked at the center of the sting.

"You've had an allergic reaction, and it's become infected. The antibiotics I gave you for your chest wound should cover this as well. I'll give you a cortisone shot for the swelling."

"Thanks," he murmured.

She rose, got the medicine housed in a small medical refrigerator. As Laurel prepared the syringe, Willow returned, swinging the door wide. It hit the edge of his chair, blocking him from view. His eyes popped open.

She inhaled sharply. "Where is he?"

Laurel flicked her wrist toward the door and Willow swung around. Her eyes held relief as they roved over his body. Color crept from her chest to tinge her cheeks a rosy red.

Laurel glanced up from the filled syringe as she tapped out the bubbles. "Willow, what are you doing?"

Willow jumped, and the color in her cheeks deepened. She cleared her throat and ran a hand down her ponytail. She'd showered and changed into a pair of ripped jeans, and a pink *Bring Me the Horizon* band T-shirt.

"Hey," he greeted. A teasing smile lifted his lips.

"I'm glad you're awake." Her brows drew together. "I wanted to be here, but —" She trailed off and sighed.

Should he tell her the truth? He'd never been honest with girls. But with Willow, things were different.

"You were here," he acknowledged, watching her reaction closely.

When she realized he'd heard her conversation with Scott, anger flashed in her eyes.

"Why didn't you say anything?"

He considered her for a moment, then scrubbed a hand

over his face. Rough whiskers scratched his hand. He needed to shave.

"I didn't want to interrupt your conversation. Make it awkward."

"And this isn't awkward?" she asked, waving her hands at him.

He didn't know whether she meant the conversation or his almost naked body.

"You deserve better," he said quietly.

She crossed her arms over her chest. "You don't know what you're talking about," she retorted. "Scott —"

"Don't defend him," he shot back, cutting off her next words.

He had no desire to hear her excuses for the asshole. Scott didn't deserve them, and he sure didn't deserve her. True, he didn't know the guy, but come on. Who treated women that way? Maybe they did things differently in Texas.

"I don't need to defend him. He's done nothing wrong," she sputtered.

"Willow," he said with quiet intensity.

"He hasn't," she insisted, voice rising in volume.

Like a tractor beam, he locked his gaze with hers. "Do you really believe that? Deep down?"

She turned her head. "I've got to go."

Without another word, she walked out the door, slamming it shut.

Laurel said nothing as she walked over and prepped his arm for the shot. Medicine burned a path from the needle into his muscle. He wanted to ask Laurel about Scott, but the woman didn't give him the chance.

"Follow me," she ordered.

"Where to?" he asked, a little cynical. He'd watched the movie *Misery*, and he didn't trust Laurel. He could imagine her swinging a sledgehammer at his ankles like Annie Wilkes.

"You can't recuperate here. You'll rest a few days in our spare bedroom."

He followed her through the clinic, down a small concrete path to the back door of the modern two-story home. She held the door open, and he slid past her into a large kitchen area. Laurel marched through the kitchen to a set of stairs. He followed her up and then down a hallway.

She opened a door to a sparsely furnished bedroom with a slanted ceiling. A twin bed, covered with a simple blue quilt, sat along the left wall. Under the dormer window, there was a charming little writing desk with a white wooden chair. A vintage Tiffany lamp was turned on and illuminated the room with a yellow glow.

"I'll bring you some soup in a bit."

Her no-nonsense attitude bothered him. "Did my sister say when she'd be back?"

"No," she returned in a curt voice.

He sat on the twin mattress. The springs squeaked and popped.

"Rest," Laurel commanded, then sailed out of the room.

His body sank into the mattress, and he groaned in appreciation. Anything was softer than the steel table he'd spent the last day on. He wondered if Willow would seek him out. How angry was she? It would be for the best if she kept her distance.

Leaving her would be difficult, and his heart already balked against it. How was he supposed to walk away?

35

Leaving AJ was harder than Lacy thought it would be. He was still unconscious when she picked up his limp, warm hand to say goodbye, yet she talked to him like he could hear her. She explained her plans, and why she had to go, even though he didn't comprehend anything she said. Which made it worse. The sickening feeling she'd abandoned him settled in her stomach like a funnel cake with powdered sugar she ate once at the county fair. They might be amazing going down, but once there, they turned into a greasy ball of misery.

They were about an hour into the drive to San Antonio, a straight shot up I-35 from Cotulla. She let out a sigh and leaned her head against the seat's back rest. Thirty minutes left of the monotonous ride.

Thirty minutes until go time.

She was going to kidnap her aunt.

Her stomach clenched, then pitched that greasy ball of misery into her throat. She covered her mouth and swallowed it down.

"You okay?" Bryan asked, eyes tight with concern. "What's on your mind?"

"I'm good," she muttered.

He gave her a sidelong glance. "Lacy, you've sighed about five hundred million times since we left Cotulla."

"Okay, fine. It's just …" She rubbed at the tension on her forehead. "I miss my brother. I can't remember a time we were separated for more than a few weeks. I feel like I'm deserting him." She pivoted to face him, frustrated, and feeling guilty for leaving AJ. "Don't you have some military motto, 'no man left behind' or some shit?"

"We're not *deserting* AJ," he said in a placating tone. "We left him to recover. Soldiers are left in hospital units to heal all the time. A platoon can't haul wounded men around because they don't want them left behind."

What he said made sense but didn't make her feel any better. She made a noncommittal grunt, then fell silent.

He reached over and covered her hand with his warm, consoling one. "I'll go back and get him. I promise."

She nodded once, then rubbed her hands over her eyes, angry at the familiar, rising urge to cry. She hated it. When things settled, she'd never shed another tear.

Buildings began to appear along the road. They passed an oil business, their semi-trucks parked in row after row behind a high chain link fence. Interstate 35's two lanes transitioned into four. Freeway panels materialized over the empty roadway, directing traffic.

Her uncle's boastful words about preserving America flooded back and confusion flooded her.

Where was everyone?

The freeways should be packed, but the traffic was next to nothing. A red, old-school Chevy pickup hauling an empty horse trailer was the last vehicle that'd passed on the four lanes opposite side, and that was a while ago. The deserted, empty landscape painted a dismal picture of the city. She'd assumed Texas still ran like a state. Had her uncle put everyone in work camps the same way the president had done? It sure looked that way.

They'd left most of San Antonio behind when Bryan exited onto an off-ramp. He made a right turn and drove into the suburb of Live Oak. It had all the charm of quaint, small-town living, but with all the big city conveniences.

They passed a park with an updated playground. A blue and red plastic jungle gym, surrounded by fake mulch, sat in the center. Metal benches, in a semi-circle around the equipment, gave tired mothers a place to rest while their children burned off excess energy. Giant oak trees, stripped of their leaves, towered over the park like mammoth sentinels set to safeguard all who entered.

She envied the peace the park promised. All she wanted was to lie in the grass, a warm wind against her face, and feel safe. Was that too much to ask? Probably, her cynical inner self chirped without missing a beat.

Lost in her depressing thoughts, she didn't notice Bryan had parked along a curb until he nudged her shoulder. The quiet neighborhood spoke volumes, not only of its past, but also its present. The upper class would've resided in the luxurious brick homes lining the street. They looked deserted, a testament to the decimated economy being the great equalizer between classes.

"Which one's my aunt's?" she asked, voice pitched low.

"Fourth house down on the right," he whispered back.

She twisted in her seat to face him, pulled her legs up, and crossed them. "Why are we whispering?" she asked, grinning. "There's no one here."

He let out a gruff laugh. "You started it."

She smiled at him, thankful she wasn't alone. "Guess I did. What time it is?"

He twisted the watch circling his wrist face up. "Two thirty-five."

"When does her bodyguard leave for his run? Have we missed it?"

A leaf skittered down the street on a gust of wind forceful enough to rock the truck. Another followed. She gazed out the windshield at the grey sky and grimaced. They better get her aunt before it started raining. Getting pelted by cold rain, then sitting in wet clothes all the way to Oklahoma, did not sound appealing.

"Nah. He'll leave in about an hour and drive to the track around the city lake. Geneviève likes to take an afternoon nap," he responded, calling her aunt by her first name.

"Life of leisure," she sneered. "You know I've never met her? I wouldn't know her if I passed her on the street. Weird, right? I bet you know all your aunts and uncles."

The expression on his face shuttered. "Yeah, I know them."

"You have a big family, huh," she continued.

When nerves hit, she filled the silence with empty, nervous chatter.

"Mm-hm," he murmured noncommittally.

"You have two brothers and a sister. But aren't they all older than you?" she asked, oblivious to his discomfort.

"Yes," he replied curtly.

"Baby of the family," she mused. "Like me. I knew you were the youngest because you're the only Rash I knew in high school."

"I'm the runt," he agreed.

She scrunched her face. "The runt?"

"Yeah. Well, according to my older brothers. And Dad. They tower over me." He scratched his jaw. "Been called that my whole life."

Bryan was no scrawny pup. Well over six feet and built like a heavyweight boxer, she couldn't imagine anyone towering over him. It lent insight into why he always acted like he had something to prove in high school.

They fell into uncomfortable silence. She stared out the window at the tree branches bending to the force of the wind and let her mind wander. It dashed from one thought to the next, and she made no effort to hold on to any of them.

Bryan's low curse snapped her back into the present. "Duck," he ordered, slouching down.

She hunched, then rolled forward thinking the back of her shoulders would hit the glove box and hold her steady. Instead, she ended up sandwiched between the dash and her seat, resembling a human roly-poly.

"Oh my God," she gasped. "I'm stuck."

Bryan reached over, grabbed her shirt, and pulled her up. A white Jeep SUV rolled by, and she ducked back down.

"You think he saw me?" she gasped.

The diesel engine rumbled past without slowing and she let out a relieved breath.

"Will you cut that shit out?" Bryan barked, as he put the truck in gear. "That was the bodyguard leaving. If he's worth his salt, he would've stopped to investigate. Be glad he didn't. I don't feel like getting my ass kicked by an ex-Navy Seal."

He pulled into her aunt's drive and shoved the shifter into park. Rolling his shoulders, he rotated his head from side to side, then cut the engine.

Her eyes widened. A Navy Seal? Her uncle had deeper connections than she realized. Impatience boiled to the surface. They'd better hurry if they didn't want a run-in with a Navy Seal. Plus, getting this lady loaded up got her one step closer to her goal. Jace.

"Let's go," she said, looking back at him, hand on the handle.

He eyed her up and down with a skeptical look. "Maybe you should just stay put."

"Why?" she snorted.

"Your aunt might get suspicious if you roll in with me. She'd know something's up. You said you'd never met her. It's going to take a lot of convincing for her to leave without her bodyguard. And, we don't have much time."

"Fine," she agreed testily, waving a hand in the air. "Go."

He jerked the door open, grumbling under his breath. Closing the door on a quiet click, he jogged toward her aunt's house.

She leaned her head against the side window and watched Bryan knock on the door. It opened after the third knock, and he disappeared inside. She breathed in and out, willing her racing heart to calm. How many years were taken off her life due to trauma and the never-ending adrenaline cycling in her system? The heaviness in her chest intensified and she willed Bryan to hurry.

The stiff wind continued to blow, rolling in darker rain filled clouds. A fat drop hit the windshield, splitting into several rivulets as it rolled downward. She wrung her hands together, nerves on pins and needles. If Bryan didn't come out soon, she was going in. What could be taking so long?

As the question posed in her mind, the white SUV pulled into the drive next to the truck.

Oh shit!

She dropped face-down in the seat. Had Bryan left a gun or weapon in the truck? She rolled into the floorboard, searched under the seat for anything to defend herself.

The SUV's door slammed shut. The sound kicked her heart into overdrive. She shoved her hand further under the seat, fingers spider-crawling along the carpet.

Sweat beaded her brow. "Come on, come on," she muttered under her breath.

At the very back along the seat's metal track, her fingertips met cold metal.

"Hey!" the bodyguard shouted as he opened her door.

Her hand grasped the smooth handle of a hidden revolver. In one swift motion, she pulled the gun out and rolled onto her back, pointing the gun at the open door.

"Back up," she ordered, punching confidence into the command.

The guard stepped back, a look of confusion and anger marked his broad, square-cut face. His short mousy-brown hair blew sideways in the wind. She caught his gaze as his hand moved to his side.

She shook her head. "Don't move. Hands up."

Keeping the gun steady in a firm grip, she rose to her waist. Using her elbow, she climbed into the seat, then scooted to the edge. The man backed up another step as she stepped out of the truck.

"What do you want?" the man asked gruffly. "There's food and supplies we can give you if that's what you're after."

He thought she was there to rob him. An unnatural giggle bubbled out. It sounded more like the strangled cackle of a hyena.

Seeing the calculated look in his eyes, she anticipated his next move. He lunged for her outstretched weapon, but she sidestepped him with ease. He grasped at empty air. The bodyguard righted himself, jerking on the ends of his shirt. She caught a whiff of cheap whiskey on his breath.

"I don't know who you are, but you better move on out of here."

She smirked. "Or what? I'm the one holding the gun."

"I'm a Navy Seal," he boasted, puffing his chest out like a banty rooster. "I could take that gun from you before you could get a shot off."

If the man had been sober, she knew he could've disarmed her, or even drawn his own weapon, which he must've forgotten about. She just needed to buy Bryan a few more minutes, then they could get out of here.

"Clearly," she said on an eyeroll, continuing to aggravate the man. "And its *ex*. Ex-Navy Seal."

"Listen, missy —"

"Missy?" she mocked. "I haven't been called that since my grandpa passed away."

His face passed red on the color wheel, well on its way to purple.

"Why are you here?" he asked, punching out each word.

The sound of luggage wheels scraping concrete stopped her from her next snide remark. A woman chattered non-stop as she walked down the sidewalk next to Bryan, hands moving expressively in the air.

An amused smile tipped his lips as he listened. When his gaze lifted and landed on her, the smile died, the same way a car battery dies in the bitter dregs of winter.

"Well shit," he muttered, coming to a stop.

"You know this lunatic, Bryan?" the ex-Seal asked, pointing a shaking finger at her head.

Bryan's eyes narrowed and she shrugged a shoulder.

"Where'd you get the revolver?" Bryan asked, ignoring the man.

She grinned. "Under the seat."

Geneviève halted and gawked at her. She gave the petite, dark-haired woman a cursory glance, then turned her attention back to the linebacker frowning at her.

She lifted her brows. "What? The colonel came at me. Oh, and he's had a few nips," she added, turning her hand up at her mouth.

Bryan shook his head. "You're disaster prone."

Her mood sank to the depths of Davy Jones' Locker. "Don't say that."

Bryan opened his mouth, then snapped it shut.

"Will someone please tell me what's going on?" the ex-Seal demanded.

Geneviève gave the disgruntled man a nervous look. "Tommy wants to see me. Bryan said he wanted you to head on up to the cabin and get it ready. Bryan will bring me along later."

Convenient lie, Lacy thought. She watched the man mull it over. His expression and the way he worked his jaw, reminded her of a cow chewing cud.

"I'm not sure about this," the man said, shifting from one foot to the other. "My orders state I'm not to leave Gen for any reason."

"Monroe said there'd be some needed repairs to a bathroom." Bryan said, building lie upon lie.

The Seal rubbed his bulbous nose. "I don't know."

"It will be fine, Jerry." Geneviève reassured. "I'm safe with Bryan."

Dammit. Did she have to say that? Lacy shot Bryan an apprehensive look.

"Okay," the man finally decided. "See you up there. I'll go lock up."

Bryan stepped over and extended a hand to Jerry. "Later, man."

Jerry slapped his hand into Bryan's. "Later."

"Let's go," she mumbled, deflated.

Bryan's disaster-prone comment stuck like an arrow straight to her chest. She opened the passenger door and climbed in the backseat. Lying down, she dropped the revolver onto the floorboard, then threw an arm over her eyes. Bryan tossed the luggage over the side of the truck bed. It landed with a bang and a thump. She bet the luggage he tossed into the back was a Louis Viton or some other expensive brand.

Bryan and her aunt loaded into the cab and the diesel engine ground to life. He put the truck in reverse and pulled out of the drive. He drove down the street back toward the interstate while Genevieve chatted about the rain starting to fall.

Like a slide projector, her mind flipped through scenes from the past five days. It seemed like a lifetime ago, but the images of all she'd done to survive were in technicolor. God's version of hell had nothing on those memories.

She craved a dreamless sleep, but uncertainty and fear of failure kept her eyelids wide open. Deep sleep was all that seemed to disconnect her from the misery of time. After she ended this hellish nightmare, she'd have to come to terms with her actions.

She'd exchange her aunt for Jace. It was a transaction, nothing more. Then they'd get the hell out of Dodge.

36

Jace peeled his cheek, caked with blood and drool from the tent floor, and raised his head a few inches. *Open,* he silently commanded his leaden eyelids. Damn, his head *hurt.*

His hands reached up to explore his battered skull. How had this happened? Gauze, crusty with dried blood, met his fingertips. Someone had bandaged it while he was unconscious. How long had he been out? He wrapped his hands around the back of his head. Dried blood matted stiff, crunchy hair to his neck.

He hadn't moved since the senator's military men tossed him inside the governor's old tent. He remembered that much. The tan vinyl, stretched over steel poles, was bigger than the living room at Cooper ranch. He rolled over and gasped. Pain burst in bright stars behind his eyelids. His bones creaked like an old rocking chair.

His muscles had stiffened, as if he'd aged overnight. The tent reeked of blood and sour sweat and the smell coated the inner lining of his nasal cavity. A Glade plug-in couldn't even conceal this kind of pungency. It was infused into the vinyl.

He turned to one side, pushed up with his elbow, until he

was sitting with his legs crisscross. He tried to sketch out his surroundings, but fiery pain exploded when he turned his head. As if a hairpin trigger attached to his neck had detonated a land mine, blowing bits of his brain all over the tent. He tried to block out the constant ring in his ears, but it droned on and on, making him nauseous.

A thick fog settled over him. Any attempt to think was like trying to see through a winter white-out. Worry bored worm holes through his heart, but he couldn't puzzle out why. Governor Deschene's SUV driving away from the Love's station was the last thing he remembered with clarity. What had he done after that?

He concentrated and memories burst forth in strobe light fragments. A flash of being struck from behind came and went so fast he almost missed it, but he managed to latch onto it.

Dylan.

The traitor had hit him with a stupid rock! Then he had the nerve to drag him back to the farm. But where was he trying to go before he got caught? The memory was right there. Like a locked filing cabinet, he just couldn't access it.

He swiveled a slow one-eighty on his butt, since moving his head hurt like a bitch. This tent had to have a bed, or a cot, something he could lie down on. Six cots lined the walls on both sides. Blond wooden TV trays sat at the head of each one. Scattered playing cards covered the top of a long, fold-out table at the front. He lifted his gaze to the highest point. It had to be at least twelve feet high.

He eyed the nearest stripped cot. If he stood, he'd tip over, so he scooted along the dirty vinyl floor until he reached it. Placing both arms along the edge, he managed to lift himself onto the thin foam mattress. The plastic outer shell had cracked along the side, leaving the exposed foam to turn a brownish yellow. He laid on his back, arms splayed out, feet dangling over the edge. Air whooshed out of his lips, and he closed his eyes, willing his muscles to melt into the cot.

The niggling worry returned as soon as he relaxed. He couldn't help feeling like he was in danger but couldn't remember why. Outside noises filtered through his ringing ears. Men moved in and out of tents going about their day-to-day chores and activities. They spoke to one another with comfortable familiarity. A low, raspy voice belted out song lyrics off key, which was answered with hoots and laughter of men standing within earshot.

"Stop!" someone shouted through his snickering.

Another yelled, "Don't quit your day job!"

A short, wiry, man wearing a black suit and tie, pulled back the flap and entered the tent. Jace eyed him warily. What was he supposed to remember? Something about a spider? No. He shook his head. That wasn't it. He'd dreamed of spiders.

The man carried an old-fashioned black doctor's bag. He stared at Jace with uncomfortable intensity. Had he patched up his head?

The man styled his pitch-black hair with a part down the middle. Gel plastered each strand of hair to his head with meticulous care. This is what a thirty-something Alfalfa from the old television show, *The Little Rascals* would look like.

The doctor's bag looked out-of-place in the man's petite, lily-white hands. The whole image the man projected unsettled Jace. The hardness in his flat, brown irises contrasted the soft femininity his physique portrayed.

The man strolled toward him with an unhurried, refined gait. He stopped at the cot, set his bag on the floor, and peered down at Jace. Disconcerting eyes met his.

"Hello. I'm glad you're awake."

The man's baritone voice startled Jace, but he recovered enough to offer a nod in response.

"Do you have any questions before we get started?" the man asked with false politeness.

Unease crept through him.

Started with what?

"Did you bandage my head?" he asked, avoiding the more disturbing questions his mind conjured.

"Yes," he murmured. "You were unconscious over thirty-six hours."

The man responded with the ease of old acquaintances getting together for tea. The time lapse threw him a little off kilter. He'd slept a whole day away. The severity of his injury struck him with the intensity of a freight train. Dylan could've killed him with that damn rock.

Another memory flashed through his head of the militia man who'd tossed him into the tent. Then the image of a black spider replaced the memory.

What was it about those damn spiders?

He closed his eyes. His heart thumped against his rib cage, pumping blood and fear through his veins. He swallowed against the rising bile in his throat.

"What's your name?" he rasped.

"My name is Geoffrey Widdowson. But," he added and coldness crept into his smile, "people call me Widow for short. Maybe you've heard of me?"

Widow. The militia man warned him about a man with that name. That's why spiders had starred in his nightmare. Black widows.

"My memory's sort of sketchy," Jace responded. "Are you a doctor?"

"I am," Widow confirmed. "Harvard degree. You should recover your memory in a few days."

Jace opened his eyes and stared at the tent's tan textile ceiling. Why did his heart ache as if he missed someone? Then like lightning flashing across the sky, he remembered and bolted upright. Lacy. His head rebelled against the sudden movement, and his stomach lurched.

He was trying to get to California when Dylan caught him. Had AJ and Bryan rescued her yet? Sweat beaded his brow. The man beside him might kill him today and separate him from Lacy forever. His heart knocked against his ribcage in an irregular, staccato rhythm. He couldn't let that happen.

The glaring fact he wasn't bound to the cot or in handcuffs wasn't lost on him. They thought him too feeble to put up a fight or try to escape. He did a mental check on his physical condition. They weren't far off. He'd lost too much blood. His body was weak.

"What do you do for the senator?" Jace asked through parched lips.

His tongue stuck to the roof of his dry mouth. He needed water. He needed to get the hell out. But how?

"I'm the resident doctor. He uses me for other things as well," Widow said cryptically.

Jace crossed his arms, trying to project a confidence he didn't feel. "What other things?"

Widow shrugged. "I have a knack for extracting the truth from people."

A spike of adrenaline shot through him, then centered in his head. It felt like someone split his skull in half with an ax.

"What are you going to do to me?" he asked, trying to squash the quiver in his voice, but it bled through anyway.

Widow eyed him with the hunger of a starved lion. "I could do so many delicious things to a pretty boy like you." He feigned a forlorn sigh. "But I have orders from the senator."

Jace raised a wary brow. "Which are?"

"I'm to teach you a lesson." His voice lowered and a thunder cloud of anger appeared on his face. "I can't kill you, but you'll pay for killing Corporal James."

Widow's sudden turn-on-a-dime switch from blasé to fury, shocked him.

"He was my associate in military matters such as these," Widow continued. "And the best mercenary I've ever worked with."

Interesting information. Jace wondered if Widow had intentionally let it slip. If Corporal James had done all the dirty work, then who would do it now?

"So, he did all your dirty work? What's the matter?" he asked forcing a smirk on his face. "You're a doctor. I'm sure you've been desensitized to blood and gore. Is it the violence you can't handle?"

Widow threw his head back and laughed. "My dear boy, you've got it all wrong. The corporal was my muscle." He waved a hand down his body with a flourish. "He did what I could not. Fortunately, the senator gave me a replacement."

A feeling of foreboding settled on his shoulders. "Who's that?"

"I'm so glad you asked," Widow responded, rubbing his hands together in anticipation.

Widow sauntered to the front and flipped open the flap. He motioned for someone to enter, then turned and walked back.

Jace raised his head and watched Dylan enter the tent with a chair, a length of rope, and a gunny sack.

He snorted. "Why am I not surprised?"

Refusing to acknowledge him, Dylan stomped out, then returned hauling two silver feed buckets. Water sloshed over the edges and puddled on the vinyl floor. He repeated the process until ten buckets surrounded the chair set in the center of the tent.

What the hell was going on?

"Thank you, Dylan." Widow tapped his index finger against his pursed lips. "I think I'm going to need the Widow pole. It's in my tent. Will you get it?" he asked Dylan.

"Sure," Dylan responded sullenly and skulked out of the tent.

Jace didn't dwell on Dylan or his poor life choices. He had bigger things to worry about. Like what in the hell was a Widow pole?

Widow picked up his black bag and set it on a wooden TV tray beside the cot. Jace watched as he opened it and pulled out a syringe. He plucked the lid off the needle, tapped the barrel, then expelled the excess air.

Jace's throat bobbed convulsively. "What is that?" he managed.

"Phenobarbital. Just a little anesthetic I like to play with," Widow said breezily.

Before Jace could try and avoid the shot, Widow reached over and stabbed the needle into his leg. His thumb pressed down on the plunger, then he extracted the needle.

Jace jumped up and shoved Widow away from him. "Get the hell away from me."

He staggered, then fell to his knees grasping his head. He couldn't function like this. There was no way he could escape on his own in his condition. No one would come and save him. All hope of surviving vanished. He needed a miracle.

Two men dressed in militia gear helped Dylan carry a pole inside. One end had a shorter pole sticking out horizontally creating an L shape. A diagonal piece of steel acted as a support brace underneath it. Jace stared at the vertical pole in disbelief. A Gallows pole, like hangman, the word game kids played.

"Where you want it?" Dylan asked Widow.

"Right here," he said walking to the tent's center.

The men dropped the pole. It hit the ground with a muted thunk. They turned and walked out, then returned with a heavy piece of square cut steel with a hole in the middle. They lifted the pole and dropped it into the base's center.

The little hairs on the back of his neck stood up as chills raced through him.

They were going to hang him.

Dizziness blurred his vision. He tried to speak, but someone switched everything to slow motion. Even his thoughts slowed.

Willow circled the pole, hands behind his back. He tested the crank that hoisted the pole up and down.

"Very good," he told the men. "String it up, please."

Dylan sighed, grabbed the rope he'd brought, muttering under his breath, "Wish you would've told us before."

It took all three men to lift the pole out of hole. They lowered it, strung the rope through eyelets welded to the pole, then raised it again.

Widow turned to Jace with a glint in his eyes. "Are you ready?"

He managed a slurred, "Leh mee go."

Widow smirked. "No. I'm ready to have some fun. It's been a while and I have all this …," he sucked in a deep breath, puffing out his chest, "pent up energy."

Widow nodded at the men. They sidled up next to Jace, one on each side, and grabbed him under the arms. He tried to fight as they hauled him to his feet, but his feeble slaps didn't faze them. They dragged him under the pole and circled the noose dangling from the rope to his neck. He grabbed it and yanked, but it didn't budge.

Widow turned the crank until the rope was taut. "Let the fun begin!"

37

"Here's a fresh change of clothes and a towel," Laurel said, whipping through the door with businesslike efficiency.

"Thanks," AJ murmured as he watched her deposit the bundle onto the foot of his bed.

He'd slept most of the day, something he hadn't done since his childhood. His body better heal fast because he couldn't hack another day in bed, much less a week or more. Laurel said it would take that long, but he'd prove her wrong. His mom often commented, 'You're standing by the sheer force of your will,' when he was sick or hurt.

"The bathroom's down the hall, to the right. You can bathe but try to keep your chest area dry. The shower head detaches. You can use it to wash your hair," she explained.

"Okay," he agreed, grateful for the chance to clean up. His scalp itched from gritty desert sand.

She started to leave, then stopped midstride. She turned, lasering her brown eyes on him, until he squirmed.

"Can I ask you something?" she finally asked.

He lifted a brow. "Depends."

She leaned against the door jamb. "How much do you

know about what happened to my sister? I've asked her but she's not talking."

He rubbed a hand over his jaw's lengthening whiskers. "Not much," he admitted. "You should wait until she's ready to talk."

She shook her head with vehemence. "I can't do that."

"Why not?"

She shoved off the jamb and began an agitated pace from the door to the window. "I have my reasons."

"I don't think it's …"

She turned from her pacing to face him. "Just tell me what you know," she hissed.

He frowned. "I don't know the details of her abduction, but I know who took her."

She stiffened. "Who?"

"A human trafficking ring based in Mexico City. A powerful man heads it up. I saw him from a distance."

"Do you know his name?" she asked, stepping toward the bed.

His expression hardened. "His last name's Nieto."

"Do you think your sister knows how to get close to him?"

He understood the need for revenge, it roiled inside him too, but he wouldn't sacrifice his sister in any way to get retribution.

He glanced up. "Why do you want to know?"

"Do you know where the man lives? I mean someone's got to know …" she trailed, and her expression turned thoughtful.

"Do you always answer a question with a question?" he asked, annoyed with the whole conversation.

She snapped her gaze to his, her brown eyes liquid heat. "Do you know where Nieto lives or not?"

His lips pressed into a fine line. He tried to block out the pain as he rose to his feet. Standing felt good. He was tired of lying around. Rest didn't assuage his wrung-out emotions.

He'd avoided thinking or dealing with the trauma his sister

went through, both at the farm and with Nieto. But it lurked in the background, his subconscious prodding him to deal with it. Vegetating gave those dark, messy feelings a chance to surface, and Laurel was making it worse. He grabbed the towel and clothes and took a step toward the door.

"Hey." She snagged his arm. "Answer me."

He pried her fingers off, one by one, then said, "Maybe. But I won't let you interrogate my sister. She's been through enough. Why are you asking all these questions anyway?"

Her arm dropped to her side. "Don't you want to make him pay for what he did to our sisters?" she asked, her voice barely audible.

"Of course, I do," he responded, gentling his tone. "He's a monster."

"Then help me," she begged. "Just answer my questions. That's all I ask."

He raised his eyes to the ceiling and sighed. Killing Nieto wouldn't take down the trafficking ring. Someone else would rise and take his place. It was that way in the drug cartel and he suspected it would be no different with a trafficking ring.

No official governmental department like the FBI or CIA was around to ask for help. The president was busy restructuring the country into a totalitarian government. Regardless, he doubted they'd be an effective solution. Nieto had his talons in the Mexican government, so asking them to take care of the problem wasn't a viable solution either.

"As much as I'd love to see Nieto dead, killing him won't solve the trafficking problem," he explained.

Her upper lip curled in a snarl. "I don't care. I want him *dead*."

"Can I take a shower?" he snarked. "While I'm still young?"

"Great," she muttered. "Sarcasm."

They faced each other. She scrutinized him again with a ruthless eye, and he let her. Her judgment of him might be false, if based on what she'd seen so far. He didn't care. As soon as his sister or Bryan came back for him, he'd never see Laurel again.

Or Willow.

The thought was a sharp barb and stuck in his heart. He shut down the introspection and stalked out the door to the bathroom.

After his shower and a long overdue shave, he donned a pair of dark grey sweatpants, and a burnt orange Texas Longhorn's T-shirt. Fog coated the mirror. He took his towel and wiped it off, then examined himself. The T-shirt hid the bandages and made him look normal. His face looked younger without all the scruff he'd managed to scrape off with the dull razor in the shower. He'd missed a couple spots under his jawline, but otherwise was satisfied with the results.

An oval brush sat on the counter, and he made use of it. Water droplets clung to his hair, then fell to his shoulders, darkening the orange T-shirt's material. He took the towel and scrubbed his head, then brushed and parted his hair on the side. Messing up the brush job with his fingers gave him a classic bed head look. A look he loved because it delivered an, 'I don't give a shit,' vibe. Most of the time he didn't. Unless it involved Lacy.

He hung the wet towel over the curtain rod to dry, then walked downstairs. No one seemed to be home. He wondered where the three sisters had gone as he examined the empty living and dining rooms.

An archway off the living room led to an alcove, that served as a small library. The walls were covered floor to ceiling with books. He perused the titles, looking for a story to distract him. He picked up a novel by Stephen King. *Skeleton Crew* was a compilation of short horror stories full of dead corpses, blood, chills, and thrills. Perfect.

A pair of blood red, wingback chairs sat around a small

round oak table. He took a seat in the soft, velvety chair, leaned back, and cracked open the book.

He didn't hear Willow and Scott enter the living room, until their voices bled through the story he was immersed in. His head shot up. He almost followed his first instinct to rise and make his presence known, but something in Scott's tone stopped him. He'd never been an eavesdropper, but this would make his second time today. Shameful. But that didn't deter him. He left his butt right where it sat.

"Come on, Will. You gotta get out of the house sometime."

Scott's words weren't guilt-filled, but there was something underlying his tone. Willow hadn't been back a full day and the guy wanted her out of the house. To go where? She needed to feel safe again. Dragging her to God knew where wouldn't help her feel secure.

"I don't know," Willow dithered. "Laurel won't like me leaving so soon."

Anyone could hear in her tone, she didn't want to go. The guy needed to back off.

"Laurel's not your boss. You're an adult. Make your own decisions," Scott shot back.

"Okay," she said, dragging out the word. "I'm not comfortable going back to Laredo."

Scott muttered something incoherent, then said, "You just don't want to spend time with me," he accused.

"It's not that," Willow denied hotly.

"You want to break up then, don't you?"

AJ's hands contracted into fists. The guy was gaslighting her. Scott's outward smarmy appearance screamed narcissist, and he just confirmed it.

"I ... I don't know what I want, Scott."

"Fine," Scott growled. "Let me know when you figure it out."

Scott stomped to the front door, opened it, then slammed

it shut.

He held his breath. Willow walked into the alcove and sat in the empty wingback to his right.

He gathered his courage, then turned to look at her. "Did you know I was here the whole time?"

"No." She lowered her head, picking at her thumbnail. "I wish you hadn't heard that. Or the conversation this morning," she added, in an accusatory tone.

He reached over and placed a hand over hers. "Stop. You'll make it bleed. Why do you wish I hadn't heard?" he wondered.

"Well, for one thing, it was a private conversation," she spouted, giving him a reprimanding scowl. "And Scott's not like this. Don't judge him harshly for it."

He retracted his hand and snapped the book shut. "Do you really not see it?"

"See what?"

"He controls the conversation in a way that makes everything your fault. And it's not. Let me ask you something." His eyes drilled into hers.

"What?" she asked, biting a fingernail.

"Were you kidnapped in Laredo?"

Blood drained from her face. "Yeah," she whispered.

"And Scott knows that?" he pressed.

"Yes. I was with him when it happened," she uttered through short, uneven breaths.

Her admission sent a shock through him. Why would Scott ask her to return to the place that had to scare the bejesus out of her? He couldn't believe the guy was that dumb.

"So why in God's name would he ask you to go back there?"

She shook her head. "Just let it go, okay? That wasn't Scott's fault either."

He blew a breath out of his nose. "The guy has to be the

most insensitive asshole I've ever met."

"I said drop it," she said, jumping to her feet. "Lacy was right about you."

He raised an eyebrow. "Why? What'd she say?"

"She said you'd steamroll right over me if I ever met you." She let out a huff. "She was right."

He smirked. "I've never done that."

"Oh really?" she challenged. "Did you stand up during a football game she was cheering at and threaten to break a player's hand?"

He tipped his head back and laughed. "The handsy jerk deserved it."

"You're accusing Scott of controlling our conversations, but aren't you doing the same thing?"

He slammed the Stephen King novel on the round table with a thump, wishing his sister hadn't shared that story. It did make him sound overprotective.

"Not at all." He stood and stalked toward her. "I'm simply pointing out the fact that your boyfriend's a self-absorbed, insensitive, conceited …"

She raised a hand. "Stop."

He took a step toward her, and she took one back. They repeated the process until she bumped into a wall.

He leaned in. "I protect those I care about, and for some reason I feel connected to you."

Her chest rose and fell in rapid succession. Her lips parted. He backed up, not wanting her to view him as a threat, and swallowed hard. The urge to kiss her rode him hard.

"I'm not trying to control you, darlin'. I'm trying to protect you. There's a difference."

He turned and left before she could respond, needing a minute to regain his composure. He'd never met a woman who affected him the way she did. Reminding his heart not to get attached, he climbed the stairs, and returned to his room.

If only his heart would listen.

38

Sleep eluded Lacy. No matter how hard she tried, she couldn't find the off switch to her noisy brain. She feigned sleep, avoiding any conversation with Bryan or Geneviève. Her aunt had turned and looked at her several times. She'd felt, rather than saw, the scrutiny. What was the woman thinking? Relaxing facial muscles on command, wasn't easy. She didn't know if she succeeded in easing the V between her brows. The whole charade gave her a tension headache.

Bryan laughed at something her aunt said. She strained to hear, but their words sounded muffled, like watching a television show with the volume too low.

Darkness crowded the truck's interior. No artificial light glowed from the rural towns they sped past, leaving the landscape in obscurity. The half-moon and glittery stars, hidden by clouds, cast down little light. Only the truck's headlights swathed through the solid black night.

The glow from the dashboard gave Bryan's profile a greenish, ghost-like appearance. Fatigue weighed him down. She should take a turn driving the tedious nine-hour drive, but just thinking about stilted, uneasy conversation with her aunt, made her want to chew off an arm.

Her aunt was a stranger. Her uncle, an enemy.

She had nothing to say to either of them.

Thinking of her uncle strained her thinly constructed composure and lit a fire under the boiler inside her. She thought it'd be a great adventure when Thomas Monroe asked her dad if he'd stay at the farm instead of moving to California. Her dad had given him a hard pass, but she hadn't. How naive she'd been. Seven harsh months had passed since then. That young girl vanished like Houdini's elephant, and left a wizened, morally jaded woman in its place.

Bryan slowed the truck then turned. She raised up on her elbows and looked out the passenger window. A giant green dinosaur loomed overhead.

He cut the engine and looked at her over his shoulder. "Truck needs gas."

She nodded, afraid to speak. It might invite unwanted conversation. Her eyes shifted to her aunt. Geneviève leaned her head on the seat's headrest and closed her eyes.

Bryan scrubbed a hand over his face, staring out at the darkness.

"Want me to try and get you an energy drink?" she asked.

He let out a frustrated growl. "How? The station's closed."

She jumped out of the truck and inspected the area. A pop machine, set beside an outdoor ice freezer, glowed bright red and blue. A beacon for all things caffeinated. Giving Bryan's shoulder a nudge, she scooted by him and hefted herself into the front seat. She opened the ash tray, looking for spare change, dollar bills, anything to feed into the dispenser of sugar water and carbonation.

The ash tray gifted her nothing but a few worthless pennies. She snuck a glance at her aunt. Her eyes remained closed, so she snaked an arm by the woman's knees and opened the glove box. And hit paydirt. Dollar bills were stuffed inside like the truck's owner had frequented stripper bars. She grabbed a handful then jumped out and waved them in Bryan's face, grinning like an idiot.

"I'll get us some caffeine. What do you like?" she asked, bouncing on the balls of her feet.

Bryan rolled his eyes and grinned. "You get excited about the weirdest stuff."

"Maybe," she hedged, although he did speak the truth.

She craved Coke like a crack addict.

"Come on, what do you want?" she pressed, walking backward toward the machine.

"Literally anything but Sprite."

"Got your back, Jack," she quipped.

Her enthusiasm dimmed a little when she realized the machine boasted the Pepsi symbol. She wasn't so picky she'd pass up the opportunity for bubbly goodness though.

"You better work," she muttered as she walked up to the appliance.

She fed two dollars into the machine. The mechanism inside hummed then with a clank, dispensed a cold bottle of Pepsi. Almost heaven. Two more dollars disappeared, then a green Mountain Dew bottle clunked down to the opening, bumping into the Pepsi.

She scooped up both bottles, ran back to the truck, then handed Bryan the Mountain Dew. He grunted his thanks before unscrewing the cap. The yellow liquid reminded her of antifreeze or some other type of chemical. She never could make herself drink it, but it provided more caffeine than the others.

He gulped down the whole bottle then chunked it into the truck bed. A comical look passed his face. He placed a hand against his chest. Then belched like lit TNT blowing rocks from a mountain.

She pinched her nose. "Gross."

"Classic," he said with a self-satisfied smile.

"You're a such a goon," she muttered, shaking her head.

He ran a hand through his hair. "I need to sleep a while," he admitted.

"Want me to drive?" she offered.

"No," he said, voice firm. "You need sleep just as much as I do. We won't be any good to anyone if we crash."

He turned, finished fueling the truck, then replaced the handle.

"We better ask *her*," Lacy jabbed a thumb in her aunt's direction, "if she needs to use the bathroom."

"Okay," Bryan agreed. "I'll go around the building first. Check it out and hit the head."

She rolled her eyes as he jogged around the corner, then jumped into the front seat.

"Do you need to use the restroom," she asked, shaking her aunt's shoulder.

Geneviève opened her eyes, focused on Lacy's face, and smiled. "Yeah," she said, stretching out, "I think I do."

Lacy fingered the remaining dollar bills in her pocket. "You want a drink?" she offered, trying to ease some of the guilt she still felt.

"Water would be good," her aunt replied, getting out of the truck.

Bryan jogged back into view.

"Go around the building," she instructed her aunt. "I'll get your water."

Her aunt walked with a dignified glide around the corner. She was much younger than Lacy had expected. She walked to the pop machine, fed more dollar bills inside, then punched the Aquafina button. The bottle rattled inside the machine, then fell out. She grabbed it, ran back to the truck, and deposited it into Geneviève's seat.

Her aunt returned and climbed into the truck. She picked up the water and uttered a small thanks.

Lacy jogged around the building. Brown weeds grew up, untouched, along its side. Spray paint in bubble-lettered graffiti tagged the back side. She read the message as she unbuttoned her pants and squatted. 'Dream' was written in bright green and yellow, and 'choose kind' was bubbled up in pink and purple. Had church kids tagged the building? Whoever did must've drank the Kool-Aid.

She pulled up the too-large pants, cinched the belt, then made her way back to the truck.

Bryan stretched out in the front, an arm over his eyes, already snoring. Her aunt had crawled into the back seat and curled up in the fetal position.

She made her way to the passenger's front seat, then climbed onto the running board, eyes unfocused, staring into the darkness. They'd lose hours stopping to sleep, but Bryan was right. If they didn't take the time to rest, mistakes would be made. And she couldn't afford a mistake. They could get hurt or killed. This plan had to go off without a hitch. Otherwise, they'd all be at the mercy of Thomas Monroe.

LACY OPENED groggy eyes and looked around, getting her bearings. Bryan snored as if he were in a logging contest. She peeked over her shoulder at her aunt who was still slept soundly. She reached over and tapped Bryan's shoulder. He mumbled something she didn't understand, then turned his back on her.

Some people didn't respond well when awakened abruptly, so she proceeded with caution. She tapped his back. Still nothing. Geez, the guy slept like the dead. She scooted closer, tapped his back again, then leaned toward his ear.

"Bryan," she whispered, lightly shaking his shoulder.

"What?" Bryan snorted, then lunged forward, smacking

his head against the side window. "Shit," he muttered, rubbing his forehead.

Lacy covered her wide grin with a hand.

He turned and glared at her. "What are you smiling about? And what was so damn important? You about shook my shoulder off."

She burst out laughing. "I did not. I tried to wake you like a normal human, but you sleep like a noisy corpse."

He grunted, massaging his temples.

"What time is it?" she asked, letting out a huge yawn.

"Bout five, I think," Bryan guessed without consulting his watch.

She considered. "Okay, that puts us there about nine, then?"

He straightened, buckled his seatbelt. "Yup. Let's hit it."

They'd slept longer than Lacy intended. Bryan gunned the engine and pulled out of the Sinclair Station. Awake now, he looked bright eyed and refreshed. It didn't matter how much sleep she gained, her face still carried cuts and bruises from Miguel and Nieto using it as a punching bag. She knew without glancing in the mirror, she looked like a hot mess. Only time would cure it.

She slumped back, but before she could lean her head against the backrest and close herself off, Geneviève leaned forward so she could see her from the back.

Lacy sighed. She didn't want to talk to or get to know her aunt. If she could keep the woman objectified and not see her as an actual person with feelings, it would be easier to use her. That thought alone turned her into someone she didn't want to be. But desperate times …

"I haven't seen you since you were a tiny tot," Geneviève said softly, eyes drinking her in as if Lacy mattered to her.

"I don't remember you at all," Lacy returned curtly.

"I wouldn't expect you to." She hesitated as if she wanted to say more.

Lacy studied the woman as she waited for her to continue. Black hair flowed over a slim shoulder and pale green eyes stared at her with sorrow. Geneviève appeared so young. She thought her aunt and uncle were around her own parent's age, but Geneviève had to be in her late thirties.

She let out an involuntary humph. Her uncle must've married her as a young, naive teenager. It figured her uncle would be some perverted cradle robber.

"I'm sorry for what you've been through. Helping Tommy," she said in a tentative voice.

Lacy crossed her arms. "What do you know about it?" she bit out coldly.

Geneviève pulled manicured fingers through her long hair. "Tommy tries to keep me in the loop. It's shocking Nieto had the nerve to kidnap you."

She sucked in a sharp breath. "Did he tell you that he *knew* Nieto would kidnap me and sent me anyway?"

Her aunt averted her eyes. "He wouldn't do something like that. He's not capable of hurting you."

The last sentence lit her fuse and her carefully constructed composure evaporated. She lifted off the seat like it had ejected her.

Bryan looked at her, worry lines creasing his forehead.

"You have no idea what he's capable of," she shouted.

Her aunt jerked back as if she'd been struck, eyes wide with shock.

A fire burst from within, her face radiating heat. Unwanted tears pricked the back of her eyelids. A guttural noise escaped her lips. She wanted to scream, call her uncle every foul word she could think of, but she couldn't lose it now. Not when she was so close to obtaining her goal. She bent over, hiding her face between her hands. She had to get a grip, lock it down, because if the tempest brewing inside erupted, she'd break apart with it.

Every mile the rolling tires ate drew her closer to Jace. She had no idea if he'd be at the farm. Her uncle could've thrown him in a military prison, sent him to a work camp, or given him another mission. But she'd find him. The thought of seeing Jace calmed her. His handsome face, eyes full of twinkling mirth, swam in front of her closed eyelids.

She breathed in deep and whispered to the image, "There you are."

"I'm sorry," her aunt commiserated. "I had no idea. I still think maybe you've misinterpreted the situation."

She lifted her head, staring at her aunt. So deluded. Too trusting. The air of innocence swirled around Geneviève. Maybe that's why she looked so young.

"Lacy," Bryan warned, glancing at her. "Don't."

In other words, now's not the time. She got the message.

"I haven't misread anything," she sniped.

Biting her tongue, she cut off the spiteful words begging to be released.

Her aunt sat back against the bench seat and closed her eyes. She wanted to unload on the woman, but Bryan was right. She needed to prioritize. Getting themselves untangled from her uncle's sticky web, getting Jace back. Those things came first.

She leaned back against the head rest, then closed her eyelids. She needed a teleporter machine that would whisk her straight to Jace. Why had no one invented one yet? The thought faded into another, just as irrelevant. What if they were all living in the Matrix? Her thinking slowed, then drifted into a heavy sleep.

A few seconds later Bryan's demanding voice penetrated the darkness of her dreamless state. "Lacy. Wake up," he urged.

She strained to open her eyelids. They felt puffy and opened into slits. Dappled sunlight shone through the glass. She recognized the familiar curves of the road, the trees through the glass.

Home.

Emotion bigger than Mount Everest, more momentous and far-reaching than any other she'd experienced in her lifetime, side-swiped her. Violent sobs shook her entire body and then it dawned on her. She never thought she'd make it back. She tried to regain her composure, not wanting to explain her meltdown.

"What's wrong with her?" she heard her aunt ask in a low voice.

"You have no idea what she's been through." Bryan returned harshly. "No one does. She's probably just so damn glad to be home. Let her cry. She needs to."

Snot ran from her nose. The side of her face and the hair behind her ears were soaked with tears. Her heart felt like it would burst out of her chest. She lifted her head at the familiar click, click, click of the tires striking the bridge's concrete deck. They were crossing Kaw Lake.

"We're almost there," Bryan informed her, voice gentle, but firm.

She lifted the bottom of her shirt, wiped her nose, then scrubbed her face with her hands. The cuts stung from salty tears and the bruises along her cheekbone throbbed. She focused on the pain, let it wake her mind and body. Throwing off the last of her sluggishness, she steeled herself for the battle ahead. Her emotions were still a raw mess, but she locked them away to think about later.

Bryan pulled the truck into the farm's long, gravel drive, then cut the engine by the farmhouse closest to the highway. Geneviève reached for the door handle, but Bryan punched the locks.

He turned and stared at Lacy. "How do you want to play this?"

His grave tone settled deep in her bones. Her eyes met his.

Geneviève leaned forward. "What's going on, Bryan?" she asked, bewildered.

A debate warred within her. Informing her aunt of her plans and why they were necessary, would be the right thing to do. She wouldn't do it. Cowardly? Without a doubt.

She nodded once at Bryan. He punched the lock button and the door locks clicked open. She opened the passenger door and hopped out in one fluid motion. She opened the back passenger door, grabbed the pistol from the floorboard, then waited for her aunt to climb out.

Her aunt stepped down, careful not to scuff her shoes on the truck's running board. Gravel crunched under her patented block heels.

Lacy snuck behind her aunt, wrapped an arm around her neck, jerking her backward. She squeezed her forearm against Geneviève's throat. The woman's arms flailed at her sides, like a goose flapping its wings.

"The less you struggle, the easier it will be on you," Lacy whispered in a calm even tone. "I don't want to hurt you."

Bryan jumped out of the truck and jogged toward the smaller farmhouse where her uncle stayed.

"Why are you doing this?" Her aunt's voice trembled.

She tightened her grip, jabbing the pistol's barrel into her aunt's ribcage. "Ask your husband," she snarled.

Bryan's swift appearance cut off her next venomous words. He prodded her uncle out the back door and down the steps. Her uncle's eyes bulged at the sight of the gun embedded in his wife's side.

"Gen," he gasped.

Her uncle's fear sent tingles racing over her body. The plan was going to work. She'd make him feel fear. She wanted to shock Thomas Monroe to his core. He deserved this, and more.

"What are you doing?" he shrieked, racing forward.

"Don't come any closer," she growled, wrenching her aunt back a step.

Her lip instinctively curled into a snarl. Her baser instincts knew how to instill fear.

Monroe skidded to a halt and raised his hands. "Okay, okay. We can talk about this."

The bitter morning wind blew across Lacy's heated face. "No!" she screamed. "I ought to blow her brains out right here! You had *no right* to screw with our lives the way you have. And now you're gonna pay."

She raised the gun to her aunt's temple.

"Please," her uncle begged, dropping to his knees.

She heard the painful thump of his kneecaps against the frozen ground. Wind blew his salt and peppered hair sideways. In this position, he seemed more like an old man than the monster he'd proven himself to be.

"Why should I show you any kindness at all when all you've done is use me, Jace, and my friends?"

His hands came together, supplicating. "I'll do anything."

Geneviève cleared her throat. "Tommy, you've got to tell her."

His hands fell to his sides, face crestfallen for a scant second. If she'd blinked, she would've missed it because a hardness swiftly crept over his features.

"What's she talking about?" Lacy questioned, eyes narrowed.

"Nothing," her uncle deflected. "Just let her go. Now."

His fear dissipated in a snarl, and the evil monster rose to the surface.

"Not until you give me what I want."

Her emotions settled like silt at the bottom of a pool. She knew what she wanted. This was a transaction. Nothing more. Her aunt's body trembled underneath her hold. The woman wouldn't take much more before collapsing from sheer fright.

"What do you want?" her uncle asked, rising back to his feet.

"I want to be free from you. Let Jace and Bryan, and all my friends go. I never want to see you again."

"Tommy, please." Her aunt began to cry.

"Fine," he said, eyes boring into hers.

"Where's Jace?" she finally asked, fearful of the answer.

Monroe turned to Bryan. "He's in the senator's old tent. Tell them I sent you, and to let him go."

Bryan raced down the drive, out of sight.

"Now let her go," he demanded.

"No. Not until I see Jace."

Her aunt stiffened, breathing erratic. "Tommy, tell her!" she shrieked.

"What is she talking about?" Lacy demanded.

Monroe's shoulders slumped forward, and defeat dimmed his eyes. "Gen, let's not walk down this path."

"If you don't tell her, I will," she threatened.

"Fine," he conceded grudgingly.

He took a hesitant step forward.

Lacy shook her head for him to stop.

"Lacy." He rubbed the back of his neck, averting his eyes.

"What?" she shouted. "Just say it."

Her aunt took a sharp breath.

"Okay." He lifted his eyes to the cloud-leaden sky. "You're our daughter."

39

It was horrifying to think men like Widdowson existed. The media showcased, even glorified men like him. But it never hit home until now.

Until he became the victim.

Click … click. The sound of metal teeth popping into place hurt Jace's ears. The rope dug into his neck. With every turn of the pole's crank, it squeezed his airway shut a little more. He stood on the tips of his toes, struggling for breath. Widow circled the pole with an unhinged glint in his eyes.

He shuddered to think of all the women who'd been abducted by men like Widow. The terror they faced. The terror he faced now, overwhelmed him. It was the nightmare's salty ocean water, stealing oxygen from his lungs.

"Hmm," Widow purred. "I'm loving this look on you, pretty boy. You're so helpless." He clapped his hands like child at Christmas.

Click. Widow turned the crank again.

Jace gasped.

The weak attempt to draw in air excited Widow. "Oh yeah, pretty boy," Widow growled, low and guttural. "I want to hear you scream."

The hairs on his neck stood up. He fought to drag in one last breath. Darkness spread from the corner of his eyes, darkening his vision. His hands dropped, dangling at the sides of his torso. He closed his eyes. Lacy's image swam into view. His heart ached over the goodbye he sent to her, wherever she might be.

The rope suddenly gave, and Jace crumpled to the ground. Widow dragged him until he lay prostrate on the tent's floor, then pinched his nose, and gave him a breath. Jace's chest expanded. He dragged in oxygen, grabbing his neck as pain ricocheted over his body. Darkness receded from his eyes, and a painful tingling sensation circulated to his limbs. He sucked in a sharp breath, then another, until his body calmed.

"Get him in the chair," Widow ordered.

Dylan grabbed him under the arms, hauled him to the chair by the pole, then hefted him up. When Dylan let go, he fell to the side, unable to keep himself upright. The muscles in his neck strained under his head's weight. Dylan righted him, keeping a hand on his shoulder to steady him.

Widow disappeared from his view. The nightmare's ocean roared in his ears. Before he could react, Widow shoved a wet rag into his mouth, then thrust the gunnysack over his head. A rope wound around his neck, securing it. Another rope encircled his forehead, wrenching it backward. He reached up to free himself, but Widow grabbed both hands, forcing them behind the chair. A zip tie cinched his wrists together. His left shoulder popped, sending a jolt of pain down his arm.

He couldn't see. The oceanic crash and boom in his ears impaired his hearing. But he sensed Widow standing behind him. His brain, still fuzzy from the injection, refused to function. He couldn't see a way out. The one thing he saw was his death. The time he'd spent with Lacy might've been fleeting compared to a lifetime, but he'd hang onto those memories until the end.

"This technique," Widow began, "is called waterboarding. It was invented in the 16th century by the Chinese."

"Who cares?" Dylan mumbled.

Unfazed, Widow continued his diatribe on the effectiveness of water torture.

A bucket's bail handle clanked behind him. Sweat pricked his forehead. Drowning was one of his greatest fears.

The memory of a little idyllic pool hidden along Salt Creek sprang to mind. Best fishing hole in the county. Lily pads grew in abundance, floating on the surface of the brackish water. His father thought it would be the perfect place for Jace to learn to swim. He was six when his dad tossed him into that water, fully clothed, and unsuspecting.

He sank like a lead ball to the bottom. When he tried to push upward toward the surface, his foot caught on an old tree root. Panic set in. He struggled to free himself, but his shoe wouldn't give. He pried his foot out of the shoe and shot to the surface. His mother had been furious when she found out. It took many years before he'd go near water again.

Water poured over his head, saturating the rag in his mouth. The memory faded. Water filled his mouth and nose, trailing down his throat. He swallowed, then swallowed again. He held his breath but couldn't stop his body from sucking water into his lungs. He coughed, gagged, sputtered.

The empty bucket clattered to the ground. Jace caught a few breaths, then it started all over. The lack of oxygen began weakening his body. He saw his mother standing at the tent's opening, a hand stretched out, a smile on her face.

"Mom," he whispered.

He blinked, and she appeared in front of him. "Son."

Her soft, lilting voice comforted his soul. He'd missed her.

"You have a choice," she continued.

Warmth stole over him, his body's every cell responding to her words.

"What choice?" he managed, keeping tears at bay.

"You can come with me," she said with a smile.

Shock rippled through him. "Die?"

A spark lit inside him. The will to fight for his life sang in his bones for the first time since Widow began his torture.

His mother's smile slipped a little. "Or you can choose to stay."

Her eyes roamed over him as if committing every part of him to memory.

"Mom, I —"

The tent flap flew open. Cold air burst inside, chilling the water, and sweat on his skin. Muscles contracted, as uncontrollable shivers raced over him. His groggy mind wondered what was happening.

"Stop," a stern voice commanded.

He recognized the man who'd given the order. He couldn't believe it.

"I'm not finished," Widow objected.

"I don't care, you sick bastard. Cut those ropes," the voice demanded.

The smack of a fist on flesh came from behind him, then a body thumped to the ground. The metal click of a knife opening was his only warning before the rope went slack around his forehead. His head slumped forward. The man ripped the gunnysack from his head, removed the rag, then cut the zip tie holding his hands. With their release, he tumbled out of the chair sideways.

"Get out, Dylan," the man growled, disgust dripping from every syllable. "You're lucky I don't shoot you," he added with a snarl.

Another gust of bitter air blew in as footsteps hurried out.

The man squatted beside Jace. "Come on, we've gotta go."

Jace opened his leaden eyelids. "I can't buhleeve …"

"They give you something?"

He nodded, unable to get his thick tongue around another word. The man hefted him over his back, rose to his feet, then walked out of the tent.

"Man, she's gonna detonate when she sees you," he muttered.

40

The words her uncle spoke bounced out of her ears like a rubber ball. The arm she'd wrapped around her aunt's throat slackened and she stumbled back a step.

What did he just say?

An apprehensive voice spoke. "I know you must have a million questions."

Her aunt's guarded voice sounded far away. As if spoken in a wind tunnel, the words whirled away like autumn's desiccated leaves.

"No," Lacy denied, casting her eyes to the ground.

She couldn't grasp the words long enough to process them. They were a phantom, there, then gone, with a lingering whisper of the truth to haunt her.

"It's true," her uncle continued in a flat, resigned voice.

All strength fled from her arms, and they fell to her side. Her aunt pitched forward as she dropped on all fours, landing with a painful thud onto the gravel. The gun skittered away from her like a rock skipping across a pond.

Thomas Monroe ran, whisked his wife into his arms,

placing kisses on her head and face, murmuring soft words of comfort.

They were … *what?*

Sobs tore from deep inside her. Tremors ran through every nerve, agitating her stomach. What little remained of yesterday's soup and the Pepsi she'd drank, gushed out.

How could this be possible?

Their *daughter?*

Her mind tossed the revelation out of her head, but her uncle's haunting words rushed back.

It's not true.

AJ's my brother.

Emmett and Lila are my parents.

That was final.

Her uncle was just trying to mess with her head. But the second her heart agreed with her rationale, her uncle's words came back like a boomerang. With sharp, throwing star points, it sunk into her heart so deep, she didn't think it could be dug out.

Dry heaves surged out of her until her mind blurred. In one second, her whole life crumbled. Three devastating words. Three. That was all it took to level her world.

Everything she thought she knew about herself was gone. Poof. She wasn't Emmett Monroe's daughter. Emmett. The kind son. Less ambitious, therefore less valuable to her grandmother. But he was the one who'd instilled Christian values into her. Values she'd tossed aside when it came to survival.

Was she born bad? Like her uncle? Would her brother have made the same decisions she had if their places had been reversed?

Her chest heaved as more dry heaves forced their way up. Someone squatted down beside her, then a gentle hand ran down her back.

"Lacy." Bryan's quiet voice broke through the tumultuous storm raging inside her.

She hadn't even noticed his return. She turned, raised a hand, and wiped her mouth. Whimpering, she fell into his chest, grabbed his shirt, and clung to him. With everything they'd suffered together, he was like a brother, and she held on to the comfort he offered.

"What did you do?" Bryan thundered at her uncle.

His head dipped to hers. "What happened?"

She shook her head, unable to admit the truth.

He stroked her hair. "Lacy, I have Jace."

Her head jerked up, searching for him. Her lifeline. Where was he? She started to rise, but Bryan held her in his arms.

"Tell me what happened," Bryan urged. "You were fine when I left. What did he do to you?"

"He said," she hiccupped, "that I … I'm their daughter," she stuttered.

Bryan's head turned to the couple huddled together a few feet away. "Is it true?" he demanded.

"It is," her uncle confirmed.

Bryan swore, wrapped his arm around her waist, and helped her off the ground. "I'm so sorry," he said, guiding her toward Jace. "Lacy." He halted, grasped her red, swollen face between his hand. "I know this is a lot to take in all at once, but Jace is in bad shape. I don't know what all that bastard, Widow, did to him, but —"

Her head whipped from Bryan to Jace, crumpled on the ground, eyes closed. His washed-out features made him look like a corpse. If it weren't for his chest rising and falling, she would've sworn he was dead. Her anger intensified, singeing her veins.

The nail had been clinched. Her uncle had gone too far. Like a jet, her heart raced faster than the speed of sound, breaking the barrier of her self-control. An internal sonic boom reverberated through her.

She wrenched away from Bryan, eyes searching for the weapon she'd dropped. Her eyes landed on the metal glinting from the sun's morning rays. She ran and scooped it off the ground, flicking rocks and dirt from her hand.

Her face burned as she turned and rushed toward her aunt and uncle. "What the hell did you do?" she screamed.

Before she could reach the couple, Bryan grabbed her by the waist. "Lacy don't do this," he said, hands firm against her hipbone.

She fought his hold on her. Eyes still on the senator, she cursed him.

"Why did you do it? Why? You almost killed him!" she shrieked.

His body went rigid, and the look he gave her was stone cold. "He killed an important man of mine. He had to be punished."

"He isn't yours to punish, you sick bastard!" she shouted, then rammed an elbow into Bryan's ribs. "Let go of me!"

Bryan grunted but didn't let go. His grip tightened. "No. Think of Jace. He needs rest. Is there anywhere we can go?"

She stopped struggling. Jace. He needed her. "Yeah."

Her throat felt raw, as if she'd swallowed sandpaper. She handed the pistol to Bryan, then rushed back to Jace. She dropped to her knees, eyes roaming over his familiar features. Black bruises marred the perfect lines of his face. The dirty bandage wound around his head sagged with water, blood, and dirt. He was wet from head to toe and shivering. Her eyes landed on his throat. A slash of red encircled his neck.

"What have they done to you?" she whispered.

"Don't move, Senator," Bryan threatened, then walked over and knelt beside her.

"Why is he wet?" she asked him, confused.

Bryan's brows slashed down. "Water torture."

Shock sent wave after wave of pin pricks over her skin. Why had he been treated like a spy? She'd seen water used as a torture device in movies. Who in their right mind would make another human suffer that way?

"Why?" she asked, horrified. "He wasn't a spy."

"Because Widow's a sadist," he spat.

The back door slammed. Bryan's head shot up. They were beginning to draw attention. Dylan walked from the pasture, several militia men in tow. His hand rested on his side piece as he sidled up beside the senator.

The senator's assistant, William, walked out the back door, hair matted to the side of his head. Bare feet slapped the ground as he descended the porch steps. He rubbed his eyes, looking around owlishly.

"Everything okay?" he asked Monroe.

A bubble of panic rose to the surface. She glanced at Bryan. "We need to get out of here. Now."

Bryan bent down, looped his arms under Jace's armpits, then hefted him up. Jace, barely conscious, wobbled, trying to plant his feet on ground.

She pressed a firm hand on his back, then leaned over and rested her head against his shoulder. The last six days seemed more like six years, and all she wanted was to climb into a bed with him, and sleep in his arms. Forget her uncle's devastating words. Forget the last week ever happened.

She raised her eyes to Bryan's. "We need to get him loaded in the truck, then find another vehicle."

Bryan gave her a quizzical look.

"You need to go back to Texas and get my brother," she reminded him quickly. "Jace and I can't wait for you to get back."

Bryan nodded, guiding Jace forward. "We'll get AJ's truck. It's over at Diehl's."

He grunted as he helped Jace into the back seat.

"Lacy," Geneviève called.

She whirled around. "What?" she shouted, flinging her arms in the air.

The woman disentangled herself from the senator's embrace.

"Gen," the senator warned, "don't do this."

Her aunt wrung her hands together. "I've loved you your whole life. I want you to know that."

She shook her head as a strangled noise escaped her lips. A lump wedged in her throat, and the hot, salty tears she'd stayed, started to fall again.

Her lips trembled and she pointed at her aunt and uncle. "You'll *never* be anything to me. Emmett and Lila are my parents. They'll always be my parents."

A thundercloud passed over her uncle's face. "Do not disrespect your mother."

Disgust welled within her. It was easier to feel anger, disgust, contempt, than to acknowledge the hurt trying to rear its ugly head over why they'd thrown her away like a piece of trash.

She jabbed a finger at them. "You're nothing to me. Got it? I never want to see either of you again."

Her aunt gasped, crestfallen. "No," she begged. "Please … I'd like to explain."

Heat flooded her system. She didn't want to hear their excuses. "You don't get to explain. If I decide I want to know, I'll ask my *real* parents. As for now? I just want to get as far away from the both of you as possible." Her eyes lasered on her uncle. "And if you ever try and find me again, I'll kill you."

He narrowed his eyes but kept his mouth shut. She couldn't help her parting words for all the tea in China.

She lifted a brow. "If you don't believe me, ask your friend, Nieto. I stabbed him and killed two of his men."

The shock covering her uncle's features was worth the confession. She buried the small amount of guilt she felt over her aunt's distress, turned her back on them, then jumped into the back seat with Jace. Bryan revved the engine, then threw the truck in reverse. Tires ground into the gravel leaving ruts in their wake as he tore out of the drive. He turned onto another gravel road, headed for AJ's truck.

Jace's breath stuttered. He bent forward, coughing, grabbing at his neck. She scooted forward. His eyes bulged in fear and panic.

She wrapped her arms around his shoulders. "Hey," she said in a calm, even tone. "It's okay. Calm down."

He turned his head and looked at her as if she'd appeared out of thin air. A ghost.

"Lacy?" he rasped.

"Yeah," she said on a shaky breath, trying to smile through her tears.

The whites in his eyes had turned blood red, causing the blue irises to glow. With surprising strength, he wrapped his arms around her and drew her close.

He nuzzled his head into her neck. "Thank God. I thought I was going to die," he managed.

His vocal cords crackled with the word's vibration as if they'd been crushed into bits of gravel.

Wet tears ran down her neck and her heart faltered.

He was crying.

She touched his cheek, then laid her head on his chest. "Me too."

"I'm so sorry. I never should've …" He cleared his throat, then continued, "left you."

Tears burned her eyes. "It's okay," she whispered.

He shook his head. "No. I should've fought for you. For us. I'll never forgive myself —"

She raised her head and placed her lips against his, cutting off the rest of his self-degradation. Her lips feathered against his, light and sweet. When she'd gained his full attention, she leaned back.

"You have nothing to be forgiven for, Jace," she said softly. "I'm just so damn grateful you're with me now."

She echoed his words from the day they'd been separated.

He studied her face with a peculiar expression, then ran his hands through her hair.

"What is it?" she asked.

He cupped his hands around her warm cheeks. "I'm wondering if you're a dream."

Her lips tipped up. "I'm real."

His chest rose and fell in broken sobs, whispering "I love you," over and over.

Emotion, bright and big as the sun, swelled within her, pushing out the dark, and the ugly. She snuggled against his chest, never wanting to leave.

Bryan pulled up beside a huge, weathered barn. Time and neglect had caved in the back side, leaving it open to birds, and other critters, wanting shelter from the elements. AJ's truck sat inside the structure's sturdier section. Birds swooped from under the roof, cawing their angst over being disturbed.

He eyed her through the rearview mirror. "Where are we going? You okay to drive?"

"Hitt's old cabin, and yeah, I'm good," she murmured, head still nestled against Jace's chest. "Just give us a minute."

Without another word, Bryan opened the door, hopped down, shutting it behind him. Jace hadn't relented his hold on her yet, and she wouldn't force him to.

She didn't know how long they stayed, their souls repairing the bond between them. But when they broke apart, the sun had disappeared over the barn's decrepit roof. His body shuddered, reminding her he was wet.

"We should go," she reluctantly suggested. "You need out of those wet clothes."

He bent his forehead to hers. "I don't want to. I'm so sorry I let you go. I'll never make that mistake again," he swore.

She disentangled herself then slid over and opened the door. He grabbed her hand before she had a chance to step down.

"I meant what I said," he whispered, rubbing a thumb over the back of her hand.

Their eyes met. "I know."

Promises.

That's just what it was. A promise. But the difference between a promise kept and a promise broken was circumstance. Her uncle had taught her that.

41

B ryan was sound asleep, curled into a sleeping bag by the fireplace when Lacy nudged the door open with her shoulder. Jace leaned on her, almost toppling them both as she'd half-dragged him up the porch steps.

She led him past the threshold to the bed. They both tumbled onto it, his weight, and the death grip around her waist, forced her down with him. They landed with a bounce on their sides. The old springs creaked in protest. She would've laughed if his condition hadn't been so serious.

Jace's eyelids closed, his hand around her waist falling lax against her side. She needed to get him out of his wet clothes.

"Jace," she whispered, touching his cheek. "Wake up."

He mumbled something incoherent, turned his head, and kissed her palm. His gentle lips against her skin sent her heart racing. Her eyes traced the lines of his face. Stubble sprouted along his bruised jaw. His body trembled, reminding her of his wet condition.

She rose and knelt beside him. "We need to get you into something dry."

Grasping the hem, she tugged the damp T-shirt to his armpits.

"Raise up," she grunted, trying to slide the shirt over his head.

As the fabric covered his face, he jerked upright, knocking her out of the way with his arm. She landed with a thud, striking her hip against the footboard.

She clenched her teeth. "Shit," she muttered, sitting back up.

Jace's chest heaved. "Get it off! Get it off!" he shouted, as he fought to free himself of the shirt. His nails scraped up one arm, breaking the skin in his struggle.

Startled out of sleep, Bryan bolted to a standing position, forgetting the sleeping bag zipped around his body. Bryan's leg tried to step forward but got caught in the web of the sleeping bag.

"Umph," he grunted, falling flat on his face. "Damn, that hurt," he complained, fighting the bag to free himself.

Lacy scrambled on her knees to Jace.

She placed a cautious hand on his arm. "Hey," she said in a soothing tone, "let me help."

He gasped through the shirt's cotton fabric, body radiating tension. "Okay," he agreed hoarsely.

She stretched the arm hole down, then bent his elbow and slipped his arm through. His shaky hands freed himself from the rest of the stretched-out shirt, then he flung it across the room. Eyes still wild, he ran a hand through his hair. He touched the gash at the back of his head and winced.

"I'm a little spooked," he admitted, falling back against the mattress.

"Well, that was fun," Bryan scoffed.

He unzipped the sleeping bag, shoved it down to his ankles, then kicked it off the rest of the way.

She fought the amusing smile turning her lips up and stifled a laugh. "It was for me."

"Shut up," he said muting his own laugh.

"Can you find Jace some clothes?" she asked, returning to

the problem at hand.

"Sure. I noticed AJ's bag in his truck. I'll go get it," he said, grabbing an old flannel jacket from a peg by the door.

He returned, bag in hand, and set it by the bed. "I'm gonna go out and gather more firewood," he said, then walked back out.

She never would've pegged Bryan as a sensitive person. He didn't seem to be in high school. The short conversations she'd had with him as they fled Mexico, led her to believe his home life wasn't great. Away from that environment, his real personality shined through. He must've known they needed privacy, if only for a while, and she was grateful for it.

She reached down and pulled the bag onto the bed. Her brother's old gym bag had seen better days. She unzipped it, pulled out a pair of jeans, ripped at the knees, and a black and white flannel button down.

She turned to Jace. "Can you sit up?"

He rose on an elbow, then pushed himself up. He shrugged on the button down with her help. She left it unbuttoned, not wanting him to feel anything constricting around his neck. She tugged on his wet boots, chunking them on the floor, then peeled off his socks.

He unbuttoned his jeans, pushed them down to his knees. She pulled them off, then placed them by the fireplace to dry. He pulled down the comforter and got in.

She pointed at the jeans. "You don't want them on?"

"No," he said, stretching his hand out for her. "Come here."

She walked to the side of the bed. He pulled her down against him, then sighed deeply. They lay in silence, listening to the cabin creak as gusts of wind battered against its north side.

The fire crackled and popped, shooting embers out of the grate. They smoldered on the stone hearth, then died. Jace kept sucking in air as if it were his last. Whoever Widow was messed with not only his physical body, but his mind as well. She should've shot her uncle. If she thought it would make a difference, she might've.

But killing her uncle didn't change what had already happened. She'd been kidnapped and Jace had been tortured. Killing him wouldn't turn back the clock. Although revenge tasted sweet, it was short-lived. Still, the temptation to go back to the farm and make her uncle pay for using them in his political game was strong. She forced her thoughts back on Jace, refusing to go down that rabbit hole.

"Jace," she said his name reverently, snuggling closer, wrapping an arm around his waist, mindful of any unseen injuries.

"Mh-hm?" he mumbled.

"What happened?" she asked tentatively.

He turned toward her until their bodies lay flush, then opened his eyes.

"I thought …" His throat caught and his eyes sheened brightly. "I thought I'd lost you for good."

"But what —"

He pressed his battered lips against hers and all thoughts of talking fled. His hand wrapped around her neck, deepening the kiss. She melted into it, surrendering.

JACE KNEW the kiss would divert her from asking the battery of questions she held. They needed to talk, but he needed time to process the torture Widow had inflicted upon his mind and body. Losing his shit over the T-shirt rattled him more than he was willing to admit.

His abused body needed rest, but Lacy needed him more. He didn't know what she'd been through, but his situation would no doubt pale in comparison.

He concentrated on her, deepening the kiss. Tasting,

exploring what he thought he'd lost forever. He reveled as he felt her surrender with no hesitation, no reservations. His hand ran down the side of her neck, feather light. They needed this connection more than they needed to talk, more than he needed rest. More than he needed air.

After several minutes, Lacy drew back. He felt her reluctance as she placed both hands against his cheeks. His eyes locked on hers, searching for the reason.

"You need rest and if we keep going ..." she trailed off with a smile.

"If I moved on to the next life making love to you, I'd have no regrets," he stated simply.

Color tainted her cheeks, and she dipped her chin. "But I would."

He gave a soft laugh and released his hold on her. "Okay."

As soon as he relented, his eyelids closed, and his body relaxed into the mattress. She leaned over him, her black hair falling over her shoulders.

"Do you need Cat to look you over? I can't tell how serious your injuries are," She hesitated. "We could go back and try to get her."

Worry saturated the air around her.

"Cat and the others aren't at the farm," he explained, fingering a lock of her hair. "They should be at Edwards' place by now."

Surprise lifted both brows. "Oh. That's good though."

"It is," he agreed.

She leaned back on her knees. "Jace, if you need a doctor or something, you need to tell me. How's your head? That gash needs staples. And your voice ..."

He cleared his throat. "I'm —"

She pointed a finger at him. "Don't you dare say fine. You're not *fine.*"

"There's nothing a doctor can do. I just need to rest. I'll admit, Dylan cracked my head pretty good."

She frowned. "Dylan?"

"He's in the Texas militia now doing whatever the senator wants."

"Figures," she muttered. "And Gracie?"

"With Cat and the others."

She sighed in relief. "Well, that's something."

"Stop worrying and lay down with me," he coaxed, holding open his arms. "You can help me recover."

She shook her head, smiling but before she could relent, Bryan opened the door, his arms loaded down with firewood. He dumped the load by the hearth, then brushed off his coat sleeves.

"There's a stack of wood by the door. That should do ya for a day or two," he said striding back to the door. "I'm gonna head out, go get AJ."

"You need to sleep," Lacy objected.

"I caught me a good couple hours. If I get tired, I'll stop," he assured her.

Jace watched sadness creep over her face. "Okay. Tell him I love him."

"You going to see your parents when Jace is up to travel?" he asked.

"No," she stated flatly.

Jace searched her face. "Why?"

He thought that would be the first thing she'd want to do. It was all she could talk about six days ago. What changed?

She flicked her hair back over her shoulder. "I want to see the Pacific. Sink my toes into the sand."

"What do you want me to tell AJ?" Bryan asked.

"Tell him everything," she said, darkness edging her voice.

He gave a short nod, hand on the doorknob.

"Bryan," she started as he opened the door. "Don't be a stranger."

He grinned. "Aw, don't go getting soft on me now, Monroe. You'll destroy your bad ass image."

She flipped him the bird which made him throw his head back and laugh.

"Seriously," she said rising from the bed. She walked over, wrapped her arms around him, and squeezed. "Thank you."

"Anytime," he quipped. "And hey, I'll be around."

She stepped out of the embrace. "Good."

He closed the door on a soft click.

She turned around facing the bed where Jace laid, waiting for her. She bent down, unlaced AJ's boots, then toed them off her feet. She unbuckled the belt holding up the oversized pants and let them fall to the floor. Stepping out of them she walked to the bed and slid under their shared blanket and snuggled against him.

"I wish I'd been there," he murmured. "It killed me not being able to go get you."

"I know," she soothed, running a soft hand down his arm. "Sleep. We'll talk later."

He turned into her, buried his nose against the crook of her neck and dropped into sleep.

42

It was ironic how days seemed to meld together into one giant string of events, indecipherable in their own scheduled twenty-four-hours.

AJ placed both arms behind his head, stretching his pierced mid-section. He breathed through the pain, staring at the morning sunlight dancing a happy, carefree jig along the ceiling. When had he and Bryan left the farm? The harrowing, nighttime flight to Mexico City from New Mexico still raised the hairs on the back of his neck. It was safe to say he'd had enough mad cap rescue missions to last a lifetime. He'd happily stick to cows and horses.

The lumpy twin mattress kept him restless. Its springs played Dig Dug into his back all night. He placed his hands down on the mattress and pushed himself up to the headboard. He detested the inconvenience of being shot. He ran both hands through his hair, swung his legs over the side, and stood.

His heart pounded painful thumps that vibrated in his ears. He searched the bedside table for painkillers. Two white tablets sat in contrast to the small table's black surface along with a glass of water. Laurel must've brought those during the night. That was considerate. Then he remembered their conversation from the day before and frowned.

Being nice still wouldn't get her the answers she sought. He plucked the pills off the table, threw them into his mouth, then greedily gulped the water down.

It wasn't just Lacy he worried about when it came to Nieto. If Laurel, by some miracle, managed to get close to the man, he still doubted she'd be successful in killing him. Nieto was smart. It would be foolish to underestimate him. It was a damn miracle they escaped. If Laurel failed and was captured, he didn't want Lacy's name embroiled with the fiasco.

He ran his hands down his wrinkled shirt, made a quick bathroom stop, then made the painstaking descent down the stairs. He white-knuckled the banister all the way to the bottom.

The three sisters sat around the kitchen table in a heated debate. He didn't hear what they said, but tension hung thick in the air. Laurel shushed an animated Olive as he entered. She sat back, face red, arms crossed. Willow looked exhausted.

Had she not slept well? He made a mental note to check on her later when Laurel and Olive weren't around.

The country kitchen, decorated with farm animals, exuded a cheerful warmth. Coffee percolated in a Bunn machine, its pungent aroma filling the air. One carafe, halffull, sat on the machine's warmer. He walked to the dish drainer by the sink and plucked a mug from the rack. He'd gotten over the disgusting stink from the helicopter ride much faster than he'd thought possible. Plus, he needed the caffeine.

"Talk to him again, Laurel."

Olive's attempt at a whisper sounded more like an angry cat's hiss.

He poured the steaming coffee into his cup, then debated whether to go back up to his room or sit down with the trio.

"Have a seat," Laurel offered, hand outstretched toward an empty seat to her left.

He let out an audible sigh, ambled over, and plunked himself down.

"Brave choice," Willow commented with a half-smile.

He chuckled. "Maybe."

"Are you going to answer my question?" Laurel asked with a raised brow.

He blew into his coffee, berating himself for sitting down, but Willow looked like she needed some support. *Sucker*. He should've known Laurel wouldn't drop the subject. Instead of answering her inquiry, he asked a question of his own.

"Does Willow know what you're planning?"

"What does that matter?" Laurel snapped.

"You're doing it again," AJ smirked, deflecting.

"What?"

Now she looked flustered as well as frustrated. He was beginning to enjoy this.

"Answering a question with a question," he replied.

"You did it first," she sputtered. "Just answer the damn question."

He crossed his arms, leaned back onto the chair's spindled back, and smirked. "Which one?"

"You're being a dick," Olive interjected, mimicking his actions by leaning back and crossing her arms. "Why won't you tell us where Nieto lives?"

His eyes darted to Willow who'd blanched at the mere mention of that foul man's name. Why were Laurel and Olive pursuing this? Any idiot could see this conversation distressed her.

"Willow was there," he said evenly. "Did you ask her?"

If he forced them to address Willow, maybe they'd see how upset they were making her. And stop.

"You know she can't tell us. She doesn't know the area. You figured out where he lives, and I know you can tell us *how* to get there." Laurel said through clenched teeth.

The doorbell's three-note chime sounded from the hallway.

"I got it," Willow said, jumping up. Her chair teetered on its back legs, then righted itself back to the floor with a solid thunk.

He watched her retreating with knitted brows. His jaw muscle ticked. Scott was probably on the other side of that door, and he wished he'd stay there. Some innate part of him didn't trust the man and not just because of his interest in Willow. He couldn't put a pin in it. The guy was, he searched for a word to match his gut feeling but came up empty. He was just off somehow.

"Well fuck a duck," Olive said, slapping a hand down on the table.

He jumped, then jerked his head from the doorway back to the two women at the table. Olive stared at him with a shit-eating grin on her face.

"What?" he asked, raising a mocking brow.

She waggled her eyebrows. "You got a thang for Will."

"Don't be ridiculous," Laurel admonished.

AJ felt heat extend to the tips of his ears. Everything about him exuded Cool Hand Luke. He could bluff a card shark, unless they knew his one tell. His ears. Damn, he wished he could figure out a way to control it.

"Look at him," Olive swung a hand his direction, then jumped up.

She circled the back of his chair, clucking her tongue, then stopped. She touched the tip of his ear.

He slapped her hand away. "Cut that shit out, will ya," he said with a testy tone.

"Olive, what are you doing?" Laurel asked, watching her sister with an annoyed look. "Leave him alone."

"The tips of his ears are on fire!" She burst into peals of laughter.

Laurel's mouth twitched with a smile.

Fuming, he used the table to push up from the chair. Why had he sat down again? Oh yeah, Willow. The girl who'd ran to the door for another guy.

"Aw, come on," Olive giggled, patting him on the shoulder. "Sit back down. I'll behave."

Shrugging off her hand, he took a step back from the table.

"Sit," Laurel commanded, pointing at his chair.

He could tell by her stern, military tone, and hard facial expression, she was used to people following orders. Not him.

"I don't think so. I'm not going to tell you where Nieto lives. Whatever you're planning, you'll just get yourselves killed." He sighed, then muttered under his breath, "let sleeping dogs lie."

Olive turned to her sister with a self-satisfied look. "Told you being nice wouldn't work."

"Shut up, Liv," Laurel snapped, rising from her seat. She turned her heated stare on him. "Willow told us what happened to her. I'm not willing to let sleeping dogs lie."

Vengeance burned, liquefying the brown in her eyes. Standing at the table's head, she looked like a Gypsy queen sentencing a man to death.

"Do you know what he did to her?" she continued in an angry growl. "He kept her for one of his associates from the states who raped her, choked her, bit and beat her. She was held captive in an underground cell for months, living on nothing but drugged food."

Silent tears streaked down Olive's face.

He shook his head, trying to clear the unwanted, loathsome images. Had Lacy experienced the same horrors? Rage rose to the surface, but with it came something he refused to admit. Fear. Nieto had unfathomable connections. They'd already made an enemy out of him. Nothing good would come from poking that bear.

"You don't stand a chance against him." AJ tried to reason with both Laurel and himself.

"If you and your friend help us, we might," Laurel countered.

He took a step back. "What?"

"You and your friend could help us," she repeated, each syllable uttered with boldness.

"We're not special ops guys," he said, voice rising. "You'd need a special team for that. We wouldn't stand a chance against Nieto and his men."

"If we planned carefully," she began in a reasonable, self-confident tone.

"I'm not going back," he said resolutely.

Olive walked around the table and stood by her sister.

She cocked her head. "Would you do it if Willow asked you?"

Would he?

He contemplated, shifting from foot to foot, then rolled his eyes at himself. What was the point denying it? Yeah, he'd go if she asked. He'd turn himself inside out if the girl wished it.

He stared at Olive. "Maybe."

It was all he'd admit to them.

"Okay, then," Laurel said, looking hopeful.

"Whatever," he mumbled, walking out.

No way. He wasn't going back to Mexico.

He rounded the corner and made his way toward the stairs. He'd wait for Bryan in his room and he better hurry his ass up.

Voices caught his attention as he grabbed the stair railing. He stopped. Two men were talking in low tones. He stepped to the corner and peered around the wall.

Scott and another man stood in the foyer. Where was Willow? And who the hell was the stranger talking to Scott?

"We've got to give her back," the dark-skinned man insisted, with an urgency that rose AJ's hackles.

"I know. I tried to talk her into a drive to Laredo, but she wouldn't go for it," Scott responded, shoving both hands into his pockets.

What the actual hell was going on here? Shit. Did Scott have something to do with Willow's abduction?

A knock on the door interrupted their disturbing conversation.

Scott opened it and Bryan sauntered in.

"What are you doing back here?" Scott asked, waving an irate hand around.

Thank God, Bryan had come back for him. He limped around the corner into the foyer.

"Ready to go?" Bryan asked, stepping around Scott without answering his question. "You're looking better."

"Thanks," AJ muttered. "Look, I need to talk to you," he paused, eyeing the two men. "Alone."

"Okay," Bryan said, giving him a confused look.

He grabbed Bryan's arm and led him upstairs to his room. Once inside, he closed the door, then leaned against it.

"What's going on?" Bryan demanded.

"I don't think we can leave yet," AJ said.

Whatever Scott was planning, it didn't sound good for Willow. He couldn't stand the thought of leaving if she was in any sort of danger. He needed to be sure of her safety before he left. He wouldn't stay because of his growing interest in her.

He just couldn't.

43

One Week Later …

The Pacific's crashing surf along the shore washed up foam, tickling Lacy's toes. She burrowed them into the wet sand and reveled in the little girl feeling it granted her. The sun glided across the sky, gilding the water's endless expanse across the horizon a white, shiny gold. It felt amazing to sit in the warm sun, feel sand and water at her feet. It made her want to believe the world could glisten like the water again.

Jace had slept most of the twenty-two-hour drive from Oklahoma to Coronado Beach, California, in the back seat of AJ's truck. The brief moments he was lucid, he'd talk. Sharing chilling details of time spent with Widow. Hopeless anger surged through her when she thought of the torture her uncle had put him through. She'd taken what revenge she could, but it didn't seem like enough.

They'd talked about staying at Hitt's cabin longer than the two days they were there. Lacy needed distance between her and her uncle but didn't want to jeopardize Jace's health. He insisted all he needed was sleep, and he could do that in the truck as easily as he could at the cabin.

The drive hadn't been easy. They'd driven across Oklahoma's panhandle, avoiding Texas altogether. A precaution. She didn't think her uncle would stop them from leaving, but who knew?

The sun, the salty scent of ocean water, the warm sand, distracted her in brief interludes. Her mind kept dredging up events of the past six days, begging her to deal with it. But could she? She didn't want to see her parents any time soon.

They'd never told her she'd been adopted, and it hurt. The fact she wasn't their real daughter sliced her heart into ribbons. The revelation Thomas and Geneviève Monroe were her real parents, just blew her mind. Thomas Monroe had traded his daughter to a Mexican human trafficker. She didn't know where to begin to process or make sense of that.

Sensing his presence, she swung her gaze to Jace, who walked down the shoreline from the beach house they'd found abandoned. Shirtless, with swim trunks slung low on his hips, he looked like a Billabong surfer model. She ogled him without shame as he leisurely strolled toward her. She wanted to melt into him, her heart ached to be close to him. They'd loved each other long into the night, returning to each other's arms again and again. They couldn't get enough.

Coronado Beach was deserted. They'd seen no one in the few days they'd been there. A key to the place was under the front door's welcome mat. She loved it and hoped the owners didn't come back and kick them out anytime soon.

The house was small compared to other lavish homes along the shoreline. One open room served as kitchen and living room. Glass walls faced the ocean with a deck to sunbathe or cook out. The loft above boasted a king size bed, a dresser, and nightstand. A small bathroom sat off one side, complete with a garden tub. The slanted roof had a skylight and they'd enjoyed stargazing as they bathed together.

Jace sat down beside her and smiled. He wrapped an arm around her, scooting her closer to his side. The heat of his body soaked through the simple pink tank top she'd thrown on that morning, causing her heart to race.

He tipped her chin, kissing her lightly on the lips. "Hey beautiful."

Her cheeks heated. "Hey."

As she gazed into his eyes, a troubled look crossed his face.

"What is it?" she asked, instantly concerned.

Was he in pain? He still had problems talking. He'd told her about the pole Widow used to stretch and strangle him. The trauma might've caused permanent damage to his vocal cords. She didn't mind, thinking the lower gravely register of his voice, sexy.

His eyes tightened in concern as he brushed a strand of hair from her eyes.

"You wanna talk about it?" he asked gently.

Instant tears sprung into her eyes, and she snorted through the sob rising in her throat.

"Which part? The one where Thomas Monroe," she spat, "is my *father*, or all the crazy, screwed up things I did to escape Nieto?"

"Wherever you want to start," he said.

"Well," she began slowly, digging a hand in the sand. "I don't want to tell you what happened in Mexico."

He cocked his head. "Why?"

She raised her eyes to his, letting the warm sand slip through her fingers. "Because if you knew, you might —"

"Nothing," he stressed, "will make me walk away from you. Not even," his voice cracked. "Not even if you had to do things …"

"No," she denied, guessing his thoughts. "I wasn't raped. Nieto tried getting close to me, but I stabbed him."

He shook his head, a slight smile tipping his lips. "That's my girl."

"But Jace," she paused, looking away.

He grasped her chin and turned her head back. "Continue."

She inhaled, letting the air escape through her lips, then told him about the underground cell, and meeting Willow.

"The man who brought us to the hotel was hurting Willow. I took a ..." she paused, shaking her head.

Might as well spit it out. Rip the band aid off.

"I ... I killed him."

Sobs, one after another, rose and spilled out at the confession.

"I bashed his head with a lamp," she wailed.

Tears ran down her face. She bent over at the waist as a keening cry ripped from the deepest part of her. She rocked back and forth, weeping, unable to control it. How could she live with herself knowing she'd taken a life? The worst part was knowing it didn't do a damn bit of good.

She hadn't escaped. Miguel might've been the worst kind of criminal. But he was someone's son, husband, and father. Someone out there mourned his loss. And the fault lay at her feet.

Jace wrapped both arms around her middle and shifted her into his lap. He cradled her, wiping tears from her cheeks. She buried her head in his shoulder, breathing erratically.

"Listen to me," he said, voice firm.

She raised her head and tried to focus her blurry, tear-filled eyes on him.

"You are the strongest, most tenacious, amazing woman I've ever had the privilege of knowing." He placed gentle hands around her face, brushing tears away with his thumb. "You did what you had to do. Is that what you're worried about? That I'd condemn you for killing the man who held you hostage and trying to escape?"

She gave a silent nod.

Unshed tears brightened his eyes. "I am so sorry you had

to do that. I know how it eats at your soul. I'd never judge you, sweetheart. You know who helped me reconcile what I'd done to Zach?"

"No," she sniffled into his shoulder.

He ran a loving hand down the length of her hair. "Edwards did. So, I'll ask you what he asked me. If it were possible for you to turn your captor over to the authorities and let them handle their punishment, would you?"

She wiped her nose with the back of her hand. "Yeah."

"You were in an impossible situation. No one, not even the law, would blame you for what you did." He kissed the top of her head. "Try thinking of it that way."

She leaned back. "Thank you. That does help. A little."

"What else is bothering you?"

Why did he have to be so damn intuitive?

She slipped out of his embrace and stood. "I'm not sure I want to talk about that either."

Bitterness laced the words. The idea, the concept of Thomas Monroe being her father, was like acid burning her heart to ash.

Jace rose to his feet. "It would help if you did."

"I don't see how," she retorted, folding her arms across her chest like a shield.

"Tell me how you feel," he coaxed.

She turned her back on him, facing the great expanse of water. Wind raised the hair off her back, cooling her neck. Saying how she felt, *out loud,* made everything real. If she kept it bottled inside, she could pretend it wasn't. Pretend she was still Emmett and Lila's daughter by birth. But make-believe castles built in dusky corners of the imagination always crumbled in the light of reality.

"I feel lost," she admitted in a quiet voice. "I feel like I'm parentless, like an abandoned orphan. Pathetic, maybe."

"Not at all."

His warm, raspy voice settled over her, diminishing some

of the anguish roiling inside her. She swung around, let the love radiating from his eyes draw her in like a magnet's north pole.

He was her true north.

"I don't even feel like a Monroe anymore." Her voice broke.

It killed her to say it, to think AJ wasn't her brother, and that her whole life had been built on a lie.

"You don't feel like a Monroe anymore because you're not," he said with a smile that puzzled her.

"What do you mean?"

He moved toward her with slow, deliberate steps, until his bare toes touched hers. He brushed a soft hand down her cheek.

"You're not lost, baby. You're mine. You're a Cooper."

Her heart exploded. A cry escaped her as she crashed her body into his. Her arms wrapped around his waist. His body's light and warmth soaked into her. It chased away the cold, bitter darkness that had settled in her core, and she swore her heart knitted back together.

She lifted her eyes to his. "You mean it?"

His eyes darkened with desire. "You know I do."

"Then marry me, Jace," she pleaded.

He lowered his lips to hers. The slow, reverent kiss turned desperate. His hands tightened on her hips as he brought her closer, deepening the kiss. Her hands ran up the length of his back, tangling in the hair around his neck.

Out of breath, she leaned back and smiled. "Is that a yes?"

He grinned. "Hell yes, it is. I don't care if we have to drive to Canada. We'll find a preacher, a priest, a rabbi."

She laughed, feeling lighter in the knowledge she belonged to him. She'd take his name, and they'd build a life together on their own terms. A tingling sensation washed over her. They might even start a family.

"I love you," she said softly.

"I love you," he returned, lacing his fingers with hers.

They walked hand in hand up the shoreline, toward the beach house, talking of lighter things. They'd make the future their own. She'd loved him six days ago. She couldn't express how much she loved him now. That four-letter word, too often thrown around without care, wasn't enough. With Jace, she could face anything.

Maybe even the parents who raised her.

AUTHOR'S NOTE

Human trafficking is the fastest growing global crime affecting every continent and economic structure in the world. The National Human Trafficking Hotline received 50,123 signals in 2021 alone. The same year, there were 180 cases of human trafficking reported in Oklahoma. The majority were sex trafficking in nature. Truck stops and motels are the most used venues. Be aware of your surroundings when you travel. There might be someone you cross paths with that needs your help.

Visit A21.org for more information on human trafficking.

If you suspect you or someone you know is being trafficked, call the Can You See Me? hotline, 1-800-THE-LOST, or your local authorities.

The Oklahoma Human Trafficking Hotline: 1-855-617-2288

Can You See Me? 1-800-THE-LOST

Thank you for reading *Ascendant*! I hope you enjoyed the continuation of Lacy and Jace's story. AJ and Willow's story continues in book three of the *Asylum* series.

Remember to leave a review! Stay tuned to all the upcoming news by joining my Facebook page, SusySmith-Writer4Life, or visit my website susysmith.com to sign up for my newsletter.

AUTHOR'S PLAYLIST

1. Save Us by Atreyu
2. Lifetime by Three Days Grace
3. Anywhere But Here by SafetySuit
4. Silent Lucidity by Queensrÿche
5. I Was So Sure by Former Vandal
6. Daylight by Shinedown
7. Coming Out of the Rain by Greek Fire
8. Can You Hear Me Running by Alan Whole
9. Bad Things by I Prevail
10. Ghost by Badflower
11. Bulletproof by Godsmack
12. Just Pretend by Bad Omens

Music that inspired me as I journeyed through *Ascendant*. You can find this playlist on Spotify.

ACKNOWLEDGMENTS

Acknowledgments are hard for me to write. I'm always afraid I'll leave someone out who deserves the shout-out. I would be remiss not to mention my best friend, Judy Stohr, first. I cannot express how much she helps me through the writing process. I wouldn't be this far in my writing journey if it wasn't for her. She challenges me every step of the way and strives to make me the best writer I can be.

Second, I'd like to thank Bill Bernhardt and the Red Sneaker Writers who make the writing conference every year such a wonderful experience. Bill has the biggest heart for authors, and I am grateful for his guidance.

I'm also beyond thankful for my family's encouragement. Wíblaha^{n}, and I love you all!

Lastly, I'd like to thank my readers who've invested their time in reading Jace and Lacy's story. They aren't finished yet! The third installment of the *Asylum* Series is in the works!

ABOUT THE AUTHOR

Susy Smith has a bachelor's degree in English and is a language teacher for the Kanza Tribe. Her debut novel, *Asylum*, won the 2020 Writer Con contest in the novel category. She loves creating a home on paper for the characters in her head and dabbling in poetry. She lives in a small Oklahoma town with her husband, four grown children nearby, and two spoiled dog-children. Learn more at susysmith.com.